THIS POISON HEART

Also by Kalynn Bayron

Cinderella Is Dead

THIS POISON HEART

KALYNN BAYRON

BLOOMSBURY
LONDON OXFORD NEW YORK NEW DELHI SYDNEY

BLOOMSBURY YA
Bloomsbury Publishing Plc
50 Bedford Square, London WC1B 3DP, UK
29 Earlsfort Terrace, Dublin 2, Ireland

BLOOMSBURY, BLOOMSBURY YA and the Diana logo
are trademarks of Bloomsbury Publishing Plc

First published in the United States of America in 2021 by Bloomsbury YA
This edition published in Great Britain in 2021 by Bloomsbury Publishing Plc

A catalogue record for this book is available from the British Library

ISBN: PB: 978-1-5266-3279-1; Exclusive edition: 978-1-5266-4271-4;
eBook: 978-1-5266-3274-6; ePDF: 978-1-5266-3729-1

2 4 6 8 10 9 7 5 3 1

Typeset by Westchester Publishing Services

Printed and bound in Great Britain by CPI Group (UK) Ltd, Croydon CR0 4YY

For the plant lovers

CHAPTER 1

White roses. Genus *Rosa*. Family *Rosaceae*. Common name "Evening Star."

Mr. Hughes took a dozen of them to his wife's grave every weekend, rain or shine. He had for the past year. He didn't care about the genus or the species, only that there were twelve of them waiting for him every Sunday, wrapped in brown paper and tied with string. My mom was going to have to tell him that the delivery truck hadn't arrived last night like it was supposed to—it flipped over on the Brooklyn-Queens Expressway. The driver was okay, but our shipment of Evening Star was scattered across six lanes of traffic.

"I'm so sorry, Robert," Mom said as Mr. Hughes, dressed in his Sunday best, came into the shop. "There was an accident, and we didn't get our regular shipment. We should have a new delivery in the next few days."

He gripped the lapels of his freshly pressed navy blazer, his bottom lip quivering as he ran his hand over his mouth and sighed. He looked like he might fold in on himself. Grief was heavy. It could do that to a person.

"We've got some beautiful peonies," Mom said. "The Ann Cousins variety. They're gorgeous, Robert. I could put them together for you right now."

I pushed my glasses up and peered around the arrangement I was working on.

Mr. Hughes's brow furrowed. "I don't know, Thandie. The white roses, they were her favorite."

My mom closed her hand over Mr. Hughes's as he pulled out a tissue to dab at his eyes. We had a single white rose in a vase on the back counter, a remnant of a wedding bouquet I'd put together the day before. I looked down at my hands, opening and closing them. I wanted to help. But I couldn't. It was too dangerous.

"I miss her so much, Thandie," Mr. Hughes said, his voice choked with sadness.

"The people we love are never really gone from us," Mom said. "Try to remember that. I know it's hard. It feels like the whole world should just stop spinnin', but it doesn't. And we've gotta find a way to pick up the pieces."

Mom always knew exactly what to say. Mr. Hughes and his wife used to come into the shop together. Now, it was just him, and it made me so sad I could hardly stand it. The arrangement on the table in front of me began to wilt.

"Hang on, Mr. Hughes," I said.

He looked at me quizzically. I glanced at my mom for a second longer than I needed to. Her face grew tight with concern.

I plucked the single rose from the vase, rushed down the short hallway and out the back door. The eight-by-ten square of dirt our landlord had the nerve to call a garden was where we kept the bigger plants that couldn't fit in the shop. Our recent shipment of chaste tree crowded the space, their spiky violet blooms just beginning to open in the damp heat of summer.

My hands trembled as I knelt and stripped the rose of its velvety petals, down to the pistil, the seedy heart of the flower. Any part of the plant would have been enough to make another like it, but having the pistil made it easier. A familiar tingling sensation crept down my arm. It started in my shoulder and trickled toward my elbow, then into my forearm. I glanced at the newly installed wooden pickets of the rear fence. They reminded me of what could happen if I lost control, even for a second.

I scooped a little hole in the ground and set the pistil inside. Covering it with loose earth, I placed my hands over it, sinking my fingers into the dirt, and closed my eyes.

Just breathe.

The tingling spread into my fingertips, warm and oddly comforting. A swell of anticipation crashed through me as a stout evergreen stalk broke through the dirt and immediately sprouted several small offshoots. They pushed their way up between my outstretched fingers. Sweat dampened my back and forehead. I clenched my teeth until the muscles in my temples ached. The new stalks reached toward the sun, their stems thickening, thorns sprouting, but never close enough to prick my fingers. Buds bloomed white as snow between new leaflets green as emeralds. Right before their petals unfurled, I pulled my hands back, clutching them against my chest. Dizziness washed over me. Orbs of light danced around the edges of my vision as I sucked in a breath, filled my chest with the sticky summertime air, then pushed it out. My heartbeat slowed to a normal rhythm.

Six white roses dotted the newly formed branches. I took stock of the rest of the garden. The chaste tree had sprouted new roots like tentacles, cracking open its plastic planter. Its bright lavender blooms craned toward me. I couldn't chance growing another set of roses to give Mr. Hughes the dozen he wanted. These would have to work.

Taking a pair of pruning shears from my apron pocket, I clipped the roses and hurried back inside. As I handed them to my mom, Mr. Hughes's face lit up.

"First you tell me you don't have any, then Briseis goes and finds the best-looking flowers I've ever seen," he said happily.

"I was keeping them special, just for you," I said. "I only have six. I hope that's okay." The smile on his face made the little white lie worth it.

"They're perfect," he said.

Mom flashed me a tight smile. "I'll wrap them up."

She tucked the roses inside a layer of ivory tissue and brown paper, then pulled a length of white jute from the big spool on the counter and tied a knot in three turns.

"Angie and I are here if you need anything," she said, handing him the flowers. "Don't hesitate to call us."

"I don't want to bother you," he said.

"Don't," my mom said firmly. "Don't do that. It's not a bother and neither are you, understand?"

He nodded, dabbing at his eyes. "Tell Mo I said thanks for dinner the other night. I owe you."

"I'll tell her," my mom said. "And you don't owe us

anything—except maybe some of your world-famous peach cobbler."

Mr. Hughes laughed, his eyes still damp with tears. "I got you covered. I make it from scratch—my grandmama's recipe. Nothing like it in the whole world."

He beamed. My mom went around the counter and gave him a hug.

I ducked back behind my flower arrangement and took a deep breath. I'd been able to help this time, but it couldn't be a habit. The last time I'd pushed my abilities to their limit was after an argument I'd had with my mom. I didn't even remember what it was about, but my overdramatic ass was upset and decided to sit in the garden and grow some chamomile as a distraction. I took a handful of loose-leaf tea and scattered it in the dirt.

And then, I'd pushed too hard. I grew dozens of the daisy-like chamomile plants, but I also brought the roots of our neighbor's Norway maple tree up through the ground, tearing apart the landscaping and busting a hole in the fence. Mo told the guy next door that sometimes trees go through a growth spurt, like kids when they hit puberty, and for some reason that was beyond me, his dumb ass believed her.

I helped Mo patch the fence, but every time I looked at the new, pale pickets, a stab of shame coursed through me.

The flowers in my arrangement craned their soft petals toward me. Any time I was sad or scared or happy, they took notice, reacted in kind. Grief and sadness made them shrivel; happiness made them perk up; and fear and anger made them lash out.

I'd been growing plants in recycled plastic milk cartons and empty glass jars since I was a kid. Mom said I had the greenest thumb she'd ever seen, even as a toddler. She found out exactly *how* green when she left me in the sunroom of my grandma's house when I was three. She went to grab her purse, and when she came back, I was tangled in the vibrant green vines of a velvet-leaved philodendron—a plant that had been dead and withered when she'd stepped out.

From that point on, Mom and Mo gave me little tests. They'd put me near a dead plant, and it would turn green and grow new sprouts if I paid attention to it. When I was older, they gave me seeds that I would plant and bring to bloom in minutes. They didn't know how or why I could do the things I did, but they accepted it, nurtured it, and let it grow, just like the plants—until I was about twelve.

Everything changed after that. I had a harder time keeping my power in check. Everywhere I went, if there was something green and growing, it was like an alarm went off, alerting it to my presence. The flora wanted my attention, and if I was being honest, I wanted to give it to them.

The bell on the door clanged as Mr. Hughes left the shop, and I went back to work on an arrangement that was scheduled for pickup in less than an hour. I clipped a few sprigs of baby's breath and stuck them alongside bundles of fuchsia crape myrtles, St. John's wort, and blush-colored roses in a tall vase. I ran my fingers over the roses and they plumped up.

Mom flipped on the Bluetooth speaker and Faith Evans's voice rang out as she bobbed her head to the beat.

"Lookin' good," she said, eyeing the arrangement in front of me. "I love the colors."

"Thanks. I've been working on it since yesterday. I should be done soon."

She came over and put her arm around my shoulder. "Thank you for doing that for Mr. Hughes. It means a lot to him to have those flowers, but . . ." She looked down the hall toward the back door. "You have to be really careful."

"I know," I said, reading the worry in her eyes. "I was. I got all six from a single pistil."

"Really?" Mom lowered her voice and leaned in close, even though we were the only two people in the shop. "That's some kind of record, right?"

I nodded. She had always been fascinated with what I could do, but her curiosity was tempered with concern. I couldn't blame her.

She looked me over. "How you feeling? Dizzy?"

I nodded. A shadow of unease crossed her face.

"Anything else you need me to do today?" I asked, avoiding her eyes.

"No, but there's something you can do after you finish this arrangement." She rested her hand on my cheek. "Try relaxing a little. School's out for the summer, baby. I know this year was tough."

I raised my eyebrows in mock surprise.

Mom narrowed her eyes at me. "Okay. 'Tough' is the understatement of the century."

This past school year had put my acting skills to the test. Not because I wanted to be on stage, but because the row of potted plants my English teacher kept on her windowsill grew roots as long as I was tall; the trees in the courtyard arched toward the window next to my assigned seat in science—and everybody noticed. I had to pretend like I was shocked, like I thought it was weird. I had to speculate loudly about the cause. It could've been chemicals seeping into the ground from toxic runoff. Maybe all the hormones the government put in our food were leaking out of the lunchroom trash and into the ground, making the trees grow in strange and unusual ways. It made zero sense, but some people latched on to the idea, and now I had to show up at protests demanding the soil around our school be tested, like I didn't make up the whole thing to keep from being found out. If anybody had been paying close enough attention, they would have seen that every school I'd ever attended had a similar "contamination."

"I love having you in the shop," Mom said. "I really do. But don't feel like you have to be."

"I love working here," I said. "You know that."

"I want you to have some fun this summer. We can manage."

"But I can *help*. You know what I mean."

Mom shook her head. My parents liked to pretend they were fine with me slacking off for the summer, but the truth was, they needed the extra help. Orders were coming in and walk-ins happened all the time, but even though business was steady, gentrification rent was erasing our gains. They couldn't afford to hire any more people, so I took on the responsibility.

The bell clanged again, and Mo came in balancing a plastic container full of croissants on top of a flimsy cardboard tray with three cups of coffee. I ran over to grab the coffees before they toppled over.

"Good save," Mo said. She kissed me on the forehead and set the food on the counter.

"It's busy today," said Mom. "I got a call about the basic wedding package. They wanted to know if we can do it by Friday?"

"We can do it by Friday." Mo clapped her hands together and turned to me. "You workin' today, love?"

"Yup."

"Nope," Mo said. She took my hand and pulled me out from behind the counter, scooting me toward the door. She untied my apron and took it off, tossing it to Mom. "I love you, but you need to get out of here and go do some teenager stuff."

"Like what?" I asked.

"I don't know." She turned to Mom. "What do kids do these days?"

"Don't ask me that like I'm old," said Mom. "They like to Netflix and chill, right?"

"I'm leaving." I grabbed one of the coffees and two croissants. "Please never say 'Netflix and chill' ever again."

"Oh, they also like to make dance videos on TikTok," said Mo. "What's that one called? The Renegade?" She did some weird move with her arm, then grabbed her shoulder, wincing in pain. "I can do it, but the way my ligaments are set up—"

"I'll never be able to unsee that, Mo," I said. "Thanks."

"You welcome, love." She grinned.

While Mom and Mo laughed themselves to tears, I closed the door to the shop and took the stairs to the third floor of our building.

Mom bought almost every piece of furniture in our

apartment from IKEA. Mo hated it because even though the products were solid, putting them together sometimes required a level of patience neither of them actually possessed. Still, Mom was obsessed with making the space feel more open, which was hard to do in less than eight hundred square feet.

I straightened the mismatched pillows on the couch and organized the unopened mail into a pile on the table before heading to my room. As I opened the door, the warm, damp air hit me in the face, fogging my glasses. Air conditioning was on an as-needed basis, and Mom had a sticky note taped to the switch that said, "You got A/C money?" I didn't, so it stayed a balmy seventy-nine degrees. My posters and playbills that I'd tacked to the walls were curled at the edges. Everything was perpetually damp. The only plus was that my plants loved the tropical conditions.

The plants under my window turned toward me. The bluebells opened like tiny gramophones, and the bush of baby's breath that had taken over an entire corner of my room looked like it was breathing. The marigolds and snapdragons all shifted toward me. These plants were quiet. Quiet plants might perk up around me, but they didn't uproot themselves or destroy a fence to get close to me. They didn't turn obscene shades of their natural colors when I was around.

I plopped down on my bed. The ivy I'd grown by the window snaked toward me, slithering across the floor and up the bedpost, sprouting new leaves and curled tendrils as it reached for me. Ivy wasn't a quiet plant. It was reactive and loud. The only place I could keep it was in my room, where no one would see it but me and my parents.

Being wound up all the time, constantly watching my every move, and being careful not to provoke a response from a red oak or potted fern was exhausting. Ignoring them was the only thing that worked—and sometimes, that didn't even help as much as I wanted it to. The worst part was that it felt wrong to ignore them, like I was denying something that was as much a part of me as the color of my eyes or the coil of my hair. But in the confines of my cramped bedroom, I could let go, and the relief that came with that was something I looked forward to more than anything else.

The sun slanted through my window, shining a large, sallow rectangle onto the wooden floor. The gauzy light saturated my room. I let the creeping vines encircle my fingertips, then wind their way up my arm. I always wondered why the plants preferred me to the sunlight when it was in a plant's nature to reach for it. Mo told me once it was because I *was* the light. She was sentimental like that and I loved her for it, but I thought it might be something else, something I didn't have an explanation for yet, which was the reason I'd applied to take a college-level botany course at City College over the summer.

Mom gave me a book on botany when I got into middle school. She thought if I became a scientist, I could figure out where my power came from and what exactly it was for. It seemed like a good idea when she first brought it up, but as I got older, the "how" became less important than the "why." I wasn't sure the answers I needed could be found in a textbook but I didn't know where else to start.

I opened my laptop and logged into my school portal to check my email. A new message from my advisor sat in the inbox.

During the regular school year, her messages were always one of two things: a reminder that I needed to work on getting my grades up if I wanted to graduate on time, or telling me I was excelling in environmental science and suggesting I apply that same energy to my other classes. But since school was out for the summer, this had to be about the botany class. My heart ticked up.

Hi Briseis,

I hope you are having a wonderful summer. I received your request to enroll in City College's Introductory Botany class, but unfortunately, the class requires participants have a GPA of 3.0 or better. It's a college-level course for college credit. Your GPA was 2.70 at the end of the semester, so I'm afraid you don't qualify. However, you are a wonderful environmental science student, so let's make a plan to raise your GPA so that you can take this class at a later date. Please don't give up hope, Briseis. Keep pushing. You're going to do great your senior year.

Best,
Cassandra Rodriguez
Academic Counselor
Millennium Brooklyn High School

I closed my computer and shoved it across my bed, biting back tears. The baby's breath puffed up, the snapdragons twisted around, and the ivy gripped the metal frame of my bed so hard it groaned in protest. I took a deep breath and the plants settled.

Nothing went right this past school year. Being really good at environmental science and botany workshops didn't get me out of PE. I tried to convince Mom and Mo that running laps and playing badminton was a form of torture, but I still had to dress out and be within smelling distance of dudes who thought wearing deodorant was optional. But PE was the least of my issues with school. The fear that I carried around with me that someone would discover what I could do—or worse, that I'd lose control and get someone hurt—was heavy.

I glanced at my desk, which was little more than a wooden shelf propped on top of some plastic crates Mo had found at a thrift shop. My microscope sat there with my research journals and notepads, colorful Post-it notes sticking from between the pages. The botany book Mom had given me lay open, its pages worn and dog-eared, entire passages highlighted and underlined. I didn't want to make a career out of being a scientist. I just wanted to understand myself better, and something I'd come across in my research struck me in a way nothing else had—raised the hairs on the back of my neck.

Near the back of the botany book was a section labeled *Poisonist*—a subdiscipline of botany that involved the study of poison plants. It piqued my curiosity and stirred something deep in the pit of my stomach—a mixture of fear and excitement.

When I was eight, a girl named Tabitha Douglass dared me to eat five bright red berries off a low-hanging tree behind our elementary school. The fruit was sour and stained my lips and tongue, but I did it. I ate all five. Tabitha ate six just to one-up me. By the time our teacher came to bring us back to class, Tabitha was curled in a ball, screaming in agony, puking her guts up. We were both rushed to the hospital. Mom burst into the emergency room like somebody told her I was at death's door, hollering and crying with Mo at her side, but I was fine. No stomach cramps, no headache, no irregular heartbeat. Tabitha had uncontrollable diarrhea for a week and couldn't eat anything other than soup and Jell-O.

The doctor concluded that I hadn't ingested as many berries as Tabitha. Technically, that was true. I'd eaten exactly one less than her. But I should have had the same symptoms. I should have felt something.

The incident stuck with me. I thought of it every time I handled anything even slightly toxic—ragweed, poison ivy, jimsonweed. They all made me feel like I'd stuck my hand under a cool tap, and a similar cold feeling had spread from my stomach the day I ate those yewberries in second grade. I hadn't explored every aspect of this strange gift yet, but that piece was always at the back of my mind—the poison plants.

A burst of excitement rippled through me as the memory swirled in my mind. That was the only other thing I had to look forward to this summer—tending to a very specific, very toxic plant. I grabbed my bag, went down to the shop, and stuck my head in the door.

"I'm going to the park for a while," I said.

Mom's face grew tight. "The park?"

The fear in her voice was too subtle for anyone but me to recognize. For her, being in a place as green as the park with all its open fields and trees and wildflowers was too much of a temptation, or maybe a threat. She worried that I'd push myself too far and make something happen that couldn't be ignored or fixed. Mo wasn't sure I needed to be so careful all the time. She and Mom bumped heads over it. They both wanted me to be safe, but there was always fear—of what might happen, of what the limits of this power might be, of where it came from. They didn't have answers and neither did I. Not yet.

"Got your phone?" Mo asked as she wrapped a dozen parrot tulips in gold foil paper.

"Yup," I said.

"See you at dinner then."

CHAPTER 2

I stood in front of the Marquis de Lafayette memorial outside Prospect Park working up the courage to go in. A man in a safari hat positioned his kids in front of the statue and snapped pictures as they grinned. Tourists buzzed around the park entrance taking selfies, being generally annoying and completely unaware of how much danger they were in by being so close to me. I stared at my sneakers and the brickwork of the path beneath them.

Stay focused. Keep my head low. Go straight to the Ravine.

I marched around the Lafayette statue and into the park. The grass was laid out like a wide green carpet, dotted with softball fields and outcroppings of trees. I took a trail that cut through the Long Meadow, the expanse of green space where people were already doing the absolute most. I understood why people did yoga, went for a jog, or bird-watched in the park, but I had to shake my head over a group of Park Slope parents staked out with cardboard signs, ready to run off the ice cream and gelato vendors so their kids wouldn't be tempted by dairy-based treats.

I stopped at the tree line on the opposite side of the meadow where the Ravine began. It was Brooklyn's only forest, and it was the one place secluded enough to test some of my more dangerous theories about what I was capable of.

I ducked onto the main trail and kept moving. The place I was going wasn't on the marked path, and my heartbeat kicked up as I got closer.

Keep it together.

The trees flanking the path shook themselves like they'd been roused from a sound sleep. Their thick, leafy canopies knitted together high above my head. I ignored the groan of their branches as they reached for me.

Keeping my eyes down, I took a sharp left off the marked trail through a thick patch of bracken that nobody other than me would have bothered to walk through.

When I reached my destination, the tree I stood in front of was just as ordinary looking as it had been the last time I was there. The towering elm looked identical to dozens of others standing nearby, but that was the point. I didn't want anyone to come across what I was hiding. Not gelato-less children in search of sweets, not dogs off their leashes. There wasn't anyone or anything that deserved the kind of painful death my secret would bring. I shouldn't have been growing it at all. Going into the park was a risk, but I couldn't keep the plant at home, where Mom and Mo would realize what it was and make me get rid of it. The shadowy, untraveled, unmarked trails of the Ravine were my only option.

At the base of the nondescript elm, far enough from the main path, through enough underbrush that even the most curious wanderer wouldn't have come close, I knelt and parted the tall grass, revealing a small bush dotted with white umbrellalike flowers. The parasols reminded me of lace. They looked like the kind of flower I might add to a bride's bouquet back at the shop.

But only if I wanted to kill the bride.

The previous two days of rain had turned the dirt to a muddy soup, but the plant was hanging in there. I took pictures of it with my phone, adding them to a Google Doc I'd created called *Water Hemlock*. I kept track of its growth, what it looked like through the different stages of its development, what conditions made it grow better, and noting what didn't work.

I'd been growing the water hemlock for a month and trying different variables. Damp, sandy loam worked better than rocky dry soil, and when I dug my fingers into the earth near its roots, the bush would grow fuller, taller. If I concentrated hard enough, new blooms sprouted, though not as easily as they did in plants that weren't poisonous. It took a lot more effort to grow the water hemlock, and I had to concentrate harder to make sure nothing went wrong. The exhaustion and dizziness that came after was so much more intense. That should've been enough to make me abandon the treacherous work, but I couldn't. I was drawn to it.

My phone buzzed. A text from Mo hung at the top of the screen.

Mo: We're getting takeout later. You want pad Thai?

Bri: Sounds good. Veggies only please!

I slipped my phone into my pocket and took a plastic grocery bag from my backpack. This was what my month of work had come to. I was going to harvest one of the smaller stalks and take it home to study. I'd only keep it long enough to take some notes, write down my observations, and then I'd get rid of it. A few hours. That was all I needed to do the research.

Running my hand down one of the stems, a cool, tingling sensation blossomed in my trembling fingertips. The petals and leaves stretched toward me with an urgency I didn't see in other plants. It was as if the water hemlock couldn't wait to make contact with my skin. I plucked the entire thing out of the ground, being careful not to touch the root, and placed it in the bag.

I left the Ravine with the bagged plant hidden in my backpack and walked home. I peeked in at Mom and Mo, who were busy loading premade arrangements into the floral cooler, before heading up to my room.

I'd debated cultivating the hemlock for months before I actually worked up the nerve to do it. I worried about being in the park and not being able to keep the other plants from noticing me. On top of that, I was scared my parents would find out. I was pretty sure that growing a poisonous bush in the park wasn't what they had in mind for how I should spend my summer. They wanted me to hang out with the few friends I had and do whatever it was they thought other kids my age were doing. Except I didn't think they understood how hard it was for me to balance friendships with the need to be near my plants, keeping what I could do a secret, and navigating the world in a way that didn't draw the attention of every single blade of grass, every tree, every shrub.

In my room, I closed the door and set my backpack on the bed. I thought about locking the door, but I pictured Mom taking it off the hinges and decided not to. I flipped on my microscope and sat at my desk. I switched out my glasses for a pair with a built-in magnifier and pulled on a pair of plastic gloves. Removing the hemlock from the bag, I broke off a sprig and tossed it into a metal tray on my desk. I opened a notebook to write down my observations.

The taller plants could grow up to seven feet tall, but this sample was only about a foot, its leaves six inches long with alternately arranged oval leaflets. It was sharp-toothed and its leaf veins terminated at the bottom, not the tip.

The root was the deadliest part. Over time, as the blossoms grew taller, the poison pooled in the bottom third of the plant, leaving the leaves and flowers fairly harmless as long as they weren't ingested.

I pulled the roots apart. They looked like small, pale carrots and smelled like them, too. They oozed a thick straw-colored liquid as I sliced into them with a scalpel. This was the substance that would bring on nausea, vomiting, seizures, and ultimately, death.

A set of hands clamped on my shoulders.

The scalpel slipped and sliced through my glove. Into my thumb.

"Oh shit, Briseis! I'm so sorry!" Mo blurted out. "I was trying to scare you a little. I didn't know you were studying."

I ripped off my glove. The gash on my thumb bloomed like a rose. Blood trickled into the palm of my hand and down my arm in thin ribbons.

I looked up at Mo. I couldn't think straight. "I—I need—"

"I'll get the first aid kit." She hurried out of the room.

Fear gripped my chest. My breaths came in quick, shallow bursts. A cold ache pushed its way from my thumb to my wrist and up to my forearm. I looked at the time on my phone.

Seconds ticked by.

Mo came back with the first aid kit and reached for my hand. I jerked away from her. She couldn't get the poisonous liquid on her or she'd die, the same way I was about to.

"I need to see it, love," she said.

"No—no, it's— Can you hand me some gauze?"

She handed me a few pieces and I pressed them against the cut. I didn't care about the wound or the pain. The poison was already working. There was no stopping it, no way to reverse it. I couldn't form the words to make her understand. She didn't even know what I'd been doing. A rush of guilt swept over me. When I died, she'd blame herself.

The ivy suddenly burst from its clay pot, shattering it with a loud crack. Mo jumped back as the plants doubled their length to reach me, encircling my ankles.

"Hey, Mo," I managed to mutter. "I—I love you. A lot."

She sidestepped the tangle of vines at my feet. "You okay, love? It's only a little blood. I don't even think it'll need stitches. Wait." She touched my cheek. "Are you in shock?"

I shook my head. "Can you get Mom?"

"Uh, sure," she said, still looking confused. She left and I checked the clock again. Three minutes had gone by. The poison only needed fifteen minutes to kill me. This was my own stupid fault. I'd given into my curiosity instead of being careful the way Mom and Mo had taught me.

Four minutes.

All the plants in my room had turned toward me.

Mom came barreling into the room. "Let me see— Oh, God! Is the finger cut off? Where is it? If we put it in ice, they can reattach it!"

Mo came in behind her. "Thandie, it's a cut, not an amputation."

Five minutes.

I stared at my hand. The tingling had stopped and was now confined to the tip of my thumb. I tried to breathe slower so I could take stock of how I felt.

I couldn't tell if my pulse was faster because of the hemlock or because I was scared. Still no sweating, no seizures, or blurred vision. The scalpel lay on my desk. The blood smeared on it had begun to turn black. That was the poison acting on the cells, breaking them apart. If it was doing that inside my body, I should've felt something by now.

Six minutes.

Mom knelt next to me. "Bri, baby, are you okay?" She eyed the tangle of ivy around my ankles.

I held my hand away so that she couldn't touch it. "I—I think so." I actually wasn't sure at all.

"Let's take a deep breath and calm down," Mo said. She took Mom by the arm and guided her to my bed. She turned to me. "Briseis, love, I am so sorry."

"No, it's my fault," I said. "It's okay."

Nine minutes.

Something was wrong, but not in the way I expected. Nothing was happening.

"You scared the crap out of me," Mom said to Mo.

"You sit there and breathe," Mo said. "You look more shook up than Briseis."

Mom shot her a pointed glance, then turned to me. "You sure you're okay, baby?" I nodded. "Put a Band-Aid and some ointment on that."

Mo came over and cupped my face in her hands. "I'm gonna get you a sign to put on your door that says Future Botanist At Work so I know not to walk up on you like that."

I forced a quick smile.

"Love you," she said.

She and Mom left. I disentangled myself from the ivy and bandaged my finger. I swept the plant parts and the bloody scalpel into a plastic bag, shoved the whole thing into an empty shoebox, and dropped it down the trash chute in the hallway.

I sat on the edge of my bed in a haze of confusion. Thirty minutes had gone by and . . . nothing.

I grabbed a book from the stack next to my bed and flipped to a page with an illustration of the water hemlock. Contact with the liquid in the root was deadly and it went right into my bloodstream through the cut. According to everything I knew about the plant, I should've been dying an agonizing death. The walls of my cells should've been disintegrating. My blood should've been unable to clot, running like water and spilling from every orifice. But with each passing moment, I breathed easier. The tingling had stopped altogether. Only a dull ache remained.

Hours passed. Mom closed up the shop, brought me pad

Thai and a bottled water, then went to watch reruns of *Penny Dreadful* with Mo in the living room. I picked at my food but couldn't stomach eating. I scrolled through my phone and found Gabby's name in the contacts. I started to text her, changed my mind, and called instead.

"Hey, Bri. Long time no speak," Gabby said, a slight edge to her voice. "What's goin' on?"

"Nothing," I said. "I just wanted to call you."

It had been a month since we last spoke. There were some texts in between, but hearing her voice brought up a bunch of mixed feelings I'd been avoiding.

Gabby knew some of what I could do but liked to pretend she didn't. At junior prom, I'd been standing next to her when her boyfriend gave her a corsage that looked like he'd pulled it out of a dumpster. It had plumped right up and looked freshly cut after a few seconds in my presence. Gabby's boyfriend was too busy lookin' at her boobs to notice, but she'd seen it.

It became this unspoken thing between us. We didn't talk about the grass literally being greener wherever I stood, or why the maple tree growing in front of our building stayed green so much longer than any of the other trees on our street, or how the flowers I'd given her mom when she graduated nursing school had lived for almost a year. I'd been tryna tell her the whole truth of what I could do for years, but it never seemed like the right time to go into more detail.

"It's been a weird day," I said.

"Every day is a weird day for you, Bri."

That hurt. I wanted to tell her about the hemlock. I guess this wasn't the right time either. I decided to tell her the version that left any mention of my strange ability out. "Mo scared me while I was dissecting a plant. I almost cut my finger off."

"Damn," she said, laughing. "You okay?"

"Yeah. I think so."

"Hold up. What are you doin' dissecting plants on summer vacation?"

"It's kind of my thing."

"It doesn't have to be, you know," she said. "You could do something that doesn't have to do with plants at all. Have you ever tried, you know . . . not being weird around plants?"

There was an awkward silence. I thought about cussin' her out. She would've gave it right back to me, then I'd be mad at her instead of just disappointed.

"My parents own a flower shop," I said. "I can't exactly get away from them—from the plants, I mean."

Gabby huffed. "So does that mean you're working there for the summer?"

"That was the plan, but Mom and Mo want me to take a break."

"I wish my mom would let me take a break," she said. "She said I gotta pay for my own phone this summer, so I'm babysitting for the people upstairs."

"Babysitting? I mean, I guess that's pretty low-key. Easy money, right?"

"Nope. That kid is a whole demon. He told his grandma to shut up the other day and nobody said anything. He's mad disrespectful. My grandma would've snatched my soul right out my body."

I wondered if I could survive telling my grandma to shut up.

Probably not, but I'd never chance it. "Oh hell no. You better watch out."

"*He* better watch out. I'll put his little ass in the cozy corner."

"What's a cozy corner?"

"Girl, it's a corner of his room with pillows and blankets where he gets sent to think about his behavior. It's like bougie time-out."

"Does it work?"

"No. He just thinks about how he's gonna be even more terrible when he gets up."

We both laughed. I looked at the cut on my thumb. It throbbed, but it wasn't too bad.

"Hey, Briseis?"

"Yeah?"

She sighed. "I don't know, Bri. Maybe listen to your moms. Try to have some fun this summer? You don't have to grow bean sprouts or potatoes or whatever. At least not all the time. That's not what most people are doing anyway. We can go to a show or a concert or something. I know you've seen everything already, but still."

I didn't grow potatoes or bean sprouts. I liked to grow flowers, vines, and the occasional deadly bush of hemlock. The words to tell her were on the tip of my tongue. I could lay it all out and maybe—just maybe—she would finally understand.

Gabby laughed. "If you can tear yourself away from your weeds—"

No. Nothing had changed. That's exactly why we didn't talk the way we used to.

"Have you talked to Marlon lately?" I asked.

"Yesterday," said Gabby. "You?"

"It's been a minute."

Marlon moved to Staten Island with their grandma over spring break and we talked less and less. But with Gabby, our friendship had hit a rough patch that didn't have anything to do with distance. It felt like the whole school year had been a countdown to the end of something. Like we were about to get off a roller coaster we'd been on since fifth grade when we'd met and become best friends. We damn sure weren't best friends anymore and we were slowly becoming something that looked less like friendship and more like people who didn't even halfway like each other.

I lay back on my pillow, watching the baby's breath in the corner of the room expand and contract. For a minute, I tried to forget about my thumb and the water hemlock. I tried to pretend that what I could do hadn't pushed its way into every corner of my life like an invasive weed. I wanted to get ahold of whatever this thing was, help my parents in the shop, and maybe have friends who understood me better. It didn't feel like too much to ask.

"We could find something to get into," I said, trying desperately to hold back a wave of sadness. "The library or the museum? Someplace quiet."

"And without any plants," Gabby added.

I sighed into the phone. That was a dig and she knew it.

"Yeah," I said, feeling defeated. I moved on to something else. "Did I tell you our building got sold? Rent is going up for the shop and the apartment, again."

"Damn. What are you gonna do?"

"I don't know." There were a lot of things up in the air and I was worried about what would happen if we couldn't bring in some more money. Everything was a mess.

A voice came screeching through the phone. "Gabby! You didn't take the chicken out the freezer?"

"Shit," Gabby said. I knew that ring of terror in her voice. Her mom, Miss Lindy, didn't play when it came to food. If she told Gabby to take out the chicken and she didn't, it was gonna be a problem.

"You better get the hair dryer or something."

"Mommy, I'm sorry! I'm taking it out right now!"

"I've been at work all day, and you couldn't take out the chicken?" Miss Lindy said in the background.

"Gotta go, Briseis," Gabby said, and hung up.

I lay across my bed, feeling the beat of my heart and listening to myself breathe. Maybe the poison hadn't gotten into my cut; maybe it was such a small amount that I wasn't affected. I looked at my thumb. The gash was oozing through the Band-Aid.

I thought back to when I met Gabby and Marlon. Our gym teacher, Mr. Cates, put us in the same group for relay races around the blacktop. We all pretended to be injured after the first lap and spent the rest of class sitting on a bench in the cool fall air, talking about our favorite movies and roasting Mr. Cates because he wore gym shorts that were way too small and his knees and elbows were forever ashy. The trees that crowded the gated outdoor area were leafless, preparing for the winter—all except the one we were closest to. It bloomed as we laughed together. Gabby was the first one to notice. She clapped her hand down on Marlon's shoulder and pointed to the trees. Their eyes were wide and fearful. If they were scared of the trees, they'd be scared of me too. I knew right then I'd have to hide what I could do.

I hated it. I should have let it all go and made the trees green or made the grass grow and owned it. Maybe that would've been better than pretending. I wanted to know what it would be like to be myself, fully, right from the jump. No secrets, no hiding.

But it was too late for that. My friends were pulling away from me, my parents were worried about me, school was a mess, and this power squatting inside me was trying to break free. How much more of this could I take before I reached a tipping point? Before I did something I couldn't take back?

CHAPTER 3

The next morning, I sat on the edge of my bed with my bare feet on the floor. As I looked around my room, wiping the sleep from my eyes, the cut on my finger throbbed. In a rush, the terror from the day before washed over me.

I should be dead.

In the night, tangled ropes of ivy had made their way across the floor and knitted themselves together like a rug of leaves. I stumbled over them to grab my glasses off my desk and went down the hall to get a jump on my morning routine. I brushed my teeth and fished through an endless hoard of hair products in the cabinet for some leave-in and a spray bottle. My six-day-old twist-out was lookin' extremely rough, but I thought I could get away with a poof for at least another day or two. I slicked up the sides with some Eco Styler and a paddle brush. If my edges were laid, it was okay if the rest was a little messy. Worst-case scenario I'd throw it in a wrap and call it a day.

"How?" Mom's voice rang out from the living room, her tone clipped. "We can't afford it."

I crept closer to the bathroom door.

"We'll figure it out. We always do," Mo said.

"We can't make money appear out of thin air," Mom said. "We're already cutting corners. We can't keep on like this."

"I know," said Mo. "Ordering costs are going up. The main case needs a repair, too. It's not cooling like it should and wasted inventory costs us more money. But it's the rent the new owner is charging that's gonna kill our profit margin. I'll go back over all the billing, make sure we're not paying too much for supplies, and then we need to get with our accountant and double-check taxes, write-offs—"

"We've done all that," Mom said.

Mo answered her with a heavy sigh. Their talks about money had gotten more and more desperate over the last few months.

"I can work nights, weekends, whatever I need to do," said Mo.

"I can pick up some more freelance work," Mom said, her voice tight, like she'd been crying. "I'll check in at the college. I know they've got some adjunct positions opening in the fall." She sighed. "I wanna know when we're supposed to enjoy life a little. Take Briseis on a vacation or somethin'."

"I don't know, babe," Mo said. "I want that too."

I finished up in the bathroom and walked into the living room. "I can get a full-time job for the summer."

"No," Mom said. "Absolutely not. You've been struggling in school and I know it's because you're stressed. You need to sit down somewhere and relax."

"I'll be less stressed when I know we can pay the bills," I said. "Whoever said money doesn't solve your problems was a liar."

"This isn't your problem to solve, you brilliant, beautiful child," said Mo, her eyes misting over. Mom was the crier, not Mo. She was emotional in a different way. Seeing her on the verge of tears put a knot in my throat. "We're going to have to make some sacrifices to keep things afloat after the summer. New rent goes into effect in the fall, so maybe we keep the shop and move to a smaller place."

"We can get a one-bedroom," said Mom, glancing at Mo. "Briseis can have the room, and we can get a foldout."

Mo nodded. "We can give up the paid parking, too. Maybe give up the car altogether. We hardly use it anyway."

"Um, sleeping on a foldout? Getting rid of the car? Are things that bad?" Those were big decisions. Maybe this wasn't just a bump in the road. Mom and Mo looked at each other solemnly.

"Everything is gonna be fine," said Mo.

"You don't have to lie to me." I sat down between them. "I know you're doing it because you don't want me to worry but it's too late for that. So, let's stop pretending everything is okay if it's not. What do y'all tell me all the time? 'It's okay to not be okay.' That's us right now."

Mom nodded and Mo beamed. We both had big brown eyes. People said we favored each other, and it was nice to have someone that kind of looked like me. Me and Mom didn't have any similar features, but we had the same sense of humor and the same laugh.

"Let's get bagels and open the shop," Mo said, resting her hand on the side of my face. "This is heavy. We can figure it out later, but right now, I'm starving."

Mom batted at her eyes and I squeezed her hand. I was

thinking of telling them about what happened with the water hemlock and how I couldn't piece together why I was still alive, but now was not the time.

We got dressed and walked to the bagel shop on Bergen Street. The morning air was warm and thick, and we held hands with me in the middle for the first block.

"I feel like I'm five years old," I said.

Mom held my hand tighter. "You'll always be my big-head baby."

The thing about walking around in Brooklyn was that people were so busy tryna get where they needed to be, they didn't always pay attention to what was going on around them. They didn't notice the oak trees perking up as I went by or the drooping flowers that spilled from hanging baskets, blooming anew. The mixture of concrete jungle and preoccupied New Yorkers was the best combination for me to keep a low profile.

Two big maples flanked the train station directly across from the bagel shop and there was one scrawny oak up the block, but other than that, there wasn't much else to worry about. If the line had been out the door, we would have turned around and left. But it wasn't, so I squeezed inside and stood with my back to the big plate glass window. Hopefully, the trees would mind their business.

The shop smelled like fresh bread, bacon, and coffee. People were talking among themselves as they waited on line. I kept my eyes forward. When it was our turn, Mo ordered and we moved to the side to wait for our food. A delivery truck rumbled by and I looked out at the street. It was a natural reaction to the loud noise, but I hadn't meant to look. I caught sight of the two towering maples. They leaned forward, their branches scraping the pavement. Roots broke free from under the sidewalk, sending chunks of rubble flying. I quickly turned away. A murmur moved through the shop, hushed whispers and confused glances. Mom's body went rigid. Mo inhaled sharply.

"Should we go?" Mom asked in a frantic whisper.

I ignored the trees as people began pulling out their phones and snapping pictures. A woman shrieked as branches dragged themselves across the store front. I shut my eyes tight, balled my fists.

Not now, please. Not here.

Dizziness overtook me. I staggered to the side. Mom slipped her hand around my waist.

"They're moving back," she said.

Mo grabbed our food and ushered us out of the bagel shop. The crowd spilled out of the shop to gawk at the twisting trees as we hurried down the street. As we turned off the block the sick feeling in my stomach let up, but behind me I heard the distinct sound of wood creaking, groaning like it was being twisted, about to snap. It took everything in me not to look back.

Work was nonstop till about one in the afternoon, when there was a lull. I checked my phone. Gabby had texted that she probably wouldn't be able to get together with me and Marlon. We hadn't even picked a date yet. It was an excuse. I shoved my phone back in my pocket and went to the sink to pick pollen and bits of plant clippings from my nails while I tried not to cry.

My mom's phone rang.

"Hello?" she answered.

She glanced at me and gave me a quick wink before her face abruptly changed. A look of utter confusion gave way to recognition. She drew her mouth into a tight line, let her gaze wander to the floor. "Can you hold on a minute?" she asked. She squeezed Mo's shoulder and stepped around the counter. "I need to run upstairs real quick." She hurried out.

A few minutes later, the bell above the door clanged.

"Hey, Jake!" I said.

"What's good, Briseis?" Jake said with a big smile.

Mo used to babysit Jake on weekends when his dad was out of town on business, and now, he came into the shop to help out two or three times a week. He refused to take any money, so we paid him in bagels, free Wi-Fi, and Mo's world-famous Sunday dinners. He was happy with that.

"How's school?" he asked, giving me a big hug.

"Out for the summer."

"I should have taken off for the summer," he said. "I'm doing three online classes."

"That's a lot of work," I said.

"Who you tellin'?" Jake asked. "I'm taking a calculus refresher for no credit because I have to take it in the fall and I suck at college-level math. It doesn't have anything to do with my plan to be a beauty guru."

"What's that?" Mo asked.

"I don't know, but I know they make money," said Jake. "How hard can it be? Paint your face, eyebrows. Powder. Done."

"Yeah, I'm pretty sure there's more to it than that—but hey, follow your dreams," I said.

"See," said Jake. "That's why I come over here. Y'all don't judge me."

Mo's phone rang in her pocket. When she answered, she had the same look of concern that Mom had.

"Briseis, can you come with me?" She turned to Jake. "Can you watch the shop for a few minutes?"

"Yeah, sure," he said, looking back and forth between us. "Everything okay?"

Mo nodded, motioning for me to follow her upstairs. She took the steps two at a time.

"What's wrong?" I asked as I scrambled after her.

She continued up the stairs without answering me.

When we walked into the living room, my mom was sitting on the couch with her hands tented under her chin.

"What's going on?" I asked, sitting down next to her. She took my hands in hers and squeezed them. Another wave of anxiety washed over me. "Mom, you're scaring me. What's wrong? Is it the rent? Do we have to move sooner?"

She shook her head.

"Did—did somebody die?"

"No, baby, it's nothing like that." She took a deep breath. "I got a call from an attorney who represents the estate of your birth mother's sister."

I heard what Mom said, but it didn't make sense. My birth mother had passed away when I was little. I didn't know she had a sister.

"I don't understand."

Mom gripped my hands tighter. "According to the attorney, she passed away, and she left you her estate."

My mind went blank. "Her estate? What does that mean?"

"I'm not sure what's involved," said Mom. "The attorney got in touch with the adoption agency, who just passed the message to me. Your—your aunt didn't want to disrupt things here for you, but it sounds like you're her only living relative. She left you something sizable enough for an estate lawyer to be involved."

Mo was quiet. I waited for her to speak because she always had good advice, but she only stood there with a worried look on her face.

"I don't really know what to say," I said. My adoption was open, but my birth mother never made contact. It wasn't a huge deal. It was just the way things were—but now, someone related to her, to me, was leaving me an estate? I couldn't wrap my mind around it.

"That's okay, baby," said Mom. "I don't know what to say either."

Mo hung by the door, watching us, then looked down at her clasped hands.

"We don't have to do anything," Mom said quietly. "We don't have to respond or we can—if you want. I don't want to jump in front of you to make a decision." Worry bloomed in her eyes and in the faint lines around her mouth.

"So someone who shares my DNA left me something in her will. Cool." I glanced toward my room. The door was cracked and I could see the tangle of ivy slinking its way up my bedpost. "Let's see what it is."

My parents were the two people I loved most in the world, and it made me sad that they were stressed over this. Bringing up my birth family was always a little stressful for them, mostly because they loved me and didn't want me to be upset. I was curious when I was younger, and they answered all my questions as best they could. As I got older, the topic came up less, but it was never off-limits.

"Maybe it's a pile of money and y'all won't have to moonlight as exotic dancers to pay the bills," I said. "I wouldn't judge you if you did but I know nine thirty is y'all's bedtime." Mom laughed, and I leaned in to put my face in her neck like I used to do when I was little, breathing her in, feeling calmed by the beat of her heart. "Let's get all the facts and then go from there. No more stressing, okay?"

Mo sat down and wrapped us both up in her arms. We sat quietly for a while before Mom and Mo went back downstairs. I stayed behind, listening to the vines rustling behind my bedroom door.

CHAPTER 4

A few days later, we waited anxiously in the living room for the estate attorney, Mrs. Redmond, to come by. As we sat on the couch, my bedroom door creaked open and a tangle of vines crept across the floor. I jumped up and shoved them back inside, closing the door.

"They're not gonna come out while she's here, are they?" Mom asked.

"I don't think so," I said, even though I wasn't entirely sure. "Have you been in my room? It's a jungle in there. All my plants are coming out of their pots."

"You think it's because you're anxious?" Mom asked.

I shrugged. "Maybe?"

I hadn't stopped thinking about what an inheritance might mean for us. I Googled what it meant when somebody left you an estate and had gotten all kinds of answers, from sprawling mansions and car collections to piles of useless junk. Some man in Florida made headlines when his long-lost uncle willed him an entire storage unit filled with creepy old dolls. I was not tryna have my life ruined by the real-life Annabelle, so I told myself that we'd walk away if there was any mention of dolls.

The doorbell rang.

We all stared at the front door for a few seconds before Mo got up.

"Okay," she said. "Think positive."

On the other side of the door stood a tall woman in an ill-fitting tan skirt suit. She had her dark hair slicked back into a bun, a streak of gray down the center of her head. She had a deep brown complexion, small dark eyes, and a wide full mouth.

"Hi there," she said. She stuck out her hand and the briefcase she was holding popped open, sending a shower of papers onto the floor. "Ugh. Sorry." She knelt and started stuffing them back inside, stealing a quick glance at me as Mo helped her gather the rest of her things.

"Please come in and have a seat," Mom said.

The woman stumbled in and sat in the armchair across from me.

"Can I get you something to drink?" Mo asked.

"Oh no, I'm fine," said the woman. "You must be Briseis." She smiled warmly at me. "Briseis. That name sounds so familiar." She strummed her fingers across the top of her briefcase. "It's from the Greek mythology, right?"

"Yes, ma'am," I said.

"Mythology lovers, huh?" she asked.

"Not really," I said, glancing at my mom.

"Sorry," said the woman, looking flustered. "I'm already getting sidetracked." She opened her briefcase, shuffling some papers around. "I'm Melissa Redmond. I represent the estate of

Circe Colchis. I understand her younger sister, Selene, was your birth mother."

"We weren't aware that her birth mother had any living relatives," Mom said quietly. She crossed her legs and started to shake her foot back and forth rhythmically, like she was keeping time. She did that when she was stressed or nervous. I scooted closer to her.

"Oh, you didn't know?" Mrs. Redmond asked, looking surprised. "Well then, this is probably very unexpected." Her brow furrowed and she shook her head. "I'm sorry to spring this on you. Usually when people inherit an estate, they know it's coming. This is a unique situation, isn't it?"

"I'd have to agree," Mo said.

Mrs. Redmond nodded. "I have limited background information, but if you didn't know about Circe before now, am I right to assume you don't know anything about this property at all?"

"This is news to us," Mom said.

Mrs. Redmond sighed. "Well then, I'll get right to it." She pulled out a stack of papers and set them on the coffee table. "The estate is sizable, which is why I was brought in. It was left solely to you, Briseis."

"So, it's a house?" I asked. "Like, a big house?"

Mrs. Redmond laughed. "Yes. A large house. But there are also personal possessions and the land it all sits on. About forty acres."

Mo gasped.

"Forty acres? How big is that?" I asked. "We measure things in city blocks around here."

Mrs. Redmond thought for a moment. "Think a football field without the end zones. That's about an acre."

"And we've got forty?" My mind raced. That was a lot of land, and that probably meant a lot of living, growing things.

Mrs. Redmond nodded. I could feel my mom's hand trembling on my leg.

"Where is it?" I asked.

"Upstate. Right outside of Rhinebeck."

"And it's mine?" I asked.

"It's yours," Mrs. Redmond said. "This is exciting, isn't it? Like I said, most people are expecting something when it comes to wills and estates. But you all look genuinely shocked. Forgive me. It's nice to not have to watch people argue over who gets what."

Mo shrugged. "Sounds messy."

"Legacies are a complicated thing," Mrs. Redmond said. "Especially when something of value is involved." She returned her attention to the stack of paperwork. "Everything was arranged before Miss Colchis passed away. We're able to skip probate altogether if you have a legal guardian who can sign the paperwork for you. And when you turn eighteen, everything will be put in your name." She handed me a large manila envelope. "I would ask that you keep an open mind when you go to see the place. Miss Colchis was an eccentric person. In the envelope are notes and keys that she asked be provided to you, Briseis."

"What kind of notes?" I asked.

"I'm not sure," said Mrs. Redmond. "They are intended for only you to see. My job is to make sure her wishes are followed to the letter, and I am very good at what I do." She smiled proudly. "I once had a woman leave an entire house and several million dollars to three tabby cats and a basset hound. Her actual children tried to contest the will, but it was ironclad and I made sure those animals got everything they were owed."

"Lucky pets," Mom said in disbelief.

Mrs. Redmond nodded in agreement.

Mo took out her phone. "The estate is near Rhinebeck? That's two and a half hours from here."

"It's a little out of the way," Mrs. Redmond said. "Maybe a lot out of the way, but it's all yours. There are a few stipulations that I have to go over with you." She read from a sheet of yellow notebook paper. "Miss Colchis asked that you not sell or otherwise change the property until you're at least eighteen. She seemed to think you'd find it agreeable once you've had a chance to go see it. The property has been in her family for many, many generations."

"What kind of taxes would we have to pay on a place that big?" Mom asked.

She was already thinking about this from every angle.

"Taxes, insurance, and utilities are paid through a trust," Mrs. Redmond said. "It's been done that way for many years. It's easier when a house is completely paid for, less to worry about."

I opened the envelope and two keys fell into my lap: a small, modern-looking one, and a larger one that looked much older, like a skeleton key.

"It's a big house—lots of rooms," Mrs. Redmond said. "I think the big key should open most of the doors inside. You'll have to do some cleaning, maybe some redecorating, but I'm sure you'll love it."

I held the keys in my hand. A big house sounded nice but going there meant I'd have to leave Brooklyn where I could avoid green spaces if I wanted to—and even then, it was hard to simply exist. This new place sounded like it was literally in the middle of forty acres of wilderness. I'd been open to hearing what Mrs. Redmond had to say, but now that I had, I didn't know if I wanted to deal with it.

A scratching noise sounded from behind my bedroom door. I didn't even glance in that direction.

"What's the catch?" Mom asked. "It sounds too good to be true, which means it probably is. So, what's the catch?"

"Nothing's ever as good as it seems, right?" Mrs. Redmond said. She straightened her skirt. "I'll be honest with you. Rhinebeck is picturesque. It's a touristy spot. But once you get past that you'll see that it's not quite what you expect."

"What do you mean?" I was looking for an out. With everything going on, this wasn't what I needed. I didn't want to go someplace where the day-to-day would be harder for me. "Not what we'd expect? That sounds kind of scary."

Mrs. Redmond laughed and her face relaxed. "Look at me, scaring you off before you even get there. What I mean to say is, Rhinebeck is full of colorful characters, but you shouldn't let that put you off."

"I've lived in New York my entire life," Mo said. "I've seen my share of colorful characters."

Mom turned to Mo. "I'm a pessimist. Give it to me the way you see it. You're always looking on the bright side."

Mo thought for a moment. I hoped she'd tell Mom this was too much to think about and that it'd be better if we stayed in Brooklyn. "Maybe this is exactly what is supposed to happen right now."

My heart sank.

"We've been struggling," she continued. "And we're about to struggle a whole lot more with this rent hike. We're gonna be paying forty-two hundred a month."

"Are you serious?" I didn't realize it would be going up a thousand dollars. I looked around the apartment. It was cute, but not forty-two hundred dollars' worth of cute, and a rent hike that big sounded illegal but landlords were always doing some shady shit.

"One of your parents will have to sign for you, and I brought duplicates of all the documents," said Mrs. Redmond. "As soon as you sign, you can go look around."

"We could go for the summer," Mo said. "Check it out?"

"Wait," I said, standing up. "We don't even know anything about this place. It's far. And—and it's in the sticks? In the *sticks*."

Mom caught my meaning and immediately came to my side. "She's right. This is too much. I don't think—"

"Please," Mrs. Redmond said gently. She came over and set her hand on my shoulder. "This place belongs to you now. If you don't take possession, it'll all go to the county and they'll do whatever they want with it. Sell it, auction it off to developers." She looked like the thought bothered her. "I'd hate to see that happen. So many old places end up getting razed for new housing or retailers. The estate is part of Rhinebeck's history, and it's away from the incorporated town. You'd have privacy and a chance to explore in peace."

"Some privacy sounds nice," said Mo, nodding at me. "I'm sick of knowing exactly what our neighbors are always arguing about. When I see them in the hall, I feel like I gotta pick a side."

"Who's going to look after the shop?" Mom asked.

"Jake can do it," Mo said. "We'll have to pay him, but I'm sure he'll do it."

Mom pinched the bridge of her nose. "We can't afford to pay him, Angie. I wish we could but we just can't."

I looked back and forth between Mom and Mo. Mo's eyes were lit up and Mom was trying to comfort me, but I could almost see the visions of a big house that was paid for bouncing around in her head. They needed this. *We* needed this.

"We could pay Jake if we cut back on inventory," I said.

Mom sighed. "Baby, if we cut our inventory, we won't make enough to keep—"

I gently squeezed her arm and she stopped, exchanging worried glances with Mo.

They could cut back on what they bought for the shop if I built up our stock, but it'd require me to use my power, which always felt like a gamble. They'd never asked me to produce flowers for the shop, and I'd been too scared to try. If I messed up, it could jeopardize their whole business.

"I—I want to try," I said.

Mom pulled me into a hug, and we sat on the couch.

"Let's go over everything line by line," said Mo. "Like Mom

said, this all seems too good to be true. I don't want to sign on to something crazy."

"I can stay as long as you need me to," Mrs. Redmond said happily. "I'd be glad to answer any questions you have."

Four hours later, after combing through the entire document, asking questions, and taking a break to go downstairs and convince Jake to work in the shop for the summer, Mo signed the documents. Jake agreed to help out on a more regular basis and in exchange we agreed to let him stay in our apartment for the summer so he didn't have to pay rent to sleep on his friend's couch.

In the early evening, Mrs. Redmond gathered her things and went to the door. "I'm so glad I got to meet you all."

"Good meeting you too," Mo said. "I hope this works out."

"I'm sure it will," said Mrs. Redmond. "Remember, call me if you have any additional questions. I'll be in touch after I've filed all the paperwork with the county. The property title will need to be changed in person, but I can walk you through that when the time comes. For now, take a minute to let all of this sink in."

After she left, we sat in silence for a long time before Mo spoke.

"We've got rent covered through the fall. That's when it goes up, but we don't have to re-sign the lease. We can move out if we want."

"I think we're getting ahead of ourselves," said Mom. "We don't know what kind of shape this place is in, if it's even livable. And the commute? Thinking about it makes my head hurt."

"Mom, you spend two hours in traffic tryna get to Home Depot and it's, like, four miles from here." I wasn't sure how any of this was going to work, but my family needed me to be okay with this. Leaving Brooklyn wasn't something I wanted to do. It was my home. But if we went to Rhinebeck, if this estate was something we could work with, my parents would be less stressed and I could get away. I could start over where nobody knew who I was or what I could do.

"What about your friends?" Mom asked. "And school?"

"You mean Gabby and Marlon? The friends I never see because I weird them out?" A knot grew in my throat. I swallowed it, trying to push away the ache. "And the classes that I'm barely passing because I can't focus. I'm scared to death I'll lose control and hurt somebody. All I wanna do when I'm not there is go to the park and grow—" I caught myself before I gave too much away. "There's nothing here that I don't mind leaving behind for a while. As long as I got you two, I'm good."

"I knew something wasn't right with your friends, baby," Mom said gently. "Y'all used to be together all the time but I haven't seen Gabby or Marlon or anybody else around lately. I don't even hear you talk about them. At least not the way you used to. I just thought it was because y'all are growing up, focused on school, maybe growing apart. But it's more than that, isn't it?"

I nodded, biting back tears.

She held my hand tight. "Maybe getting out of here for the summer will do us some good. Let's see what all this is about and go from there. Okay, baby?"

I rested my head on her shoulder. "Okay," I said. "Let's go."

Mo clapped her hands together, scaring the crap out of me

and Mom. "Let's pack up and leave in a few days," she said. "I can commute a few times during the week to help Jake. All the billing is online anyway. We can make this work for us. This might help us get back on track."

Her enthusiasm was infectious but even as I allowed myself to imagine this all working out, I couldn't shake the uneasy feeling building inside me. I didn't know if I could keep my abilities controlled in a place that far from the towering concrete buildings and paved streets of the city, but it looked like I was about to find out.

CHAPTER 5

Mom and Mo spent the next days planning our trip to Rhinebeck. When Jake came by, they went over everything that needed to be done while we were gone. Mo told him she'd come back on Mondays, Wednesdays, and Saturdays to help.

Mom insisted we keep up our regular order for most of our stock, but I told her I wanted to replenish our supply of red roses because we sold more of them than anything else. I stole away to the back garden and lined up pots, filled them with soil, and set fully bloomed roses in the dirt. Mom offered to keep me company, but I didn't want her or Mo anywhere nearby if something went wrong.

Stirring the soil with my fingers, the familiar prickling brought my skin to gooseflesh. I closed my eyes and concentrated as hard as I could on the warm feeling in my fingers.

Just grow. Only these flowers. Nothing else.

The stem of a rosebush pushed its way up through the dirt. My heart raced and my head pounded as I moved to each of the other pots. The back garden transformed into an oasis of crimson petals and dark green leaves and stalks. There must've been two hundred flowers ready for harvesting, so perfectly formed they looked fake. I knew they'd stay that way for weeks, maybe longer. I hoped Jake wouldn't question the peculiar longevity of the roses.

My vision blurred. I was winded, like I'd run a mile, and so dizzy I couldn't keep my balance when I stood up. I leaned against the back wall of the shop and slid to the ground, cradled my head in my hands, my palms damp with sweat. I just wanted this to work without having to be afraid of what might happen.

The door to the shop creaked open. Mo poked her head out, took one look at me, and pulled me inside. I slumped into a chair behind the counter and took off my glasses. Mo filled a paper cup with water and handed it to me. I sipped it slowly, worried it might come back up if I drank too fast.

"We're done with that," she said. "No more. We'll be fine."

"No, I can help," I said. I stood up and a sweeping rush of nausea knocked me right back down. "I need a minute to get it together."

Mo dampened a paper towel under the faucet and laid it across my forehead. She handed me my glasses and slipped her hand under my chin. "No. Let it be. We'll order what we need. Don't waste another minute thinking about it, you hear me?"

Mo glanced down the hall, then back to me. There was something in her eyes that scared me. It was uncertainty, fear. Of what? It could have been fifty different things, but I was afraid in that moment it might be me. She took me by the arm and led me out of the shop.

The next morning, we loaded the car up. I gave Jake my house key and asked him to water my plants before we took off.

Navigation said we'd get to Rhinebeck in two hours and twenty-three minutes. Mom pointed out that was the exact length of the *Hamilton* soundtrack, and I knew what we'd be listening to on our trip. Mo was Hamilton, Mom was Eliza, and I was Angelica, Peggy, and Mariah Reynolds—but they asked me to chill during "Say No to This" because apparently, my ho impression was too spot-on. It was only a bunch of gyrating and overdramatic hand gestures, but they weren't having it.

We kept the windows down and the volume up the whole way. When we pulled into the town of Rhinebeck, the closing chords of the final song played out. Mom sobbed through Eliza's farewell as Mo dramatically held her hand like she was the actual sad ghost of Alexander Hamilton, with me dying of embarrassment in the back seat.

"What key are y'all singin' in?" I asked. "I don't think any of those notes exist in real life."

"It's in B-quiet," Mo said, turning to Mom. "We're almost there. You okay?"

Mom nodded, wiping her face on her shirt.

Google said Rhinebeck had a population of seventy-seven hundred people. I told myself that was enough to keep us from feeling like we were moving to the middle of nowhere. But as we drove through the shop-lined streets of a literal village, I realized that their seven thousand, compared to our over two million in Brooklyn, was like moving to the moon. There wasn't any traffic. People strolled along the sidewalks like they didn't have anywhere to be. There were bike lanes and the cars actually yielded to the cyclists.

And there were trees. So many trees lining the streets.

Everywhere I looked were red maple and white ash in full bloom. Their beauty held my attention for only a minute before I understood how difficult this was going to make things for me.

"I don't know about this," I said.

Mom laughed. "Baby, this is heaven."

"Is it?" I asked. I was thinking of someplace else.

We drove the twenty-five-miles-per-hour speed limit through the town and several people waved to us. I stuck my head between the front seats. "Should I wave back?"

Mo shrugged. "I guess?"

I waved to an old man, who smiled and gave me a thumbs-up. I leaned back in my seat.

"Nah. See? It's like *Get Out*," I said. "I don't want a white woman living in my body, Mom."

"Girl, stop," said Mo, as she and Mom chuckled. "I know we're all used to being real guarded, but it looks like that's not how they do things up here."

"I already hate it," I said.

Mom looked at me in the rearview mirror. "Wanna turn around?" She was dead serious, and she would have done it if I'd asked her to.

I leaned against the door and thought of Gabby, of Marlon. "No, ma'am."

We took a series of turns that put us on a narrow, two-lane road leading away from town. After a few minutes, there were no other cars in sight, and the blue triangle on our GPS started to twirl in a circle.

"Great," Mom said. She reached under her seat and pulled out an actual map. She handed it to Mo.

"Yeah, okay," Mo said. "Let me just—" She flipped the map around a bunch of times, then smoothed it out on her lap. "If that way is north—" She literally pointed up and I clapped my hand over mouth to keep from hollering. "Then we have to keep going this way and—what direction does the sun set in again? Never mind. These numbers on the side, that's latitude, right?"

Mom let the air hiss out between her teeth. "I don't need to know the latitude."

"No?" Mo asked. "Okay, so I think we're, like, four kilometers away."

"Kilometers?" I sat back. "We're about to be so lost."

"I don't wanna get turned around out here, Angie," Mom said.

"I haven't read a map since I was in school," Mo said. "And after that we had MapQuest so—"

"What's MapQuest?" I asked.

Mom groaned. "Bri, baby, you been making me feel real old lately and if we're being honest, I hate it."

Mo stifled a laugh. "MapQuest is printed directions."

"Like on paper?" I asked. "You had to read it while you were driving?"

Mom gave an exhausted sigh.

The woods grew thicker the farther we went, crowding the road, their canopies so dense they blotted out the sky. Through their trunks I caught glimpses of the darkness that hinted at the vastness of the forest beyond. It unsettled me.

My stomach turned to knots as the road twisted through the trees and came to a fork about two miles in. Mom veered to the right. The mile markers disappeared, replaced by handwritten signs that read No Trespassing and Private Property.

"You sure this is the right way?" Mo asked.

Mom turned to her. "You're the one with the map."

The road narrowed then stopped abruptly at two towering pillars. It looked like there had once been a gate, but that was long gone and the faded brick pillars were now crumbling. Mom pulled into the driveway and the house came into view.

"Is this it?" Mom asked. "This can't be right."

It stood like it had sprouted from the ground, like a living thing. Its foundation was covered in thick green moss. A latticework on the side was completely encased in a tangle of leafy vines. Hundreds of tendrils jutted off, stretching across nearly every surface of the slate-gray house. They wound around its conical turret, laced themselves through the banister, traced the pointed arches over the windows and doors like picture frames. The inky black trim highlighted all the angles. A big green dumpster sat on the side of the house and from what I could see of the grounds somebody had slacked off on mowing.

"Did I—did I inherit the Addams Family Mansion?" I stammered.

Mom put the car in park and got out. Mo followed, but I hung back. We were pretty far from the town, and I could see the land the house sat on stretching away from us, bordered by forest on all sides. I didn't see any other houses or buildings. If I accidentally made something happen, nobody was around to see. I expected that possibility to send me spiraling into thoughts of controlling my power, of worrying about keeping myself and my parents safe. Instead, a quick burst of excitement pulsed through me. It caught me by surprise to feel anything other than fear and uncertainty.

Mo motioned for me to get out so I grabbed my bag, took a deep breath, and opened the door.

As I slipped out of the car, the vines closest to the front door rustled and sprouted dozens of velvety pink blooms. I immediately looked away.

Mo reached out and took my hand. "It's okay. Hang on to me. Breathe."

I took out the keys Mrs. Redmond had given me. That burst of excitement had run its course and all I wanted to do was get inside. I went up the front steps, across the wide porch, and put my key in the lock. A rush of stale air greeted us as I pushed the heavy, old-fashioned door open. Mom put her arm around me as Mo searched for a light switch. When she found one and flipped it on, the entryway was bathed in a gauzy yellow glow.

The inside of the house reminded me of the brownstones rich folks in the city lived in, with all the original wood inside, built-in bookshelves, and wide staircases that led to sprawling upper floors. Each room branching off the entryway was as big as our entire apartment, and they were filled with furniture draped in dingy drop cloths. Sunlight filtered through the squares of blue-and-green stained glass set in geometric patterns above each of the narrow windows that flanked the front door. Dust hung in the air. The mineral-like taste stuck in my mouth.

Mom kicked a stack of papers and a mouse scurried out from underneath. "This place is a fire hazard."

"It needs some TLC," said Mo. "A good cleaning, but it's paid for, so let's try to look at the silver lining."

Mom sighed heavily. “We should start by moving some of this trash out,” she said, eyeing a big plastic bag that seemed to be squirming. Probably more rodents.

I shivered at the thought. “Nasty.”

“Let’s do a walk-through,” said Mo. “Stake out bedrooms—”

“Get possessed by the ghost of an angry white man,” I said jokingly.

Mom’s eyes grew wide. “Do not play with me.”

Mom came up in a family, headed up by my grandma, whose folk magic practices stretched back generations. She wasn’t as into it as my Auntie Leti or Granny, but she respected it. Fully. She didn’t mess with ghosts, spirits, haints, none of that, and not because she thought it was silly, but because she knew there was probably something to it.

As we wound our way through the house, checking out each room, I expected to feel out of place, like I was intruding on someone else’s space, but a sense of calm settled over me. The house was old and a mess but it had that lived-in feeling. Like people had laughed and loved there, shared meals and stories, celebrated birthdays and holidays. It felt warm. I wondered how long it would be before reality came to steal this moment of wonder and excitement from me.

The main floor had two separate living rooms, a formal dining room, a huge kitchen, a bunch of big closets with winter coats and boots for at least two or three people. There was only one bathroom and I prayed to Black Jesus that there was another one upstairs somewhere.

Near the rear of the first floor, the hallway seemed to narrow and the runner that ran down the center was faded and worn almost completely through. The hall terminated in front of an enormous wooden door, the surface carved with wide leaves of canna and Persian ivy. I ran my hand over the intricate woodwork.

"This is really beautiful." I tried the ornately engraved handle. Locked.

"Let's keep moving and come back to it later," suggested Mo.

"Seriously?" I asked. "Mo, that's how you miss the room that used to be a morgue or whatever and then, boom—we're all possessed by demons."

"Would you stop with the possession stuff?" Mom said, gripping Mo's arm.

"Don't worry, babe," Mo said, shooting her a devilish grin. "I'll protect you."

"How?" Mom asked. "How you gonna protect me from a ghost?"

Mo pulled her close as I took the two keys Mrs. Redmond had given me and tried them in the lock. The skeleton key worked. The door opened with a creaking groan.

The room beyond was the size of the flower shop—maybe even bigger—and set up in a similar way. A wide counter, scattered with different kinds of scales, measuring cups, and scoops of varying sizes, ran the length of the room. Behind it and along the back wall, shelves went up two full stories, the height of the house. A ladder ran along a track that circled the entire room like in an old library, but there weren't any books on the shelves, only glass jars. Dozens and dozens of glass jars of all different sizes and shapes.

"I'm so confused," said Mo, her gaze darting around the room.

We filed in, Mom still clinging to Mo for dear life. The air was sweet and smoky, something like the lingering scent of incense. A fine layer of dust covered everything. I set my bag on the counter and walked to the ladder, pulling it in front of the wall of jars behind the counter. I put my foot on the bottom rung.

"Please be careful, baby," said Mom. "I don't know how far away the hospital is."

I tested my weight on the step. Mo came over and steadied the ladder as I climbed up about halfway. It wobbled and creaked and I grabbed the shelf, glancing down at Mo.

"You gotta hold it still," Mom said.

"This thing is rickety as hell," Mo huffed. She planted her foot next to the small wheel at the bottom.

When I was sure she had a handle on the ladder, I leaned over and plucked a big glass jar with a silver lid from the shelf. I read the peeling, faded label aloud. "Wintergreen." I set it down and examined the labels on the other jars. "Winter's Bark. Witchgrass. Witch Hazel."

"Witch what?" Mom asked.

"Witch hazel," Mo said. "Comes in a liquid. You can use it for hemorrhoids."

Mom scrunched up her nose. "Excuse me?"

I laughed. "I mean, you're not wrong. It's a natural anti-inflammatory."

"Okay. But what's witchgrass for?" Mom asked.

I shrugged. I wasn't entirely sure. I continued up the ladder, reading labels as I went. Thyme. Spiderwort. Orchid. Myrrh. It went on and on in reverse-alphabetical order. There had to be two hundred jars, and most of them were full.

"What is this place?" I asked. Whatever it was, it felt familiar.

At the top of the ladder, I stepped onto a narrow platform that wound around the top part of the room, allowing access to the highest shelves. A sturdy mahogany banister was anchored to the balcony-like structure. I gripped it as I shuffled along the walkway, examining the rest of the jars. A nondescript built-in cupboard sat in the wall near the end of the walkway. I slid the door open. Inside were three shelves, all lined with glass jars, painted black, obscuring their contents. I pushed up my glasses and picked up the container closest to me.

Water Hemlock Root.

I fumbled the jar but caught it before it crashed to the floor below.

"You good?" Mo asked.

"Yeah," I said as images of the dissected hemlock root flashed in my mind. "It's just more dried plants."

I read the names on the other jars to myself as my heart threatened to beat out of my chest. Oleander Leaves and Stalks, Wolfsbane, White Snakeroot, Angel's Trumpet, Rosary Pea, Little Apple of Death, Castor Oil Beans.

They were all poisonous.

Deadly.

I shook the jar. I didn't think there was anything inside, but I didn't want to chance opening it. My stomach twisted into a knot. I closed the cabinet door and climbed back down on unsteady legs.

Mo rummaged through a drawer under the counter. "Look. There are labels, bags, twine, like we have at the shop. Were the people who lived here selling this stuff?"

"It's an apothecary," Mom said. "I think. Or some kind of old school natural medicine dispensary. My grandma used to go to a place like this when I was little."

Maybe that was what the larger part of this place was for—natural medicines or teas or something—but that couldn't be all. I glanced up at the small cabinet of poisons. Those plants couldn't even be handled with bare hands, much less ingested as medicine, not without fatal consequences. I rubbed my finger over the cut on my thumb.

"Should we check out the rooms upstairs?" Mo asked.

I nodded, grabbed my bag, and closed the heavy door behind us as we went out.

The wall along the stairs that led to the second floor was lined with paintings and photographs of people—families, children, and a trio of women smiling and hugging one another. I paused to take a closer look. They all had the same big brown eyes, and two of them wore glasses. They shared the same toothy smile, the same mass of tight coils crowning their heads in varying lengths, their brown skin beaming in the sun. They looked happy standing arm in arm in front of this very house. They looked like me.

Mom put her hand on my shoulder. "You okay, baby?"

"I've gotta be related to them, right?"

"I'd think so," Mom said, leaning in and studying the photo. "They're gorgeous. Like you, baby." She turned back to me. "You sure you're okay?"

"Yeah," I said. But everything suddenly felt heavier.

Other photographs and artwork crowded the wall. A large painting of a black dog with yellow eyes hung in a silver frame. In a smaller painting, a man was shown lying under the ground as vines grew out of the soil above him, twisting into a strange-looking tree. Mom nudged me up the last few steps.

On the upper floor we found another smaller living room, and a laundry room with a washer and dryer. Mom almost cried at the sight of it. No more venturing into the stank-ass basement of our building to wash clothes. Finally, there were four huge bedrooms, all furnished with big four-poster beds and matching linens and pillows. Huge dressers and armoires sat against the walls, and each bedroom had its own bathroom. The thought of being able to complete my wash-day routine in peace made me deliriously happy. Back home, Mom always seemed to have a craving for ice cream right in the middle of my twist out, knowing she's been lactose intolerant her entire life, and knowing we all had to share the single bathroom. Living out in the middle of nowhere might be worth the trouble if I could have my own bathroom.

Mo discovered a claw-foot tub in the bathroom of the largest bedroom, and she and Mom did a whole-ass praise dance to celebrate.

I wandered into the room next to theirs and flipped on the light switch. The bulbs buzzed on in an uneven pattern, slowly illuminating the room. Even when they'd reached peak brightness, it was too dark. I pulled the heavy navy blue curtains away from the windows, which sent a cloud of dust into the air. I took stock of the rest of the room.

There were two narrow windows, a dresser and matching armoire, and a chest near the wall that held neatly folded blankets and sheets. A fireplace was set in the rear wall, and on the marble hearth were a dozen pots housing the remains of shriveled plants.

"Y'all look pitiful," I said as I stirred the dirt with my fingers. They came back to life, greening up and sprouting a few new leaves. African violets, pastel pink geraniums, jasmine, and a half dozen others woke from their slumber. Lots of quiet plants, like the ones I kept in my own room back home.

I unlocked the windows and pushed them open. A warm breeze swept through the room and cleared out some of the stuffiness. I tried to see around the back of the house but couldn't get a good view from my room. I went down the hall and peered through a window that overlooked the rear yard.

A large expanse of open grass with a few small outcroppings of trees butted up to a dense tree line. Beyond that was forest as far as I could see, with a few paths snaking into it. Something stirred in the pit of my stomach. I thought I noticed a subtle shift in the tilt of the trees. I quickly stepped away from the window.

A quick series of a half dozen sneezes cut through the air. I went back to Mom's room to find her sneezing her face off as Mo shook out the curtains in their room.

"I'm gonna need Zyrtec," Mom said. "Maybe a biohazard suit."

I jumped onto the bed, sending a plume of dust into the air.

Mom shrieked and pulled her T-shirt up over her face. "You tryna kill me?"

I carefully scooted off. Her allergies were a mess in the summertime and being out in the sticks was only going to make them worse.

"What are we gonna do with the extra bedrooms?" I asked.

"We can turn one into an office or something," Mo said. "Make the other a guest room so your grandma can come visit."

"She'll love this place," I said. Staying here for the summer—or maybe longer—was looking more and more like the right move.

"*If* we stay," Mom added. "We haven't gotten that far yet."

"Just keep an open mind, babe," said Mo.

"I'm trying," Mom said, but there was a clear ring of worry in her tone.

"Let's finish looking around," I said.

I moved toward the door, but Mo knelt and looked up into the chimney of the fireplace. She reached in and pulled a short chain. The flue groaned as it opened, spilling a pile of rotted leaves and a dead bird into the hearth. Mom looked absolutely done.

"At least it's clear," said Mo. "We can put some logs in there, get a bearskin rug. It'll be romantic."

Mom rolled her eyes and shoved her hand down on her hip. "Nothing romantic about a roasted chicken in the fireplace."

Mo inspected the twisted pile of feathers. "I'm pretty sure it's a crow, but I'm gonna clean it up. Don't worry."

While they fussed, I went out to the hallway to look around. More paintings and photographs lined the walls—some in color, some in black and white, and some were paintings that looked like they should be hanging in a museum. At the end of the hall was a narrow door with a bronze handle. I pulled it open and found myself at the foot of a short flight of stairs."

"There's another floor," I called out.

Mom and Mo joined me at the bottom of the staircase. A dim light streamed down from somewhere above.

"Want me to go up first?" Mo asked.

She didn't have to ask twice. Me and Mom stepped aside to let her through.

"Man, y'all are cold blooded," she said, shaking her head. She trudged up the stairs. A few moments later she called down to us. "Come on up."

CHAPTER 6

I climbed the stairs, ducking so I didn't hit my head on the stairwell's slanted roof, and emerged in a small room with a conical ceiling.

"We're in the turret," I said, peering out a small oval window that overlooked the driveway.

Shelving went around the entire room. Every nook was filled with books, boxes, and a bunch of old furniture. Paintings hung on the walls, but unlike the ones downstairs they all featured the same person—a woman, her skin rendered in the warmest golden brown, her hair and eyes dark. In one gold-framed portrait, she sat at a table scattered with an assortment of strange items. A small fire burned in a dish in front of her as she poured liquid from a cup into the flames. Next to the dish sat a large green toad, an abalone shell, and a coiled red string. The woman stared out at me, her full lips parted, like she was about to say something.

"Do you think she's related to them?" I asked. "To Circe and the other people in the portraits in the hall?"

Mo studied the painting. "Maybe. She looks a lot like them, like you."

"We should probably start moving some of the junk out of the bedrooms and get the sheets in the wash so we have a clean place to sleep," Mom said.

"Good idea," Mo said. They went to the stairs.

"I just need a minute," I said.

Mo nodded and ushered Mom down the stairs. I didn't want to leave yet. Not until I'd had a chance to look at the other painting of the mysterious woman. In it, she was seated next to a man, her right hand extended over a small copper-colored dish, eyes fixed on her work. I could see the painter's brushstrokes in the red of her dress. The woman looked absolutely focused on whatever was in the dish, and the man next to her sat in rapt attention, his brown eyes wide, regarding her with some mix of fear and intrigue.

I looked around, trying to imagine the people who had lived here before, what they might have been like. It was clear they loved books and had a soft spot for the woman in the paintings. I pictured them standing where I was standing, deciding which books to read and which pieces of old furniture they were going to stow in the turret. A wave of curiosity like I hadn't felt since I was younger overtook me.

I fished the manila envelope Mrs. Redmond had given me out of my bag and opened it. Inside was a smaller white envelope. My first name was written across the front. I slipped my finger under the lip of the seal. As I pulled it open, a scream cut through the stuffy attic air.

My heart jumped into my throat. I shoved the letter in my pocket and scrambled down the stairs as the scream rang out again. The front door sat open. I raced onto the porch and jumped, bypassing the four steps and landing on the driveway's cracked pavement. I couldn't see Mom or Mo anywhere.

A groan sounded from the side of the house. I rushed toward it, skidding around the corner. The toe of my sneaker caught on a rock and I fell face-first next to the big green dumpster.

Mom lay in a heap next to me, newspapers scattered all around her. Mo stood next to the dumpster, doubled over, laughing hysterically.

"I'm gonna piss myself!" she said.

Mom sat up. Bits of grass and leaves stuck out of her hair. She brushed herself off. "It's not funny!"

I rolled to a sitting position and readjusted my glasses. My knee throbbed and my elbow was scraped up. A cool, tingling sensation spread over my palms and down the side of my neck.

I glanced at Mom. The leaves clinging to her were familiar to me—something I'd used in a bouquet? Some other arrangement maybe. I looked closer.

"Oh no."

It was all I could say before deep, ruddy splotches bloomed on Mom's face and neck, her outstretched arms, her bare legs. The spots turned to raised welts and the area around her left eye began to swell.

She clawed at her skin. "What the hell is this? Why am I so damn itchy?"

We'd both tumbled into a tangle of brush. Clusters of leaves in groups of threes numbered in the hundreds.

"It's poison ivy," I said.

"Oh shit," Mo said. All the joking was over. She reached out to help Mom up.

"No, wait," I said. "Don't touch her. The poison can spread to you too."

Mom stood up and looked me over. "You okay? I don't see any welts."

"Yet," I said quickly. "It could take a few minutes to show up." I knew I should've felt something already.

"What do we do?" Mom asked.

"We have to wash it off," I said. "The oil in the plant is what causes the reaction. We have to get it off us." The cool sensation on my skin dissipated as images of the hemlock root splayed open on my desk flashed in my head. This feeling was nothing even close to that.

"Come on," Mom said.

I followed her to her room. She went into her bathroom and turned on the water in the tub. Mo was furiously Googling Mom's symptoms on WebMD, asking her if she was having trouble breathing or swallowing. She wasn't, so at least we didn't need to go to the ER.

"I'm gonna go wash off in my bathroom," I said.

"Okay," said Mom. "Hurry before it gets too bad."

I went to my bathroom and closed the door. I turned on the faucet in the tub. The water spurted brown for a few seconds before clearing. I took off my shirt and stared at myself in the floor-length mirror that hung on the back of the door. I waited for the hives to appear.

I turned and tried to get a look at my back—nothing there,

nothing on the curve of my belly where my shirt had risen up when I fell. No splotches on my legs. The cool feeling had completely disappeared. Maybe it was because the poison ivy was less toxic than other plants, but even still, welts and blisters should have been popping up all over me by now. I sat on the edge of the tub, watching the water swirl into the drain, feeling like I was missing something. Something important.

"Briseis?" Mo called from outside the bathroom door.

I turned off the water. "Yes, ma'am?"

"I'm gonna have to go into town and get some calamine lotion for Mom. She's a mess."

"Into town?" I laughed. "Sounds real country."

"Right?" she said. "We're already fitting in. How much calamine lotion do you need, love? You need a whole bottle?"

I looked at my reflection again. "I don't think it got me as bad as Mom. I'm good."

"Okay. Text me if you change your mind. Be back soon."

I heard her leave and close the door. I stripped off the rest of my dirty clothes, washed my cut elbow, and changed into a pair of leggings and an oversized T-shirt I'd shoved in my bag before we left home. I went down the hall to check on Mom. I knocked on her door.

"Don't come in here," she said. "I don't want you to see me like this."

I could tell by her tone that she was only half-joking, so I turned the handle and went in. She was sprawled across her bed in her underwear, staring up at the ceiling. Every inch of skin that wasn't protected by her tank top or shorts when she fell was covered in welts.

“I want to scratch my skin off,” she said.

“Don’t,” I said. “That’ll make it worse.”

“It can get worse? Great.” She turned her head to look at me. “You’re not scratching. You didn’t get any on you?”

“I guess not,” I said, looking at the floor. An entire triplet of leaves had gone in my mouth when I fell, but I wasn’t going to tell her that.

“Lucky,” she said.

“Mo’ll be back soon. What can I do?”

“Nothing, baby,” she said. She gave in and scratched her forearm. Relief spread across her face. “Why don’t you go look around some more? See if the fridge works so we can pick up some groceries. But text Mo and tell her to grab takeout for tonight.”

I went downstairs to explore the kitchen. Everything we needed was there: dishes, glasses, silverware, pots and pans, but the appliances looked as old as the house itself. A huge black contraption with a bunch of rectangular doors on the front was set into a tiled alcove in the rear wall. I sent Mo a text and asked her to grab some food on her way back.

My thoughts wandered to the letter Mrs. Redmond had given me. I took the crumpled note from my pocket and went out onto the front porch. I opened the letter and read the handwritten script.

Dearest Briseis,

I hope this letter finds you well. I realize how strange all this must seem to you, and I am sorry it has come to letters and wills and lawyers. I should have told you these things face-to-face, but it was not meant to be.

I have lived my entire life here in the very house I intend to leave you. I was happy here with Selene. I find it ironic that, even with these gifts, we are not impervious to suffering.

I paused.

"Gifts."

I hope you will make your home here, because there is no one else this place could belong to. It is yours, by right. There are things that I cannot fully explain. Selene had hoped to save you, but we cannot escape our fate. This was always meant to be.

In the turret, behind the portrait of Medea, you will find a safe. The combination is 7-22-99. More answers will be provided for you there, but you must not, under any circumstances, share the contents of these instructions with anyone. You will have questions, but everything you need to know is contained within these walls. There are, I would imagine, things transpiring in your life that you have questions about—and you may find yourself set apart. Please know that, in time, you will come to understand it all.

Always,
Circe

I stuffed the letter back in the envelope. I was about to run to the turret to see if there really was a safe behind the painting, when the car came up the drive.

Mo parked right in front of the door. "I need a hand, love."

I helped her bring in two plastic containers of takeout and a paper bag filled with stuff from the pharmacy. We set the food on the kitchen counter and Mo caught sight of the stove.

"Look at that," she said, smiling. "My great-grandma had a stove like that when I was a kid and even then it was old as hell. You have to start a fire in the middle part to get it going."

"Like, with wood?" I asked.

"Yup," said Mo. "That should be fun. Can you do me a favor and pull some of the covers off the furniture in that front room so we can sit and eat? I'd say let's eat at the table but I saw a mouse skipping across those fancy place settings a little earlier."

"Gross," I said. The curiosity about what might be in the turret wasn't loud enough to drown out the noises my stomach was making. I was starving.

Mo took the stuff from the pharmacy up to Mom and I pulled the drop cloths off the living room furniture. Everything looked like it belonged in a castle in the English countryside, not in a house in upstate New York. The couch and chaise were covered in matching emerald green fabric with yellow begonias stitched on them. There was a coffee table and an ottoman under the other cloths. I washed off some plates and forks from the kitchen and carried them to the front room with the takeout. I hooked up my laptop and put on a movie.

Footsteps on the stairs drew my attention. Mo walked down first, her finger pressed to her lips, signaling for me not to say a word. Mom came down after her, covered head to toe in pink calamine lotion, her bright red bonnet sitting halfway off her head. I laughed anyway and Mo let her hands fall heavily at her sides.

"I know, I know," said Mom. "Laugh it up." She lowered herself onto the couch like she was made of glass. Mo got her settled, but she kept switching her position every few minutes, huffing and puffing because she couldn't get comfortable.

"What was that stuff Grandma put on you when those mosquitoes tore you up last summer?" I asked.

Mom tilted her head back and sighed. "I don't know, baby, but I wish I had some right now."

I took out my phone, glancing at the time. "You think it's too late to call her and ask?"

"She's a night owl," Mom said.

Mo raised an eyebrow. "'Owl' isn't the right word. Maybe 'night creature'? 'Night demon'?"

Mom was trying so hard not to smile. Mo and Grandma loved each other, but they had a funny way of showing it. Grandma was always giving Mo a hard time about putting sugar in her grits, and Mo was always telling her that her wig was crooked. It was jab after jab, and then they'd end up on the couch cry-laughing over episodes of *Judge Mathis*.

I dialed my grandma's number, and she picked up on the second ring.

"Hey, my sweet baby," she said. Her voice was a familiar song, her thick Southern drawl like honey. "How's everything goin' up there, baby? Your mama said you was goin' up for the summer to some place called Rhinebeck."

I stood and walked into the hallway. "Yes, ma'am. We're here. But Mom fell into a patch of poison ivy."

"She did what now?" She let out a deep, throaty laugh.

"Granny, she's jacked up. She was wearing shorts and a tank top. She's got welts and blisters everywhere. Mo got her some calamine lotion, but she's still hurtin'."

"Calamine lotion ain't gon' do it, baby."

"Can you tell me what you put on her last summer? The stuff for the bug bites?"

"I made that myself. Little bit of this, little bit of that."

I glanced toward the apothecary. "I've got a bunch of herbs and stuff here. I could probably make it if you tell me how."

"Hmm," she said. "You know, your auntie Leti was always real good at puttin' together salves and balms and such. Your mama tried, bless her heart, but she never really took to it. You got a mind to do somethin' yourself?"

"Maybe," I said, honestly.

"You need to get you a dish, somethin' wide to put everything in."

I went into the apothecary and put Grandma on speaker. I found a large glass bowl on the shelf and set it on the counter.

"Got it," I said.

"Baby girl, you not gon' have all the things you need."

"I might," I said, looking up at the wall of jars. "I'll write it down if I don't have it."

"You need calendula flowers, a little jojoba oil, salt, lavender oil, and some clay."

I pulled the ladder over and found jars with everything she'd mentioned. There were two larger jars labeled Clay. I opened their lids and peered inside. "Grandma, is clay supposed to look like powder?"

"Yes, baby," she said. "You need some that's a sandy color and smells like outside after it rains. You got that, baby?"

One of the jars was full of a light brown powder that smelled damp and earthy. That had to be it.

"I got it, Grandma."

"Really?" she asked, sounding surprised. "What y'all getting into up there that you got everything you need right in front of you?"

"It's an old house," I said. "But there's a shop with all kinds of natural stuff in here."

She huffed. "Wait till I tell your auntie. She gon' be on the first flight out to visit."

I gathered up the other ingredients she'd mentioned. "How much do I use?"

"Just put a little in at a time. You'll know when to stop."

I laughed. That's the way she did everything, by feeling, by her gut.

"When you got everything together, mix it all up in the bowl. Use your hands though, not no spoon or nothin' like that."

"I have to use my hands?"

She laughed. "Can't be done no other way. You fixin' somethin' for somebody you love, for healin'. Gotta do it with your bare hands and your whole heart. Understand?"

I didn't need to fully understand to know she was right. If that was how she would do it, I'd take her word. "Yes, ma'am."

"I gotta go, baby," she said. "Tell your mama to sit her narrow behind down somewhere, and tell Mo I said *Judge Mathis* moved to eleven in the mornin'."

"I will," I said.

"You take care. Be careful. I dreamed about Mama Lois. She only comes around when there's about to be a problem. Nothin' strange goin' on up there, is it?"

My heartbeat ticked up. Mama Lois was Grandma's grandma, and she'd been dead since way before I was born. When Grandma dreamed about her, it meant something was off. "Not yet, but I guess we'll find out."

There was a long pause. "I love you, baby girl. Call me on the weekend, okay?"

"I will. Love you more."

I hung up and finished mixing the herbs and oils together in the bowl, pressing them together with my bare hands. I added the ingredients until they formed a sticky paste that resembled the thickness of the batch my grandma had made for my mom last summer. As I sank my fingers into it, warmth bloomed in my palms. The dried calendula turned from brown to vibrant yellow and the pungent, earthy aroma of the petals wafted up. My grandma was right. Everything came together and something in my gut told me it was ready.

I washed my hands and carried the bowl to Mom.

"This is it!" she said excitedly. "Baby, you did it!" She turned to Mo. "Babe, get a paintbrush. You about to paint every inch of me with this."

Mom kissed me and took the bowl with her as she waddled up the stairs. Mo looked like she wanted to scream.

"I guess I'll be upstairs, painting your mom," she said.

"That's y'all's business," I said, laughing.

"You staying up, love?"

"Yeah, for a little while," I said.

She hugged me and went upstairs mumbling something about not having a paintbrush.

I muted the volume on my laptop. As soon as I heard their door close, I crept up the stairs, past the portraits and pictures that seemed to come alive in the darkness. The black dog's big yellow eyes followed me as I hurried by. I went to the turret with a million questions tumbling through my head. Was there really a safe behind the painting, and what could possibly be inside that warranted this kind of secrecy?

A single bulb illuminated the cramped space now that the sun had set, and the portrait of the woman Circe called Medea hung on the wall, looking more ominous than she had in the daytime. Her expression was serious, maybe even angry and her eyes were steely, painted in a way that made me feel like she was looking at me no matter where I stood. I lifted the painting off the nail and set it on the floor. Behind it was a silver wall safe with a combination lock.

I turned the dial. Right, left, right. 7–22–99.

It popped open.

"Please let it be a million dollars," I said to myself.

A single folder sat inside. It wasn't thick enough to have a million dollars in it. I was disappointed. I took it out and sat in a rocking chair under the light bulb so I could see.

There were three envelopes in the folder. Each one had my name, and they were numbered one through three. It was the same handwriting as the letter Mrs. Redmond had given me. Clearly this woman, my birth mother's sister, wanted to communicate with me, but I hesitated. Circe was a stranger. She didn't know my favorite color, or my favorite food, or that I couldn't sleep if I had socks on. She didn't know anything about me and I didn't know she existed until a few days before. The house was going to help my family, but these letters, whatever they were, felt like a burden I didn't want.

I shoved the envelopes back in the safe and rehung the picture. As I reached up to turn off the light, something outside the window caught my eye.

There was someone standing in the dark, looking at the house.

I moved closer to the window to get a better look. It was a young woman with a crown of silver-gray hair, blown out in a way that made it look like her head was surrounded by a luminous cloud. I had to blink a few times to make sure I was really seeing her.

She met my gaze like she knew I'd be standing there, staring down at her. She smiled, and I bolted downstairs to tell my parents there was a stranger in the driveway.

CHAPTER 7

I knocked on my parents' door.

"Come in," Mom called.

I opened the door a crack. "There's someone outside."

"What?" Mo called from the bathroom. "It's almost midnight."

"I know, but she's standing in the driveway. I saw her from the window upstairs."

Mo came barreling out of the bathroom in her tank top and sweatpants.

Mom jumped up and pulled her taser from her purse. She pushed the button and a bolt of static electricity split the air with a loud crack. "I'm not playin' games. Get in the closet."

"Mom! I'm not going in the closet."

I quickly turned and followed Mo down the stairs before Mom forced me to hide. Mo went to the window next to the front door and peered out. She reached for the doorknob.

"What the hell are you doing?" Mom asked as she came racing after us.

"I see somebody," Mo said.

"You just gonna open the door?" Mom asked, peeking through the window next to her. "Investigating weird people in the driveway will get your ass sliced up, Angie. You've seen *Us*. Come on now."

"She could be hurt or something," Mo said. She unlocked the door and pulled it open a crack. "Can I help you?"

I didn't hear an answer.

Mom sighed. "'Can I help you?' Really, Angie?" She brushed past Mo and wrenched open the door. She hit the button on her Taser again. "You're on private property!" Mom shouted. "You ain't never met nobody like me—" She stopped short.

"What?" I asked anxiously. "What is it?"

She stepped out onto the porch, her Taser crackling in the dark. "There's nobody here."

"What? No," said Mo, rushing outside. "I saw somebody." She quickly steered Mom back inside and closed the door, locking it. "Maybe we should call the police."

Mom shook her head. "Do we want to do that? Do we need to? We see all kinds of weirdos back home." She held up the Taser. "I can handle this."

"We're new," Mo reminded her. "We have no idea what kind of weirdos they got up here. Could be nothing to worry about, could be everything."

One of the handful of times I had actually seen Mo call the cops was right after she witnessed a car swerve off the road and hit a guy on the sidewalk. She was trying to get an ambulance, but the cops showed up and made everything so much worse than it needed to be. She avoided calling them unless it was absolutely necessary.

"She was there, and then she was gone," Mom said. "She disappeared."

"People don't disappear, Thandie." Mo sat on the couch, massaging her temple. "I saw somebody and so did Bri. Maybe she ran off when you came out of the house screaming like a banshee."

"I wasn't screaming," Mom said. She looked at me. "Was I screaming?"

"Define 'screaming,'" I said. "Your outfit was probably what scared her off." She was covered head to toe in the salve I'd made. Her ugly leather house shoes with the heel folded down were sliding off her feet as she shuffled around the entryway. Her droopy red bonnet topped off the terrifying ensemble.

Mom looked down at her outfit, paused, then shrugged like she knew I was right. "Okay. Maybe I scared her off, but who was she, Flo-Jo? She was gone."

I found a non-emergency number for the Rhinebeck police department online and handed my phone to Mo. We waited for almost an hour before the doorbell rang.

Mo hopped up to answer it and I grabbed the pile of paperwork Mrs. Redmond had left with us to show that that we were allowed to be there. Mom set down her Taser, then took to pacing the floor.

Mo led a tall woman into the front room. She wasn't wearing a uniform, but had a name badge hanging from a lanyard around her neck. She was put together—black slacks, button-up, and a blazer—and had a walkie-talkie clipped to her belt. "I'm Dr. Khadijah Grant. I run the civilian Public Safety Office here in Rhinebeck. How are you all this evening?" When she caught sight of Mom she bit back a smile.

"We've been better," Mo said. "Public Safety Office? So, you're not a police officer?"

"No, ma'am," Dr. Grant said kindly. "I'm a licensed social worker, and my department handles incidents called in on the non-emergency line."

"I have a Taser," Mom said, pointing to the coffee table. "Just so you know."

Dr. Grant glanced at her, her smile like a mask. She probably used it to put people at ease while she observed everything around her. She'd already spotted the Taser. "As long as you aren't planning on zapping me, it shouldn't be a problem."

"I wasn't planning on it," Mom said. "But I'm glad I have it. Took y'all a while to get here."

"I apologize," Dr. Grant said. "We've recently begun defunding the local police department. Several officers have proven themselves to be more of a problem than an asset to the residents here. As such, we've cut back the number of officers on the force and diverted funding to programs that better serve the community. My department acts as a buffer between what's left of the police and the community to ensure everyone's safety."

"Well, damn," Mom said. "Sounds like y'all are ahead of the game out here in the sticks."

"I'd like to think so," said Dr. Grant. "No one has lived at this address for a while, so we don't have anyone on regular patrol this far out. I'll make sure we add a trained community patrol partner to the route. You have my word." Her expression turned to one of concern. "Dispatch said you had a prowler?"

"Yes," said Mo. "Someone was standing in the driveway. They took off when we opened the door."

"What did this person look like?" Dr. Grant asked.

"I didn't get a good look at her," Mo offered. "I saw her through the window, but she looked about my size, around five foot eight, maybe."

"Briseis saw her," Mom offered.

Dr. Grant was taking notes on a small pad of paper but stopped abruptly. She didn't look up but her pen stopped moving. "And what did you see, Briseis?" she asked, eyes still downcast.

"It was dark," I said. "It was a girl. Maybe. I'm not sure but somebody was definitely out there." I knew what I'd seen but I found myself holding back on the details.

Dr. Grant took the walkie-talkie from her belt. "I need a community patrol to sweep the outside of 307 Old Post Road." She holstered it and went to the front door.

"She's probably not hiding outside, right?" I asked.

"I hope not," said Mo, glancing at Mom. "For her sake."

Mom huffed.

A few minutes later, a car marked with a Rhinebeck Public Safety decal pulled up and two people got out. They went to opposite sides of the house with their flashlights drawn, casting long columns of light into the dark. Dr. Grant opened the door as they circled around and came back.

"We did a quick sweep," one of them called out as we followed her onto the porch. "But the property is huge. You folks buy it recently?"

"It was left to my daughter in an inheritance," said Mo. "We came up for the summer to check the place out."

Dr. Grant turned to me and there was concern in her eyes. "I've lived in Rhinebeck my whole life. When I started my own practice, I networked with people on the police force. They used to get all kinds of calls about this place, but it's been quiet for the better part of ten years. Not a single call out here—until today. When I saw the address dispatch sent over, I thought it was a mistake."

"Let's hope this doesn't turn into a regular thing," Mom said. "I don't play when it comes to the safety of my wife or my daughter."

Dr. Grant nodded. "I understand."

"Do you know anything about the people who lived here before?" I asked.

She shifted where she stood. "They were a pretty private family. Rhinebeck is a small town. People like to talk. A bunch of foolishness if you ask me, but like I said, there were always complaints of strange people coming and going."

"Strange people?" I asked. Her tone echoed what Mrs. Redmond had said to us before we left Brooklyn—colorful characters. It didn't sit right with me.

"Rhinebeck is a community within a community," she said, measuring her words. "Outside of the tourists, there are all sorts of people here. Artists, celebrities, people just trying to make a living." She stopped on the verge of saying more. "I'm sure it's just local kids. They probably thought this place was still empty. I know I did."

"It's not empty anymore," Mom said.

"No, ma'am. And I'll be sure to let police and fire know so there's no further confusion."

"So it's all clear out there now?" Mo asked.

"I think so," Dr. Grant said. "I'll do a walk around the perimeter before I go. I suggest you make sure everything is locked up tight. I'll give you a call in the morning to check in, if you'd like."

"Not necessary," Mo said. "But we appreciate the offer."

Dr. Grant handed Mo her card. "If there's any trouble, anything at all, call this number to reach me directly. I'll come right over. Rhinebeck is unique, and I wouldn't want you getting run off before you've even had a chance to settle in. I hope you'll like it here."

After she left, we walked through every room in the house and made sure all the doors and windows were locked. The house seemed more ominous as the night pressed in on us. The dark corners deeper, the hallways longer. I grabbed a blanket and balled up at the end of my parents' bed, trying to pretend everything was fine. Mo said it was fine. Even Mom tried to tell me it was fine but Mo kept glancing toward the window and Mom put her Taser on the nightstand in a way that would let her grab it at any moment.

Strangers in the driveway, a house that was mine and not mine at the same time, my friends back home probably not thinking about me at all, and a dead woman thinking about me so much she'd left me a house and all the stuff that went with it.

Everything was not fine.

As soon as the sun lit the room through a crack in the curtains, Mom got up and stood in the shower for half an hour trying to relieve her itchy skin. I was still rash-free. Mo ran out to get breakfast and came back with griddle cakes, fruit, and coffee that we ate in the front living room.

The morning light and delicious food had blunted the unease from the night before. Mom was still on edge, but had put her Taser away, which was a good sign.

"I say we start cleaning at the top and work our way down," said Mo. "We can use that dumpster on the side of the house. There's a number on it. I'll call and see if they can come switch it out when it's full."

I preferred a plan that involved napping, Netflix, and maybe ordering a pizza but that would have been too easy. We made our way up to the turret with trash bags and empty boxes we'd salvaged from the first floor. I avoided looking at the painting on the wall. I didn't want to worry about what was in the letters stashed in that safe.

We filled bag after bag with old newspapers and magazines. I organized empty plant pots into stacks and swept up the dust and mouse droppings. I helped Mo carry out a broken chair then turned my attention to the bookshelves.

I pulled collections of poems and stories by people with names like Euripides, Eumelus, and Pausanias off the shelves. Every single one was worn, their pages dog-eared and marked up with pencil in the margins. I dusted them off and reorganized them on the shelf in alphabetical order.

"I think Circe had a thing for Greek mythology," I said.

Mom picked up a copy of *The Metamorphoses*. "I remember

reading some of this in college," she said. "It didn't really stick. I know the Orpheus myth, though."

"Seeing *Hadestown* doesn't count as knowing the Orpheus myth," Mo said.

Mom put a hand on her hip. "I paid a hundred dollars apiece for those seats. It counts."

"Check this out." Mo pulled a beige drop cloth off what I thought was another stack of boxes, but underneath was a book the size of a poster, sitting on a waist-high pedestal. Mo studied its proportions. "This thing's gotta weigh fifty pounds."

I grabbed a rag and dusted off the leather cover where the title had been pressed in crimson. *Venenum Hortus.*

"Latin?" Mom asked.

"'*Venenum*' is poison," I said in a whisper. My skin turned to gooseflesh under the sleeves of my shirt. A tickle at my ankle drew my attention downward. One of the plant pots wasn't empty after all. Something I didn't recognize at first was wrapping itself around my leg, turning from brown to green while turtle shell–shaped leaves with thin white veins crisscrossing their surfaces sprouted by the dozens.

"*Peperomia prostrata*," I said.

"There was nothing left of that thing," Mom said, her voice tight. "Those pots were empty. There was only dust inside. I've—I've never seen you bring something back that was *that* dead."

I tried to think of a time when I'd done something like that, either purposely or by accident, but she was right. I'd never brought back a plant from its dusty, decayed remains. Avoiding her worried gaze, I gently untangled the tendrils from my leg, pushed the pot back against the wall, and turned my attention to the massive book.

"Plants are classified in Latin," I said. "So I recognize that part. I think the other word is—" I took out my phone and Googled "*hortus*." I wanted to be sure. "'*Hortus*' means 'garden.' It's 'poison garden.'"

We huddled around the book as Mo pulled open the front cover. The spine cracked like a set of aching knuckles. The first page was a semitransparent piece of paper. Through it, I could make out the outline of a plant. Mo gently uncovered the picture underneath. The details were sharp, the colors vivid, like a photograph. The only clues that it was hand-drawn were the hints of pencil where the artist had painted over their sketch.

"It's beautiful," Mom said.

I didn't need to read the Latin inscription to know what it was. The white parasol-shaped blooms gave it away. It was the same plant I'd grown in Prospect Park. The very same plant that should have killed me. *Cicuta douglasii*, the water hemlock. I took a deep breath, pushing away the memories of what had happened in my room with the plant—or more importantly what *hadn't* happened.

Mo flipped through the pages, revealing more beautifully detailed drawings of every poisonous plant I knew of and some I didn't. I recognized the velvety pink petals of oleander and the white orb with its blackened pupil of the Doll's Eye, both capable of stopping a heart in less time than the hemlock. But there was a vine with tendrils black as the night sky, dotted with indigo leaves and hundreds and hundreds of bloodred thorns that I'd never seen before. The Latin classification was listed as *Vitis spicula*, but the common name was Devil's Pet.

"Don't like that," Mo said quietly, shaking her head. "No, ma'am. Let's go on ahead and flip that page." She turned the page so hard the pedestal rocked to the side.

There were brackets alongside the drawings labeling the parts in intricate detail. There were measurements and deconstructed drawings of the plants from their surfaces to their insides. It was all diagrammed, from the minuscule trichomes—little coverings of hairlike structures some plants had—to the points of every leaf, every vein, every node.

At the bottom of each page, sectioned off by a thick black line, were detailed instructions for the care and cultivation of the plants, printed in perfect penmanship. It listed how much sun, shade, and water each plant needed, what kind of soil, and when to harvest each one.

There was something else, something I didn't normally see in books about the care and cultivation of plants: a small box labeled *Magical Uses*. It was different for each plant. For the foxglove, the passage read *for protection, use dye to create a crosshatch on the floor of a dwelling.* For morning glory, *place seeds under pillow to stave off nightmares; root can be a substitute for High John the Conqueror.*

"Magical uses, huh?" Mo asked.

I had some idea of what that meant. Lots of plants had medicinal uses, like the salve my grandma gave me instructions for, but I didn't know how that worked when it came to poison plants.

When we turned to the last page Mom gasped. "Wait," she said. "What is this?"

At the top of the page was the name *Absyrtus Heart.* The vibrant drawing of the plant was the strangest thing I'd ever seen. It had thick, ropelike stalks and tufts of black leaves, but the top of the plant resembled an anatomically correct human heart, complete with valves, lobes, and what looked like veins running across its fleshy pink surface. In the bottom right corner of the page was the artist's name in black ink. Mo ran her finger over it.

"Briseis, baby," Mom said as she looked at the book. "I think your birth mother drew this."

I stared at her name. The curl of the capital letter S, the crook of which was lighter, like her pen had come away from the surface of the paper for a split second. Mom put her arm around my shoulder and a nervous flutter settled in my stomach.

"I know we came up here in a hurry," Mom said, her voice low and measured. It was how she talked when she was dead serious, when she needed me to really pay attention to what she was saying. "Maybe we didn't think this through." She exchanged a worried glance with Mo. "This is a lot to deal with all at once. This house, this town, and now these hints of the people who left this to you. If this is too uncomfortable, if you're having second thoughts, we can pack up and leave. No questions asked."

I sighed and ran my hand over the drawing, over Selene's name. "You say that, but the rent is still going up in September, and we still have bills for the shop, and—"

"No," Mo said. She'd switched on her serious voice too. "We won't stay here if it's hurting you, understand? Nothing that's going on with our bills is worth that. We will make it work, with or without this place. Don't you dare ignore your feelings on this."

"I'm okay." It wasn't the whole truth. I didn't want to go back to Brooklyn and deal with all we'd left behind but being here was overwhelming and more complicated than I thought it would be. Selene was always at the back of my mind but now she was more real, more present. "It's a lot to think about but I'm okay. Really."

"You sure?" Mo asked.

"Say the word," Mom said, "and we'll go."

"No," I said. "I'm good. Promise."

Mo gave me a big hug. She was good at reading the room and knew I needed a minute alone. "We're gonna go have some of that coffee." She steered Mom down the stairs while I hung back.

I couldn't look away from the drawing of the Absyrtus Heart. The black leaves and the bloodred stalk, the pink lobes of the upper part, the bluish veinlike structures on its surface—Selene must have put a lot of time into drawing it. Every other plant in the book was deadly. This one would have been too, based on the coloring alone, but I was positive it didn't exist in nature. It was too strange. I would have seen it in other books. Somebody would have mentioned it in some scientific journal or article. Maybe she'd conjured it from her own imagination.

I glanced at the painting on the wall. The woman, Medea, stared back at me, like she was daring me to open the safe and see what was inside. I felt a stab of guilt. If I was being real, I *wanted* to know more, but I worried that meant I was being disloyal to Mom and Mo.

I shook my head. I was overthinking it. I had an opportunity here, in this secluded house in the middle of nowhere, to do something I'd never been able to do—let go. I eyed the potted *Peperomia prostrata*. It turned toward me and instead of trying with everything I had to pretend it wasn't happening, I took a long, deep breath and let my shoulders relax.

The plant sprouted three more lengths of stalk and knocked over its planter as it stretched toward me. I let it wrap itself around my leg, gently touching the soft leaves. I felt a sense of calm, of belonging. Circe knew something about my power, and I decided right there to find out exactly how much. I took down the picture of Medea and gave in to a curiosity that hadn't left me since Mrs. Redmond had showed up at our doorstep. I twisted the lock on the safe, pulled out the letters, and opened the first one.

CHAPTER 8

The envelope marked *1* contained an intricate, hand-drawn map, not a letter. A single sentence was scrawled at the bottom.

Follow the map and open the second envelope
when you get to the gate

Taped to the corner was an ancient-looking key. I gently peeled back the tape and held it in my hand. Questions about Circe's secrecy and where she was leading me took root in my mind. I allowed them to grow and branch off into a hundred new possibilities. This woman had to know something about me, but why not just tell me, since she seemed to like writing letters so much? There had to be a reason she couldn't simply say what she meant, and curiosity bloomed anew as I thought about what that reason could be.

I closed the safe and rehung the picture, untangled the vines from around my leg, and righted the pot. I grabbed my bag from my room, stuffing the other letters inside, and added the new key to the ring with the two others Mrs. Redmond had given me. I barreled out of my room and crashed right into Mo. She stumbled back, stunned.

"Something chasing you?" she asked.

I readjusted my glasses. "No. I—I'm gonna look around outside."

"Oh, okay," Mo said. "This property's big enough to get seriously lost, so don't go too far. You got your phone? You wanna take Mom's Taser?"

"Got my phone. And I don't need the stun gun. I have mace though."

"That's my girl," Mo said. She narrowed her eyes at me. "It's a lot of open space, and you've never been in the sticks like this. We're so far from town, from other people . . ." She trailed off.

I looked at the floor. Would she ask me to be extra careful? To make sure I didn't do anything that might put us all in some kind of danger? She slipped her hand under my chin and leveled my eyes with hers. "Stretch. Be careful, but not too careful. This is the perfect place to let your guard down."

It was permission I didn't know I needed. I grabbed her and hugged her tight before slipping on my shoes and circling around the back of the house.

A wide plain of half-dead grass that looked like it hadn't been cut in years sloped away from the house. I took out the map. A red line traced the path Circe wanted me to take, straight through the center of the rear yard. I took a few tentative steps into the knee-high grass. It bent toward me as I waded through, cutting a swath of vibrant green into the brown.

As I approached the tree line, a series of low aching groans cut through the air. The trees twisted back on themselves. They had noticed me.

Stretch.

That was what Mo had told me to do. I wanted to let my guard down, but I didn't trust myself not to make something terrible happen, so I turned my attention back to the map. I could hear the trees righting themselves as I put my thoughts elsewhere.

Three paths led into the dense forest, but the map said I should take a fourth. I flipped the map around, and in that moment, I was pretty sure I'd learned my map-reading skills from Mo.

After a closer look, I noticed a depression marked the ground where the other path might have been at one point, but it was completely overgrown. Hundreds of Dutchman's-pipe vines tangled together to obscure the way. Smaller leaves with razor-sharp serrated edges—stinging nettle—interlaced with them, forming an impenetrable curtain. They weren't deadly unless you were allergic, but their leaves and stalks contained microscopic barbed darts tipped with a mild poison. Contact with the skin caused rashes and pain that could last for days. I didn't want to have to douse myself in calamine lotion, but after my encounter with the poison ivy and the hemlock, I wondered if I even needed to worry about it.

I looked at the map again. Even the drawing included the overgrowth of plants, but the red ink cut right through them. I took a step forward. Testing my theory, I reached out to stroke the leaves of the stinging nettle, then braced myself for the pain. It didn't come.

A cool sensation washed over my hand, more intense than it had been with the poison ivy, but nowhere near the numbing pain I'd felt with the hemlock. It spread to my wrist, stopped, then retreated to my fingertips.

I took another step. The tangled curtain of ivy and nettle unwound before me. The layers of foliage parted, revealing the well-worn fourth path. I paused, and the plants responded to my hesitation. They curled back over the opening, making it impossible to see.

"Okay," I said aloud, trying to calm my racing heart. "Okay."

I stuck my hand out again, fingers trembling. The vines pulled back. I stepped onto the path, and the cloak of leaves and vines closed behind me.

The late afternoon sunlight slanted through openings in the canopy. The black spruce and red pine groaned as they shifted like hulking shadows, creating a corridor for me to walk through. The ground flattened as if it was making a way for me. Walls made of twisted branches bordered the trail. The red line on the map snaked through the woods before running into some sort of open space marked with an *X*.

Fifteen minutes passed before I came to the clearing. It was surrounded by ancient, towering oak trees. All across the glade, small, black creatures stared up at me with their wings spread, eyes shining, whiskers hanging from their chins like goblins. My heart jumped into my throat and I let out a choked scream, stumbling back.

It took me a few seconds to realize that they were a type of flowering plant. I was glad nobody else was around to see how quick my mind had jumped to goblins instead of plants.

I gathered myself and crouched to touch one of the inky black blooms. It immediately bent toward me, caressing my palm. These flowers weren't poisonous. There was no cool feeling in my hand. Taking out my phone, I Googled "black bat shaped plant" and found that I was looking at hundreds of *Tacca chantrieri*, the black bat flower. Their petals looked like a bat's wings in flight. They had a dozen whiskers dangling from their centers and white seedy pods that looked like glowing eyes.

The red *X* on my map was positioned at the other side of the glade and according to the drawing, beyond it was a large rectangle with a bunch of smaller rectangles set inside it. A building? Some kind of enclosure? I couldn't tell. The trees on the far side of the clearing were tightly packed, huddling together, but as I drew closer, they shifted. The oak trees bent unnaturally, groaning loudly as they leaned away from the facade of an overgrown stone structure.

A towering iron gate peeked through the tangle of mulberry-purple bougainvillea like a wicked, rusty smile. Thick, thorny vines crawled along the top of the wall like giant snakes. I craned my neck to see if this led to someone else's property, but the wall wasn't longer than maybe two buses parked end to end. It was some kind of enclosure.

I took the second letter out of my bag and opened it.

Briseis,

Behind this gate is a garden with all the plants needed to stock the apothecary. I have no doubt that you've seen inside the shop, and while you might not understand completely, I trust you will . . . in time. It has been a pillar of this community for generations.

Open the letter marked #3 when you come to the moon gate. This is where I'm sure most of your questions will be answered.

Something snapped in the woods behind me. I spun around as a man emerged from the trees on the other side of the glade. Blood trickled from a large cut on his forehead. His bottom lip was split clean open. His clothing hung off him, torn to shreds. He stumbled forward.

"You—you're here," he gasped, his chest heaving.

I backed into the gate and palmed my Mace, pointing it straight at him.

Welts bubbled on his skin as he limped closer. His breaths rattled, tight and labored, like he was breathing through a straw. "After all this time . . . so many years," he said. The gashes on his skin opened like budding flowers, blood dripping like crimson sap.

I'd walked so far into the woods that no one would hear me if I screamed. With my back to the gate, I couldn't run. I'd have to have to spray him—maybe fight him. I squared my shoulders as he approached. He was taller than me, but very thin, and he was much older. His outstretched fingers were swollen and blistering and as he angled himself toward me, his other hand came into view.

He was gripping a long, machete-like knife.

"Get away from me! Get back!"

"I—I need—I need it," the man stammered. He was an arm's length away, and I couldn't back up any farther. "Please, Selene."

"Selene? I'm not—"

A rustle over my head drew my attention. A duo of vines slithered off the top of the enclosure and struck out like giant arms, catching the man in a tangle of poisoned barbs. He screamed as they lifted him off the ground and tossed him into the tree line like a rag doll. His head hit the trunk of a maple tree with a sickening thud, and the knife bounced from his hand. Rolling onto his side, he clawed at the dirt. His groans turned to panicked yelps as the vines found him again and wound around his ankles.

I ran to the path leading away from the glade and looked back, only once, to see the man's terrified face as a blanket of stinging nettles pulled itself over him like a shroud.

I sprinted down the path toward the house, my heart in my throat. I crashed through the woods, burst through the curtain of nettle, and ran up the sloping lawn. Racing to the front door I all but kicked it in and slammed it shut, locking it behind me.

Mom came into the hall. "We slammin' doors now?" she asked, her eyes narrow.

How was I supposed to explain what I'd seen? "There's a guy out there! In the woods!"

Mo came barreling down the stairs. "What? Where?"

Mom sprinted to her purse and grabbed her Taser.

"Outside! By the back of the house!"

Mo peered out the window as Mom dialed Dr. Grant's number, cursing under her breath.

"Are the other doors locked?" Mo asked, her voice rising.

Mom rushed off to check while she yelled into the phone. "You said to call you directly, and somebody else is creeping around the house. How fast can you get here?"

Mo turned her attention to me. She clenched her jaw as she looked me over. "Are you hurt?"

"No," I said. "I'm okay. Just a little freaked out." I was still trying to catch my breath, still trying to put together what had happened.

Mom came rushing back to the entryway and we stood together, silent, until the sound of sirens echoed in the distance. The screeching of tires skidding across the pavement and car doors opening and slamming shut drew Mo to the door. She yanked it open, and Dr. Grant came in as several officers in uniforms broke off and went around the side of the house.

"Another prowler?" Dr. Grant asked, concern on her face. "I notified RPD this time. What happened?"

Mom looked to me to fill in the details.

"Uh—there was a guy out back. He was all messed up. He came toward me—he had a knife."

Mo sucked in a quick breath. Mom put her arm around me, her entire frame trembling, but I couldn't tell if it was from fear or anger.

Dr. Grant spoke into her walkie-talkie, telling the officers to check the rear of the house, warning them that the man had a knife. The muscle over her temple flexed and then relaxed. "Did he hurt you?"

"No," I said. "I was gonna Mace him but he—" I stopped short. "I—I ran away."

Dr. Grant let out a long, slow breath. "I'm glad you weren't hurt."

"But she could've been," Mom said. "Anything could've happened out there." Rage invaded her voice as she turned to Dr. Grant. "She could've been seriously hurt—or worse."

"I understand your concern," Dr. Grant said. "Briseis, you said the man was 'messed up'? What does that mean, exactly?"

"He was cut up," I said. "He had a bunch of open wounds and sores like—" I stopped. Mom was wearing a sleeveless top and shorts, and her skin was all puffy where the poison ivy had touched her. The man had similar patches, but worse. So much worse. Like he'd come in contact with something a lot more poisonous than oak or ivy. Images of the plants that lined the path to the hidden garden flooded my mind.

"What is going on?" Mom demanded. "This is the second weirdo who's shown up." She turned to Mo. "We shouldn't have come up here. This was a mistake."

My heart sank. I was scared to death, but I was more afraid of leaving without finding out what was behind that locked gate.

"Babe, don't do that," Mo said gently. "Don't make a snap decision."

"Angie, this is scaring me," Mom said. "I don't like this."

It was weird to see my mom so fearful. Mo was always levelheaded, and Mom was the one with the slick mouth and zero tolerance for bullshit. She didn't mind confrontation—and she didn't scare easily. Seeing her this shaken rattled me.

A voice crackled from Dr. Grant's walkie-talkie. "We have the suspect in custody. Run an ambulance to our location."

Dr. Grant walked out the front door. Mom and Mo

followed her, fussing about whether we would stay or go. A few moments later, a siren blared somewhere in the distance, and I peered out the window as an ambulance sped up the drive.

A group of officers emerged from the side of the house, carrying the man I'd seen between them. He looked like he was unconscious. His body was limp, his face swollen, and a trail of spittle hung from his chin.

"What the hell happened to him?" Dr. Grant asked as the officers hoisted the man onto a gurney.

"No idea," said an officer. "He was laid out near the tree line. He said something about being attacked, but he lost consciousness before he could tell me the rest."

"'Attacked'?" Mom asked, shooting me a glance. "He's the one who came after my daughter." Her fear had ebbed, and I could see the anger taking over as she shifted back on her heel and crossed her arms over her chest. "He's lucky I didn't catch him."

"He got stung by something?" one of the medics asked.

"I have no clue," said Dr. Grant. "He was out here harassing the property owners. Make sure you keep an eye on him. We'll follow you to the hospital. Northern Dutchess?"

The paramedic nodded and the ambulance sped out of the driveway with the other officers following in their patrol cars. Dr. Grant stayed behind to take my statement. I told her exactly what happened, except for the part about the plants coming alive and snatching the man into the trees. I kept that to myself.

"What's going to happen to him?" I asked.

Dr. Grant stepped up onto the porch. The hollows under her eyes were deep and dark. I didn't recall her looking so dead tired the last time I saw her. "They'll probably cite him for trespassing and possibly criminal mischief. You said he had a knife? If I can get a few of my people to go back out and find it, that would be another charge."

"I don't think anybody should go back out there. I mean, it's our place now. People shouldn't be wandering around." I didn't want to have to explain my reasoning in too much detail, but Mom and Mo both nodded like they agreed with me and that was good enough for now.

"We can get a restraining order against him too, if you'd like," said Dr. Grant.

Mom tilted her head to the side. "And what are we supposed to do with a restraining order when he comes back? Throw the paper at him?"

Dr. Grant shook her head. "I know it's not much. I'll go up to the hospital to speak to him, see if I can find out what motivated him to come out here in the first place." She shifted her weight and sighed, tucking her pad of paper into her breast pocket.

"I don't know if we're staying or not," Mom said, her tone clipped. "So maybe we won't need a restraining order."

"The man in the woods called me Selene," I said quietly. I thought Dr. Grant should probably know that detail.

"What?" Mo asked. She turned to Mom and then back to me.

Dr. Grant stared at me, a blank expression on her face.

"My birth mother's name was Selene. She lived here. That man thought I was her."

A look of utter shock gripped Dr. Grant's expression. She quickly put up her arm and coughed into the crook of her elbow.

When she turned back to us, she exhaled long and slow, avoiding my gaze. "So you inherited this place from your mother?"

"Selene was my birth mother. They're my moms," I said, gesturing toward Mom and Mo. "And I guess technically, I inherited the house from her sister, Circe."

"Of course," said Dr. Grant. She stood quietly for a minute.

"So, uh—yeah," I said. "That guy in the woods, he called me Selene, but I don't know why he'd think that. She died a long time ago."

"You look like her," said Dr. Grant. Her commanding voice was softer, but her mouth was pulled into a tight line like she was biting the inside of her lip.

Mom lifted a brow. "You knew her?"

Dr. Grant suddenly seemed much less sure of herself. She straightened up and cleared her throat. "I went to school with Circe. I was very sorry to hear that Selene had passed. I'm still sorry. Rhinebeck is a small place. Word got around—" She stopped short, shaking her head and swallowing hard. "That's the past, isn't it? No use bringing up painful things."

Was it painful for her? She'd known Selene through Circe, but she seemed pretty wrecked talking about her death.

"I'm going to head over to the hospital to see what I can find out about your trespasser," she said. "I'll call you when I know more and we can discuss your options."

Mo sighed, letting her shoulders roll forward and shaking her head. "Fine."

Dr. Grant left, and we retreated inside.

Mom fell into the couch. "We need to talk." I sat next to her as she ran her hand over my cheek. "We need to seriously consider packing up and getting the hell out of here."

"I don't want to leave," I said.

"Baby, I know, but this is ridiculous," Mom said. "Who are these people and why are they descending on this house? Did a memo go out? A signal to all the weirdos? What?"

"I don't know, but that old man was confused," I said. "And he got pretty jacked up out there. I don't think he'll come back."

"About that," Mom said. "What the hell happened to him?"

"He looked like somebody two-pieced him a few times over," Mo said, shaking her head. "You sure you didn't touch him, love?"

"I would never hit an old man," I said. "Unless he really deserved it."

Mo and I laughed, but Mom sat quiet.

"I just don't know," she said. "I think we should leave."

I started to protest but Mo patted my hand and jumped in before I could say anything.

"We'll sleep on it," she said. "We don't wanna make a decision we'll regret, one way or the other. Sleep on it. Then we'll talk in the morning. Deal?"

Mom huffed but nodded reluctantly. Mo gave me a nudge and went to lock up for the night.

I slept at the foot of their bed for a second night. I dreamed of the gate, of the strange man in the woods. My restless mind conjured images of sentient plants surrounding me as I stood in shadowy woods. The man swung his machete, barely missing my head.

I awoke with a start, gasping for breath, my heart thudding. Mom and Mo slept soundly, but I was done sleeping for the night.

CHAPTER 9

"How about we go into town for a while?" Mo asked the next morning. "Get some food, look around."

Mom was less upset than she'd been the night before but I still sensed that she was on edge.

"Y'all wanna go right now?" I asked. I'd spent my sleepless night thinking about what was behind that gate. I wanted to get back out there.

"Yeah," said Mo. "Come on. If we're gonna stay the summer we need to see what else this place has to offer, because mouse turds and dust bunnies is not gonna do it for your mama."

"Damn right it's not," said Mom, smiling. "I need food. I'm starving."

I got dressed and followed Mom and Mo out to the car. I glanced back at the house and the grounds beyond. Whatever was behind the gate would have to wait a little longer.

We drove into town and Mom parked the car on a side street. We walked over to the main road that ran through the center of Rhinebeck. Shops and restaurants lined Market Street on both sides. People walked together, sipping iced drinks and holding hands.

"This is so . . ." Mo searched for the right words to describe it.

"Quaint?" Mom offered.

Mo's eyebrow shot up. "I was gonna say white but I guess quaint works too."

We stopped in front of a shop whose display window was crammed with all kinds of candles. The smell that wafted out made my eyes water.

"Ooh!" Mom's face lit up. "Let's go in here. I love smelly-good stuff."

Mo looked like she was going to throw up. I scanned the shops, looking for an excuse to get out of going inside. Across the street was a small bookshop with a sign in the window that said Buy One Get One Free.

"I'm gonna go check out the bookstore," I said.

"Sure, baby," Mom said as she hooked her arm under Mo's. "I'll text you when we're done so we can figure out where we're gonna eat." They disappeared into the candle shop.

My phone buzzed as I crossed the street. I took it out of my pocket and checked the text.

Mo: How dare you

She was staring out the front window of the candle shop, a pained look on her face. I shot her a grin.

An older woman in an orange apron walked up to Mo and handed her a basket. Mo nodded and waved me on. The woman followed her gaze and as she made eye contact with me, she did a double take. Her eyes grew wide with what I could only figure was shock, and then she smiled the cheesiest grin I'd ever seen.

Manically grinning ladies, old dudes with machetes in the woods, and strangers in the driveway—I was starting to understand what Mrs. Redmond and Dr. Grant were hinting at. Some of the people in Rhinebeck were clearly on some other shit. I turned and hurried toward the bookshop.

Almost every single shop I passed had potted plants outside or hanging from their awnings, and I could feel them rustling in their containers as I went by. Maple trees rooted in squares of dirt dotted the sidewalk for as far as I could see. Ignore. Breathe. I couldn't stretch here, not out in the open.

The bookshop sat tucked between a tailor's shop and a pharmacy, the door propped open with a half-dead cactus. As I went in, it greened up and stretched toward me. I nudged the container away from the door and let it clang shut behind me.

Dust floated in the shafts of sunlight shining through the shop window. As I wandered through the closely fitted stacks, the musty smell of books, most of them more than gently used, stuck in my nose. I spotted a stack of old Audubon field guides in a plastic crate on the floor. Priced at $2.50 each, they were in perfect condition. The pictures were still bright and I'd always loved the rainbow-colored covers.

A huge crash suddenly rattled the shop. I spun around to see a young guy, probably my age, sprawled on the floor. A stack of books he'd been holding lay scattered around him like fallen leaves.

"Are you okay?" I asked as I took ahold of his arm and helped pull him to his feet.

"Yeah," he said, avoiding eye contact as he brushed himself off. Embarrassment radiated from him like heat from the sun. I picked up a few of the books he'd dropped and handed them to him.

"Are you sure you're okay?" I asked again.

For a moment, he didn't answer. He stared at me, his brown eyes wide. "Yeah. I, uh—I tripped." He gathered the rest of the books. One of them was titled *Botany for Gardeners.* Without thinking I plucked it from his hand.

"Is this part of the buy-one-get-one sale, too?"

He nodded. "You into gardening?"

I almost cringed. I set myself up for it but did we have to start there? I should have left the book alone. "You could say that." I gestured toward the field guides. "What about these? They on sale, too?"

He craned his neck to examine the titles. "You want those? They're really old."

"But the pictures are great," I said.

He grinned and ran his hand over the top of his head. "You can just take them."

"You serious?" I asked.

"Yeah." He brushed past me and scooped the whole stack out of the crate, hauling them to the counter.

"What's the catch?"

He blinked a few times. "Uh, no catch."

"Sounds like a scam, but okay," I said.

As he smiled something about him struck me as familiar. I couldn't place it.

"So, you new in town or visiting?" he asked.

"Not sure yet," I said. I grabbed a copy of *The Changeling* and set it on the counter. I felt bad that he was giving me the field guides for free so I figured I could at least find something to pay for.

"You a horror fan too?"

"I don't discriminate when it comes to good books. I'll read anything. But yeah, I love scary stories, especially when they're about us, you know?"

"Have you read *House of Leaves*?" he asked.

I couldn't keep from smiling. "I have. But see. That's what I'm talkin' about. Couldn't have been me. The first time a creepy door appears in my house, I'm out." I paused. I was the new owner of an old house tucked away in the woods at the edge of an unfamiliar town. It sounded exactly like the beginning of a horror novel and talk of strange doors and myths made real hit a little too close to home.

He entered the price of the book into the register. "So, do you like me so far?" He pursed his lips, flustered.

I raised an eyebrow. "Excuse me?"

"Rhinebeck." He shook his head like he was disappointed in himself. "I meant, do you like Rhinebeck so far?"

"Oh—um, it's different." I bit back a smile. "Quiet. Except for random people showing up where we're staying, but whatever."

"Where, uh—where are you from?" He bagged up my books and handed them to me.

"Brooklyn," I said.

"Oh, wow. The city, huh?"

Technically, no. Not Manhattan, but whatever. "What about you? You from around here?"

"I grew up here," he said.

"So you'd know where I can get something to eat with my parents?"

"Have you tried Ginger's yet?"

"No. What kind of food is it? Is it good?"

He rolled his head back and clapped his hands together. "It's so good. It's real deal Southern food. You know the kind that makes you dance when you eat it? It's like that."

I laughed and he laughed, and I suddenly felt sad. Gabby and I used to get pizza from this joint around the corner from school all the time. I missed my friends. Or, because of the way things had been, I missed the *idea* of my friends.

"I can take you over there, show you where it's at," he said.

I needed a minute to assess the situation. He was a stranger and my guard was pretty high when it came to new people. I could put up a wall like I'd done with everybody else or I could do something different. Mo's words echoed in my head. *Stretch a little.* "That's really nice of you," I said.

"Lots of good places around but there are a few spots that think salt counts as a seasoning. I don't want you to have to deal with that. We can go now if you want?"

"Okay," I said. "But hang on a second."

I shot Mom a text.

Bri: Let's go to this place called Ginger's

Mom: Sounds good. Meet you there in ten?

Bri: Yup

He pushed open the door and flipped the sign to Closed.

"Aren't you worried about losing business?" I asked.

"Nobody except you has been in here today," he said, a twinge of sadness in his voice. I glanced at him expecting to see him frowning but instead he looked extremely confused. I followed his gaze to the cactus, now green and flowering. My heart sped up as he grabbed the pot and held it in front of his face. "This thing was dead."

I tried to think of some excuse for its hardiness that sounded halfway true. "Cacti are pretty resilient. They can go without water for a really long time."

"Yeah, but it was all brown and shriveled up."

The cactus moved toward me slightly. I did't think he saw, but I turned and walked away immediately.

"I'm sure I can find this place if you don't want to take me," I called over my shoulder.

He quickly set the plant down and locked the door. He jogged to catch up with me as I power walked away from the shop. "I'm Karter, by the way."

"Briseis."

"Oh. That's pretty," he said.

"Thanks." His voice was soft and he was a little awkward. It was kind of nice. It didn't feel like he was trying to be anybody but himself. I wished I knew what that was like.

My phone buzzed. Mo was waiting at Ginger's with Mom.

"This way," Karter said. Making a quick right turn, we cut through an alleyway between two shops. All along the ground were plants in terracotta pots. Karter walked ahead and I tried to pretend like I didn't see the lemongrass and lavender growing fuller. I bumped into him as we emerged from the alley.

He turned and smiled at me. "Here we go."

Ginger's was a hole-in-the-wall place tucked away off the tourist route. I hoped that meant it would be good.

"You coming in?" I asked.

"Oh," Karter said, his eyebrows pushing up. "I wanted to show you where to go. I don't wanna bother you."

"If you don't want to—"

"I do!" Karter said, louder than he needed to. "I mean—I'd like to."

"C'mon," I said.

Karter opened the door for me and I stepped into the magical little place. It smelled like warm cornbread and the familiar vinegary aroma that went with greens stewed in a pot for hours. That smell, the laughter coming from the kitchen, the woman who poked her head out that looked like my grandma—it all felt like home.

Mom and Mo sat at a table near the front window. Mo beamed at Mom as she tilted her head back and laughed. They seemed really happy in that moment, which made everything else that had happened feel less important. Mom's face lit up as she caught sight of me and Karter.

I turned to him before walking over. "Just so you know, my parents are mad extra."

"How extra?" Karter asked. "My mom's like that too."

Mo snagged a chair for Karter. "Have a seat," she said, a little too eagerly.

Karter sat and stuck out his hand. "I'm Karter. I work in the bookstore up the block. It's nice to meet you."

"He's so polite," Mom said, like he wasn't sitting right there.

She reached out to shake his hand. Splotches of ointment dotted her forearm. "Don't you worry about that. I'm not contagious. Some poison ivy got me." She drew her arm back. "I'm itchy in places I didn't even know existed."

I could feel the heat rising in my face. I was hoping they'd wait until we ate to start embarrassing me.

"We practically had to use a paintbrush to put on the ointment," Mo said as she nonchalantly scanned the menu.

I sank deeper into my seat. Karter grinned.

Mo whistled. "Lookin' like a young Trevante Rhodes, so handsome."

Mom nodded in agreement and I looked into my lap. This was so much worse than I imagined.

"So, Karter, what's good here?" Mo asked.

"Everything," he said. He was trying very hard not to laugh.

Mom opened her mouth to speak, and I shook my head. "Please. Don't." I didn't even know what she was going to say, but I knew it would be embarrassing.

She smiled, pressing her lips together. We ordered and since it was nearly lunch, Mom got catfish and greens and Mo got the same thing, but with baked mac 'n' cheese on the side.

"If there are breadcrumbs on top, I'm gonna lose it," Mo said.

"Breadcrumbs?" Karter asked. "That should be illegal. They'd never do that here."

"Ooh, I like him so much," said Mo, nudging my shoulder.

"I found some field guides at the bookstore," I said, trying to change the subject. "The old ones with the bright covers. Perfect condition, too."

"Oh yeah?" said Mom. She turned to Karter. "We run a flower shop back home, so Briseis has a love for plants."

"Really?" Karter asked. "That's what's up. What's it called?"

"Bri's," Mom said, beaming at me.

I'd always thought it was sweet, naming the shop after me. It was another way they tried to embrace what I could do. It was all good when I was using my power to grow daffodils in plastic pots but it had evolved so much since then. The look of shock on their faces when that plant in the turret came back from practically nothing bothered me. They'd always been supportive, but they didn't know all the ways this power could manifest, and neither did I. Each time something new happened, I braced myself. It was one thing to be afraid *for* me, but it was something else to be afraid *of* me.

I tried to push all that aside as the waiter brought our order to the table.

Karter was right. The food was so good that Mom kept humming and doing a little dance in her seat. Mo started six different conversations but kept getting sidetracked by how delicious everything was. When we were done, we sipped lemonade and sweet tea while Mo talked about the flower shop and how being in a place like Rhinebeck was so different from Brooklyn.

"It's a big change," Karter said. "Rhinebeck is small."

"Does it feel small? You know, since you grew up here?" Mom asked. "I didn't realize how small my hometown was till I moved to Brooklyn."

"Yeah. Too small sometimes. Kinda wonder what I'm missing." Sadness danced behind his eyes as he turned to me. "I gotta get back." He pulled out his wallet to pay and Mo waved it away.

"I got it," she said. "Our treat."

"Thanks," he said. "I owe you. It was really nice meeting you."

"It was nice meeting you, too, Karter," said Mo.

I scooted my chair back. "I'll walk you."

Karter jogged ahead of me to open the door.

"Baby, he's so polite!" Mom called after me. "Don't be too mean to him, okay?"

I quickly walked out.

Karter stifled a laugh. "Your parents are the best."

"Oh my God, I'm mortified," I said. I could feel them looking at us through the window.

"I guess that's kind of their job, right? To embarrass you? I know my mom does."

"They act like it's their job," I said. "And they deserve a pay raise, because they're really good at it."

We walked to the bookstore and found the attorney who'd come to our apartment, Mrs. Redmond, standing outside. She was speaking loudly into her phone.

"Are you serious?" she asked. "That's not going to work." She smiled wide when she saw me. "I'll call you back."

"Mrs. Redmond?" I asked.

"Briseis, how are you?" She reached out and gave me an awkward side hug.

"You two know each other?" Karter asked.

I looked back and forth between them and it dawned on me why he looked so familiar. It was clear Mrs. Redmond was his mom. They shared the same deep-set brown eyes, the same square chin.

“Through work,” Mrs. Redmond said. “But how do *you two* know each other?”

Karter stared at his mother. Something silent passed between them.

“We just met,” I said quickly. “I was checking out the shop.”

Karter gave me a stiff smile.

Mrs. Redmond put her hand on my shoulder. “My office is right upstairs if you ever need anything. Are you having a good time? Have you been able to explore? Get a feel for the place?”

“Not really,” I said. “We’ve had some issues with random people showing up at the house.”

Mrs. Redmond’s face grew tight. “Really?”

“Yeah. We had to call the police. A woman named Dr. Grant had to come out.”

“Dr. Grant?” Mrs. Redmond asked. “I didn’t realize she was still running things up there at the Public Safety Office. These small towns are like a trap sometimes. People never leave, even when they should.”

“I’m gonna get back to work,” Karter cut in. “It was nice meeting you and your family, Briseis.”

“You met her family?” Mrs. Redmond asked. She had the same enthusiasm as Mo. “That’s wonderful!” She seemed genuinely thrilled, but Karter rolled his eyes so hard it looked like he was being possessed.

He turned to me. “See? You’re not the only one who has parents who embarrass you.”

“Please,” Mrs. Redmond said dismissively. “If anything, it’s the other way around, but you don’t see me complaining.” She checked her phone. "I'm going to grab lunch. Karter, please get in the shop in case any customers come by."

Karter huffed. "I don't think you have to worry about that."

She put her hand on Karter's shoulder and squeezed. "Don't be a pessimist. We can make a way out of no way but only if you try harder." She turned and walked off, texting furiously on her phone.

"Business is tough, huh?" I asked.

"Yeah." He didn't offer anything else so I left it alone.

"Do you work every day?" I asked. "I work in our shop all the time even though my parents wish I'd go out and do something else. I think they want me to be a juvenile delinquent."

Karter laughed. "I'm here a lot in the summer, mostly in the afternoons. It's quiet. I got my phone and I use the free Wi-Fi from the place next door." He unlocked the door and slid the cactus in place to hold it open. I followed him inside. "Me and my mom take turns running things."

"And she's a lawyer too? How does she find the time to do both?"

"She puts in a lot of hours. Too many, sometimes. She's one of those people who's constantly grinding, you know? She never stops."

"That can be a good thing," I said.

"Sometimes." The sadness in his tone had returned. "There's such a thing as too much work though."

As much as I was enjoying my first trip into town, my mind drifted back to the iron gate in the forest and what might be behind it. Circe had implied it was a garden but I wanted to see it for myself.

"I gotta get back to my parents," I said. "But listen, it was really nice meeting you."

"You too," he said, smiling. "Can I, uh—can I call you?" As he leaned on the counter, his elbow slipped off and his wrist hit the countertop with a loud crack.

I bit the inside of my cheek to keep from smiling.

"Maybe we can get coffee or something?" He rubbed his arm.

He definitely wasn't flirting, but I was still trying to figure out his angle. Maybe he was just a guy with friend potential, even though dudes like that were few and far between. The thought sent a wave of panic through me. I didn't know if me and my parents were staying and if we were, would a friendship with him be any different from Gabby or Marlon when he inevitably found out what I could do?

But he was easy to talk to even if he was awkward as hell, and my parents already liked him way too much. If I was being honest, I needed a friend. Maybe more than I needed anything else.

"Coffee sounds good," I said. "Let's do that."

We exchanged numbers and I left. As I headed back toward Ginger's, my parents came strolling around the corner.

Mo gazed over my shoulder. "Where's Karter?"

"He went back to work," I said. "And thank y'all so much for embarrassing me like that."

"I'm sorry, baby," Mom said. "It's good to see you doing things with kids your age. He seemed nice."

"He is nice," I said.

Mom and Mo raised their eyebrows in unison and exchanged mischievous glances.

I shook my head. "It's not like that. Y'all are the worst."

"Are we though?" Mo asked. "I kinda think we're the best."

"The absolute best, if you really think about it," said Mom. She and Mo exchanged nods.

"I'm ready to head back if you are," I said.

Mom pulled me close and kissed me on the side of my face. "My big-head baby."

We drove to the house, and Mom decided she needed to take an oatmeal bath to deal with her rash. Mo fell into a food coma on the couch, and I spent the late afternoon debating whether I should go back to the garden or not.

I put on and took off my sneakers three times. My procrastination skills were legendary when it came to schoolwork and sometimes my chores, but this was on a whole other level. The incident with the man in the glade was fresh in my mind, but beyond that there was fear. Fear that I might find something I couldn't walk away from. When I finally worked up the nerve to go back, it was already dark, and that seemed like a perfectly good excuse to put it off for one more night.

CHAPTER 10

The next morning, I was up before Mom and Mo. I sat on the edge of my bed and weighed my options—stay in and help my parents clean, or maybe face somebody's knife-wielding pawpaw in the woods on my way to a secret enclosure where I was told answers would be waiting for me.

What happened had shaken me. He'd called me Selene, said he needed something, and then got laid out by a tangle of poisoned vines. I had to get out there but I wasn't going back underprepared. I'd had Mace before, but this time I slipped Mom's Taser into my pocket, grabbed my bag, made sure my phone was fully charged, and left out the door.

The sloping length of grass was green where I'd walked through it the day before. I took a parallel route to try and even out the color but it only made it look worse. As I approached the tangle of vines at the edge of the forest, they drew back before I had a chance to reach out. Did they sense my presence and respond, or was I willing them to reveal the path to the glade and the strange enclosure? I didn't know but both possibilities intrigued me enough to continue on. I glanced back at the house before ducking into the trees and following the trail.

When I got to the clearing, I scanned the entire area. As far as I could see, no one was lurking in the shadows. I was alone aside from the trees and flowers, but I didn't really feel alone. I was meant to be there. I didn't know how or why, but it had to be true.

In front of the gate I stood on shaky legs as the carpet of black bat flowers curved toward me like they were waiting anxiously for me to open it. A thousand thoughts tumbled through my head. I didn't know what was behind the gate or why Circe felt it was so important that I find out, but I couldn't walk away from this.

I held the key that had been taped to the map in my trembling hand. As I put it in the lock, the bougainvillea curled down and encircled my wrist, twisting around it gently before snapping itself off, leaving me with a beautiful bracelet of purple blooms. Few things shocked me when it came to what foliage might do around me, but this left me in awe.

The lock clicked open and the vining plants gripped the gate's iron bars, pulling them apart. I took a few tentative steps inside.

The gate suddenly clanged shut and I almost jumped out of my skin. The trees righted themselves, covering the entrance so that I couldn't see through the gate's bars. No one would be able to follow me, but what exactly had I walked into?

Dead leaves crunched under my feet as I followed the path through a stone corridor that terminated in a sharp left turn, like an entrance to a maze. I rounded the corner and found myself looking at a large rectangular courtyard. A tree stood in the center, its gnarled trunk—as wide as a car—led up to a canopy that fanned out like a giant umbrella. Pressed into the inner walls of the stone enclosure were metal pegs that held rakes, small shovels, and coiled hoses. Several watering cans of various sizes littered the ground. A rusted spigot stuck out of the wall.

Raised beds filled the courtyard in a checkerboard pattern, each divided into quarters by wooden planks. Every bed was full of plants, but they were all dead, their leaves yellowed, their stalks broken. A short wooden pillar with a plaque affixed to the top stood in front of each bed. I walked to the closest one and scraped off a thick layer of green moss to read the words under it.

ANGELICA
Angelica archangelica

I weaved my way through the beds, cleaning off the other signs. Each of the dozens of plots had a label that matched one of the jars from the apothecary. I studied the map again. The rectangles represented the raised beds, and a thick black line drawn through the center represented a wall that divided the front of the garden from another area behind it. I followed the path, passing under the enormous tree.

Three-quarters of the way back, a circular archway sat in the center of a high wall. The wall itself was blanketed in a writhing mass of black vines dotted with dark purple leaves and crimson thorns. It was the vining plant I'd seen in the big book, the Devil's Pet—and it was even more terrifying in person than it was in the illustration.

I took out the letter I was supposed to read when I got to this point and tore it open.

Beyond this point is the Venenum Hortus, the Poison Garden. Every plant grown in this bit of poison earth could kill a full-grown person five times over. Most people who wish to come in contact with these plants would have to cover every inch of exposed skin, and even then, it might not be enough to protect them. While you may not yet understand why, I trust you will understand what I mean when I say that you, dearest Briseis, need no such protections.

She knew.

Circe, a dead woman I'd never met, knew my biggest secret—a secret I'd only just figured out myself.

Your mother, Selene, tried to spare you this responsibility, but fate has a way of catching up to us. You must decide if you can continue this work, because you are the only one left who can, and it is more important than you can possibly imagine.

The vines twisted around one another like a tangle of snakes. Something deep in my bones, in the same place where this power was seeded, urged me to keep moving forward. I stepped through the archway into the deadly garden.

My nose burned, my eyes watered, and cold spilled down my throat like a glass of ice water. I coughed, trying to force out the chill, wiping my eyes with the back of my hand. The feeling slowly subsided, leaving a tingling sensation on the inside of my nose and mouth.

"Okay," I said aloud, steadying myself. "I'm fine. I'm okay." The way the cold hit me meant something poisonous, something deadly, lingered in the air.

The stone walls were covered in thick, hunter-green ivy, its tendrils curling around each craggy brick. Smaller than the front portion of the garden, the Poison Garden was arranged in a similar way—raised beds, all labeled with the names of the plants they held, all their contents wilted and brown.

DEADLY NIGHTSHADE
Atropa belladonna

WHITE SNAKEROOT
Ageratina altissima

CASTOR BEAN
Ricinus communis

ROSARY PEA
Abrus precatorius

OLEANDER
Nerium oleander

WATER HEMLOCK
Cicuta douglasii

In the far corner stood a short tree in a circular plot. Its label read Little Apple of Death (*Hippomane mancinella*). This tree was so deadly, people weren't supposed to breathe the air around it, much less eat the apple-shaped fruits it bore.

I stepped back and nearly tripped over something on the ground—a dead bird. All around me were dozens more, their broken bodies in varying stages of decay. Most of them had been reduced to piles of yellowed bone and feathers. I looked up. What I thought were the tangled limbs of trees outside the garden was actually a canopy of twisted nettles, ivy, and roses—with petals as black as ink, thorns longer than my fingers—interlaced with a scaffolding of curved metal arches.

As I wandered between the beds, rereading the letters, it was obvious that Selene had made a choice. She didn't want me to have anything to do with this place, and for some reason, Circe was trying to get around that, even from beyond the grave. I wasn't sure I cared what Circe thought I should know. *This* was something only I could do? But what was I supposed to do, exactly? Run their shop for them? It didn't seem like Rhinebeck had a population eager to sustain an herbal remedy business.

Rustling sounded above me as the tendrils of a vine crept down from the top of the wall and produced the prettiest purple calla lily bloom I'd ever seen. It felt like a gift, like the bracelet of bougainvillea. I plucked the flower and stuck it behind my ear as the vine retreated.

I left the garden in a daze. Circe and Selene were growing the deadliest plants on earth in this garden. From what I could tell, they were harvesting their parts to store in the apothecary along with plants that had more common uses. I had more questions than answers—and nobody to tell me the whole truth. I took out my phone and called Mom.

"Hey," she said.

"Hey, can you text me Dr. Grant's number? I wanted to see if she had any information about the guy who was out here."

"Uh, yeah. I can call if you want."

"No, it's okay. I know the guy was a creep, but I hope he didn't die." My phone buzzed as Dr. Grant's number popped up on my screen. "Thanks, Mom."

"Love you, baby."

"Love you more."

I hung up and called Dr. Grant.

"Dr. Khadijah Grant," she answered.

"Hi, Dr. Grant. This is Briseis Greene."

There was a long pause. "Hello, Miss Greene. Is everything all right?"

"Yes, ma'am, everything's fine. I was wondering about that guy you picked up out here at the house. Is he okay?"

"You're worried about him?" She sounded surprised. "He's hanging in there as far as I know. He's heavily sedated due to the nature of his injuries, which were pretty severe."

"So he's at the hospital?"

"He is. Northern Dutchess Hospital. But don't worry, we've got a guard on him. We'll question him when he's more coherent."

"Do you know his name?" I asked.

There was another pause. "Alec Morris. He's seventy-three years old and has lived in Rhinebeck his whole life. That's about all I've got at the moment. I have no idea why a man his age would be running around in the woods with a knife, but trespassing on private property is a no-go. Like I said before, I don't want anyone running you and your family off before you've had a chance to get settled."

According to Mom, we may never get settled. She was one incident from packing up and rolling out.

"Thanks," I said. "I really appreciate it." I'd gotten the information I needed without having to lie too much.

"Not a problem," Dr. Grant said.

I hung up, but before I could stick my phone in my pocket, it buzzed.

Karter: I found some more field guides. Thought you might want them.

Bri: How much?

Karter: It's on me. Can I drop them off for you?

Bri: Sure. 307 Old Post Rd. GPS doesn't really work out here so be careful.

Little dots appeared, then disappeared a few times before another text came through.

Karter: Ok. See you in 15?

Bri: Yup

I locked the main gate to the secret garden and watched as the trees hid the entrance, making it nearly impossible to see. The entire walk back to the house, tangles of poisonous plants undulated along the ground, a shallow wave of green and black leaves and gleaming thorns. At the tree line they hung back, twisting over on themselves. The vines parted, and I slipped out.

Glancing back, I felt eyes on me, like someone or something was watching. That had been true before—a man with a machete had been waiting, watching me. That should have been enough to keep me from returning to the garden, but what had happened to him, the way the forest had come alive to attack him and protect me, made me feel safe in a situation that was obviously . . . not. The vines closed behind me and I quickly walked up the sloping lawn toward the house.

Before I got up the hill, Mo came strolling across the grass with a big smile plastered on her face. Karter bobbed along behind her.

"Look who came to visit," Mo said.

"Hey," I said.

Karter looked me over. "Hey. Uh, what were you doing?"

The question caught me off guard. I looked at my clothes and realized I'd sweated out the pits of my T-shirt and was wearing flowers like other people wore jewelry. "Exploring. But listen, I gotta change real quick. Wanna come in?"

"Yes, he does," Mo said. She ushered him inside and I ran upstairs. I set the flower bracelet and the calla lily on the bathroom counter and showered. I pulled on a pair of jeans and a semi-clean T-shirt I had in my bag, threw my hair in a yellow headscarf, and went back downstairs to find Karter in the front room, laughing himself to death with Mom and Mo.

Mom wiped tears from the corners of her eyes. "She used to take off her shirt and run around the shop like nobody would notice! I've never seen a kid who wanted to be naked as much as Briseis."

I cleared my throat. "Wanna go?" I slipped my arm under Karter's and pulled him toward the door before my parents said anything else. "We can lose them if we run," I whispered.

Karter grinned.

"Where are y'all headed off to?" Mo asked as we walked out to the front porch.

A beat-up old truck sat in the driveway. The front bumper was gone and the once-red paint had aged into a patchwork of rust.

"We're going for a drive," I said.

"We are?" Karter asked. I gripped his arm. "Oh, right. Yeah. Goin' for a drive."

"Okay, well, wear your seat belts," said Mo. "And keep your phone on so you can check in."

"Yes, ma'am." I climbed into the passenger side as Karter slid into the driver's seat.

Mo made sure that we could see her eyeing the front of the truck. "I got your license plate, Karter."

Karter looked nervously to me. "Is she serious?"

"Yes."

"Did I miss something?" he asked. "We were laughing and joking a minute ago." The entire vehicle rumbled as the engine turned on.

"My parents like to joke, but they play zero games when it comes to me. Especially Mo." I shooed her away from the truck. She walked backward to the house, keeping eye contact with Karter until he looked away to adjust his rearview mirror.

He pressed his lips into a line. "She doesn't have to worry. Really." He seemed concerned and I felt bad for him.

"Mo's pretty harmless," I said. "I think you'll be okay."

Karter handled the truck like it was trying get away from him, roughly pulling at the steering wheel to keep it in line. Every bump we hit made the cab shimmy and creak. It felt like there was nothing between me and the road, and if we hit a pothole it was gonna be over for my tailbone.

He glanced at me, his eyes kind. "Sorry. The truck is old."

"It's fine," I said. "My spine might need to be realigned when we get out but it's cool."

He laughed and the tension eased.

"Sorry again about Mo. This is all new to us too so she's feeling extra protective right now."

"You call your mom Mo—mind if I ask why?"

"I mean, they're both 'mom,'" I said. "I call them both 'mom' depending on the situation, but Mo is short for Mom. It works for us."

"That makes sense. I thought maybe it was her first name or something."

"Yeah, no." I laughed. "Call her by her first name? Never in my Black-ass life."

"Got it," said Karter, nodding. "So where are we going?"

"Can you take me to the hospital?"

He looked me over, his brow furrowed. "You good?"

"I'm fine, but there was this man—" I stopped short. I wasn't sure how much to tell him. "There was a guy on the property earlier. He was hurt pretty badly, and I wanna check on him."

Karter stared ahead as we drove. "Some random guy?"

"Yeah," I said. "He got into something poisonous and we had to call an ambulance."

He grimaced. "Wow, welcome to town, right? Weird guy in the woods on what, day two? The hospital's not too far. I'll take you if you think it's a good idea."

"I don't know if it's a good idea or not, but I wanna go." That part was the whole truth.

A paper bag sat on the seat between us and Karter nudged it toward me. "I think there's four or five in there."

The field guides were in perfect shape, just like the ones he'd given me before. "You sure you don't wanna sell these? I can pay you."

"They're just sitting on a shelf. Think of it as a housewarming gift."

"Thanks," I said.

"Have you had a chance to look around?" Karter asked as he turned onto the main road.

"Not really," I said. "Coming into your shop and eating at Ginger's was our first trip to explore."

"Wanna swing through downtown? I can point out a few spots."

I wanted to get to the hospital, but I was enjoying my time with Karter more than I thought I would. If this was going to be a repeat of every friendship I'd ever had, this would've been the start of me putting my defenses up, watching my every move, steering clear of any place where I might lose control, and taking zero chances. But if I was going to make a fresh start . . .

"Sure," I said. "That'd be nice."

CHAPTER 11

Karter steered us toward town and we talked like we'd known each other for more than a day. He'd struck me as awkward and kind of clumsy before. I thought he was just shy but as we spent more time together, I got the sense he was just a soft-spoken dude. He was laid-back and funny. It was easy to be with him.

"This is Montgomery Street," he said as we pulled into town. "Once you get south of downtown, it turns into Mill Street." We passed a farmers' market with a bunch of colorful tents and bustling stalls. "Market Street is where most of the shops are. Samuel's Sweet Shop is my favorite place." He pointed to a shop with blue trim and a red bench out front. "The guy who plays Ant-Man is the co-owner or somethin'."

"Really? Paul Rudd?" Mo thinks Paul Rudd is the finest white man she's ever seen.

"He's aight," Karter said laughing. "At Samuel's they got these candies called Clodhoppers. It's peanut butter, pretzel, and graham crackers covered in milk chocolate. So good."

"See, now I'm hungry," I said.

"I'll take you if you wanna go," he offered. "I mean, only if you want to," he said quickly, keeping his eyes forward.

"I'd like that, I really would, but maybe another day? I wanna get to the hospital before it gets too late."

"Oh yeah, sure," said Karter. "It's not going anywhere."

I smiled and as we drove through town, I imagined what the sugar maples that lined the streets would look like in the fall when their foliage would turn a kaleidoscope of golds and reds. We were driving slowly enough that I caught their subtle movements, gestures I wasn't sure other people could pick up on. These movements were like taking a deep breath—a gentle rounding of the leaves, an almost imperceptible elongating of the branches—and they were doing it because of me. For the first time in a long time, it felt more like a gift than a burden.

"This place doesn't feel real," I said.

"It takes a while to get used to."

"What was it like growing up here?" I asked. "Because I'm not gonna lie, I've seen exactly six other Black folks since we got here, and you and your mom are two of them."

"The fact that you've seen all of us already is pretty much the only thing you need to know." He shook his head. "Nah, but for real, it's okay. People are cool for the most part. The ones who live here all the time keep to themselves. The tourists are annoying, especially in the summer, but hey—what're you gonna do?"

We drove past a stately house with a sign that read Beekman Arms Inn. "Everything looks like something out of a history book. How old is this place?"

"Pretty old," he said. "The town, I mean. And the people

here are old as hell, too. I think the average age gotta be like sixty-five."

"Serious?"

"Probably." Karter grinned. "There's a bingo hall off Market Street that's packed every weekend."

"So that's where the party is on Saturday nights? Good to know."

"If by 'night' you mean five thirty in the afternoon, then yeah." Karter made a loop and headed back toward the house. "The hospital's this way."

By the time we got there, it was midafternoon. Karter parked the truck and turned to me. "Do you want me to come in with you?"

"Sure, but I don't even know if they'll let me see him."

"I guess we'll find out, right?"

We walked inside and a woman in a floral-print button-down, the collar neatly pressed, eyed us suspiciously from her perch behind the information desk. "Can I help you? You look lost."

"I'm looking for a patient," I said. "His name's Alec Morris. He came in by ambulance yesterday."

She clicked around on her keyboard and read from the monitor in front of her. "He's in room 316. It looks like he's under guard, so you won't be able to see him without a police escort."

I sighed. That made sense. Dr. Grant said they were keeping an eye on him.

"Thanks," I said, feeling a stab of disappointment.

I turned to walk toward the door, but Karter hooked his arm

under mine and pulled me in the direction of the elevator. "We should go pick up your meds while we're here," he said.

"Huh?"

He gently squeezed my hand.

"Oh," I said, picking up on the ruse. "Good idea."

Karter smiled at the receptionist as we got into the elevator. As soon as the door closed he let go of my arm.

"They're not gonna let us see him."

He thought for a moment. "I can cause a distraction and you can sneak in."

"Wait. What?"

"I'll slip and fall or something," he said with a smirk. "I might not have to pretend. I have two left feet."

"I hadn't noticed." I had definitely noticed. It was kind of funny that the person who was going to help me stealthily sneak in to see the stranger from the woods was probably the most uncoordinated person ever. I pushed my glasses up. "So you're good at scamming people? Should I be worried?"

"Nah." He smiled that big toothy grin of his. "But keep me in mind if you ever need to make half-assed plans that probably won't work out."

The elevator climbed to the third floor. The doors slid open and we followed the signs to room 316. It was the last room situated at the end of the east hall, and a police officer sat outside the door scrolling through his phone. I ducked behind a crash cart and pulled Karter down next to me.

"What are we gonna do? I can't just walk in there."

Karter bit his bottom lip, scrunching his bushy eyebrows together. Suddenly, he clapped his hands. "Okay."

He stood up and marched out from behind the cart, drawing the officer's attention.

"Shit," I said under my breath.

Karter's left ankle suddenly twisted and his leg folded under him. He fell to the floor, moaning, and started rolling around.

The officer leaped up and a nurse came skidding around the corner. I ran after her, hoping it would make my approach to room 316 less obvious. The nurse knelt at Karter's side as he clutched his ankle. A thin film of sweat blanketed his forehead. He wasn't kidding when he said he might not have to fake it. I caught his gaze and he jerked his head toward the door before letting out another groan. I crept past as the police officer and nurse both tried to comfort him. I backed up until I reached the door, then quickly slipped inside, closing it behind me.

The patient was shackled to the bed rails and sleeping soundly. The room was small, with a single window overlooking the parking lot. The drab monochrome decor made the space feel cramped.

I cleared my throat. The man stirred with a start. Lifting his head off the pillow, his gaze settled on me. His right eye was swollen shut, but the gash in his lip had been stitched closed. The monitor tracking his heartbeat beeped loudly.

"What do you want?" His voice was gravelly, strained. I took a step closer. He squinted his bloodshot left eye. "Oh, it's you."

"You don't know me," I said. "You called me Selene before, but I'm not her."

His face, swollen and bruised as it was, softened. "I'm sorry. You look so much like her. It's uncanny."

"Did you know her?"

He nodded. "And her sister, Circe. They're gone now. They're all gone." His eye misted over. "I apologize for scaring you. I was confused. I got turned around out there."

"About that," I said. "How did you get to the gate? It's on private property, and it's—"

He raised his left eyebrow, a simple gesture that seemed to cause him a disproportionate amount of pain.

"It's hard to get out there," I said.

He eyed me carefully. "I know how difficult it is." He readjusted himself in the bed, wincing with every movement. "That's why I brought the machete. I had to chop my way through, and still . . ." He held up his hands in front of him. The skin had peeled off several fingers, and the nails had turned black. He leaned back on the pillow and gave a dry, rasping laugh. "I should've known better. There's a reason nobody can get out there. I thought there were booby traps, maybe some kind of elaborate security system. I knew it would be overgrown. I had no clue the damned forest was going to come alive and try to kill me."

If there had been a plant nearby, it would have found me, drawn in by my racing heart.

"Don't worry," he said. "I won't go back out there. I barely survived as it is. No sense testing my luck."

"Why were you out there in the first place?"

"The house was dark for years. After Selene died, Circe shut down the shop."

"The apothecary?" I asked.

The monitor beeped and a cuff on his arm tightened. "Natural medicines. Remedies. Other things too, but I'm not the right person to ask about that." He glanced out the window.

The natural medicine part made sense, but what other things?

He turned onto his side and the sheet slipped off his bare foot. It was covered in deep, painful-looking sores. He quickly readjusted the sheet. "That's what I need the herb for. Diabetes damages the blood vessels, makes it harder for wounds to heal. I've tried every ointment and cream my doc recommends but nothing works like comfrey. But it has to be the comfrey Circe and Selene were growing. It's just better. I knew they were growing the herbs somewhere on the property, so I went to find out where. I've been without it for so long, going on ten years. I was desperate. I didn't know you'd moved in. I saw you go into the forest and I thought—I thought you were Selene. Back from the dead to help me out."

"Not tryna be rude, but death is pretty permanent," I said.

"If you say so." He shook his head. "Never mind. I was confused. Maybe I still am. I'm sorry. Truly."

My gut said was he was telling the truth and I felt bad. "Listen. I can get the comfrey for you. There's still some at the house."

He turned to me. "You'd do that? Even though I trespassed and probably scared the life out of you?"

"It's not a problem."

"You look like Selene." He smiled, sadness in his voice. "You have her gentle heart, as well."

"I'm not her," I said, firmly. "My name is Briseis."

His eyes widened. "Like the Greek myth."

I nodded. "I'll get you the comfrey if you promise not to sneak around the house anymore. It's not safe." Not for him, anyway, and not only because of the plants. Mom and Mo might put his ass back in the hospital if he showed up again.

He lifted his right hand. The sores on his forearm were open and oozing. "Scout's honor."

"Come by when you're better."

I exited Mr. Morris's room. The officer had retaken his seat outside and whipped his head toward me.

"How'd you get in there?"

"Sorry, it—it was the wrong room."

He narrowed his eyes at me as I rushed down the hall and made a quick turn into the waiting area. Karter sat there in a chair facing the nurse's station, his ankle propped on a coffee table, a bag of ice strapped to it with an ACE bandage. He held his phone to his ear.

"It's a sprain. It's not bad. It's not gonna mess anything up." He slumped in the seat.

I stuck out my hand. He had to be talking to his mom. "Let me talk to her. This is my fault."

He shook his head. "Mom, I gotta go. I gotta take Briseis home." She said something and he grunted in return, then hung up.

"I'm so sorry," I said.

"It's fine," Karter said. He got to his feet, testing his weight on his injured ankle. "She's worried I'm gonna miss my shift at the bookshop. She don't care about the ankle."

"What do you mean she doesn't care? She's your mom."

He tilted his head, his brow arched. He opened his mouth to say something, then changed his mind. "Come on."

Karter limped toward the elevator. I ducked under his arm and slid my hand around his waist so he could put his weight on me.

He smiled. "Thanks."

"I got you."

"How's the guy?" he asked. "Still alive, I'm guessing?"

"He's a mess but I think he'll be okay."

I helped Karter outside and into his truck. "I'd offer to drive, but we'd probably end up right back in the hospital with somethin' a lot worse than a sprained ankle. I don't even have a license."

"I'm good," Karter said. "Really."

I climbed in on the passenger side. I felt guilty for dragging him into this. "She was pretty mad, huh? I am so sorry. I didn't mean to get you in trouble."

"Like I said, not your fault."

"I'm the one who asked you to come up here."

He cocked his head to the side. "Maybe it is your fault." He narrowed his eyes, and we both laughed. "Our relationship is . . . complicated. It always feels like I'm fuckin' up, like I'm not doing or saying the right thing."

I sat back as he turned on the truck and pulled out of the parking lot.

"Sorry," he said, staring straight ahead. "That was too personal."

"No, it's okay," I said. "So, you guys have a tough relationship?"

He hesitated before letting his shoulders fall and shaking his head. "I wouldn't say tough. I love her more than anything. She expects a lot from me. Makes me feel like I'm always letting her down."

"Because you twisted your ankle?"

"It's not just that." He sighed heavily. "It's nothing. I need to stop being so emotional."

"Nah, don't say that," I said. "Emotional is good."

His mouth drew up into an amused smile. His phone buzzed in his pocket as we pulled up to the house. He put the car in park, then glanced at the screen and sighed. "She don't know when to quit."

I hopped out, grabbing the bag of field guides. "Whatever's happening between you and your mom, I hope it gets better," I said. "And you can absolutely talk to me if you need to."

He smiled, but it was all mouth and no eyes. "Wanna get breakfast tomorrow?"

"Or you can come over and I can make you breakfast!" Mo came bounding toward the truck, rubbing her hands together.

"How did you even hear what he said?" I asked. "Were you waiting on the porch?"

"Yes," said Mo, unapologetic.

"Sounds like a plan to me," said Karter.

"Come by about nine. I make a killer Belgian waffle."

"You've never made a waffle in your whole life," I said. I'd never met anybody who could cook lunch and dinner so well but couldn't make breakfast food to save their life. That was why the people at the bagel shop knew us by name. "Didn't you burn the scrambled eggs last time you—"

Mo caught me in a bear hug so that I couldn't say anything else.

"See you tomorrow, Karter. Bring your appetite, hun."

"I'll be here," he said. "Bye, Briseis." He turned the truck around and took off.

Mo grinned as I wriggled free of her grasp and pushed up my glasses.

"Really?" I said. "Why are you acting like this? Are you okay? Do you need to lie down?" I put my hand on her forehead to see if she felt hot.

"Girl, stop," she said, smiling. "I'm happy to see you getting out of the house and making friends."

"Are you really gonna make waffles?" I asked Mo. "We just moved in. Mom'll be pissed if you burn this place down."

"It'll be fine. Tell me more about Karter. You like him, huh?"

"He's really nice," I said, pausing to consider what she was hinting at. "I like him as a friend and honestly, that's what I need right now."

"That's just as important as anything else," said Mo.

I could always tell if I liked somebody straight out the gate. People didn't really grow on me. I either liked them right away or not at all, and I liked Karter. But that meant at some point I'd have to decide how much to tell him or how much I had to hide, and I hated that part.

CHAPTER 12

I found Mom in the kitchen, scrubbing the open shelves like her life depended on it. Her eyes were rimmed with red like she'd been crying.

She caught the concern on my face. "It's my allergies. This place is so dusty. Where did you run off to?"

"I drove around with Karter for a while."

"See anything interesting?" she asked.

"Sort of. We drove past this place called Samuel's Sweet Shop. Looked cute. They serve coffee and stuff. Maybe we could go there another day."

"Tomorrow?" Mom asked.

"No, Mo is making waffles tomorrow."

"Wait. *Who's* making waffles?" Mom asked.

"Karter is coming over for breakfast tomorrow, and I'm gonna make waffles," said Mo as she walked into the kitchen, shooting me an overexaggerated scowl. "Look what I found earlier." She went to the cabinet and took out what seemed like the first waffle iron ever made. She put it on the counter with a heavy thud. "It inspired me."

Mom stared at Mo like she had two heads.

Mo crossed her arms over her chest. "I'm so mad that y'all think I can't make waffles. It's not rocket science."

"I know," Mom said. "But, babe, have you ever actually made waffles?"

I tried to stifle my laughter but couldn't. Neither could Mom. Mo turned and walked out.

"I'm gonna prove y'all wrong in the morning," she called over her shoulder. "And then you're gonna want me to make you waffles *all the time*, and I'm gonna say no."

Mom sighed and knelt down to clean the lower row of cabinets. "Make sure you have your camera ready when she starts cooking, but also be ready to call the fire department."

"Oh, I'm on it," I said. "I'm gonna start going through some of the stuff upstairs. I, um—I found something when I was out looking around."

"Oh yeah?" Mom asked. "What is it?"

I wanted to tell her everything, but I stopped myself. I was still trying to figure out what Circe was trying to communicate through her letters and understand what my immunity had to do with the work she'd mentioned. "A garden," I said. "It's overgrown and mostly dead, but I think I can fix it."

"If anyone can do it, you can." She sat back, her legs folded under her. "Do you like it here, baby? I know it's not Brooklyn. It's different. But I gotta be honest, if we could get a handle on these random people showing up and this dust, it might grow on me. I heard birds chirping this morning, baby. *Birds.* And not stank-ass pigeons either."

"Pigeons don't even chirp," I said.

"No, they're too busy stealing people's food and shitting on everything to chirp. But that's what I'm sayin'. This place has actual birds, and even though this pollen is tryna murder me, it's beautiful up here. I think I love it."

Mom was a city chick to the bone, a New Yorker, the queen of minding her own business. She didn't believe jaywalking was a real thing and I didn't think she could live without her favorite Cuban sandwich from the bodega down the block. I never thought she could be happy anywhere except Brooklyn, but here, she was less stressed than usual. She smiled wider and was giving me more freedom than I'd ever had before.

All of a sudden, my throat tightened up. It had been so long since we could worry about anything other than how we were going to pay our bills, and just the possibility of not having to do that anymore was enough to bring me to tears because I knew what it would mean to her, to all of us.

She stood and took my hands in hers. "Listen, I talked to Mo and she got me thinking. Maybe you can let your guard down while we're out here."

"What?" I said, surprised. I wasn't expecting that from her at all.

"Maybe we should both relax a little. I get so worried about you and this power. All I ever wanna do is protect you. I love you so much." She gently traced the lines on my palm, and tears welled in her eyes. "But you have this gift for a reason, right? So maybe keeping it bottled up isn't the right move. Go explore, grow some plants. Find me something pretty to put in the window, okay?"

I buried my face in her shoulder. "It's really nice to see you like this."

She held me close. "Like what?"

"Happy. Not worrying so much and asking me to put flowers in the window."

She traced the side of my face with her fingers. "I guess we've all been wound up, stressin' ourselves to death. Now that we've got this place, maybe we can let some of that go. But we'll see, baby. Let's take it one day at a time."

"I love you, Mom."

She kissed the top of my head and squeezed me tight. "I love you more. Now get out in that garden and grow me some peonies. You know I love them."

"Hang on." I left the kitchen and went to the apothecary. I climbed the ladder, searching for a jar I'd seen when we first arrived—dried peony root. I fished out a chunk and took it back to the kitchen.

I gently set the root in her palm and cupped my hand over hers. I took a deep breath. A warm sensation flowed from my fingertips. A wave of dizziness washed over me, but I relaxed into it. I unclenched my jaw, set aside thoughts of this going wrong, and let the energy move through me.

The dizziness disappeared immediately. The root shifted. Mom inhaled sharply. A single green stalk pushed through my fingers and sprouted a foot high. A bud bloomed, revealing the blackest petals I'd ever seen, the seedy center as red as blood.

"It's an onyx peony," I said. "It's the rarest kind of peony there is." I was in awe of the unique plant, but I was also stunned that my own resistance to this power—worrying so much, trying to control it—seemed to be the thing that caused the dizziness and exhaustion I always felt after bringing flowers to bloom. There was none of that now. When I looked up at Mom, she was staring at me. "What is it?"

"You, baby." She looked at me like she was seeing me for the first time. "You're some kind of actual Black girl magic."

She put the flower in a tall glass of water and as I went down the hall, her Bluetooth speaker chimed on. The familiar notes of Josephine Baker singing "Blue Skies" in her signature breezy way wafted through the house.

Mo poked her head out of the front room. "Is Mom playing that music?"

"Yeah. She said this place is growing on her."

Mo's mouth curved into an ecstatic grin. "Who'd have thought?" She went back to dusting the shelves and windowsills, humming along with the music.

I went upstairs and took out the map Circe had left me to study the checkerboard setup of the plots in the garden. They would grow better if I transferred the plants that shared the same soil needs into the same beds. The ones that needed more acidic soil would thrive in beds with similar plants instead of sectioning the individual plots off with wooden planks.

I laid a piece of blank paper I had stuck between the pages of my notebook on top of the map, thinking I might trace the positions of the beds and sketch out the way the plants should be reorganized. The bright white printer paper stuck up a full three inches above the top of the map. I ran my fingers over the rough edge. It looked like it had been cut with a pair of dull scissors.

I jumped up and grabbed my glasses with the built-in magnifier out of the small box I'd shoved all my research stuff into before we left home. I slipped them on and examined the ragged edge of the map. A piece was missing. And near the center, the tiniest bit of ink had bled down from whatever had once been above. There was something beyond the far wall of the Poison Garden.

I put my sneakers on and ran downstairs. Mom and Mo were occupied, so I left out the front door and went around to the hidden path. The curtain of vines pulled back as I approached, but this time, I didn't worry about how the trees or grass might behave. The surrounding forest responded by creating a rolling wave of shrubbery, clearing the path of sticks and pebbles, making way for me. I gripped the map in my hand as I headed through the shadowy confines of the forest.

The trees bowed away, allowing me to unlock the gate. I quickly ducked inside, marching straight back to the moon gate. I'd been braver in the forest, but I didn't know if I should be as confident in this part of the garden. A mistake now could be fatal.

I stepped into the Poison Garden. Again, the feeling of ice water being poured down my throat caught me by surprise. The icy hot feeling stung at first but faded faster than it had during my previous visit. I swallowed hard. The tingling sensation lingered, but it didn't hurt.

I slowly approached the rear wall. Treetops pushed down through the metal arches overhead. The wall was covered in poison ivy and Devil's Pet so thick I could barely see the stones underneath. I touched the leaves, testing my immunity once again.

As my fingers grazed the foliage, vines shot out and twisted themselves around my wrists. I yanked my hand back, but they only gripped me harder. The long, toothlike spikes flattened themselves, lying against my skin but not puncturing it. My heart galloped into a furious rhythm as I tried to disentangle myself. Some of the purple leaves came off in the struggle but bloomed again under my touch. Another tendril encircled my waist and squeezed me so hard I couldn't breathe. They dragged me across the ground, knocking my glasses off, then held me upright, my feet dangling above the ground.

"Stop!" I cried out.

The poisonous vines loosened their grip, sitting me down gently but not letting go. The Devil's Pet and poison ivy parted like a theater curtain in front of me. There, in the stone wall, was a rusted metal door. At its center was a coat of arms or crest of some kind.

The Devil's Pet unfurled, releasing me from its grip. I rubbed my aching wrists. A single curl of ivy slithered along the ground. It sprouted three skinny tendrils and used them like fingers to pick up my glasses and hand them back to me.

"Uh, thanks?" I didn't know what else to say, so I wiped my lenses clean on the bottom edge of my shirt and moved closer to the newly revealed door to examine the symbol.

In the center was a woman's face or—as I realized leaning in—three faces. One stared out from the center and the other two were turned to either side. Above the faces sat a crown of intertwined vines. All of this was rendered within a shield-shaped border that was encircled by tendrils of plants and curling leaves. At the very top, a key crossed by two torches was emblazoned in intricate detail.

The backplate where the keyhole sat was beautifully carved with a swirling pattern that reminded me of the Devil's Pet.

I pulled out my keys and tried all three of them in the lock with no luck. I stepped away from the door and the vines fell back into place, concealing the door completely.

There hadn't been any mention of another key in Circe's letters, but she had said that everything I needed to know could be found in the house. Maybe the key was in there somewhere. I heaved an exhausted sigh as I pictured the endless piles of newspapers and magazines, drawers stuffed with knickknacks, and closets as big as our apartment back home. I didn't even know where to start.

Wondering what was behind the door in the rear of the Poison Garden gnawed at me as I sifted through drawer after drawer, cabinet after cabinet. Questions crept into my head and twisted themselves around every idea I had. I couldn't stop thinking about what could be behind it and why, in a garden full of plants that would kill someone who wasn't like me, it needed to be locked behind a steel door that looked like it belonged in a bank vault.

I checked the safe one more time to make sure I hadn't missed anything and took pictures of the pages in the big book so I'd know how to care for plants in the Poison Garden that I didn't recognize. Mom and Mo had moved a bunch of trash out of the turret, so I examined the titles on the shelves one by one, checking between their pages for hidden spaces where someone might keep a key to a creepy door in a walled garden in the middle of the woods.

The books on the back shelf were older than the ones near

the front. Their covers were made from leather, their pages yellowed and fragile. I took down a small, tattered book that looked in worse shape than most of the others. On its face was the word "Medea," and in subscript, the name "Seneca." I opened the cover and read from one of the pages.

"O gods! Vengeance! Come to me now, I beg, and help me . . ."

I skimmed through the rest of the book. I'd seen *Hercules* enough times to recognize some of the characters, like Jason, leader of the Argonauts, manning the ship called the *Argo*. But the main character in the tale seemed to be Medea, the woman from the paintings hanging in the turret.

I set the book aside and continued to look through the shelves. There were more old books, some encased in plastic and falling apart at the seams, and stacks of loose pages. I came to a section full of a half dozen identical bindings. Each leather-bound volume was filled with lists of herbs and plants, all with detailed instructions on their various uses and care. Every herb, plant, tree, or shrub I could think of was detailed, along with dozens of others I didn't recognize. Next to each of them were instructions for their use. The entire tome was dedicated to the making of herbal remedies for ailments ranging from PMS to arthritis. There were salves for bruises and rashes, tinctures for upset stomachs and headaches. I put the books back on the shelf and took the copy of *Medea* with me to the table in the center of the room to read.

I spent a half hour skimming through it. Medea was a woman scorned, so full of anger and rage that she plotted against her unfaithful husband by concocting a poison to kill his new lover. I was so unsettled by the description of Medea killing her own children to hurt Jason that I had to close the book and refocus. The story made it seem like Jason was the person the reader should pity, but the tragic figure was clearly Medea. What kind of person would do that to their own kids?

I gathered some of the other books from the back shelves—*Metamorphoses*, *Fabulae*, *Heroides*—and took them to my room.

I spent the rest of the late afternoon reading and making notes. Every single book that mentioned Medea was marked up, passages underlined with pencil, notes scribbled in the margins. She was a devotee of a goddess called Hecate, Guardian of the Crossroads, Keeper of the Keys. She had a hundred names, and her mythology went back even further than Medea's, to a time before the gods in Greek myths even existed. Hecate and Medea were always mentioned in connection with each other.

Mo stuck her head in my room. "You okay? You've been in here awhile."

I checked my phone. It was almost eight o'clock.

"I lost track of what time it was." I jumped off the bed. "I told Mom I was gonna help clean. I'm sorry, I got caught up in these old books I found."

"Don't worry," she said. "We got plenty of time to clean. I wouldn't choose cleaning over a good book either, love. As long as you're okay, I'll leave you to it."

"I'm good," I said. "I have a question though."

"Shoot," she said.

"You know anything about Greek mythology?"

She pursed her lips. "I studied business in college, love. Greek mythology wasn't something I was really into, but I had a friend who was. She was a curator at the Brooklyn Museum for a few years. I don't know if she's still there but I can get you her email."

"That would be perfect. I found all these old stories. There's this woman named Medea, and—"

"Like the Tyler Perry 'Madea'?"

"Uh, no," I said, grinning. "Not *Ma*dea, *Me*dea. She was the daughter of a king, and I think a devotee of a goddess, and Circe has pictures of her all over the place. It's kind of weird, but I wanna look into it."

"A lot of things are weird around here," she said. "That guy out back? Weird. I wonder if they'll arrest him when he recovers if they haven't already."

"He's kind of old," I said. "I don't think we should press charges or anything."

Mo sighed. "You're probably right. I'll talk to Mom. In the meantime, I got pizza and some organic root beer that probably tastes like ass. It's downstairs."

The doorbell rang. I heard the front door creak open, and then Mom called out.

"Briseis? There's someone here for you."

"Is it young Trevante?" Mo asked, peering into the hallway.

"His name's Karter," I said, checking my phone for a missed text or call.

Nothing.

The stab of disappointment I felt caught me off guard. I was looking forward to hanging out with him again. I went downstairs with Mo trailing behind me.

As I peered around my mom, I recognized the person standing there.

It was the girl who'd been in the driveway the other night, the one we'd called the police on. The one who'd vanished right in front of us.

CHAPTER 13

I waited to see if Mom or Mo was going to say anything. Mo had seen someone but was fuzzy on the details. Mom hadn't seen her at all. Neither of them seemed to recognize her.

In the moment our eyes met, I took in everything about her, like my mind was purposely making sure I couldn't forget any of the details. She was the most striking person I'd ever seen. Her skin was the deep umber color of autumn leaves, and her silver-gray hair was slicked back, gathered behind her neck in a mass of tight coils. The corner of her mouth drew up as she watched me.

"I'm sorry to bother you," she said, her gaze fixed on me. She stuck her hands in the pockets of her camo-colored coat. "I know it's late. I'm Marie, Alec's granddaughter."

"Who's Alec?" Mom asked.

My mind raced to think of a lie that wouldn't get me in too much trouble. I couldn't tell Mom or Mo that I'd visited Alec in the hospital. "A guy I met in town," I said quickly. "Do you want to come in?"

Marie tilted her head and smiled. "Very much. Thank you."

She stepped into the entryway, and Mom and Mo stood there, waiting for me to explain.

"Follow me," I said, avoiding their stares. "I'll get the comfrey for you."

My parents hung back, but I could feel them watching as Marie followed me down the hall. We turned into the apothecary.

"How's Alec?" I asked. "They release him yet?"

Marie rolled her eyes. "No. He's fine, though. Annoying, but fine. He got himself into a mess, and if he suffers while he's healing . . ." She shrugged like she was saying "oh well." She put her hand on her hip and looked me over from head to toe so slowly I had to glance away out of embarrassment.

A stirring sense of confusion and, if I was being real, intrigue settled over me. She couldn't have been older than me, maybe seventeen at the most. I couldn't tell if her hair was dyed silver or if that was her natural color. She wore a fitted pair of jeans, ripped in a few places at her thigh where her skin showed through, and a white T-shirt under her camo coat. Her chunky black boots clunked across the floor as she circled the shop. There was something about the way she moved, like she was in slow motion, each movement deliberate.

I was suddenly aware that I probably looked a whole mess and quickly tried to find something to check my reflection in. I took out my phone and pretended to read my email as I flipped on the front-facing camera. As soon as I caught sight of myself, I wanted to smash my phone on the ground and disappear into the fuckin' ether. Of course this beautiful girl showed up right when I was at my most busted. I sighed. It was too late to do anything about it now.

"That was you outside the other night," I said. I kept my voice low so Mom and Mo wouldn't hear. "You scared my parents."

She smiled like it was funny. "Not the reaction I was hoping for."

"You stand outside of a stranger's house in the dark, you're probably gonna scare somebody."

"I didn't mean to," she said softly. "It's been a while since the shop was open. I heard a new family moved in, so I came to see. But you're not a *new* family after all, are you?"

"Wanna tell me what that's supposed to mean?" I asked. I scanned the shelf and spotted the jar with the comfrey near the top. I slid the ladder in place and climbed up to grab it.

"You're related to Circe." She was suddenly at the base of the ladder holding it steady with one hand. "I can see that by looking at you. Do you mind if I ask how?"

"Her sister, Selene, was my birth mother."

She made a noise like a cough, but when I looked, she stood stoic, thoughtful. I climbed down and set the jar on the counter as she walked to the opposite side.

"Can I ask you something?" I said.

"Of course."

Again, something about her struck me. She was pretty—no. More than that. She was beautiful. But it wasn't just that. I shook my head. "Uh, sorry—I lost my train of thought."

She shrugged. "It happens."

I scrambled to think of what I'd meant to ask her. "There are stores—you know, online—that sell most of this stuff."

"I don't want to buy it online, and nobody else does either."

"Why not?" I asked.

"I don't know the people selling it," she said flatly. "I have no idea what they intended when they cultivated the plants."

"Is that important? The intent of the person handling them?"

"More than anything." She glanced at the wall of glass jars, then set her hands on the counter, leaning in. "I read a study once. It said that if you have a plant and talk to it like you love it, it'll grow faster, bigger. But if you keep a plant and talk down to it, insult it, it will wither and die."

"That's true," I said. I'd read the same article and had even done an entire paper on the process for my environmental studies class. "So maybe there's something to it, to what you think and feel when you grow a plant."

She nodded. "I think so. I imagine plants are kind of like people. Tell a person they're worthless, hurt their feelings everyday—they'd wither, too." She let her delicate fingers dance over the surface of the counter, then up to her lips. Her eyes were like the centers of Velvet Queen sunflowers, brown and blazing. She held my gaze. "But imagine telling someone they're beautiful, magnetic, stunning. Every single day. Imagine how they'd flourish."

I knocked over the jar of comfrey as I shuffled papers, trying to avoid her stare.

Marie straightened, a smirk on her lips. "Anyway, the plants and herbs here are just better. They stay fresh longer. They don't rot in their containers. Why do you think that is?"

"I—I don't know," I lied. I was beginning to get some idea.

"You're new to this place, but it isn't new to you," Marie said. "It's in your bones. It's part of who are."

I couldn't look straight at her because I didn't know where my gaze would land—her wide eyes? The full curve of her bottom lip? "How do you know that it's in my bones?"

"I know a lot of things," she said. "For example, there are paper bags under the counter. And there should be a scoop and scale under there, too."

I looked down. She was right.

"I'll take eight ounces of the comfrey," she said.

"Right." I took the lid off the jar. The species was *Symphytum officinale*. "This kind of comfrey is called common comfrey. It's good, but the Russian strain, *Symphytum uplandicum,* would be better for Alec's ulcers. The alkaloid content is higher in that strain."

I raised my head to look at Marie. Her eyebrow arched, her mouth a half smile. I quickly scooped the dried comfrey leaves onto the scale, measured out eight ounces, and then dumped them into a paper bag. In the drawer to my right, I found a sheet of small black stickers and used one to seal the bag. I handed it to Marie and she pushed a twenty-dollar bill across the counter.

"I can't take that," I said.

"Why? It's what I paid Circe."

"When?" I asked. "Everybody keeps telling me this place has been closed for a long time."

"A while ago." She pushed the money closer to me. "You got bills to pay, right? I really hope you reopen the apothecary. This place is more important to people than you can imagine."

She'd sidestepped my question about when she'd paid Circe like I hadn't even asked it. Something lingered in her words, some other meaning. This place.

Marie leaned forward, rolling the beads of her necklace between her fingers. Her nails were painted fire-engine red, and a moss-colored agate in the shape of a skull adorned her middle finger. "This has been passed down through my family for generations. You see the beads? Do you know what they're made from?"

I leaned in to take a closer look at the necklace. She gently bit her bottom lip and sighed. The warmth of her breath and the closeness of her face to mine lit a fire in me. I blinked away the thoughts and I tried to refocus on the necklace.

What appeared to be wooden beads were, in fact, black and red seeds, dried and drilled straight through the middle.

"They're *Abrus precatorious*," I said. "Rosary peas."

She strummed her fingers on the counter. "Harmless in this form—"

"Deadly to cultivate."

"Exactly."

Circe had known, or at least suspected, that I was immune, and I began to wonder if she had an even deeper understanding of this mysterious gift than I thought.

"Circe replaced them for me over the years," Marie said. "See these ones?" She touched two cracked and flaking seeds near the clasp. "Maybe you can fix them for me now that she's gone."

The jar labeled *Abrus Precatorious* was empty, but she probably knew that. She wasn't asking me to climb the ladder—she wanted me to grow them for her.

"I'll pay you a hundred dollars a seed," Marie said.

The door of the apothecary bounced open. Mom and Mo fell headfirst into the room. Mo practically did a full barrel roll, then jumped up and stood at the doorway.

"I was just—just checking these door jambs," she stammered, rubbing her shoulder. "The jambs are loose. And the hinges are—are broke. We gotta get that fixed." She ran her hand over the jamb like she was inspecting it, then turned to Mom. "Babe, can you call somebody to fix this?"

Mom took out her phone and put it to her ear. Without unlocking it. Or dialing a number. She pretended to talk to someone and then paused, shoving her phone back in her pocket.

"We were eavesdropping," Mom admitted. "Sorry. We'll leave y'all alone."

They stumbled out of the room and closed the door—which worked perfectly—behind them.

I sighed. "They're a whole mess."

Marie laughed as she pulled out her phone. "What's your number?"

"You want my number?" I asked.

"Yes." She said it with zero hesitation.

It took me a second to actually remember my own damn phone number. I needed to get it together because I was embarrassing myself. After rattling off the numbers, she sent me a text so I had her info.

"Call me. We can talk more about Circe, about this place, or maybe something else altogether." Before I had a chance to respond, she swept out of the room, glancing back to look me square in the eye. "Bye, Briseis."

The way she said my name sent a flood of warmth through me—and not the kind that brought flowers to bloom. She disappeared down the hall. Not a minute later, my parents were standing in front of me.

"Spill it," said Mo. "Who was that? And why was she lookin' at you like *that*?"

"She said she was gonna pay you a hundred dollars for some seeds?" Mom looked extremely concerned. "What kind of seeds? Opium? Kids gettin' high out here in the sticks?"

"What? No. It's—it's plants." I needed to let them in on at least some of what was happening so they didn't worry. "Circe and Selene were running an apothecary. We figured that, but the thing is, they were growing and harvesting everything themselves in that garden I told you about."

"And there are already people willing to pay money for this stuff?" Mo scanned the shelves.

"That's why random people have been showing up," I said. "The place has been closed for a while, but now that word has gotten around that we're here, I think people are hoping we'll reopen it."

"Will we?" Mom asked. She turned to me. "You want to do this?"

It wasn't that I wanted to do it. I felt like I was *supposed* to. The only thing I'd ever been really good at in my life was the one thing these random people needed me to do. It wasn't a coincidence. It couldn't have been. "I want to try and reopen the apothecary. I'll take care of the plots and see if I can bring back the plants. We could run it like the shop back home. Maybe you can help me figure out the business side?"

Mom sighed. "It might be similar, but it's still a business. It's a lot of work."

Mo looked thoughtful. "We're not paying rent for the space, and the inventory would be whatever you're growing in the garden, right?"

"I'd grow everything myself," I said. "We'd only have to pay for bags, maybe labels, but that's it."

"And you're not worried about, you know, the way it makes you feel?" Mom asked.

I shook my head. "Not if I don't try so hard to control it. When I let go, it's easier."

Mo smiled. "Startup costs would be nothing. It'd be almost one hundred percent profit. I think we'd have to steer clear of making promises about what this stuff can and can't do for legal reasons, but other than that, I think it's doable."

We sat quietly for a moment. We were all thinking it through, figuring out if our plan could work. I could see Mom worrying about every detail, looking at it from every angle, and Mo seemed to have decided it was a done deal. She was already scratching out supply lists and possible business hours on the back of a paper bag. After talking it through a half-dozen times and establishing a schedule based on how quickly I thought I could restock the contents of the apothecary, we had a solid plan for reopening it.

Mom and Mo talked excitedly as they meandered upstairs and into their room for the night. It made me happy to think we could stay, that I could spend some more time with Karter, and hopefully see Marie again. Her face was emblazoned in my mind.

I closed up the apothecary and went to my room. I brushed my teeth and put on a bonnet. As I walked past the fireplace, the plants by the hearth tangled themselves together and knocked over their planters.

As I righted them, I noticed something odd. Unlike the fireplace in my moms' room, this one didn't have any debris inside. The raised grate where the logs would sit looked brand-new aside from some dust. It didn't look like anything had ever been burned in it at all. I crouched down and craned my neck to look up into the chimney. I couldn't see anything, but figured it was probably blocked like the other one had been, so I grabbed the chain and stood as far away from the opening as I could before yanking it down.

I waited for the metal on metal grinding as the flue opened and braced myself for the subsequent shower of dead birds and leaves. Instead, I was met with a low rumble, a sound that might have been mistaken for distant thunder, as a cloud of dust engulfed me. The hearth sank into the wall, then rolled to the right, revealing a small room.

I stumbled back coughing, my eyes watering. I expected Mom and Mo to come running but there was only quiet. This wasn't exactly the same as a strange door appearing out of nowhere like in the scary stories I'd talked about with Karter, but it was close enough to make me briefly consider taking a flying leap out the closest window.

The fireplace wasn't real. It was a false facade, and behind it was a space the size of a large closet. A rolltop desk sat against the far wall, a wooden chair tucked underneath. Above it, a large map was pinned to a corkboard. I grabbed my phone and turned on the flashlight, sweeping the light upward. There were three pins stuck in the map, right over Rhinebeck, and three more scattered across different continents.

The desk itself was dusty, covered with loose papers, sketches of plants, and books arranged in neat stacks. I pictured Circe or maybe Selene sitting and studying the map and drawings. Carved into the dark cherry wood of the desk's surface was a symbol I recognized—the same crest from the hidden door in the Poison Garden. I traced the lines and curves of the three faces with my fingers.

I swept my light to the wall behind me. There was only one other thing hanging in the musty space—another painting of Medea. It was bigger than the ones in the turret and set in a heavy, silver frame that was tarnished with age. Medea sat front and center, her big dark eyes staring out at me, her hair down, the tight coils brushing the tops of her bare shoulders. Her hands were cupped together in front of her, and in her palm sat six seeds.

I backed up against the opposite wall to take in the entire painting, and as I did, I saw Medea wasn't alone in the frame. Standing behind her, taking up the entire top half of the canvas, was another figure. A woman dressed in billowing black robes stood directly behind Medea. Her eyes were the color of ink and her skin was like the velvety petals of the calla lily, Black and beautiful. She had a jet-black mass of thick, lustrous hair framing her head. Set among the valleys and peaks of her natural hair was a crown of golden gilded rays.

The other portraits had made me nervous, like Medea was watching my every move, but this painting stirred in me a profound sense of unease. Like she, and the woman with her, knew exactly who I was and, maybe, what I could do. Their slightly parted lips and piercing stares gave me the unshakable feeling that they were waiting for me to *do* something. I turned and left the room, yanked down the chain, and watched the fireplace move quietly back into place.

CHAPTER 14

Karter was at the front door at nine the next morning, and I had added the room behind the fireplace to my growing list of secrets.

"How's your ankle?" I asked.

"Better. It's just a sprain." He pulled up his pant leg. His ankle was wrapped, but he didn't have too much of a limp as he came in. Down the hall, a crash of pots and pans rang out. Karter jumped.

"The hell was that?" Mom yelled from somewhere upstairs.

"Mo's in the kitchen," I called back.

She appeared at the top of the stairs. "I was hoping she was gonna forget about breakfast. Karter, baby, I apologize in advance. You don't have to eat nothin' she puts in front of you."

Karter glanced at me, clearly concerned.

I stifled a laugh. "You thought I was joking when I said she's never made a waffle in her life?"

"I did, actually," he replied.

I led Karter down the hall and as we rounded the corner into the kitchen, we saw Mo wearing a full-on chef's uniform: the white coat, the hat—everything.

"Yikes," I said.

Mo's head whipped around.

"Watch and learn, baby girl," she said. "Watch and learn."

"Where'd you even get that outfit?" I asked.

Mo waved me away. "Don't worry about it."

She laid out all the ingredients she was going to use on the counter. Karter and I sat at the narrow table at the rear of the kitchen as Mom walked in and immediately took out her phone. Mo mixed the ingredients together and poured the batter onto the waffle iron. It made a loud hissing sound.

"Is that smoke?" I asked.

"It's steam," Mo said.

A half hour later, our blackened waffles were in the trash and the windows were open so the wispy clouds of gray smoke could escape. Mo drove into town to pick up breakfast under the condition that we would never speak about her waffle-making skills ever again.

After breakfast, Karter and I went outside. It was barely midmorning but the warm summer air was already heavy. The combination of a full stomach and the heat made me feel lazy as we circled around to the back of the house. I eyed the entrance to the hidden path.

"You gotta give Mo an A for confidence," said Karter. "She was convinced she could make that breakfast. You really don't know where she got the outfit?"

"No idea," I said, laughing. "I feel bad, but she's really good at lunch and dinner. I don't know why she can't get the hang of breakfast. We usually get bagels."

"Probably a good idea." He put his hands in his pockets. "So, what now? Are you guys staying long-term or . . ."

I pushed my glasses up the bridge of my nose. "I didn't think we would. I didn't want to come up here at first."

"Why?" Karter asked.

"I was worried. This is a big change and the city is . . . familiar. Being out here is all new."

"I get that," said Karter.

"But I kind of fell out with my friends," I said. "Maybe 'fell out' isn't the right way to say it. It's more like we were one thing when we met and now we're something different. We just grew apart and I got comfortable making myself small." I stopped. "Sorry. Now I'm the one telling you all my business."

"I told you about my mom, so it's only fair you tell me about your problems." He smiled. "That's what friends are for, right?"

I couldn't keep myself from grinning. Did he already think of me as a friend? "We're here and I think we'll try to make it work. Besides, I'm having fun finding out about Rhinebeck and the house."

"The house?" he asked. "What do you mean?"

"I mean, I've been talking to people. Dr. Grant runs the Public Safety department and she said stuff has been goin' on out here forever. The house has a reputation for attracting strange people."

Karter rubbed the back of his neck. "Can I tell you something?"

"Uh oh," I said. "That can't be good. What is it? Somebody died in there, huh? Or it used to be a mortuary or something?"

He shook his head. "Nah, it's just that I've heard things about this place, too. And the people who lived here before."

"Really?" I asked, surprised. "What did you hear?"

He looked down at the ground, shifting from one foot to another. "People say the women who lived here were into witchcraft."

"What?" I laughed but Karter didn't. "You believe in that kind of thing?"

"I don't know. I guess not. It was just something I heard. Thought it might be good to know."

"In case any witches show up?" I was going to laugh again, but Marie's face pushed its way to the front of my mind. I shook my head. Witches were ridiculous . . . right?

Karter's phone buzzed, and he answered it.

"Just here with Briseis, Mom," he said, rolling his eyes. A puzzled look spread across his face. He held out his phone. "She wants to talk to you."

I took it. "Hi, Mrs. Redmond."

"Hello, Briseis. Is everything all right?" she asked. "How are things going? You liking the place?"

"Everything's good," I said.

"That's wonderful. I cannot tell you how happy I am that the house won't be tied up with the bank."

"I'm happy too," I said.

Karter rolled his head back, then whispered, "She loves to talk. Just hang up on her."

"Actually, I had a quick question," I said, giving Karter a nudge. "Was there another key you were supposed to give me?"

Mrs. Redmond paused. "I'm pretty sure I gave you everything I had. Would you like me to double-check?"

"If you get a chance," I said. "No big deal."

"Did you come across a door you couldn't open?" she asked.

I hesitated. "A couple of closets. We want to make sure there aren't mice living in there."

"I can understand that," Mrs. Redmond said. "The property is pretty big, and Miss Colchis, by her own admission, never threw anything away. Maybe there's another key in the house somewhere?"

I'd already searched the turret, the bedrooms, all the closets and drawers. But I did find a secret room, so there was still the possibility that I'd missed something.

"Listen," Mrs. Redmond said. "I'll double-check my office and see if I left anything behind."

"Thanks," I said. I handed the phone back to Karter, and he hung up after saying bye.

"You guys having trouble opening doors?" Karter asked. "Are you sure it's locked? Sometimes in these old houses the hinges get stuck and you have to—" He stopped short.

I followed his gaze to the waist-high grass surrounding us. The blades were stretching toward me like a thousand eager arms. How could I have been so stupid? Walking through the grass with him like that? I couldn't make him unsee what was happening, and to make things worse, the blades turned an obscene shade of bright, neon green. They refused to be ignored.

Karter grabbed my arm. "Why is it doing that?"

I had a choice to make. I could rush him back into the house and act like I was just as confused as he was. I could start the vicious cycle of lies and pretending, or I could do something I'd never done before. What would it be like to let everything be right out in the open? This friendship with Karter was new and I didn't want to have to hide the way I did with Gabby back home.

I studied Karter's expression. He was anxious, but he'd moved closer to me, not away. I took a deep breath.

"It's me."

He blinked repeatedly. "You're making the grass do that?" He glanced around the yard. "How?"

"I—I don't know. Please, Karter. Please don't be afraid." He stayed quiet but didn't move. I took that as a sign that he wanted to know more. "Come with me."

I took his hand and pulled him toward the hidden path. We stopped at the tree line. As if on cue, the curtain of vines parted in front of me. Karter's eyes grew wide. He stepped back, snatching his hand away from me.

"What—what's happening?" he stammered.

I turned to Karter. If he was freaked out, he could leave. I'd be disappointed but not surprised. "I know it's strange. But I need to talk to someone about what I found."

Karter's chest heaved. He was in a half-crouched stance, like he was ready to sprint away at any moment.

"Just walk with me," I said. "For a little bit?"

Karter exhaled, long and slow. "Walk with you where?"

I stepped onto the path and looked back at him. "It'll be easier if I can show you. Please?"

I held out my hand, hoping he'd take it and give me a chance to prove to myself that I was capable of this.

He took a tentative step forward, then put his hand firmly in mine.

CHAPTER 15

Before, the plants along the path had pulled back, making a way for me. Now, they stayed close to my feet, slithering like poisonous snakes and crowding the trail, ready to strike. Karter kept a death grip on my arm as I led him through the trees, which creaked and groaned as they arched toward me.

"Keep moving," I said. "And stay close."

We emerged into the clearing and Karter loosened his grip though I didn't let go of him. Images of Alec being reeled in by vines as thick as my arm tumbled through my head. He'd been a threat to me, and this place had sensed that and acted accordingly. I still wasn't sure what mechanism made that happen, but if I kept Karter close, I thought I could keep him safe.

The black bat flowers that blanketed the meadow shifted in unison. Karter looked beyond them, his gaze resting on the gate. "What's in there?"

"More plants," I said, unsure of how to tell him exactly what it was. "That's what I wanted to show you."

"If it's just plants, why is it sealed up like that?" He gestured toward the lock.

"Some of them are poisonous," I said. I took the key from my pocket and unlocked the gate. The bougainvillea pulled back as the rusted gates swung open. I took Karter's hand again and we walked into the walled enclosure.

Karter moved closer to me. "The poisonous stuff—is it like poison ivy or somethin'?"

"No, more like oleander and belladonna."

His eyebrows knitted together. "I have no idea what that means, but it sounds like something I don't want no parts of." He gazed up at the tree in the center of the garden and around at the plots. "Are these the poisonous ones?"

"No. These are pretty harmless, but . . ." I glanced toward the wall that divided the garden in half. "The plants back there are deadly. They could kill you by brushing against your skin."

He swallowed hard but kept his eyes on the gate. "For real? So we can't go in there?"

"No."

He angled himself toward me. "But if they don't touch my skin, I'm good? You've been in there, right? And you're okay."

"Yeah. But the poison—it doesn't affect me the same way it affects other people."

Karter raised an eyebrow. "Okay. So I'll be careful. And I'm not really sure what you're doin' or how you're doin' it, but I—I want to see everything."

There was a ring of excitement in his voice, but I had a vision of him tripping over his own feet and falling into a bed of stinging nettle.

"I promise I'll be careful," he said, as if he could sense my hesitation.

I wanted to share this place with him because I was done being afraid to get close to people. I didn't want to hide anymore. "We can go right inside the gate. Don't touch anything. Don't even brush up against anything, okay?"

"I swear I won't," he said, craning his neck to look past the moon gate.

I moved toward the circular opening in the dividing wall. I led him through, stopping just inside. The locked door in the back was shrouded by ivy once again. No one would have known it was there unless they were looking for it.

"Wow," said Karter. He cleared his throat.

"You good?" I asked, as the familiar cool sensation trickled down my throat.

His gaze suddenly darted to the top of the wall. A vine as big around as a telephone pole slung itself down, thudding as it hit the ground. It moved along the ground like a snake, baring its thorns like fangs.

Karter scrambled back. He coughed over and over again and his eyes watered profusely. I'd made a mistake. He shouldn't have been here at all.

"Do me a favor and don't move," I said, my heart racing. The plants were reacting to me. A frenzied sort of energy permeated the air as tangles of vines and Devil's Pet began to unfurl from the tops of the walls. I lunged in front of Karter as the snakelike vine reached for him. "Don't!" I shouted.

"It listens to you?" Karter asked, his eyes wild, his breath pumping out of him.

I didn't know for sure that it would, but I didn't know what else to do. I put my hands up in front of me. "Stop!"

The vine coiled back on itself and went still.

Karter looked around frantically. "Can we go?"

We left the Poison Garden, and as we did, the vine recoiled and retook its position at the top of the wall. Karter had backed all the way up and was standing in the shade of the big tree. His eyes were bloodshot, his face shiny with sweat. He clawed at his neck. "Am I gonna die?"

"No," I said.

"You're good? Why do I feel like I'm dying?"

He sat down, gulping in the fresh air between fits of coughing. After a few minutes, his breathing slowed, and his eyes stopped watering. He'd be okay.

"You can't go back in there. I'm sorry. I thought if you didn't touch anything you'd be okay." It was too much of a risk and I felt terrible.

"It doesn't affect you at all?"

"Not as far as I can tell. Listen," I said, before he had a chance to ask me any questions. "I know this is . . . different. I don't know what's going on here exactly, but I think it has something to do with the people who lived here before, Circe and Selene."

I thought he would freak out, maybe tell me he had to go and then never come back, but he sat quietly, lost in his own thoughts for a minute before speaking. "And they left you this place? How did you know them?"

"I didn't," I said.

He tilted his head to the side. "Then why would—"

"Selene was my birth mother."

Karter blinked. "Oh."

"It's not a secret," I said. "I was adopted. I've always known that. But Mom and Mo are the best."

"Not the best at waffle-making, but whatever." The vines atop the high walls rustled, and Karter tensed like he was going to get up and run.

"Circe and Selene were running a natural medicine shop out of the house. I'm gonna try to reopen it."

"Sounds like a lot of work," Karter said, looking around the garden. "Everything's dead."

"I'm gonna fix it," I said. "Maybe you could help me?"

"Uh, I kill plants on contact. I couldn't even keep bean sprouts alive for a science fair project. And I'm definitely not going back in there." He waved toward the Poison Garden. "I felt like my throat was gonna close up."

I sat down next to Karter. A tendril of flowers dropped down from the canopy above us. They looped around my neck and broke off, leaving me with a necklace of bright pink blooms.

Karter's mouth opened into a little O. "How—how did you do that?"

"I don't know, exactly." My heart was in my throat. I'd never been so open about what I could do with anyone other than my parents and it felt like another huge gamble.

"It's . . ."

I braced myself for what he might say. Weird? Scary? Strange?

His face softened. His shoulders relaxed and he shook his head. "I don't know. Maybe it's magic."

I blinked a few times, trying to clear my head. "I don't know about magic. I've been like this all my life, but until I got here,

I'd always been afraid that I was gonna lose control and mess up or get someone hurt."

"It's not like that now?" he asked, his gaze darting from me to the plants and back again.

"No." As I said it, I realized how much these last few days had allowed me to see myself in a way I never had before. "So much has changed since I've been here. Things have happened that make me wonder if this is where I'm meant to be." I didn't know if he'd understand but I hoped I was making myself clear. "I can show you more, if you want. I'm gonna bring all those plots back. I'll do what I have to do to stay here because it's making me and my parents happy in a way I didn't even know existed." I sighed, feeling the full weight of that. "I could really use your help."

"Sorry," Karter said.

My heart immediately sank into the pit of my stomach.

"I'm gonna have to pull weeds or rake or something, because I can't do anything special. Not like you."

I looked up at him, daring to hope that he was saying what I thought he was.

He leaned close to me, nudging me with his shoulder. His eyes lit up. "This is unreal. But I'm with it. You're like the Black Poison Ivy."

There wasn't a way to tell him how much it meant to me to feel—for the first time in forever—like I had a friend on my side. "Wanna start now?"

He pulled out his phone, dismissed whatever notification was on the screen, and shot me a grin.

We spent the afternoon in the garden, steering clear of the

poison section. Karter found a hose and connected it to the spigot in the wall. Rust-colored water shot out in sporadic bursts until it started to flow even and clear. I watered the acacia tree until the ground at its roots was soaked. I ran my hand over the rough, cracked bark of the trunk, gazing up into the twisted canopy of branches. Warmth flowed from my fingertips. The leaves doubled in size, expanding until they blotted out the sun. A hum filled my ears as the tree shifted, stretching toward the sky.

Karter watched, his mouth half-open. He didn't look away. He even clapped his hands when I brought a gathering of shriveled angelica stalks back to life.

"They need lots of water and shade to thrive," I said. Now they had both, thanks to the hose and the expanding canopy from the acacia tree. I leaned in close. A pungent, musty odor wafted up as small clusters of white blooms came to life. I put my hands in the soil beneath them, and the plants doubled in size.

"Do you even need my help?" Karter asked, smiling.

"You can rake," I said.

"As fun as that sounds, I'll get me a lawn chair, maybe some lemonade. I'll keep you company while you practice your magic."

If that was all he wanted to do, I'd be perfectly happy to let him. His company was what I wanted most.

I made my way through the front section of the garden, watering the beds and watching them wake from their slumber. In the corner nearest the entrance was a small bed with a collection of decayed and crumbling plants all crowded together. The plot wasn't marked on the map but a small metal plaque set among the broken stalks and rotted leaves read Hecate's Garden. I emptied the watering can into the bed, drenching the soil. Digging my fingers into the dirt, I breathed in the muggy air and let the warmth flow from my fingertips. Blooms as black as the night sky burst open like fireworks—black scallops, Queen of the Night tulips, hellebore, and black-purple irises.

I heard Karter gasp. When I glanced back at him, he quickly rearranged his shocked expression into an amused smile. He looked down at the sign. "Who's Hecate?"

"I'm not sure." There was that name again, Hecate. I'd read it in one of the stories about Medea, but I couldn't remember which. I stood. "All the plants look good here so far. I'm gonna transplant some of them, but we can do that another day."

"What about them?" Karter motioned to the Poison Garden. "You're gonna bring those back to life too?"

I took out my phone and looked at the pictures I'd taken of the pages in the big book back at the house. Some of the plants needed to be watered with dew collected on the morning after the first full moon of the month. I sighed. Those poisonous plants were high maintenance, and I would have to take care of them on my own to keep Karter from getting hurt. "They're gonna have to wait. I think I'm done for right now, though. Let's get out of here."

Relief flooded his expression. I hoped it was because it was hot and we were both sweaty and thirsty, not because he wanted to hightail it home and never come back.

We made the short walk home and got there just as Mom and Mo were hauling a small couch down the front steps. Its entire underside was shredded to pieces.

"I was hoping we'd left the rodents behind in Brooklyn," Mo said. "Wishful thinking, right?"

Karter's phone buzzed and he checked the screen. "I gotta go." He jogged over and gave Mo a quick hug. "Thanks for breakfast. It was great."

"Baby, you don't have to lie to her," Mom said. "She needs to hear the truth."

"You know I can hear you, right?" Mo said. "I'm standing right here."

Karter chuckled. "I'll text you later, Briseis." He hopped in his truck, gave a quick wave, and left.

"Bri, baby, you need to take my Taser if y'all are gonna be out in these woods," Mom said as I followed her inside. "There are wild animals out there."

"You want me to use the Taser on wild animals?" I started to laugh but realized she wasn't joking. "Mom, how's that supposed to work?"

Mo shook her head. "We're not tasing wild animals. We should be trying to make friends with them. We're in their territory now."

Mom sucked her teeth. "Make friends with them? Who are you, the Black Snow White?"

"Just you wait," said Mo. "By the end of the summer, I'm gonna have deer and baby bunnies eating carrots out my hand."

Mom shook her head, then turned to me. "What were you and Karter up to out there? Getting that garden in shape?"

"It's a mess, but we put a dent in it today."

"You need help?" asked Mo. "Me and Mom could come out there and help."

"Don't volunteer me for that," Mom said quickly. "You wanna

go out there, be my guest. But keep me out of it. Love you. Bri, baby, you know I do, but I'm stayin' put."

"It's okay. Karter can help, and I don't mind being out there by myself. It's kind of nice. Gives me a chance to"—I looked at Mo—"to stretch."

Mo nodded and Mom seemed happy that she didn't have to go outside. I'd shared more with Karter than I had with them, and I felt extremely guilty about that. They'd never done anything but be supportive of me in every possible way. But if Karter got upset or decided it was too much, he could walk away. I'd be crushed, but I'd find a way to get over it. My parents couldn't walk away from me—they wouldn't want to. It was better to try and make sure they never had to choose between loving me and being afraid.

Karter came over every day for the next week. I worried his mom would make him stick to his shifts at the bookshop but she covered for him most days. He helped me rig up a plastic tarp to collect dew for the poison plants, but I never brought him into the Poison Garden. He didn't want to be back there, anyway. He coughed every time he got close to the moon gate even though there was nothing poisonous in the air around him.

We talked for hours about how things had been for me growing up, how Mom and Mo had reacted when they found out what I could do, what it was like living in Brooklyn, but when the conversation shifted to him, he was always hesitant. He didn't talk about his dad at all, and his mom was a workaholic to the point of neglect. Karter always changed the subject when it got too heavy.

The plants in the Poison Garden grew with their infusions of rainwater and dew, but they took their time. They came alive under my thumb, but by the time I'd collected two full harvests from the front garden, only one was ready in the Venenum Hortus.

Karter worked in the front part of the garden while I collected the rosary peas and watered the hemlock root, castor beans, and oleander. Every time I did, I let the most toxic parts of the plants come in contact with my bare skin, just to test myself and see if Circe might have been wrong about me. I never developed so much as a rash or a welt, let alone seizures or bleeding mucus membranes—things that were supposed to happen when these poisons got in the bloodstream.

One afternoon, as we put away our rakes and hoses and as I hauled a bag of black hellebore to the gate, Karter paused. "Can I ask you something?"

"I don't think I've ever said no to that question." There was nothing he'd asked me about so far that I'd shied away from.

"I know you're happy with your parents, but do you ever think about your birth mom?"

"Um—sure. I think that's a normal, right?"

"Makes sense," Karter said. "Do you know how she died?"

The question caught me off guard. I didn't answer him right away. My mind twisted back to when I'd asked Mom and Mo that exact same question. I think I was ten or eleven. One of my classmates had gone to a funeral and they told us all about it when they came back. It got me thinking more about death than

I had before that point. I'd asked what happened to Selene right in the middle of a spaghetti dinner, and Mom told me that the adoption agency called to tell her Selene had passed away shortly after my adoption was finalized. I knew that already, but I wanted to know how. She said the agency told her she died of an illness.

"She was sick," I said.

"I'm sorry," Karter said, his voice low. "I know all this belonged to her. My dad died when I was twelve, and I used to go to this one park where we'd had cookouts to feel like I was sharing space with him after he was gone. I was wondering if that's how you're feeling now."

My throat tightened. "I'm sorry about your dad. I hadn't thought about it like that, but I think that's beautiful."

I looked around. Was I sharing space with Selene and Circe? Did Selene even want to share this with me? I didn't think so, but Circe did. Her letter made that clear, but there was still something left to be discovered. Every time I looked at the spot where the hidden door was, knowing I still didn't have the key, the pull toward it grew stronger. There was something else here that needed to be uncovered.

CHAPTER 16

Karter left for his afternoon shift at the bookshop, and I took the time to shower, turn up my music in the bathroom I didn't have to share with anybody, and give my hair the attention it so desperately needed. Two hours and one full Beyoncé *Homecoming* routine later, my hair was detangled, conditioned, twisted, and sitting under a plastic cap. I was lotioned up and feeling like a whole new me. I swore to myself I'd never let Marie, or anybody else, catch me slippin' ever again.

I found Mo in one of the bedrooms she was using as a makeshift office, with her dresser as a desk. Everything smelled like freshly washed sheets and potpourri. She set up her computer to do the billing and ordering, but she'd skipped her first scheduled trip back to the shop to help out because one of Mom's other friends had volunteered to give Jake a hand.

"Hey, Mo. Do you have that email for your friend at the university? I wanted to ask her about some of the books I found."

"Sorry, love," said Mo. "I totally forgot." She sent me a text with her email and went back to her bookkeeping.

I went to my room, opened my laptop, and wrote a short email to Professor Madeline Kent.

> Professor,
>
> This is Briseis Greene. My mom, Angie Greene, gave me your email. I was hoping I could ask you a few questions about Greek mythology, specifically the story of Medea. I've come across different stories and thought you might have some more detailed information.
>
> Thanks for your time,
> Briseis

I hit send. Before I had a chance to put my phone down, I got a reply.

> Hello, Briseis! I'd be happy to talk with you. Would it be all right if I called you?

I sent her my number and my phone rang a few minutes later.

"Professor Kent? Thank you so much for talking to me. I'm sorry to bother you."

She laughed. "It's not a problem at all. How's Angie? I've been so busy I haven't had a chance to call her lately."

"She's good. We're in Rhinebeck for the summer."

"Oh? Rhinebeck is beautiful in the summer. I've been there a few times myself. What can I help you with?"

"We're cleaning out the house where we're staying, and the people who lived here before were pretty into mythology, especially Medea. Mo said you were an expert?"

"I have a PhD in Classical Studies and a second PhD in English."

"So you're definitely an expert."

She laughed lightly. "I am and I don't ever miss an opportunity to say so. As for Medea, she is a tragic figure, but not someone people readily identify when they think of Greek mythology. She is more closely associated with opera or courses that examine narratives centering on the trope of the woman scorned."

"You mean how she killed her own children to get back at her ex?"

"That part, yes." Professor Kent sighed. "I think within most narratives, you will find the thoughts and beliefs of the author. Whenever you hear a story about villainous women, you should ask who's telling the story. Medea's tale has been told and retold a dozen times, but always by men who seem to revel in her heinous actions without addressing what caused it. Sometimes her story is used to showcase women as crazy, unpredictable, or vindictive." She sounded thoroughly irritated.

"I've been reading the stories, and it's weird to me that a fictional character—"

"Not fiction."

I paused. "Wait. What's not fiction?"

"Medea," said Professor Kent. "She's not a fictional character. Not entirely, anyway. Many of the stories we've thought of as fiction have been proven to have a basis in reality. It's the same for Medea. There are contemporary accounts of a woman who fits her description. She was considered a witch and shared her name and origins, being a daughter of the King of Colchis."

My breath caught in my throat. "Colchis?"

"Yes. A powerful family in ancient Greece. You said you've been reading about her. Not all versions of her story are the same, but she was most definitely the daughter of the King of Colchis. Sometimes that fact is omitted depending on the preference of the author."

I didn't recall coming across the name in the books I'd read so far, but there were so many others I still had to go through. "And you said she was a witch?"

Professor Kent laughed. "Yes. Being a woman was enough to get you labeled a witch in those days, but for her, it had more to do with her talent for crafting poisons."

It felt like the air had been sucked out of the room. My mind went in circles. "Can I—can I put together an email with my questions and send it to you? This is a lot to take in."

"Oh, sure. Whatever works best for you. Tell Angie and Thandie I said hello, and please feel free to call, text, or email anytime. I never tire of talking about these things."

"Thanks, Professor."

I hung up and sat quietly for a minute. Everything I knew about Greek mythology came from watching *Hercules* a few too many times as a kid, wishing a little too hard to be one of the muses. I knew the story of Achilles because I shared my name with his wife and had looked into it only to find out Patroclus was the love of his life and Briseis was probably just their homegirl. And of course, I'd listened to the *Hadestown* soundtrack more times than I could count—but they were stories. Myths. I opened a blank email and tried to put my questions for Professor Kent in some kind of order.

Professor Kent,

1) First, you're an expert on this. What's your consulting fee? Your time is valuable, and I'm not asking you to do this for free. Please send me your Venmo or PayPal.
2) Greek myths were based in reality? All of them or just some? And which ones?
3) You said Medea could have been a real person, a witch? Like the Wicked Witch of the West or Sabrina?

I had other questions, but I didn't think Professor Kent would be the right person to ask. That name—"Colchis." It was my birth mother's family name. It made me wonder if their interest in Medea had turned into an unhealthy obsession.

Going over everything in my head left me even more curious about what was behind that door in the Poison Garden. More paintings of Medea? More books? Something else?

I sent the email to Professor Kent and sat back against the pillows, gazing up at the canopy above my bed. If I was supposed to know what was behind the secret door, why didn't Circe leave me a key like she had for everything else?

I grabbed my phone and dialed Mrs. Redmond. Her voice mail picked up, but I didn't leave a message. I sent Karter a text to see if he could put me in touch with his mom, but when he didn't text back in the five minutes I was willing to wait, I decided to ask Mom or Mo to take me into town so I could stop by Mrs. Redmond's office. I found them in the extra bedroom, rummaging through an old wardrobe full of winter coats.

"Do you think we could drive into town?"

"Sure," said Mo. "I need to go to the store anyway. Where do you need to go?"

"Mrs. Redmond said she might have another key for me," I said, immediately regretting it.

"A key to what?" Mom asked.

"The closet in my room," I lied. "It's locked and the skeleton key doesn't work in it."

Mo ran to grab her keys, and I tucked my still-damp twists under a head scarf and met her in the driveway. We drove into town and parked in front of the grocery store.

"I can walk over from here," I said, climbing out of the car. The muggy air fogged my glasses, and I wiped them on my shirt. "Wanna meet up at that coffee shop we saw the other day, the one by the candle shop?"

"Sounds good," she said.

Mrs. Redmond's office was two blocks over. As I made my way there, I peeked inside some of the storefronts off Market Street—a thrift shop, a pizza joint, and a place selling handmade wind chimes and birdhouses. Tucked along a side street was a small boutique with a chalkboard sign that read Lucille's. Through the window, I saw an older woman with a head full of locs standing behind the counter. We made eye contact, and I was about to look away when I realized I recognized her from somewhere. She motioned for me to come in. I pushed open the door and ducked inside.

"I was wondering when we would run into each other," she said. Her big brown eyes were bright as she looked me over. She pressed her fingertips to her lips.

I still couldn't place where I'd seen her. "Sorry, but do I know you? I feel like I've seen you before."

"I work the morning shift at the candle shop down the block. I saw you the other day across the street."

As she grinned, the memory of seeing her with Mo that first time we'd come into town came back to me.

"I knew that face," she said. "You Colchis women are carbon copies of one another." She came around the counter and took my hands in hers, tracing her fingertips over my palm. She inhaled sharply. She seemed at a loss.

"I'm Briseis," I said, gently breaking her firm grip.

"I know," she said.

"How?"

"Word gets around. Marie was up here a few days ago gushing about the beautiful girl at the apothecary."

Heat rose in my face and I looked down at the floor.

"Ah, young love," she said wistfully.

"What? No. I—I don't even know her," I stammered.

"Just wait," said the woman, a knowing glint in her eye. "So, tell me, is the shop back up and running? I'm low on supplies. I have to source everything individually now. Mugwort from Alabama, rue from Georgia, sweet grass from California. It's exhausting."

"I—I'm gonna reopen it," I said. Now all I could think about was Marie.

"That's very good to hear." She winked at me. "People call me Mama Lucille. You feel free to do the same. Think you could set aside some lavender, vervain, and calendula? Do you have enough of those? Three ounces of each should work. That would tide me over until you get stocked back up."

"I can set some aside," I said as I looked around her shop. It was a small, cramped space, but the shelves were overflowing with candles. They weren't the fruity-smelling kind like the ones from the bath and body shop Lucille worked at in the mornings. These candles were different shapes, sorted by color, and locked inside glass cases.

"What do you use the plants from the apothecary for?" I asked.

"Lots of things," she said. "Load candles, add them to oils, make teas and soaps, you name it."

"'Load candles'?" I asked. "What does that mean?"

She thought for a moment. "It means to imbue a candle with a specific purpose using certain oils and herbs."

I looked at her again. A question sat on my lips, but I held it in. I didn't want her to think I was making fun of her in any way, but I couldn't quite grasp what she was saying without asking. "Are you a . . . a witch?" I laughed nervously.

I expected her to laugh, too, but she didn't.

"Would it bother you if I was?" she asked.

I blinked, then pretended to look at something on my phone. "I—I don't know." After what Professor Kent had mentioned about witches, after the rumors Karter had shared with me, it didn't seem like such an impossible idea. "I guess not."

Lucille handed me a crisp one-hundred-dollar bill.

"What's this for?"

"The herbs," she said.

I hadn't really thought about pricing, but this seemed like way too much. "I need to get you some change."

"That's all right," she said. "Put it on my account. Should be a book in there somewhere with my name in it. You'll be seeing quite a bit of me. I used to swing by Thursday afternoons and a few times a week around the solstices. Will that work for you?"

"I think so," I said.

"Good!" She took my hand again. "You've had some doubts about staying but you're on the right track."

"How did you—"

"Stay," she cut in. "Stay and open the shop and . . ." She trailed off. Her warm enthusiasm faded and was replaced by a look of utter confusion and then concern. "Do you—do you stock oleander? Do you have it there now?"

"No," I said. "I mean, we will, once I grow some more, but it's deadly, so I'll be careful."

"Don't," she said sternly. "Don't stock it." Lucille patted me on the shoulder, then went to the counter and wrote something on a piece of paper. "These are my numbers. I don't own a cell phone because I don't like them. Call me here or at home if you need anything." She handed me the paper.

I took out my phone and checked my messages. Still no reply from Karter. I put Lucille's info in my phone.

"I have something I gotta do," I said. "It was nice meeting you. I'll call you when I have your stuff ready."

"Sounds like a plan."

I left Lucille's and walked the rest of the way to Mrs. Redmond's. I was hoping to see Karter in the bookshop before I went up to her office, but the door was shut and a sign reading Sorry, We're Closed hung in the window.

I took the narrow flight of stairs next to the bookshop up to the second floor of the building. There were several doors to what must have been other small office spaces. A sign hung from the door closest to the front of the building. It read "M. Redmond." I knocked. No answer. It sounded like a TV was on inside.

I dialed Karter's number again and this time he picked up.

"Hey, it's Briseis. You busy?"

"Not really. Just workin'."

"Oh? Are you in the shop? I was just there and I didn't see you. I thought you went home or something."

"I have another job. My mom's running the shop today. She probably went to grab something to eat."

"You have two jobs?" I asked.

"Yeah, nothin' major. Gotta make them coins."

"Do you think you could ask your mom to call me when she gets a chance? I have a question about the house."

"Sure. Everything okay?"

"Yeah. It's not super important."

"As soon as I talk to her, I'll let her know you're tryna get ahold of her."

"Okay, thanks. Wanna link up for lunch tomorrow?"

There was a long pause. I checked my phone's screen to make sure the call was still connected.

"Yeah, I'll call you."

He hung up before I could say bye. I went back downstairs and made my way to the coffee shop. I peeked inside to see if Mo was waiting, but she wasn't there. My phone buzzed. It was a message from Mo.

Mo: Meet me back at the grocery store ASAP

I started walking toward the store, picking up the pace as another text came through.

Mo: WHERE ARE YOU?

I sprinted the last block and barreled into the grocery store parking lot. Two Public Safety vehicles were parked by our car and Mo was speaking angrily with a short, blond woman.

I raced up to her, struggling to catch my breath. "What's going on?"

The blond woman glanced at me and then down at her pad of paper.

"Look," Mo said, pointing to the car.

It sat at an odd angle, one side lower than the other. The tires had deep gashes in them, the rubber slit clean through.

"Somebody cut the tires while you were in the store?" I asked.

"Mom is gonna be pissed."

The woman took Mo's statement, which was that the tires were fine when she went into the store and flat when she came out. She didn't see anyone or notice anything strange.

Mo called the insurance company and they sent a tow truck to take the car to an auto repair shop down the street. We sat in the stuffy waiting room for two hours while they replaced the tires. While Mo was signing the paperwork and trying not to pass out from the shock of seeing the cost, my phone rang. It was Mrs. Redmond. I stepped outside to answer it.

"Mrs. Redmond?"

"Hi, Briseis. Karter said you were trying to reach me?"

"Yeah, sorry to bother you. I wanted to see if you found any other keys?"

"I've been very busy. I really haven't had time, but I'm pretty good about making sure things are organized and that my clients' wishes are fulfilled to the letter."

Her tone was sharp and I felt bad for implying that she was disorganized. "I'm sorry. The house is old. Maybe there isn't a key for some of the doors."

"I'm here at the office now. I can call you back after I've double-checked."

"Okay, thanks."

Mo met me at the car, looking exhausted. We got in, and she leaned her head on the steering wheel. "They don't let you get two new tires. You gotta get four or the car will be unbalanced, but the only thing unbalanced right now is my damn bank account. It's always something."

My phone rang again.

"Hi, Mrs. Redmond."

"Hi, Briseis. I really apologize. I don't have another key for you, but I do have something my secretary misplaced. It's a drawing. It's here if you'd like to swing by and get it."

"Be there in five minutes." I put my hand on Mo's arm. "It's gonna be okay. I'm gonna reopen the apothecary and get some money coming in."

"Always lookin' at the bright side." She smiled and leaned back.

"I get that from you," I said. "Can you run me to Mrs. Redmond's office quick? She has a paper she forgot to give to me."

"Didn't you just come from there earlier?"

"Yeah, she wasn't there, but she is now."

Five minutes later I got out of the car and went up to Mrs. Redmond's office again. The door sat ajar.

I stepped inside and an electronic bell chimed.

"Be right there," she called from another room.

The office was cramped and sparsely decorated. A small desk strewn with papers and file folders stood in the middle of the room. There was a bookshelf with only two or three titles, all having to do with law. The sound of running water and the flush of a toilet told me the only other door in the office led to a bathroom. A picture of Niagara Falls hung on the wall. A small TV sat on a file cabinet in the corner. The local news was on, and a meteorologist was warning of an impending cold front that would bring rain and wind to Rhinebeck and the surrounding areas.

Mrs. Redmond came out and gave me a quick side hug before sitting down at her desk. "I should have been more thorough when I was putting your paperwork together. I am so sorry, Briseis. Truly." She picked up a piece of paper and held it out to me. "Like I said, I'm usually very good about staying organized, but my secretary must have misplaced this. I found it shuffled in with some papers that were to be shredded."

I took the paper from her. "It's okay, really."

It was a drawing of the same crest that was on the door in

the rear of the Poison Garden and on the hidden office's desk, but there was something underneath I didn't recognize—three horizontal lines stacked one on top of the other. I was sure they weren't on either of the other crests. I sighed, frustrated. This wasn't exactly helpful, and it didn't tell me how I was supposed to find the key to the door in the garden.

"So how are things with the house?" Mrs. Redmond asked. "Is the old place treating you well?"

"It's going good," I said. "I mean, there's still a lot of work to do. The place is filled with old junk."

She shook her head. "That's too bad. Have you had a look around the rest of the property? I know there's a ton of acreage. Karter said you've been spending a lot of time in a garden? I have to be honest, I'm a little surprised by that. Gardening isn't really his thing."

"He's been helping me out," I said. "Thanks for letting him come over. I know he's got responsibilities at the bookshop."

"He does, but to hear him tell it, it's all too overwhelming, too much to handle." She shook her head. "What can I do? I'm only his mother. Not quite as exciting as the new girl in town." Bitterness stained her words, and all I could think of was how much Karter wanted to be in her good graces. "Briseis, I've been meaning to ask you something." She clasped her hands together in front of her. "Has a young woman come to the house by any chance? A woman with silver-gray hair?"

"You mean Marie?"

"Oh, I don't know her name. The reason I ask is because a few weeks ago, while I was prepping the paperwork for the house, I had to go over and make sure everything was locked up.

We've had some prowlers around town, and I didn't want anyone trespassing on the property." She lowered her voice and leaned in closer. "I saw a young woman standing out in the driveway."

My skin pricked up. "Did she—did she say anything?"

"No. It was the strangest thing, and I'll be honest, it scared me. She left before I had a chance to confront her. But you say you know her?"

"I mean—we just met. I don't *know* her."

"Right," said Mrs. Redmond. "I'm so happy that we were able to get you into the house and that you'll be taking care of it from now on. Please don't take offense to what I'm about to say, but not everyone has good intentions. You're new here and you've come into possession of a very large estate. There may be people who want to take advantage of you."

I wasn't sure what she was getting at.

Mrs. Redmond leaned back. "I'm sorry, Briseis. It's the mom in me, always worrying. You know, Karter is—" She stopped short as she gazed past me to the TV. A ticker flashed across the bottom of the screen and the reporter took on a solemn tone.

"A tragedy in Rhinebeck tonight. Longtime resident Hannah Taylor was found after an exhaustive search covering most of Dutchess County, and the result was not what anyone was hoping for." The reporter's voice cracked as he announced the details of the woman's death.

Mrs. Redmond shook her head and her eyes glazed over. "Oh no." She stared at the television, her hands trembling.

"Mrs. Redmond?"

She clenched her teeth and looked down at her desk.

"Hannah and I went to high school together. Graduated the same year."

I looked at the TV again. "I'm so sorry."

She hung her head and dabbed at her eyes. "Would you excuse me, Briseis? I need to make some calls. Hannah's mother is probably beside herself."

"Yeah, of course."

"Please be cautious," she said, her voice choked with emotion.

"I will." I reached out and gently squeezed her arm, then went to meet Mo in the car.

CHAPTER 17

"Got what you needed?" Mo asked, eyeing the drawing in my hand.

"No. It wasn't a key. It's a drawing that was with the other papers." I glanced up at the office window before we pulled off. "Mrs. Redmond just heard that a close friend of hers died."

"Seriously?" Mo asked.

"It was on the news. They found her body somewhere close by."

"That's terrible." Mo shook her head and heaved a big sigh as we headed back to the house.

"You okay?" I asked.

"It's funny how people complain about stuff that happens in the big city, but I've never had my tires cut back home. It threw me."

I angled myself toward her. "I'm sorry. We're out here because of me."

Mo reached over and squeezed my hand. "No, love. Don't be sorry."

"Do you regret coming out here?" I asked.

"Do you?"

"No," I said. That wasn't the whole truth. "Maybe a little."

"Why?" Mo asked. "You've been running around here with Karter. You seem happier than you've been in a minute."

"Yeah, but this has to be weird for you and Mom. I know we talked about it and you said you'd support me, but we're living in a place with people who knew my birth mother and her family. We're living in a house that belonged to them. That has to make you and Mom feel some type of way."

"We're being honest?" Mo asked.

I took a deep breath. That was Mo's way of saying she was willing to have a tough conversation. "Yes," I said. "We're being honest."

Mo nodded. "I don't know why your birth mother chose adoption. You were, and still are, the most wonderful thing I've ever seen. I loved you from the moment I laid eyes on you, and for the longest time, I asked myself how anyone could walk away from you."

A knot formed in my throat. Mo kept her eyes forward as she continued. "But my thinking was flawed. I wasn't as knowledgeable about the adoption process as I should have been. I have no right to judge anyone, especially when your birth mother's decision made it possible for you to come into my life. What she did, for whatever reason she did it, was a choice that allowed us to be together.

"I think about her a lot and being here makes me think of her even more. I hope she didn't come to her decision under any circumstance other than it was the right choice for her and for you." She cleared her throat. "And now we're here, in her space, making it our own, and I'd be lying if I told you I wasn't worried about how all this is affecting you."

"And I'm worried about how all this is affecting you and Mom." I couldn't keep the tears from spilling over. "I didn't come here because I wanted to know more about my birth family. I came here because I knew it could help us out."

"But that's the thing," said Mo. "You don't have to choose, love. You can do both. Of course you'd want to know more about these people, about their past, about their lives, and I—*we* support you. You love me and Mom, right?"

"More than anything."

"And the feeling is mutual, baby girl. I love you more than I love myself, and you know how much I love myself."

I laughed through the tears. Mo was the best at making a heavy situation feel lighter.

"Talk to people, research, look at pictures, ask questions. We both know that you got something running in your veins that can't be easily explained. Maybe this is your chance to get to the bottom of it. Me and Mom are here for you no matter what. We are a family. Nothing is going to change that, understand?"

Mom and Mo were so different in most ways, but not in the way they loved me—unconditionally and with their whole hearts. I reached out and squeezed her hand. "I love you."

"I love you more."

We pulled up in front of the house, and she leaned over and hugged me tight. Mom came out to meet us.

"Why are y'all cryin'?" she asked.

"Just having a heart-to-heart with our baby," said Mo.

We climbed out of the car and stood around, looking at the

new tires. Mom put her arm around my shoulder and wiped my tearstained face with the sleeve of her shirt. "Anything I need to be aware of?"

"Nah," Mo said. "We were mourning my waffles and thinking about how much better they'll turn out next time."

Mom pulled me closer dramatically. "Oh, baby, I'd cry too if I had to eat any more of her breakfasts."

"Next set of waffles is gonna be lit." Mo winked at me.

"I thought we agreed to no more buzzwords," I said.

"That wasn't a buzzword," Mom said. "She's telling you her next set of waffles aren't gonna just be burned, they're actually going to be on fire. Lit." She glanced at the shiny new set of tires and rolled her eyes. "I can't believe this. Why would somebody slash our tires?"

"The people at the tire place said it happens," Mo said. "Local kids, you know?"

"They need an ass whoopin'," Mom grumbled as we climbed the porch steps.

Billowing ash-gray clouds rolled across the sky. The smell of rain hung in the air. My plants would love that and it would give me a break from watering.

I went inside and up to my room. I studied the drawing Mrs. Redmond had given me—a black-and-white sketch, it didn't have the details of the illustrations in the big book. I wondered whether it had been Circe or Selene who drew it, and what the three lines there at the bottom meant.

After making sure Mom and Mo were occupied downstairs, I opened the hidden door behind the fireplace. I slipped inside and studied the crest carved into the desk more closely. There were no lines anywhere around it. I pulled open the drawers and searched for any markings, symbols, anything that might help me figure out what I was missing but there was nothing.

Frustrated, I slumped into the chair and stared down at the crest. The lacquered finish was dull in the area directly in front of the symbol, as if it had been worn away over time. I traced the faded mark and found it ran under the lip of the desk. Scrambling out of the chair and crouching down, I swept the light from my phone across the underside of the desk. Three lines were etched deep into the wood, and a shallow divot sat directly on top of them.

"Holy shit," I whispered, my heart thudding in my chest.

I pressed my finger to the indentation. There was a soft click and a compartment fell open with a heavy thud. I jumped, knocking my head on the edge of the desk. I clamped my hands down over the ache. The plants in my bedroom crowded in on me, stretching their roots across the floor.

A sketchbook sat tucked inside a hidden compartment the size of a small drawer. I lifted it out and paged through. The Absyrtus Heart was drawn there in even more intricate detail than it was in the big book. The inner workings of the plant were unlike anything I'd ever seen. The stalk appeared to be covered in something more like skin than plant matter. The lobes were shown splayed open and the voids inside were draped with pale, cobweb-like structures. On the last page was a recipe and some notes scribbled in the lower corner.

The Living Elixir
Absyrtus Heart

Quicksilver
Liquid Gold
Transfigure
Infuse in a draft of honey

This burden is sometimes too much to bear. The Heart must be kept, but at what cost?

We must find the pieces that have been lost to time. We must. We have to bring them together to save her. Even if it is too late, we must still do this.

Absyrtus in pieces, everlasting life.

Absyrtus made whole, master of death.

Maybe I'll set aside this terrible task and let this family pass into legend and myth like our ancestors before us.

Tucked between the last pages of the sketchbook was a single sheet of paper, sealed between two pieces of plastic casing. As I studied it under the glow of my flashlight, I thought "paper" might not have been the right word to describe it. It was more like fabric. I could see the individual fibers poking out from its uneven edges. It was covered top to bottom in lettering that looked a lot like the Greek I'd seen in the books about Medea. It was riddled with holes, so I assumed the casing was the only thing keeping it from falling apart.

I set the book on top of the desk and reached into the compartment to see if there was anything else. A wadded-up piece of cloth was shoved inside, near the back. As I pulled it free, something clattered to the ground.

I picked up the object. It was a small, ancient-looking key, made of some kind of off-white material too heavy to be plastic—maybe some kind of bone. About the size of my pinkie, its bow was a beautifully carved Valentine's Day–style heart. Another shape was set inside, molded from a glistening red stone, and this one resembled a tiny human heart.

A bolt of exhilaration shot through me and my hands began to shake. This is what I'd been looking for. It had to be the key to the door in the garden.

My phone chimed in my hand, and if I hadn't been gripping it so tightly out of pure excitement, I would have dropped it. It was Marie.

"Hello?"

"Hey, Briseis. I'm sorry to call so late."

I glanced at the clock on my screen. "You're good. It's not even nine. Everything okay?"

"I was wondering if you wanted to come over."

I looked down at the key. I really wanted to go straight to the garden, but the time and the sound of her voice were making me reconsider. "Can I ask you something?"

"Anything you want," she said.

"Right, I, uh—do you know about—"

"The garden?" she cut in.

"So you do know about it."

"I've never been inside their garden, but yeah, I know."

"Did Circe ever tell you anything? About what was in there?" I asked.

There was a long pause. "Why don't you come over and we can talk about it?"

"Right now?" I snatched the scarf off my head and touched my hair. It had been a few hours, and I'd dried it halfway before twisting it up so I could get the most stretch and cut my drying time by more than half, but it was still damp at the roots.

She laughed lightly. "Come on. It's been a minute since I've had company."

"I don't have a ride. I don't drive. And I—"

"I'll send a car for you."

"I can get an Uber or a Lyft myself. It's not a big deal."

She huffed into the phone. "Do you know how dangerous rideshares can be? I'll send my own car with a driver I can trust to get you here safely."

I hadn't heard right. "Wait. You mean like a car service?"

"Fifteen minutes."

"Gimme thirty?"

She huffed into the phone. "Okay. See you soon." She hung up.

I closed up the hidden room and stashed the newly discovered sketchbook and key under my mattress. I put the hair dryer on low heat, high air and blasted my scalp till I was sure I could safely take out the twists. I could not meet Marie in another state of crusty disarray.

Ten minutes under the dryer and the world's fastest take down later, my hair was coifed and ready to go. My eyebrows were a mess and I didn't really feel like putting on a full face of makeup, but I also wanted to look halfway cute. I threw on a pair of gold hoops and dragged a fingertip full of Vaseline across my lips. I slipped on a pair of sneakers and went downstairs. Mom and Mo were in the front room.

"Is it okay if I go over to Marie's house for a little bit?" I asked.

"Who's Marie?" Mom asked.

"That girl who came to the house the other day."

Mom raised an eyebrow. "If you want to, baby, but do you think it's a good idea? You just met her."

"She seems pretty nice," I said.

Mo gave me a look. "Nice, huh? Is that why you got on them hoops? Everybody knows that hoops mean you tryna look cute."

"Do I look cute?" I asked.

"Always," Mom said. "Do you need a ride?"

"No," I said. "She's sending a car."

They both turned toward me, eyes wide.

"A car?" Mom asked. "What kind of rich people behavior—"

"Shoot, Briseis is single. Might be a match made in heaven," Mo said.

Mom thought for a moment then nodded in agreement. "Secure the bag, baby."

I cringed. So hard. "First of all, y'all are terrible, and second, that's not what's goin' on. She knows about some of the plants in the apothecary, and she invited me over to talk."

My phone buzzed.

Marie: Car's outside.

"The car's here."

Mo scrambled to the door with Mom at her heels. I went over and peered around them. In the drive was a sleek black sedan with tinted windows. The driver's door opened and a tall, bald woman with broad shoulders wearing a bloodred pantsuit got out and came around the passenger side. I pulled the door open and walked onto the porch.

"Miss Briseis?" the woman asked.

Mom's mouth was stuck in a little O. Mo's eyebrows arched up so hard they disappeared into the one wrinkle that ran across her forehead.

I kissed Mom and gave Mo a hug. "I'll text you when I get there."

I jogged to the car and the woman opened the door for me. Only when I was standing next to her did I realize she was at least six feet tall. "Okoye got nothin' on you, huh?"

Her deep brown eyes moved over me, and she smiled, her mouth full of perfect paperwhite teeth.

"Miss Morris will see to it that she is home safe and sound," she called up to my parents, who were still standing on the porch with their mouths open.

I climbed in and she closed the door. The car's interior smelled like warm vanilla, and the upholstery was the same red as the woman's suit. The driver's door opened and closed, and the partition rolled down.

"Comfortable?" the woman asked.

I nodded.

"Help yourself to anything you'd like," she said.

A refrigerated chest filled with soda and water bottles and illuminated by a ring of white lights was built into the center console. I pressed my lips together to keep from asking, out loud, what in the entire hell was going on. I picked up a root beer.

"This is perfect. Thanks."

We turned out of the driveway and onto the road that led away from the house.

"My name is Nyx," said the woman. "I work with Miss Morris."

"Marie?" I asked.

"Yes," said Nyx.

"You work with her? Like, driving people around and stuff?"

Nyx smiled. "Among other things."

I opened the root beer and took a drink. "You probably won't be honest with me, but I'm gonna ask anyway. Is this a setup?"

Nyx raised an eyebrow. "You'll have to be more specific."

"Like, she's not trying to kill me or anything, right? My parents worry." I'd be so mad if I put on these hoops just to get murdered by the most beautiful girl I'd ever seen.

Nyx laughed. "No, you'll be safe with her."

That answer was a little weird, but so was drinking root beer in the back of a luxury car on my way to a stranger's house. I tried to make polite conversation. "So, the few people I've met since I've been here have lived in Rhinebeck their whole lives. Is that how it is for you and Marie? Are y'all from here, too?"

"Not me," Nyx said. "I came here from California years ago. But Miss Morris has lived here in Rhinebeck since it was Beekman's land."

"Who's Beekman?" The name sounded familiar, but I couldn't remember where I'd heard it.

I thought I saw Nyx bristle in the rearview mirror. "An old man. But let me stop talking before I say too much. I fear I may have already."

"It's okay," I said. "I'm new here. I don't know the town gossip."

"That's probably good. This town is full of nosy people, and now that you're in that house, I'm sure you'll be the talk of the town."

"Yeah. I'm starting to understand that."

We drove through town and crossed over Market Street. The hustle and bustle of Rhinebeck village faded as we drove south. Twenty minutes later, Nyx navigated a steep, narrow driveway. I peered out the window, but it was hard to see through the tinted windows.

"We're here," Nyx said.

She hopped out and came around to open the door. I found myself in the driveway of a very large, very expensive-looking house. The immaculately kept lawn looked like a sea of green carpet. Statues dotted the landscape and I was creeped out by the way they loomed in the encroaching blackness, their marble skin reflecting the soft light from the house. Beyond the driveway was a void, but I could hear rushing water.

"The mighty Hudson is beyond the bluff," Nyx said.

"So, Marie is rich? Or her parents are rich? Because this place looks crazy expensive."

Nyx laughed and gestured toward the door, but she didn't answer my question.

As I followed her up the wide steps to the front of the house, I heard something beyond the muffled rush of the river. Pausing, I looked in the direction of the bluff, squinting against the darkness. A rhythmic rush of air, like bird wings beating.

"This way," Nyx said, ushering me inside.

The inside of the house was just as impressive as the exterior. A floor of mottled gray marble, inlaid with hexagonal patterns of ebony tile, was polished to a glass-like shine. A painting of a regal-looking woman in a long, patterned dress hung in the foyer alongside watercolors of lush landscapes. An iron chandelier affixed to the exposed crossbeams drenched the entire entryway in a warm, undulating glow.

Nyx led me down a long hall and into a small library.

A *library*.

Inside a *house*.

A fireplace big enough to step into took up the entire back wall. The flames inside clung to the last of their dying embers, casting a dancing amber light all around.

"Please make yourself comfortable," Nyx said.

She left, and I immediately went to the built-in shelves closest to me. I pulled down a beautifully illustrated book of fairy tales and took it to the large leather couch. As I thumbed through, I gently touched the well-worn pages. Something about the look and feel and smell of old books always sparked a sense of calm in me. The books Karter had gifted me and the ones I'd found in the turret gave me the same feeling. Nyx returned a few minutes later carrying an assortment of meats, cheeses, and crackers on a large wooden cutting board. She set it on the coffee table.

"You didn't have to do that," I said. "You had to walk like a block to bring this to me, huh? How far away is the kitchen in this mansion?"

"You're not hungry?"

I stared into Nyx's face. The room was fairly dark but not so much that I couldn't tell if she'd been speaking to me or not. She had not moved her mouth at all. I followed her amused gaze to the wingback chair by the fireplace where Marie was sitting cross-legged, a half smile painting her lips.

Nyx gave me a wink before leaving the room, closing the door behind her.

"Were you there the whole time?" I asked. "I'm so sorry. I didn't see you." I hadn't even registered the chair, much less the beautiful girl sitting in it, when I came in.

Her silver hair was slicked up into a perfectly twisted topknot. She was wearing a pair of fitted gray joggers and a matching cropped sweater. Her skin glowed in the firelight. And her eyes . . . I was staring again. I shook my head.

"I was waiting for you to call so I could invite you over," Marie said. "But you took your sweet time, so I had to make the first move."

Heat rose in my face. "I was gonna call you."

"When?" she asked, her eyes locked on mine. She sounded like she genuinely wanted to know.

"When I got settled," I said honestly.

She seemed satisfied with my answer and relaxed into the chair. "It's gotta be overwhelming for you, coming into possession of the house and all its—responsibilities."

"You mean the apothecary?"

She blinked a few times, then readjusted herself in her seat. "It's a lot of work, right? To get it back up and running?"

"Yeah," I said. I looked around the room again, then back to

Marie. "This house is amazing. I've seen *Beauty and the Beast* too many times to not have thought about having a library in my house."

"You can come over anytime. Give Nyx a call, and she'll get you."

I studied her face. "I'm not tryna be rude, but this is all really, really strange. Do you live here alone? And why are you being so nice to me?"

Marie tilted her head back and let out the most melodic laugh I'd ever heard. It sounded like bells. "I don't know what you want me to say. I'm a nice person, I guess? I've been fortunate, so I like to pay it forward when I can."

"Okay, and you live here with . . . who? Your parents?"

"My grandfather, Alec. He's sort of an amateur historian. Most of the older books are his." She gestured toward the shelves. "He did most of the decorating, which is why this place looks like it's haunted by the ghost of a French nobleman or some shit. Look." She pointed to a portrait of a man in a full suit of armor sitting on a tall brown horse, his sword drawn. "Who even is that?"

"Definitely somebody's soul trapped in that painting." I grinned and I couldn't be sure, but I thought I heard her sigh. She suddenly stood and swept over to the couch, taking a seat next to me. She pulled her knee up and rested her chin on top of it. The smooth brown skin of her belly stuck out from under her sweater.

"And Nyx?" I asked, putting my thoughts elsewhere. "Is she, like, your assistant or something?"

Marie laughed again. "She's more like a bodyguard."

"Seriously?"

"What?" Marie grinned. "She could fold somebody up, no problem."

"No, I—I believe it, but what do you need a bodyguard for?"

"I have— My family has some money. People come around trying to get over. It's a precaution."

I reached down and picked up a few slices of the gourmet cheese.

"Do you like it?" Marie asked.

"Yeah. It's like a bougie Lunchable."

Marie grinned at me. "It's a charcuterie board."

"If you say so. Are you gonna have some?"

"No. I'm good. Take as much as you'd like." She scooted toward me, leaning in closer than she needed to. She smelled like vanilla and cocoa butter. She wore a thin gold chain around her ankle and her toes were painted neon green. I set down the cheese I'd picked up. I couldn't concentrate enough to eat, which I didn't realize was necessary until that very moment. Everything about her commanded my full attention.

"Do you want a tour of the house?" she asked.

Not really. I would've been perfectly happy to sit there and stare at her like a creep for the rest of the night.

"C'mon," she said. She took me by the arm and led me out into the hall. "I've lived in Rhinebeck my entire life, but I love to travel. Sometimes I just need to get away from Alec and his collection of haunted antiques."

"You're not in school?" I asked.

"I graduated early," she said. "I think I've learned more from traveling than I ever did sitting in some schoolhouse."

I'd never heard anybody use the word schoolhouse when they were talking about school. Maybe rich people did things differently.

We hung a right and she led me down another long hallway lined with more creepy paintings in gold filigree frames. She showed me an indoor swimming pool but said the one outside was much better for swimming in the summer. We came to a set of tall double doors and she pushed them open.

The room could only be described as a mini museum. Glass cases full of artifacts were crowded together at the perimeter of the room. Masks, swords, pottery, clothing, and tools were all expertly displayed.

"My collection," Marie said. "Alec and I are getting all these artifacts back to their countries of origin. Most of them were stolen, smuggled out, or sold on the black market. So much history looted." She shook her head. "Now museums charge a fee to look at things that don't even belong to them."

"How'd you get ahold of all this?"

"That's a long, boring story."

I moved to a display case in the far corner. Inside was a broken bowl that looked like it was made out of gold, and on it was the tiny figure of a woman with three faces.

"The triple goddess, Hecate herself," said Marie. "That one was a gift from someone I was very close to."

"Keeper of the Keys," I said, repeating the words I'd read in one of the books back at the house.

Marie narrowed her eyes. "You know about her?"

"Sort of," I said. "I've been doing some reading and her name is always connected with a woman called Medea." As I stared at the symbol, it reminded me of the one in the crest on the door in the garden.

"I've seen the play," said Marie. "I love the theater."

"Me too," I said smiling. "I haven't seen it, but there are some portraits of her in the house."

"Circe loved to read. And that story is tragic, really gut-wrenching. Maybe she found some parallels with her own life."

"Her life was tragic?" I asked. I turned my attention to another display full of artifacts. "She had a big house, and it's paid off. She was running a business and I'm sure she was making good money based on what you said about how much you paid her. Doesn't really seem like a tragedy."

I turned to find that Marie had moved across the room and was standing not a foot from me.

My heart jumped into my throat.

"Not everything was easy for her," Marie said quietly. "She bore a huge burden."

"What burden?" I asked. Suddenly everything seemed brighter, louder. I was aware of the rattle of hot water pipes and the hum of the electricity powering the lights in the display cases. Fear had dialed my senses to ten.

Marie took a few steps toward me. "You found the apothecary and the garden. I'm sure you've seen what lies behind those high walls."

"The plants to stock the apothecary?" My voice sounded small, hollow.

"That's part of it but . . ." She stared at me, her eyes

searching, and finally finding something that seemed to trouble her deeply. She moved closer—slowly and deliberately, the way she had when she'd come to my house. She narrowed her gaze, her brown eyes glinting in the dim light. "They were keeping an unfathomable secret."

CHAPTER 18

I had the strongest urge to leave— No, not leave. Run.

"I'm sorry," Marie said. "Please. Please don't go." She clasped her hands together in front of her. "I'm not trying to pressure you into giving me any information—"

"I don't even have any information," I said. "I—I haven't opened the door."

Her sigh was heavy with relief. "Good. Don't open it."

"Why? What's behind it?" I inched closer to the door.

"I don't know exactly." Her shoulders rolled forward as she hugged herself around the middle. She drew a long breath. "Circe looked after a very rare, very poisonous plant. The only reason I know that much is because of—" She stopped short. Pain twisted her beautiful features. "Because of Astraea. She was a relative of yours and my best friend in the whole world, like a sister."

Some of the fear had ebbed but I kept the door in my line of sight. "What did she say about the plant?"

Marie gazed off to the side like she was recalling a distant memory. "She told me it was the center of her world, that it consumed her waking days and even her dreams. Once, she told me she would have given her life to keep it safe, and I laughed." She looked absolutely disgusted with herself, shaking her head, squeezing her eyes shut. When she opened them again, tears threatened to spill over. "She didn't talk to me for six months."

"Why?" I asked. "There are a lot of poisonous plants in the garden. At least a dozen of them are deadly."

"It's nothing like those other plants. It couldn't be, or they wouldn't have kept it locked away." Her tone darkened. "And if that's true, and I have every reason to think it is, then you should never open it. Never even speak about it. Ever."

"Where's Astraea now?" I asked. "Do you think she knows I'm here? Why isn't she taking care of the house and the garden?"

Marie's face grew tight. "Astraea died a long time ago."

"Oh. I'm sorry," I said. I shook my head, frustrated.

"What's wrong?" Marie asked.

"It's like everybody who could give me any real answers is gone. That leaves me in a weird place if I'm tryna figure things out." As I went over this growing list of people who'd passed away and where that left me, something occurred to me. "How did Astraea die?"

Marie glanced at me, hesitating.

"My birth mother died, too. So did Circe and Astraea. Now that I think about it, I'm worried." What was plaguing the Colchis family line to leave me the last one standing? The question unsettled me.

"Cause of death is tricky when you're a Colchis," Marie said.

I raised an eyebrow. "You wanna tell me what that's supposed to mean?"

She crossed her arms over her chest. "It means that if I walked into the records room at the county courthouse and asked for a copy of the coroner's report for Astraea or even Selene, I promise you there'd be an issue. It's been moved, lost, caught on fire in a back room somewhere . . ."

"You don't know how any of them died?" I asked.

Marie shook her head. "No. I asked Circe about Astraea, but even she couldn't give me any real answers. For a long time, I thought it was another secret, something else she'd sworn to keep private, but I don't know anymore. Maybe she didn't know what happened to her—or maybe she did, but didn't want to tell me."

"What about the coroner?" I asked. "This is a pretty small town. Maybe you could get the information directly from them?"

"This *is* a small place. So small that our medical examiner's office and our funeral home have been run by the same family for years. I actually think that's illegal, but on top of that, the guy in charge now is an asshole. And like I said, the records always happen to be unavailable or misplaced."

"I understand what it's like to have questions and feel like you can't get a straight answer," I said. "That's how it's been for me ever since I got here."

Marie bristled. "Astraea was my friend and for somebody like me, real friends are hard to come by. If I knew what happened to her, maybe it'd make me feel less—I don't know, less lost."

My fear had ebbed completely, and I gently put my hand on Marie's arm. She seemed vulnerable, unsure of what to do or say next. "I get it. Maybe I can help. Do you know how I can get ahold of the medical examiner?"

She pulled out her phone and a few seconds later, I had a text from her.

"That's his information. I won't get my hopes up, and you shouldn't either."

"We'll see. Can't hurt to ask," I said. "Anyway, how's Alec?"

"Alive," she said.

I waited for her to elaborate and choked back a nervous laugh when I realized that the little ring in her voice sounded like disappointment.

"He's upstairs," she said quickly, noticing my confusion. "He'll probably be in county lockup soon for trespassing on your property." She looked disgusted.

"I already talked to my parents about that. Nobody wants him locked up. I'd be worried if my grandpa—"

Marie's eyes widened for a split second. I stared at her, trying to decide how I was going to say what I was thinking without sounding rude. "You're not telling me the whole truth about who he is to you. I don't know why, but after everything you just said about your friend and how you hate being kept in the dark—"

"You're right," Marie interjected. "You're right." She studied me carefully. "He's not my grandfather, but he is family, so I look out for him, even when he gets himself into trouble."

"Okay." I was happy she was willing to offer me that. "I can work with that."

"Can we leave the rest of the questions for another time?" Marie asked.

"Actually, I have one more," I said. "Were you sneaking around outside the house before I moved in?"

The corner of Marie's mouth twitched like she was holding back a smile.

"Mrs. Redmond—the lawyer who's handling all the legal stuff for the house—said she saw you in the driveway a few weeks ago. I was wondering why you were there."

"I was making sure everything was on the up-and-up. Circe wouldn't have wanted some stranger in her house."

"I'm a stranger," I said.

Marie shook her head. "You're not. Maybe you feel that way, but it's not true."

I checked my phone. No messages from Mom or Mo yet. They'd wait till the clock struck eleven to remind me of my curfew. If I didn't text back, they'd be in the car at five after, like some kind of modern-day fairy godmothers. Except instead of snatching back a fancy dress and glass heels, they'd take my free time, phone, and any thoughts I had of being almost grown.

"You have to go?" Marie asked.

"It's about to be eleven."

"That's not really an answer, is it?"

I hoped that her question meant what I thought it did—that she wanted to see me again. "I'm guessing you don't have a curfew."

"Oh right," she said. This time, her disappointment was crystal clear. "C'mon. I'll walk you out."

She led me back through the maze of corridors and to the front drive. As I walked down the steps, Nyx came striding out of the darkness from the direction of the bluff and the strange noise I'd heard earlier.

Marie cleared her throat loudly and Nyx stopped, dusted something off her jacket, and fastened the buttons.

"Call me. Or I'll call you," Marie said. "Oh, and I can take you to see them whenever you want."

"Who?" I asked as I moved to the car door.

"Selene and Circe. They're in your family's plot, not the big cemetery where everyone else is buried. It's off the beaten path. If you ever want to go, let me know."

"Oh. Right," I said. I wasn't sure that was something I wanted to do, and the topic had caught me off guard.

"It's completely up to you," Marie said.

"I'll think about it." I turned and Nyx opened the door for me.

I climbed in and Marie retreated into the house. I sat quietly in the back seat as Nyx drove me home. When we pulled up to the house, Mom and Mo were at the door, waiting.

I let myself out and Nyx met me on the passenger side of the car.

"Miss Morris asked me to leave you with this." She handed me a small card. "It's my phone number. She said you're welcome to come up to the house anytime."

"That's really nice of her," I said.

"She's taken a liking to you," said Nyx. "I think she's been without a true friend since Astraea died, and that was a very long time ago."

"Couldn't have been that long. She's only seventeen."

Nyx burst into a deep, throaty laugh. She took a second to compose herself. "Forgive me. Technically, that's true."

"I don't know what that's supposed to mean," I said. "But I

know that nobody around here likes to give me straight answers and it's irritating as hell."

"She'll fill you in, I'm sure." She readjusted her blazer and straightened up. "When Miss Morris thought they—the Colchis family—were gone, she was undone. And when she found out you were related to them . . ." She stared off to the side for a moment. "I've never seen her so relieved."

"Why? What does it matter if I'm related to them? Everybody I've met here makes it seem like that's a big deal. I don't see it like that."

Nyx looked thoughtful. "Who am I, or any of us, to tell you how you should feel? But a word of caution, if I may? Now that you're here, people will come. All kinds of people, most of them with no ill will. Try to keep an open mind."

I thought of Alec and Marie and wondered if she meant people like them or something else completely. "I can do that. I think."

"I hope so." She gave me a pat on the arm and left.

Mom and Mo made me give them a minute-by-minute rundown of my visit. They wanted every excruciating detail. We stayed up for an hour going over everything: the library, the fancy appetizers, the fancy car, the multiple pools, and Marie's affinity for old things. In the end, they could only agree that I needed to be careful and that Marie probably had a lot of money and too much free time. But I knew she had more than a passing interest in me, and it lit me up inside. I hoped I'd be able to see her again, and soon.

CHAPTER 19

I slept, but only because I couldn't sneak out of the house in the middle of the night to use the new key. When I woke up the next morning, it was barely seven. I lay in bed thinking of what Marie had said. She'd told me not to open the door, that there was something unfathomable behind it. She was worried that the plant was poisonous but that wasn't a concern for me. All I could think of was opening that door.

When I heard Mom and Mo get up, I slipped the key with the heart onto my lanyard and went down the hall to tell them I'd be back for breakfast. As soon as I closed the front door behind me, I broke into a run. I bolted around the side of the house and across the lawn, into the tree line. The pathway opened up before me and I ducked through. I followed it to the garden, and as I came to the clearing, I took out the key and opened the gate. As it swung open, a sprig of climbing snap-dragon slithered down from the wall and encircled my head, twisting itself into a crown of fuchsia blooms before breaking off and returning to the wall. This was our exchange every time I went in, and my collection of flower jewelry was deposited all around the house, not a single petal or stem wilted.

The gate clanged shut behind me and I rounded the corner, making my way straight to the Poison Garden.

The front section of the garden had come alive since Karter and I had started working on it. The foliage was lush, vibrant, and more animated than I'd ever seen it, shifting and reaching as I went to the moon gate. I braced myself for the chill of the airborne poison as it hit the back of my throat and burned the inside of my nose. It only took me a second to recover.

Where the front half of the garden had been every shade of evergreen, olive, and emerald, the Poison Garden had also come alive like never before. Blankets of belladonna intertwined with wide leaves in rippling shades of black, sable, and obsidian—just as vibrant, just as prismatic as their benign counterparts. Deadly crimson thorns protruded from the arms of Devil's Pet, which had doubled in size and now twisted through the overgrown foliage.

I walked to the center of the rear wall. The Devil's Pet cinched itself up, revealing the door. I held the key in my trembling hand, and its heart-shaped stone glinted as I inserted it into the lock and twisted until it clicked.

The door groaned as I pushed it open. I'd expected another garden or a storage area, but it was a darkened enclosure no bigger than a hall closet. The smell of damp earth permeated the air. The room had a slanted roof made of the same stone as the walls and was completely covered from floor to ceiling with tangles of poison ivy, stinging nettle, and, to my astonishment, crimson brush.

Crimson brush was supposed to be extinct. I'd only ever seen black-and-white photos of it, taken in the late 1800s when a single sprig remained in the British Museum. Its star-shaped blooms burst from their three-leafed seats and emitted a rust-colored pollen. It should have caused sores to open on my skin and closed up my throat and eyes, but once again, I was unaffected aside from an ice-cold chill. I fanned the cloud of pollen away and the brush shrank back, as if it had realized its mistake.

I pulled out my phone and turned on my flashlight, sweeping it around. The tangle of crimson brush shifted, revealing a narrow stairway that led down. Only the top few stairs were visible. I inched closer and held my phone at arm's length. The weak column of light illuminated the floor of the room below. The steps were covered in a layer of slick green algae. Water trickled down the walls, running off in delicate rivulets, dampening the stone beneath my feet. Gripping my phone, I descended into the dark.

A small, windowless room took shape as my eyes adjusted to the gloom. A glass enclosure sat directly in the center. Immediately above it, a cylindrical shaft as big around as a can of soda was cut into the ceiling. I peered into it, and while I could see some light from the outside, it wasn't strong enough to penetrate all the way down.

I turned my attention to the waist-high enclosure. Hinges ran between panes of cloudy glass. I tried to open one, but it didn't budge. I shone my light in and caught my first glimpse of what it contained. The strange plant bore an unmistakable resemblance to a human heart. My phone slipped out of my trembling hand and hit the floor with a loud crack.

I scrambled to pick it up as the flashlight flickered on and off. A spider's web of cracked glass stared back at me as I checked the extent of the damage. I sighed. I should have stayed my ass aboveground.

Turing back to the enclosure, my light glinted off something set in the stone near its base. I pushed up my glasses and crouched to read the words engraved on a rusting placard.

ABSYRTUS HEART

I slowly stood, my gaze locked on the glass housing. The plant from the big book was real, and for whatever reason, Circe had put me through an entire scavenger hunt to find it. It was behind a locked gate, a locked door, and a gathering of toxic plants that would put most people in the hospital—if they lived long enough to get to one.

The confines of the room pressed in on me. The Heart stood within the enclosure like something out of a nightmare. The plant was rooted in a small circle of dirt ringed by shining black stones, and directly next to it was a second circle of dirt where nothing grew.

I searched for a way to open the glass and found a small keyhole marked by the same crest as the door above. Using the bone-white key with the ruby heart, I unlocked the case. Without the foggy glass in the way, I studied the plant. It was even stranger up close. It looked like the drawing in the big book, but it wasn't pink and plump. It was crumbling and ashen. The artery-like stalk snaked into the bone-dry dirt. Without thinking, I reached out to touch one of the broken leaves. Maybe it would perk up like the plants in the shop back home.

My fingers had barely brushed the nearest leaf when a bolt of cold entered my arm like an electric pulse. I stumbled back, clutching my hand. A numbing ache spread into my wrist. I cried out, my voice echoing all around me. Panting, my heart racing, I fell against the wall. My hand felt like it was frozen in a block of ice. The pain was so much worse than when I cut myself dissecting the water hemlock, worse than anything I'd ever felt. It was the most toxic thing I'd ever come in contact with.

I quickly locked the enclosure and left, making sure to lock the metal door, too. My hand ached, and the cold had spread to my arm like ice was flowing in my veins. I rubbed the back of my hand, trying to push warmth into the tips of my fingers, but the pain of touching my own skin was agonizing. I paced the Poison Garden, shaking out my hand.

I was immune to the hemlock, to the poison ivy, and the crimson brush, but this thing—the Absyrtus Heart—had wounded me in a way I didn't think was possible. Did this immunity have limits?

The pain held fast, refusing to retreat. I watched the time through the fractured glass of my phone's screen. Only after thirty minutes that felt more like hours did the pain start to dissipate.

A gathering of blush-pink oleander overtook the confines of its plot and spilled across the ground and was crowding the hellebore, suffocating it. I decided to thin it right at that moment and try to put my mind somewhere else. I grabbed a mesh bag from one of the hooks in the garden wall and pulled up the oleander, stuffing it inside. I glanced back at the place in the wall where the door was hidden. I didn't know what an Absyrtus

Heart was or why it was in its own secret room, protected by enough plants to kill everyone in Rhinebeck a few times over. Marie said it was dangerous. She'd asked me not to open the door. I should've listened.

I took the oleander I'd collected and left the garden. My hand still ached as I made my way home. I wanted to keep that room locked up. If that was what Circe had wanted me to find, she'd gotten her wish. I saw it, but I wasn't going back in there. Why hold on to a plant like that? Something that poisonous was dangerous, not that anybody could even get to it—but still, why chance it at all? Dread crept in and buried itself in my thoughts.

CHAPTER 20

My phone chimed in my pocket. I was surprised it still worked. It was Karter.

"Hey, Briseis," he said. "You busy?"

I put him on speaker so I didn't have to press the broken glass to my ear. "No, just coming from the garden." I wasn't ready to share what I'd seen with him yet.

"You wanna catch a movie?"

"Sure." I was willing to do anything to get away from the Heart. Karter gave me a rundown of the movies at the local theater.

"Pick you up at seven?" he asked.

"Sounds good."

I got to the house and was climbing the front steps when a car pulled into the driveway. An older man in jeans and a V-neck sweater stepped out. He smiled warmly and gave a little wave. He was completely bald and wore a pair of round glasses perched on the bridge of his nose.

"You need something from the shop?" I asked. It couldn't have been anything else.

"I do," he said. "If it's not too much trouble."

"Come in." I opened the door, and Mom and Mo looked up from their spots on the couch.

The man waved at them. "Morning. I'm Isaac Grant."

I looked him over as Mom and Mo stood to shake his hand.

"'Grant'?" I asked. "Do you know Dr. Grant?"

"She's my daughter," the man said. "She told me you'd moved in and I thought I'd stop by to say hello and pick up a few things."

Mom eyed the bag under my arm. "What's that?"

"Weed," I said.

Mom laughed the fakest laugh I'd ever heard and looked back and forth between me and Dr. Grant's father.

"I'm joking," I said. I turned to Isaac. "Seriously. Just a joke. Please don't call your daughter to come get me."

He held up his hands. "Your secret's safe with me, but I can tell you she's not in the business of enforcing laws about weed as long as Black folks are sitting in jail on possession charges while Karen and Brad are getting rich off edibles in Colorado." He took out his wallet and flashed a card that looked like a driver's license but had the words "Medical Marijuana Program" printed at the top. "If you can get this place certified, maybe you can be my new dispensary."

For a second, I thought I saw actual dollar signs flash in Mom's and Mo's eyes.

"It's not weed," I said. "It's for the shop. Some of the stuff is poisonous."

Isaac put his wallet away. "So you're back in business, then?"

I nodded. I showed him to the apothecary and slung the bag of oleander onto the counter. "Can I ask you to stand back for a minute? I don't want you to get near this."

Isaac took several steps back.

Leave it to Mom and her raw food phase, which lasted exactly three days, to point out that the closet with racks set inside that we'd come across in the shop looked like a big dehydrator, the kind you'd use to dry fruit leather, but on a bigger scale. We realized it was for drying out the plants before transferring them to the jars.

I went to the closet and pulled out the top rack, setting it on the counter. I reached for the oleander with my bare hand but stopped. I looked back at Isaac, who was, of course, watching my every move, so I grabbed a scoop and transferred the oleander to the drying rack without touching it.

"What, uh, what can I get for you?" I sounded like I was working the drive-through at McDonald's, but it was better than asking, "What kind of wild shit can I grow in my weird garden for you?"

"I need two ounces of brimstone," Isaac said.

"Um, what?"

"From the pits of hell."

I whipped my head around.

"Forgive me," he said, pressing his hand to his chest. "My humor has been described as dry, but not always appropriate."

"Brimstone just sounds scary."

"Technically, it's sulfur," he said. "But brimstone sounds more dramatic, and I love all things dramatic."

I glanced toward the top shelves. Everything was in

alphabetical order, but I couldn't remember seeing anything marked brimstone, and it definitely wasn't something I could grow in the garden—poison or otherwise.

I slid the ladder over and climbed up. Between a jar of Brazil nuts and a container of bryony was a circular indentation in the back wall of the shelf. I ran my fingers over it and a small door popped open. The smell of rotten eggs wafted out. A covered jar sat inside the hidden space. The label read Brimstone.

"I'll assume by the look on your face that you found it," he said.

Climbing down, I tried to hold the jar as far away from me as I could. As soon as I got to the bottom, I set it on the counter.

"Wanna take the whole thing?" I asked, nudging it toward him.

"Two ounces is all I need at the moment," he said.

I searched the drawers for something to scoop the chunks of yellow sulfur from the jar. I'd never get the smell off my hand if I touched it. Shifting some papers around under the counter, I found a leather-bound book. I lugged it out and opened it on the counter.

Inside were stubs from countless receipts. A pound of mugwort, a quarter pound of powdered acacia root, twenty-six sticks of palo santo, all accounted for with names and dates—Louise Farris, October 20, 1995; Hudson Laramie, June 12, 1990; Angela Carroll, August 14, 1993.

Near the back of the ledger was a log of names and dollar amounts, and I remembered that I was supposed to credit Lucille for the herbs she was going to pick up later. I searched until I found "Lucille Paris" and penned in a hundred dollars with the date. I set the book aside, found a pair of wooden tongs, and fished out a few pieces of brimstone, sitting them on the scale.

"I don't know of many uses for sulfur," I said. "Wanna tell me about it?"

Isaac came over to the counter, pushing his glasses up the bridge of his nose. "You can make a soap out of it. It kills mites on people and pets." His voice was even, his words rehearsed.

"You have mites?" I asked. "Or your pet has mites?"

"My pet," he said.

"A dog? A cat?" I didn't think he was telling the truth.

He didn't answer, but he chuckled. He studied me carefully, and then his gaze wandered to the shelves.

"You've come into possession of this place," the man said. "What do you think it's for?"

Here we go with the damn riddles. I sighed. "It's an apothecary. Natural remedies."

Isaac chuckled. "That's part of it, yes. That's the face that's presented to the local community who has no idea what's happening right under their noses."

He sounded like he might actually give me some information that wasn't a question wrapped in a riddle.

"You have many, many ingredients here," he continued. "On their own, they're useful for natural remedies, teas, soaks, and so on. But combined, they can be much more powerful."

"Combined?" I asked, confused. "For what?"

"Any number of things. Combining what you've collected here, in the right way, can bring about changes in the real world."

"Sounds like magic," I said jokingly.

He didn't laugh. "Yes, magic."

"You're serious?" It wasn't that I didn't believe him. How could I dismiss what he was saying when I knew what I could do?

"Humor me," he said, scanning the shelves again. He gestured toward the cabinet with the poison herbs. "Wolfsbane root. And if you would be so kind as to provide me a copper dish?"

I hesitated for a moment, but my curiosity took over. I brought down the wolfsbane and fished around in the lower cabinets until I found a stack of shallow copper plates.

"Please place one root in the dish," he said.

"You want me to do it?" I asked.

"Can you?" he asked, a ring of worry in his voice. "Circe could do it bare-handed. She'd built up an immunity over the years running the shop, but I noticed you didn't touch the oleander. I thought . . ."

He said something else, but I didn't hear him. *Circe could do it, too.* She could handle the poison plants with her bare hands. What I could do wasn't unique, and Circe knew it. Isaac seemed to think it was a power she'd developed, a side effect of handling the toxic plants, but I knew better. She'd probably been born with it but that realization only left me more questions.

"Are you all right?" Isaac asked, snapping me out of my own head.

"Yeah," I said. "I'm fine."

I opened the jar of wolfsbane. He covered his mouth and nose with the sleeve of his sweater. It didn't smell, but even a little dust in his windpipe could kill him. I reached in and took out a single root. Cold gripped my fingertips and made them ache for a moment before returning to normal. I set the root on the copper plate.

Isaac reached into his pocket and produced a small vial. He uncorked it and poured a shimmering, silver liquid on top of the wolfsbane.

"What is that?"

"I dabble in alchemy," he said. "It's taken me a long time to produce this substance. It's a staple of my practice but it is nearly impossible to make. If you would be so kind as to press your hand down over it."

"What? Why?"

He smiled warmly, but there was pity in his expression, and I didn't like it. "I'm not sure how long you've been aware of what you can do, or how deeply you've delved into what you're capable of. I can assure you, however, that it is not limited to growing a garden, poison or otherwise—though that is a very useful part of it. Your skill is much more than that, which is why people like myself come to find you here. This apothecary has been a pillar of the magical community in Rhinebeck for generations."

Magical community.

Marie had hinted at something similar, and so had Lucille. I kicked myself for thinking I was going to grow some thyme, maybe a little basil, and call it a day.

Isaac looked down at the wolfsbane root. "I can't actually transfigure the mixture. I can prepare it, but it takes more than that to complete the process, something that can't be learned from a book. The ingredients I use are highly toxic—fatal to someone like me. But that isn't the case for others. Try it. I think it might answer your question as to whether I'm serious or not."

The beating of my heart was thunderous. But like I'd done so many times since we'd arrived in Rhinebeck, I let myself stretch. I cupped my hand over the mixture and pressed down hard. The cold feeling went deep into my palm. I didn't know if I should close my eyes or concentrate but suddenly, the muscles in my hand felt like they were being ripped apart. The pain was blinding and I snatched my hand away, but something had already happened in the dish. The silver liquid had dissolved the wolfsbane root.

"What's going on?" I asked.

The viscous liquid turned over on itself, giving off a warm glow. He sighed, letting his shoulders fall, and clasped his hands together in front of him. "You've done it."

"Done what?"

He carefully transferred the mixture back into his vial and stuck it in his pocket. "The true test will come in a week's time. I'll stop back and let you know if it was successful."

"If what was successful?" I was so confused. "Wolfsbane is lethal. Whatever that liquid is, it's dangerous. What are you going to do with it?"

"I will handle it with the utmost care. You have my word."

Mom and Mo poked their heads into the shop.

"Everything good?" Mo asked.

"Yup," I said.

Isaac turned to leave but paused at the door, glancing back over his shoulder. "Do guard your secrets carefully. When you can do something well, there will always be those who wish to take advantage." He pulled out a small white envelope and set it on the counter. "I'll be seeing you again soon. Take care." He turned and left.

"How'd it go?" Mom asked, glancing down the hall. "Did he buy anything?"

"Yeah," I said. I looked at my still-aching hand. "He's an alchemist."

"An alchemist?" Mom asked. "What's that? Is that like a wizard?"

"Maybe?" I wasn't really sure.

Mo came over, picked up the envelope, and peered inside. "Holy shit!" She pulled out several crisp one hundred–dollar bills.

Mom snatched the envelope. "What is this? Are these real? What did you give him?"

"Just some brimstone," I said.

Mom and Mo stared at me.

"I know how it sounds but this place is going to serve some . . . unique clientele."

"Like that girl, Marie?" Mom asked.

Marie was unique but probably not in the way Mom was hinting at. "Like Marie and that lady I met in town, Lucille. Dr. Grant's pops bought something from us, and he'll come back to buy more. We just gotta keep an open mind about the kind of people who might show up."

Mom tucked the money back in the envelope. "Not gonna lie. I don't like the way that sounds, especially after what happened before with the man out back. Remember him? Pawpaw Machete?"

Mo chuckled. "You're overthinking it. It'll be fine."

I hoped she was right.

CHAPTER 21

As we stood in the entryway waiting for Karter to pick me up for the movies, Mom fussed with my phone. She laid a piece of clear packing tape across the broken screen and tried to tell me it was basically good as new. What she was really saying was that she stopped paying for the insurance on it and I wasn't getting a new one anytime soon. I was just glad she didn't press me about what happened.

"I'm glad you're getting out of the house with Karter," said Mo. "But when are you gonna let that rich girl take you on a date?"

"Maybe I'll ask her out. But not because she's rich," I said. "I like her."

"Whatever you wanna do, baby," Mom said, smiling. "Anybody's better than that heffa Jasmine or that man-whore Travis."

"Mom! Come on. Jasmine wasn't that bad."

"You have your thoughts, I got mine," Mom said smugly.

My ex-girlfriend wasn't really ready to be in a relationship and our breakup was mutual, but all Mom and Mo saw was that she started dating a senior as soon as we split up. It was just too convenient for them. But Travis? Yeah, he deserved that title, and I broke up with his dusty ass as soon as I found out he was seeing not one, but two other chicks from different schools.

"You have your phone all the way charged?" Mo asked.

"Yup. And I'm bringing the charger with the wall piece and the car adapter." I swear, sometimes leaving the house felt like I was going on a mission from which I might never return.

"You got cash?" Mom asked. "A lot of places only take cash. And take the Mace with you too."

"Mom, we're only going to the movies." I gave her a big hug. "While I'm gone, you and Mo can watch Netflix, play Uno, whatever boring stuff y'all do when I'm not around. Don't worry about me."

Mom hugged me back. "Be careful."

"I will." I pocketed my Mace just to make her happy.

The doorbell rang. Mo answered it, and Karter tripped over the threshold.

Mo caught him by the elbow. "You okay?"

He straightened his T-shirt and smoothed the front of his jeans. "I'm good. Thanks." He held a small bouquet of daisies in his hand.

"Are those for me?" I asked.

"Yeah," he said, handing me the flowers. "Pretty, right? I—I know you like plants."

Mom and Mo exchanged a quick, worried glance.

A crinkling sound drew my attention to the flowers in my hand. The long, milky-white petals elongated, and the sunny yellow centers brightened.

"Baby, why don't you let me put those in some water," said Mom as she reached for the bouquet.

Karter stared at the flowers, then back at me, grinning, but Mom was about to flip.

"It's okay," I said. "He knows."

"You—you told him?" Mom was trying her hardest to sound calm.

"She showed me," Karter said.

Mo grinned. "Y'all have been in that garden so much I figured he had to know something. Making friends, girlfriends, *and* money? We hit the jackpot out here, huh?"

I reached into the paper and grasped the daisies by the stems. The bouquet burst to life, sprouting a dozen more blooms as roots broke from the paper and reached for the ground, looking for dirt to bury themselves in.

"I think these will have to go in a pot," I said. Mom took the flowers from me and set them aside.

"Ready?" he asked.

I gave Mom and Mo a hug and waved at them as we got in the truck and pulled off.

"I'm guessing you didn't share your talents with your friends back home?" Karter asked.

I shook my head. "I tried to. I wanted to. But it never worked out right."

"I'm glad you shared it with me," he said. "I wish I had some hidden talent to show you, but I have zero cool abilities." He laughed. "Oh, I won a spelling bee in the eighth grade, so if you need me to spell the word 'advantageous,' I'm on it."

"Good to know," I said, laughing.

"You liked the flowers?" he asked.

"I loved them."

"I had a feeling if I brought flowers, you'd show off. I've been thinking about everything you can do and sometimes I wonder if it's real, if that makes sense?"

"I get it," I said. "It's nice to not have to hide it. It feels great, actually."

After trying and failing to get a signal on the radio he switched it off. "Let's talk about this movie. We have two choices. One is a romantic comedy, and the other one is some indie horror movie. A vampire thing."

"I love scary movies," I said.

"Me too," he said. "I don't really like jump scares though, you know? I like horror movies that make you think. You seen *Get Out*?"

"Yes!" I was excited that we had a similar taste in movies. "Not gonna lie. When we first got here, that's all that was going through my head. 'Please don't let an old white lady take over my body.'"

We laughed ourselves to tears as we pulled onto Market Street, parked, and got out. Trees draped in strings of white lights lit up the block.

I felt the familiar urge to bind myself, to be hyperaware of every single plant or tree in my immediate vicinity. As we walked along Market Street, the trees rustled but didn't make too much of a fuss and I wondered if it might be because I was more at ease with my abilities than before.

"Here it is," Karter said.

I stopped and looked around. I didn't see a marquee or a ticket window.

"Here *what* is?"

"The movies." Karter gestured between two of the houses that had been turned into shops. Spanning the alley was a metal sign that said Theater, and beyond it was a set of double doors leading into what looked like the back of an old house.

"For real?"

"What? You were expecting something else?"

"Are you telling me this theater is in someone's house?"

Karter laughed. "Come on."

We passed a few people who were gathered outside on our way into the lobby, which wasn't much more than a small room. A guy was working a popcorn machine that looked like it was made at the same time movies were invented. When he saw us, he quickly walked behind the counter.

"Vampires?" the man asked.

"Yeah," said Karter. "You seen it? Is it any good?"

"It's really good," the guy said. "A little bloody but in a really artistic, thoughtful way."

I glanced sideways at Karter and he grinned.

"Let me get two tickets, then," Karter said.

I took out my debit card to pay but Karter was already handing the guy a couple of twenties. "I got you."

He paid for our tickets, two small bags of popcorn, and two bottled waters, since apparently soda wasn't allowed in the theater.

"Enjoy the show!" The guy gave an awkward salute and went

back to tending the popcorn machine. He clearly took his job very seriously.

We went down a short hallway decorated with posters of old movies and vintage film reels.

As we entered the seating area I glanced at Karter. "There are, like, twenty seats in here."

"Twenty-four," Karter said. "And all empty. Take your pick."

There were four rows of six seats each, and the screen was so close I could have thrown a piece of popcorn and hit it. I picked two seats in the middle of the second row.

"I've never seen anything like this in my life."

Karter chuckled and leaned back in his seat. "It's nice though, right?"

I looked around as two guys came in and sat in the last row.

"It's different," I said.

A few minutes in, the lights dimmed. The screen lit up as the movie started. I picked at my popcorn. It was too buttery, and I really wished I had a cold soda to wash it down.

Karter finished his popcorn and kept looking at my bag.

"Want some?" I whispered.

He laughed. "Sharing is caring. Thanks."

We huddled together, trying to keep our laughter as quiet as possible, especially since the character on screen was being torn to shreds by some kind of undead creature. Bad timing, but I was feeling happier than I had in months.

Halfway through the movie, the door at the back of the theater opened and two more people came in. They were dressed in dark clothing and one of them wore a baseball hat, the bill covering his face. They sat directly in front of us.

"What's the point?" Karter whispered. "Movie's halfway over."

One of the men in the back row cleared his throat. I turned to look at him, but he stared ahead, avoiding my eyes. The theater turned pitch-black as the characters on screen entered an underground crypt. As my eyes adjusted to the dark and Karter finished off the last of my popcorn—muttering things like "hell nah" and "stupid" under his breath—I noticed that one of the men in the front row wasn't paying attention to what was happening on the screen. He had turned so that he was looking toward the side of the theater, his left ear tipped toward me.

The screen flickered, bathing the seats in bright light as the characters moved back outside. The man turned to the screen, pushing his hat low on his forehead. I gripped Karter's arm. Something wasn't right. Karter followed my gaze to the man in the front row. Concern spread over his face.

One of the men in the back row stood up and moved to the aisle, and another man in front of us cleared his throat.

Karter was suddenly on his feet, spilling my water across the floor. He grabbed my hand and pulled me toward the exit but the man in the aisle blocked our path.

"Wanna move?" Karter asked, annoyance ringing clear in his voice.

The man crossed his arms over his chest. Karter went to push past him, but the man grabbed him by the front of his shirt. Karter shoved his hands off him as I stepped back and bumped into someone else. One of the men in the front row was right behind me. My body tensed.

Fight or flight.

I lifted my knee and drove my foot back as hard as I could. I palmed my Mace, flipped off the safety, and spun around, spraying him directly in the face. He sank to his knees, coughing and gagging. The other man in the aisle rushed Karter, but he ducked out of the way and the dude crashed into the wall. I grabbed Karter's arm and rushed to the exit.

"Get her!" someone yelled from behind us.

Karter stumbled, knocking his shoulder into the doorframe and pinballing off. I grabbed the back of his shirt to steady him and we raced down the alley. When we hit Market Street, people were still milling around in ones and twos but the street was mostly clear.

"We gotta get out of here!" I shouted.

Karter grabbed my hand. "C'mon!"

We sprinted to the truck and dove inside. Karter fumbled with his keys. Through the rear window I saw the four men running out of the alley, looking up and down the street.

"Go, go, go!" I screamed.

Karter threw the truck in drive and we lurched forward, turning off the main road and speeding toward the house as fast as his ancient pickup could take us. The entire cab rattled and the engine knocked loudly as we picked up speed.

"I gotta slow down," Karter said. "This rickety shit might fall apart."

"What the hell is going on?" I fumbled with my phone, dropping it onto the floor of the truck, where it slid under the seat. "Shit!"

"I—I don't know," Karter said. "What are we gonna do?"

As we approached the straightaway that led to my house a

pair of headlights in the oncoming lane flooded the cab of the truck. I still didn't see anyone behind us but we'd slowed to thirty miles an hour and the engine kept faltering like it might stall. I didn't want to get caught on the road alone.

"Flash your brights!" I yelled. "Flash your high beams!"

Karter flashed the truck lights and laid on the horn. The car slowed and pulled onto the shoulder.

I recognized the decal on the side of the vehicle. "It's the Public Safety people! Pull over!"

We skidded to a stop on the low slope next to the road and I jumped out as a short, broad-shouldered woman exited the Public Safety vehicle and rushed over to me.

"Are you okay?" she asked.

"No! Somebody attacked us in the theater!"

The woman's expression turned stern. "Get in your vehicle and lock the doors." As I climbed back in the truck with Karter, the woman got on the radio in her car.

"What is she doing?" Karter asked. "Is she calling the police?"

"I don't know."

A few minutes later, a car skidded to a stop behind us. Karter gripped the steering wheel and threw the truck in drive.

"Wait!" I yelled, recognizing the person exiting the car behind us. It was Dr. Grant. She rushed to my side of the truck and I rolled down the window.

"Dr. Grant!" I half screamed at her. "These guys tried to attack us at the movie theater!"

She glanced down the road, then reached for her walkie-talkie.

"Wait!" I opened the passenger door and got out.

"Briseis, what are you doing?" Karter asked.

"Just give me a second." I steered Dr. Grant toward the back of the truck.

"Miss Greene, I need to call this in. You told the Public Safety officer you were attacked—"

"I know but wait a minute. Please." A sudden rush of panic gripped me. If Dr. Grant called this in to the police, my parents would make us pack up and go back to Brooklyn, probably that same night. No amount of money or fresh air or chirping birds was enough to make them stay if they thought I was in danger. "Dr. Grant, please. If I tell my parents, they'll make me leave, and I can't do that." I looked at Karter. I thought of Marie, of the garden, and even of the Heart.

"Miss Greene," Dr. Grant began. I was prepared for her to tell me she didn't have a choice, that she had to do her job. But she sighed. "My father was up at your place earlier?"

"Yes," I said.

"And he told you what he does?"

"Sort of. He told me he was an alchemist like I'm supposed to know what that is. Mom thinks it means he's a wizard."

Dr. Grant bit down on a smile. "I think you'd have to ask him if you want an exact answer. He's been studying alchemy since before I was born. It was the same way with my grandfather, and his grandfather's mother before him. Generations of practice." Dr. Grant stared off to the side before refocusing. "Imagine their surprise when I told them I wanted to be a social worker." Dr. Grant shook her head, her face softening. "I'm sure he'll be a regular at your place. He was when Circe and Selene ran it."

"He won't be a regular because I won't be here if my parents find out what happened." A knot stuck in my throat. "You don't know what it was like for me before we came here. The way I've felt since we've been here? You can't understand what it means to me. I have to stay."

Dr. Grant tipped her head back and closed her eyes for a moment. "My only goal is to try and keep the people of this community safe. I haven't always been able to do that." Her face hardened again. "I feel like I'm failing you, Miss Greene." She straightened up and took out her notepad. "Tell me everything you can about what happened, anything you can remember. I'll look into it discreetly for now. I'll let you know if I find anything, but if I do, I have to let your parents know." She shook her head. "This goes against everything I'm trained to do, but if you leave . . ." She sighed. "You deserve to live here in peace. I'll be damned if a bunch of magical assholes think they can push you around."

It hadn't occurred to me that the people who'd come after us might have been a part of this shadowy community of magical practitioners. Lucille, Dr. Grant's father, and even Marie and Alec were cool, if not a little strange—but Dr. Grant clearly wasn't talking about them.

"How worried should I be?" I asked. "You're not telling me something. Do we need to put in an alarm or something?"

"Probably not a bad idea," she said. "For now, give me any information you can about what happened at the theater."

I ran down the details I could remember, but it had been dark and everything happened so fast. What I knew for sure was that there were four men who'd come into the theater in two pairs. They didn't say anything, and I didn't see if they got into a car afterward. The one who'd bum-rushed Karter was a white guy, stocky build, but I didn't get a good look at the others. She flipped the notepad closed and walked me back to the truck, where she turned her attention to Karter.

"You're Karter?" Dr. Grant asked him.

"Yes, ma'am," he said. "Karter Redmond."

"Are you new in town, too?"

Karter shifted in his seat. "I grew up here, ma'am."

Dr. Grant questioned him and it turned out he'd noticed even less than I did. He'd seen a few of the men go into the theater and sit down but didn't realize anything was off until I grabbed his arm. She tucked her notepad away and waved off the other Public Safety official. "I'll tail you to your driveway and then I'll be on my way." She and I exchanged a nod of silent agreement and she walked back to her car.

"What do we do now?" Karter asked. "We'll have to make an official statement, right?"

"Listen," I said. "I need a favor that's gonna sound ridiculous, but I need us to be on the same page."

He eyed me suspiciously. "What is it?"

"I don't want to tell anyone about what just happened. If my parents find out, I'll be back in Brooklyn by tomorrow morning."

Karter opened his mouth to speak, then stopped. He sat quietly for moment. "Aren't you worried about who those people were? What they were tryna do? They attacked us. That guy tried to hem me up. You're not worried about that?"

"I am. Dr. Grant is gonna handle it. I'll tell my parents later, but if I tell them now, it's over. I can't go back to the way things were. I can't go back to not having you as a friend." The tears came in a rush. "The house, the garden, the way my parents have been feeling . . . it all makes me feel like I'm where I'm supposed to be. I need to stay. Please, Karter. I need you to understand."

A low groan echoed somewhere in the dark, and a tapping sound drew my attention to the passenger-side window. Some of the smaller trees along the road had leaned over as far as their trunks would allow. Their branches elongated, scraping against my window like fingernails. I glanced back to see if Dr. Grant had noticed, but she was staring into her lap, her face illuminated by the light from her cell phone. I touched the glass and took a steadying breath. The trees righted themselves.

Karter looked at me, his jaw set. "You gotta promise me you'll let me know what that lady—Dr. Grant—finds out, because I'm worried. I don't want anything to happen to you. I don't want you to leave either. In case you couldn't tell, I don't have a lot of friends. I didn't think it was a big deal till I met you and realized how much I needed one."

I reached over and squeezed his hand. "I promise I'll keep you in the loop."

Karter squeezed my hand back, then drove me home.

CHAPTER 22

Dr. Grant followed us to the end of my driveway. Karter dropped me off and watched me go inside. I locked the door and quickly walked past the front room where Mo and Mom were playing an aggressive game of Uno, hoping they wouldn't ask me about our evening.

"Skip. Draw Four. Skip you again. Reverse back to me and BAM! Wild card! The color is blue."

"You can't play all those cards in one turn," Mom said as I slid past them. She waved in my direction but kept her gaze on Mo.

Mo smirked. "House rules say I can."

"House rules say you're a cheater."

"Never!" Mo said laughing. "You just mad. It's okay to lose sometimes, babe. I still love you."

I went to my room and changed into a pair of sweats, threw a bonnet on, and laid across my bed. I tried my best to section off what had happened at the theater from everything else that was going on. The secrets were piling up, and they were starting to feel heavy.

My gaze wandered to the top of the armoire that sat near the door. A triangle of paper stuck out over the top edge. I got up and stood on my tippy-toes to reach whatever it was. I pulled down a square book, covered in a thick layer of dust. I could tell by its shape and the crinkly sound its pages made that it was a photo album. Pressed between pages of sticky transparent plastic were pictures of a young girl, probably eleven or twelve, with thick black hair and big brown eyes. She wore glasses that were too big for her face. In one photo, she was sitting under a tree with her face turned up to the sun and her eyes closed. The grass all around her was a vibrant, almost unnatural, shade of green. In another, her eyes were open wide, a big grin stretched across her face as another person pushed a piece of cake into her mouth. A colorful birthday banner hung behind them.

I flipped through the other pages, and the girl got older with each turn. In her late teens, she wore her hair in braids, traded her glasses for contacts, and looked much more serious and focused. In another photo she sat in a rocking chair on the front porch of this same house, a potted bush of hogweed leaning toward her, its white flowers curling around the runners of the chair and around her ankles.

I flipped to the last page and pulled a small portrait of her from behind the plastic. She'd taken down her braids, her natural hair curling out from a colorful head scarf, and she'd started wearing her glasses again. She wore a long blue dress, and she smiled so warmly I could feel it through the picture. I turned the photo over in my hand. Selene, August 2004 was written on the back. I flipped it over to look at the image again. Her arm curved down, her hand cupping her slightly bulging belly. She was pregnant with me.

“Selene” wasn’t just a name. She wasn’t some faceless character in the story of my life. She had lived here, worked in the apothecary, and tended to the garden. She knew the secrets of this place, and if her sister knew about my immunity to poison plants, then maybe it was because they both shared this same ability.

Mo’s words echoed in my head. I didn’t have to choose. I could dig. I could find out more about these women and their work, and I didn’t need to feel guilty for it.

I took out my phone and sent a text to Marie.

Bri: I’d like to see her grave, if you’re still willing to show me.

A few minutes went by before my phone buzzed.

Marie: Nyx will pick you up at seven tomorrow night.

The next day, I stayed in the house. Karter texted me to check in, and Dr. Grant told me her office had accompanied the police to question the theater attendant running the popcorn machine. He’d only seen two of the men go into the theater. They’d paid, but because it was cash, there was no way to track it. She said the other two must have gone in when the theater attendant took a bathroom break. She hadn’t found anything else important but told me she’d call me if she did.

A little before seven, I told Mom and Mo where I was going and just like Mo promised, they were good with it. No questions asked. I brought a dozen onyx peonies to bloom from the one I’d grown for Mom in the kitchen, and Mo improvised a paper covering with a few of the paper bags from the apothecary. They both asked me twenty times if I wanted one or both of them to go with me for moral support, but I wanted to make the first trip by myself.

Nyx picked me up right at seven and we drove away from town, in the opposite direction of the main cemetery. When we came to a stop, I thought Nyx had gotten lost. We were in the middle of nowhere. The road we'd driven down terminated in an unpaved turnaround, surrounded by thick, black forest on all sides. But through the trees, a small clearing with a collection of ancient-looking headstones stood forgotten, untended.

"Miss Morris should be arriving soon," Nyx said.

"She didn't want to ride with us?" I asked.

"She was busy earlier this evening, but don't worry, she'll be here. She won't shut up about seeing you again."

I met Nyx's gaze in the rearview mirror. "Really?"

"Yes," she said. "It's highly annoying."

The sun dipped low in the sky, turning it to fire. The reds and oranges burned away the light and left only the smoldering darkness and draped everything around us in long shadows. A tap at the window startled me. Marie stood on the passenger side of the car. I got out to meet her, taking in the beauty of her face like it was the first time I was seeing it. She wore a pair of black jeans, a chunky black sweater, and black boots.

I looked around, expecting to see a car. "How'd you get here?"

"A rideshare," she said.

"You told me rideshares were dangerous," I said pointedly.

"Not for me."

I looked down the road. "I can tell when someone is bullshitting me."

Her eyes glinted as she narrowed them at me. "Right. If I told you it was for your own good, would you believe me?"

"Most of the time when people say something's for your own good, it's not. So, no."

Marie looked thoughtful. "What if I told you it was for *my* own good?"

My skin pricked up. A primal, instinctive fear draped itself around me, much the same way it had when I'd been alone with her in her house. "I might believe you if you said that."

"Okay then," she said. "It's for my own good."

She gestured toward the cemetery. The graveyard was fenced in by wrought iron that was badly in need of repair. The main gate looked like it had come off its hinges ages ago, and the spiky pickets sat at odd angles between the trees.

Marie slipped her hand into mine and a nervous flutter invaded my stomach. Nyx stayed by the car as Marie pulled me through the cemetery gates.

The place might have been tranquil once, but now bits of pale marble headstones stuck out of the overgrown foliage like broken, jagged teeth. It was so quiet all I could hear was the beat of my heart, which sped up every time Marie readjusted her grip.

My phone rang and Karter's name flashed on the screen. Marie paused. I tried to silence it, but accidentally declined his call.

"Making friends already?" Marie asked.

"It's a guy I met at the bookstore. The one on Market Street. He's my friend. Just my friend." I wanted to make that really, really clear.

She didn't even try to hide how happy that made her.

"Market Street?" she asked. "The used-book place?"

"Yeah. You know it?"

"It's new. Opened a few months ago."

"Oh." I thought Karter had mentioned working there longer than that. As I tried to remember what he'd said, I noticed that the overgrown grass was leaning toward me. Marie turned and glanced at the ground. I stepped back, letting go of her hand and swatting at the grass, trying to make it stop reaching for me.

"I'm not surprised by much," Marie said. "But that ability, that gift you share with the people who have come before you—it never fails to amaze me. It's nice to see it again after all these years."

Part of me understood that she knew about me. But hearing her say that and moving on like it was no big deal made me feel like I'd put down a heavy burden.

The fiery evening sky was quickly swallowed by the starry night. In the dying light, ancient-looking oaks twisted in the darkness. As we moved by, they creaked and groaned.

"Most people who've died in the last thirty years are buried over in Grasmere Cemetery," Marie said. "This place is much, much older and holds the remains of families whose lineages stretch back generations."

A granite tombstone with a sculpted angel draped over it, mourning, sat among a gathering of gnarled trees. The name and date carved on its face read Beekman 1623–1707.

The shadowy path led us to the back side of the iron fence, where two overlapping pieces didn't quite connect. Marie slipped through the opening and waited on the other side. I hesitated.

"A little farther," Marie said.

I squeezed through the fence and followed Marie into the thicket behind the graveyard.

"This is the site of the original cemetery," she said. "Watch your step."

Grave markers, most of them level to the ground and so broken they lay in heaps among the brush, dotted the ground. I stumbled trying to keep from stepping on them. Marie came to a sudden stop and I bumped into her. She set her hands on my waist to steady me. I lifted my head to meet her gaze but her eyes were downcast. I followed her mournful stare. There, among the weeds, overgrown grass, and twisted roots, was a small white headstone.

CIRCE COLCHIS
OCTOBER 31, 1970–JANUARY 12, 2020

My attention was drawn to the grave next to Circe's. It was covered in hellebore, a poisonous black flower with a bright yellow center. They crowded the grave marker.

I bent and brushed them aside. The cold tingling rushed over my fingers and then faded. I didn't immediately look at the name on the marker. Did I know who it would belong to? Is that why I had bent to clear it without hesitation? I gathered myself and looked at the name.

SELENE COLCHIS
SEPTEMBER 8, 1977–DECEMBER 24, 2007

I set the flowers I'd brought with me against the headstone, and the hellebore coiled around them. An overwhelming sadness enveloped me, stole my next breath, and brought a torrent of silent tears.

"They were always close," Marie said solemnly. "Like I said, they were private, aside from the business of the apothecary. I think it makes sense that they would've wanted to be here together, with the rest of their family."

I gazed bleary-eyed at the other markers. Every single one that was still readable bore the name Colchis. Perse, Danae, Ares, and all with dates of birth and death ranging from the mid-1800s and some even older than that.

One of the headstones didn't have a date but read Persephone Colchis and was so crumbled and broken that it probably wouldn't be legible for much longer.

"They're all here," said Marie. "This has been their plot since they came to this place. The house you live in was built on the site of their original homestead. They've been here ever since." Her eyes misted over. "Even after Circe closed down the shop, she was still there like a ghost, walking the halls, mourning every minute of the day."

I thought of what it must have been like for her. My grandpa Errol was the best man I'd ever known, and when he died, Mo didn't get out of bed for a week. For a long time, it was like she was going through the motions. She would get up, shower, eat, and go to work, but it was like a shadow was constantly hanging over her—over *us*, because we mourned with her.

It only got better when we went to counseling and got the help we all needed to process what had happened. I couldn't imagine how things would have been if we hadn't gone. Maybe

Circe didn't have that opportunity. Every new thing I learned about these people made them more real.

The trees surrounding the grave site bowed their limbs, a reflection of my own sadness.

"I didn't bring you here to make you sad," said Marie. "I wanted you to know that you have a connection here that's bigger than what happens in the shop, and the Heart is that connection. They all took their turn protecting it, but as much as I tried to understand it, they guarded their secrets fiercely. It was like they couldn't allow anyone else to share their burden."

"You don't know why they kept it hidden?" I asked. "Why is it a burden at all?"

Marie walked over to a meticulously maintained grave. A fresh vase of fuchsia orchids sat next to it. The name read Astraea Colchis 1643–1680. She knelt and dusted off the grave marker. "When I was younger, I was ready to take on the world. I wanted to leave this place so badly—until I met Astraea. I stayed here because of her. She was my best friend during a time when I had none at all." She swallowed hard. "One summer, I got sick. Sicker than I'd ever been in my life. My sister and my father had already died, and I knew I'd be next. Astraea saved me."

My heart ached for her, but I couldn't pretend that other parts of what she was saying weren't bothering me. "You just said 'when I was younger' like you're not young now. I'm confused."

Marie sighed. "I'm thinking of how I can make it clearer for you."

"See? Saying things like that makes no sense, and I'm not

gonna lie, it scares the shit out of me. Like, literally scares me to death." I recalled how, twice now, just being in her presence had sent fear rippling through me. It wasn't the only thing I felt for her, but it still concerned me.

Marie shook her head. A pained expression stretched across her face. "I don't want that."

"Then you gotta start being honest with me. How could Astraea have been your best friend if she died in 1680?"

"All I know is that Circe left everything to you," Marie said, glossing over my question. "She wanted you to pick up where she left off."

"I didn't ask for any of this. I don't even know if I want this responsibility." I was willing to grow the garden and stock the apothecary, but protecting the Heart? I didn't know what that meant. Protecting it from what? And why? Because it was poisonous? It didn't make sense.

Marie drew her mouth into a tight line. "That's your choice. But I can tell you that the apothecary is important to people around here. People like me. I've been thinking of a way to be more open with you. It might—" She stopped, and her eyes grew wide.

"It might what?"

"Shhh!" She was by my side so quickly I didn't even see her feet move, but before I could say anything, something darted between the trees. Marie tilted her head to the side, then took a long, slow breath. "If I asked you to close your eyes and keep them shut until I told you to open them, would you do it?"

"I—I don't know, I—"

A man wearing a dark jacket and a baseball cap emerged

from the tree line. Three other men stepped into the graveyard behind him.

"Nice to see you again," said the first man.

Marie glanced at me and I realized where I'd seen at least one of them before.

"He came after me and Karter at the movies," I said, my heart pounding.

Marie stepped in front of me. "Leave," she said to the men. Her voice was low, like a growl, and that terrible feeling of being in the presence of something uniquely dangerous washed over me again.

"Give her to us and we'll let you live," said one of the shorter men.

"You'll *let* me live?" Marie asked. I couldn't see her face, but the rise in her tone made it sound like she was talking through a smile.

I couldn't breathe. I balled my hands at my sides as a chorus of groans emanated from a cluster of large willow trees behind me. The unkempt grass rustled in the windless night.

One of the taller men took a step forward, and Marie held up her hand. "Last chance to rethink this." Her voice was so cold it scared me, but she didn't sound afraid. She sounded irate.

"We'll take her by force if need be," said the man.

"Take me where?" I asked. "What do you want?"

"She doesn't know?" one of the men asked.

"Shut up!" shouted the taller man.

"Close your eyes, Briseis," Marie said. "Please."

I was trembling so bad I could hardly stand up straight. The first man lunged forward, and I shut my eyes. Something impacted me from the front. I was suddenly being dragged across the ground. My eyes snapped open and I clawed at the dirt as a tangle of vines wrapped around my waist, pulling me back to the tree line. A gathering of nettle rose up like a fence, and to my utter astonishment, a rare and deadly plant called the stinger, a mustard-yellow bloom with poisonous barbed spears that, when threatened, released porcupine-like quills.

A pained moan cut through the air. One of the shorter men lay on the ground. He rolled onto his back. A sickening gurgling noise erupted from his throat, which lay torn open. He became unnaturally still. I tried to scream but nothing came out.

The vines held me tight, refusing to release me. I spotted Marie standing at the edge of the clearing with her back to me. The tall man stood in front of her.

"Marie! Run!" I screamed.

She didn't move. The man leaned toward her. Her hands held the sides of his head. The vines gripped me harder, the poison plants like guard dogs in front of me.

"Marie?" I called out again.

There was a loud pop and the man's arms went limp, dropping to his sides. Marie tossed him to the ground like a rag doll. The vines loosened, and I was able to wriggle free.

"We need to go," Marie said. Her voice had returned to its normal singsong tone.

"What the hell is going on?" The tall man lay in a heap on the ground. The space where his head should have been was a dark spot in the grass. Was it a shadow? A trick of the light? The other two men were nowhere to be seen.

Marie huffed loudly as she marched up to me. "Did you close your eyes like I asked?"

"Are you serious right now?" The plants surrounding me slunk back into the underbrush.

The smell of metal, like wet pennies, permeated the air around her. Marie's eyes were black as soot—no pupil, no white. She leaned toward me. "You have so many secrets, Briseis. Can you keep one more?"

CHAPTER 23

I struggled to keep my feet under me as Marie pulled me along the path that led out of the cemetery. Nyx was standing at the driver's side of the car, readjusting her jacket.

"Where were you?" Marie asked.

Nyx motioned to the ground by the rear wheel. A man lay on the ground, his arms and legs bent at unnatural angles. "He tried to run."

"I handled the other three," said Marie. "They already came after Briseis once before."

Nyx frowned. "That's . . . concerning."

"'Concerning'?" I almost screamed.

Marie pushed me into the car and slid in beside me. Nyx got behind the wheel and soon, we were driving toward my house.

My stomach spasmed and vomit rose in the back of my throat. I gripped the edge of the seat. "Will you please tell me what is going on? Did you—did you just kill those guys?"

Marie took a bottle of water from the cooler and spilled it across her hands and face, wiping away dark smudges with the sleeves of her sweater. "I'm going to have to be more honest with you than I wanted to be."

"No shit," I said.

"Should I call Dr. Grant?" Nyx asked.

Marie nodded.

"Wait," I said. "She knows y'all are out here killing people?"

"I wasn't planning on killing anyone. But those people in the cemetery came after you, twice. All because they want what you have."

"I don't have anything," I insisted.

Marie adjusted the skull-shaped agate on her finger and clasped her bloodstained hands in front of her. "The Absyrtus Heart."

"A shriveled-up old plant?"

"You remember what I said about Astraea and how she helped me when I was sick?"

I could only nod.

Marie looked down. "She used the Heart to heal me."

"'Heal' is not the correct word," Nyx chimed in.

Marie rolled her eyes. "Roll up the partition please."

"I think I'll leave it down."

Marie side-eyed her, then angled her body so that her back was to Nyx. "The protection of the Absyrtus Heart is tasked to your family. As a service to our community, they've cultivated plants, poisonous and benign alike, used in the work of conjurers, root workers, alchemists, witches, and others for as long as I can remember."

The image of Astraea's gravestone flashed in my mind. Her grave had been cleared, flowers had been left there, and her date of death had been 1680. I locked eyes with Marie. "What are you?"

"I couldn't explain it if I tried."

"I'm gonna need you to try before I flip." Another wave of nausea broke over me and sweat dampened my back.

Marie leaned against the seat. "That illness I told you about, the one that made me so sick I thought I would die? It was plague. Some strain of the Black Death."

"What?" I couldn't comprehend what she was saying. "You're telling me you got the plague? How is that even possible?"

"It was a long time ago," Marie said quietly.

I was done trying to be polite. "How old are you? Because I'm really, really confused."

"Three hundred and seventy-six."

A high-pitched ring sounded in my ears. I thought I was gonna pass out. "No. Nope. Nah. Stop the car." I couldn't see straight. "Let me out." I pulled on the door handle—I'd jump if I had to—but it didn't budge. "Let me out!"

"Please, Briseis." Marie put her hand on my shoulder.

"Don't kill me!" I shrieked, trying to move as far away from her as the confines of the car would allow.

Nyx burst out laughing from the driver's seat. "Miss Briseis, please try to calm down. She's entirely too taken with you to kill you."

Marie threw her hands in the air. "Nyx! Damn! I'm tryna be serious. She's scared and you're not helping."

Nyx laughed.

"I would never hurt you," Marie said. "Not for any reason,

and I'd kill anyone who tried. But I guess I don't need to tell you—you've seen that for yourself."

"Maybe we stop talking about killing," Nyx said.

I whipped around and stuck my head through the partition, seeing if I could squeeze through somehow. But Nyx was in the front, and she'd killed a man, too.

Was this some kind of joke? They both seemed too nonchalant, like it wasn't a big deal that Marie had crushed a dude's skull with her bare hands or that Nyx folded a grown-ass man into a pretzel.

I turned to Marie. I searched her face for any hint of malice, any sign she wanted to embarrass me by making me think she was some kind of monster. I saw only kindness in her eyes, which had returned to their normal dark brown color.

"Okay," I said to myself. "Okay, just—just give me a minute to think." I tried to put my thoughts together. "Those guys at the cemetery were after me because I have the Absyrtus Heart?"

She gave a quick nod.

I readjusted my glasses. "And they want it because the Absyrtus Heart is a cure for the plague?"

"It is the cure for impending death, no matter the cause," Marie said. "But the result is immortality. I'm sitting here the same as I was the day Astraea used the Heart to save me. I'll be seventeen forever."

"But it's still there, the Heart. I saw—" I stopped, remembering the patch of vacant earth next to the plant. "There were two?"

"I don't know how she did it, but Astraea used one of them

to save me. Imagine what somebody might do to have that kind of power."

"I—I don't know what to say. This can't be real."

Marie sighed and shook her head. "Sometimes I wish it wasn't true. I wasn't lying when I said I felt lost without Astraea. She knew what I'd become, even when I didn't fully understand it myself. After she used the Heart to save me, she never told me how she came into possession of the plant, why she and her family knew how to care for it, where it came from, nothing. All of this is real and terrifying, but I—I need you to know that I'm being completely honest with you now. I won't keep anything else from you. If I'd known how to tell you that I'm . . ."

"Immortal?" I cut in. "Strong as shit?"

"Yeah," Marie said. "How was I supposed to say that without you walking away?"

Walk away? Is that what I wanted to do now that I knew her secret, and she apparently knew most of mine? She was right. Nothing she said could have softened the blow of what she'd shared. "I won't walk away, but I'm gonna need a minute to think."

"That's fair," Marie said.

We pulled up in front of my house and the door lock clicked open. I grabbed the handle, then hesitated.

Marie reached out and gently closed her hand over mine. I felt a searing stab of guilt. She had saved me in the graveyard. Who knows what those guys would have done if she hadn't been there? I let go of the handle and sat back.

"Do you think I'm safe now that those guys are . . ." I couldn't bring myself to say "dead."

"I don't know," said Marie. "I don't know who sent them or what they planned to do. Astraea always said how dangerous it was to be in her position." She sighed. "Will you try to talk to the coroner?"

That was the other thing I'd been meaning to look at: why everyone else in my birth mother's family was dead. Were those guys in the woods my biggest threat? I couldn't grow the garden or protect the Heart if I was dead because of some unknown illness stalking my family tree.

"I'll go up there tomorrow," I said. "And you said you'd talk to Dr. Grant?"

"Yes," she said.

I got out of the car, and she was already standing on the passenger side as I closed the door behind me.

"Shit," I said, grabbing my chest.

"Sorry. I'm sorry." There was genuine remorse in her tone. "This night didn't go the way I planned."

"Yeah. Coffee shop meet-cute would've been nice," I said. "Instead we get, what, graveyard murder meetup?"

She laughed. After everything that had happened that night, she laughed. She leaned in and kissed me gently on the cheek, then climbed into the car and drove off.

A part of me wanted to run after her and tell her to kiss me like she wanted me the way I wanted her. She'd killed three grown men to protect me and I *still* wanted to make out with her. I went inside and tried to get my life together.

I didn't sleep. I couldn't. I'd seen things that I thought only existed in nightmares. Marie was some kind of immortal, able to kill three people without breaking a sweat, and the Heart had made her that way. Her face stayed in my mind. Her kiss lingered on my skin.

Marie and Nyx had said they'd call Dr. Grant, so she had to know more than I thought she did. Did that mean she couldn't keep me and my parents safe—or that she was willing to do just that . . . by any means necessary?

The next morning, I called Karter and asked if he wanted to come with me to the funeral parlor. Marie had said a man named Lucian Holt had more information about the deaths in the Colchis family and I wanted answers as much as she did. The address, according to Karter, was only a twenty-minute drive from the house. He picked me up and we drove over.

We parked in front but we didn't go inside right away. Karter kept looking at me, opening his mouth, then closing it and shaking his head.

"What is it?" I asked. "You look like you need to say something."

"Don't take this wrong way, but you look rough. Are you okay? Did you sleep?"

"Not really. I got a lot on my mind."

"Wanna talk about it?" he asked.

"Not right now," I said. "Sorry."

"No, it's okay. Whenever you're ready." He stared out at the funeral home. "Why do we keep ending up at the most random places? The hospital, a secret garden in the woods, a funeral parlor."

"We tried going to the movies and you saw how that turned out."

"Yeah. About that. Any word from Dr. What's-her-name?"

"Grant," I said. "And no. Nothing yet."

I didn't want to tell him about Marie or how Dr. Grant seemed to know a lot more than she was willing to tell me. We climbed out of the truck and started up the walkway. A sign that read Lou's Funeral Parlor stood in front of the house.

"Imagine having a baby and naming it Lou," I said.

"Imagine naming your funeral home after somebody," Karter said. "Like, 'Guess what, Lou? We named the place where we embalm dead people after you.'"

"It's so sweet," I said sarcastically.

We both laughed, but it was only to shake off the nerves. Karter was creeped out about the funeral home itself and so was I, but after what I'd seen with Marie, I was worried this guy was going to be a werewolf or something. I was not prepared for that.

The funeral home was run out of an old Victorian with a perfectly manicured lawn. Two enormous weeping willows flanked the walkway. Curtains of leaves swayed in the breeze. They brushed against me as I passed by and went up the front steps. A hand-lettered sign next to the door read Please Come In. I turned the handle and pushed open the door.

A bouquet of white carnations sat on a small table in the entryway. To the left was a sitting room full of comfy-looking recliners and couches. To the right was a bigger room with folding chairs set up in rows. At the front of the room was a low platform. On it, an open coffin.

"Oh no," Karter said. "There's a body in there."

Someone with dark hair and a red blouse lay inside. Bouquets of roses and tulips were arranged all around the casket. A stand-up arrangement in the shape of a heart stood at the foot end. The pink roses adorning it had begun to brown and curl at the edges. I stepped into the room.

"What are you doing?" Karter asked in a hushed tone.

"That arrangement is jacked up," I said. Mom would never have let half-dead roses get delivered to a funeral home for a service—or anywhere, for that matter. "I can't leave it like that."

The center aisle that led to the coffin was lined with bushels of carnations and white football mums. They were fresh and plump and barely moved as I walked by. Karter followed close behind. When I got to the coffin, I looked inside. An older woman lay there, her head resting on a white satin pillow.

I'd been to a few funerals in my life. The last one was for Mom's great-aunt Bernice. There were kids at the service and they were scared to death. One of their parents told them that Bernice would look like she was sleeping. That wasn't true. Dead people never looked like they were sleeping. The woman in the coffin didn't look like she was resting peacefully either. She looked like a wax figure.

Stiff.

Dead.

I ran my fingers over the wilting petals of the arrangement at the foot of the coffin. The roses regained their shape and color under my touch.

"That's quite a talent," said a voice.

I spun around, nearly knocking over the flower arrangement. Karter jumped up onto the platform, but his foot slipped and crashed into the base of the coffin. I grabbed the side of the casket to steady it.

A tall, gangly man stood in the doorway. He wore khakis and a button-up shirt, the sleeves rolled to the elbow. He was so pale I could see the spiderweb of blue veins running underneath his skin as he strode to the platform. A scattering of white-blond hair stretched across the top of his head. He reminded me of Lurch from *The Addams Family*. His gaze passed over the flower arrangement. "It looks much better."

"I'm Briseis Greene," I said quickly. "Marie gave me this address. She said there would be a man here who might be able to help me."

An angry scowl stretched across his face. "Marie Morris?"

"Yes," I said.

"That troglodyte is giving out my personal information now, is she?"

He was angry. Like, irrationally angry. "Wanna bring it down a notch?" I asked.

Marie had been irritated when she'd given me his name and address, but this guy looked like he was going to blow out his neck vein at any moment.

"Might be the wrong time to bring this up, but what's a troglodyte?" Karter asked.

"It's Marie," said the man. "Marie is a troglodyte." The man turned his attention to me, and something like recognition flashed in his eyes. The lines in his deeply creased forehead softened. He took a step toward me, and I took a step back. Karter was frozen where he stood.

"Who are you?" he asked, his voice barely a whisper, no hint of the anger that had been there a moment ago.

"I think you might already know the answer to that," I said.

He glanced at the flowers again. His eyes glazed over, like he was remembering something. "What is it Marie said I could help you with?"

I stepped off the platform and Karter stumbled down after me. "She said you're the medical examiner and the funeral director, and that it's hard to get any information out of you when it comes to the Colchis family."

The man blinked back a look of utter shock. Composing himself, he clasped his hands together in front of him. "I do indeed serve a dual role here in Rhinebeck. I am both the Dutchess County medical examiner and the funeral director here."

"I told Marie I was going to do some digging to find out what happened to the Colchis family," I continued. "And she told me not to bother because official records were destroyed, maybe not by accident. She made it seem like getting more detailed information would be a problem."

The man huffed. "She's not entirely wrong, but that girl never tells the whole truth no matter how hard she tries. She's been lying for so long, it's her nature now."

"You two have issues?" Karter asked.

The man leaned to the side and glared at Karter. "You have no idea."

"So, if the records are all gone and I can't get them, why would Marie send me here?" I asked.

"Would you mind following me? I think we've disturbed

Mrs. Oliver enough." He motioned toward the casket. "Poor woman. She fell down a flight of concrete steps. The reconstruction was difficult, but I think she looks as lovely as ever."

"Reconstruction?" Karter asked. "What's that mean?"

The man's eyes lit up. "People want to see their loved ones as they were. Mrs. Oliver's head was sunken in on one side due to contact with the steps, and her cheekbone was fractured. I had to glue the bones back into place and fix the coloring of her skin, but the work is superb, some of my best." He stared adoringly into the casket.

Karter looked like he was going to throw up. I wasn't squeamish, but it did feel like the man was oversharing.

"This way," he said, gesturing toward the hall. We followed him out of the room. "Marie gave you my name?"

"Yes," I said. "Lucian Holt."

The man stopped. He tilted his head back, letting his shoulders slump. He sighed heavily.

"That's not right?" I asked.

"No, it's not," he said sharply. "And she knows it. Lucian was my grandfather. The two of them had something of a love affair when they were teenagers. Well, when he was, at least. It scandalized the entire town, including my poor grandmother. Giving you that name is her way of twisting the knife a little more."

I could see he was angry, but it seemed misplaced and way more extra than it needed to be. "You mad at your grandpa, too? Or just her?"

He huffed again. "He died a long time ago, so I hope he's

right where he belongs. Her, on the other hand—she'll outlive all of us now, won't she?"

Karter looked like his brain was going to explode. He didn't know Marie's secret, but this man clearly did, which made everything he said sound ridiculous. We came to a narrow door that led down a short flight of stairs.

"If Lucian was your grandfather, what's your name?" I asked as we descended the stairs.

"Lucifer," he said.

"Say what?" Karter asked, way louder than was necessary. He stopped on the step. "You're joking, right?"

"In case you couldn't tell, I'm not the joking type," the man said. "It's *Lou's* Funeral Parlor. My grandfather was a Lou, so was his father before him—Lewis, Louis, Lucian. In keeping with that tradition, I now carry the moniker."

"In what universe is Lou short for Lucifer?" Karter asked.

"This one," Lucifer said. "But feel free to use Lou if it makes you more comfortable."

Karter stood there with his mouth open and I nudged him in the side. The stairs led down to a big, open room where two body-length stainless steel tables sat side by side. Various trays of instruments and tubing lay neatly organized on the counter. On the rear wall was a heavy door with a latch and a biohazard label stuck to the front.

"That's where we keep the bodies," Lou said, following my gaze. "Don't worry. They stay dead."

He turned and walked into an adjacent room.

Karter ran both hands over the top of his head and tented his fingers in front of his mouth. "What the fuck does that mean?" he asked in an angry whisper.

I followed Lou into the next room, pulling Karter in behind me.

Lou sat down at a desk piled high with papers and folders. He leaned back in the chair. "It's really not a coincidence that the Colchis family has very few written records left. They were always private, and I think most of their information was passed down from generation to generation by word of mouth. An oral family history, if you will."

I looked around the room. "So you don't have any record of how they died?"

"I am the record." He tapped his temple. "It's all right here."

Karter shot me a confused glance.

"So you know how they died?" I asked. "Marie said—"

"Marie feels like she's entitled to know things that don't pertain to her." His eyes were cold and hard as he spoke her name. "Just because she was friends with Astraea doesn't mean I'm at liberty to share her medical details with her. I have a certain way of doing things, and if she doesn't like it, that's too bad, but I won't be changing a generations-long practice because she disagrees with it."

"Can you tell me?" I asked.

Lou eyed Karter suspiciously. "I could tell you. It's clear as the nose on my face that you're a Colchis right down in your bones, but him—" He stuck a bony finger at Karter. "He's a stranger."

"I trust him," I said, glancing at Karter, who still looked highly upset.

"You don't take my meaning," Lou said. "What I mean to say is he's outside of things. An observer."

"No, he knows what I can do," I said, taking a step toward Karter.

"And you think that's the only secret worth keeping?" Lou asked.

Now it was my turn to be annoyed. "Can you help me or not?"

Lou tapped his long, sticklike fingers on the desk and tilted his head to the side. "Records have been destroyed, lost. And yes, your family is disproportionately affected by unfortunate events, but it's not bad luck. It is for a reason." He leaned forward, resting his elbows on the desk. "In any given set of people, particularly people who are related by blood, you'll find patterns, genetic anomalies that cause any number of diseases and afflictions."

My heart sank. "I knew it. There's something in my genetics, right? Something fatal? What is it?"

Lou shook his head. "Your blood relations have been blessedly free of cancers, heart disease, issues of that nature. However, your family has also experienced an unusually high number of homicides, suspicious accidents, and declarations of deaths after someone has disappeared."

My skin pricked up. "What?"

"There have been twelve unsolved homicides in the last six generations of the Colchis family," said Lou. "Four drownings. Three unsolved disappearances."

I couldn't believe what I was hearing.

"Marie's beloved Astraea was murdered." He glanced at

Karter, and thankfully didn't reveal the date of her death. "Perse Colchis in 1904 of a blow to the head. Phoebe Colchis in 1945 by drowning . . . in a dry bathtub. Adelaide in 1953 of strangulation. The murderer was never caught. Eurydice Colchis in 1984, stabbing. The list goes on and on."

"All these people were dying in this town and nobody thought that was worth looking at?" I asked.

"No," Lou said. "Because if you looked at the causes of death released to the public, you'd see nothing of consequence other than some hereditary flaw or unfortunate accident that sent them to their maker."

"Wait," I said, my head spinning. "Are you saying someone lied about their deaths? Why? Why not just tell the truth?"

"There are reasons. I assure you," Lou said. He started to say more but stopped himself.

"Do you want to go?" Karter asked me suddenly. He stood in front of me, his back to Lou. "We can leave if you want."

"No, I'm okay," I said. "Just give me a minute."

He stepped aside but kept his shoulder pressed to mine.

"I need to know what happened to Circe and—and Selene."

Lou's mouth turned down. "Selene was your mother, wasn't she?"

"My birth mother, yes," I said.

Lou took a deep breath. "I will try to be as delicate as one can be about these things, though I imagine this will be difficult to hear. Selene was found in a wooded area on her property. She suffered a gunshot wound to the upper chest. It was fatal. A homicide."

"Somebody killed her?" The room tipped and I leaned

against the wall to steady myself. Karter put his hand on my shoulder. "And nobody looked into it?"

"It was *investigated* in the same manner as the other deaths," said Lou. "I'm sorry to say nothing came of it." He actually seemed genuine. "When she died," he continued, "Selene had in her possession a photograph of a small child. On the back was the name Briseis. When Circe became aware that I knew Selene had a child, she came to me and asked that I take that information to my grave. Neither of them wanted you here in Rhinebeck. Of course, I agreed, but something must have changed their minds because you're here now, and I can't deny that I am extremely curious as to why that is."

"Me too," I said. Why leave the house to me? Why lead me to the garden and make it seem like I belonged here if they never wanted me to come? "What about Circe? How did she die?"

"She was declared dead earlier this year," said Lou. "She disappeared in 2010, three years after Selene's death. She was never heard from again."

I was taken aback. She left letters for me that long ago? "But I saw her tombstone."

"You'd find nothing in the ground below it, I promise you."

"She knew she was going to leave me the house, though. She left me letters."

One of Lou's transparent eyebrows arched up. "She did what?"

Karter clapped his hands together suddenly, startling me. "All right. Cool. Briseis, let's go. This guy is full of shit."

"Excuse me?" Lou said angrily, pushing back from his desk and standing up. Karter took a step forward. Lou was tall and lanky, and Karter was uncoordinated as hell. I couldn't imagine the two of them fighting.

I grabbed the back of Karter's shirt and pulled him toward me. I had more questions, but I couldn't let Karter beat up this wraith of a man in the basement of his funeral parlor. "Thank you for your help. We're gonna go."

Lou shifted his gaze to me and his posture relaxed. He retook his seat. "It has been my pleasure. Will you give Marie a message for me if you happen to see her?"

"Uh, sure," I said.

He smiled and his thin lips stretched across his yellowing teeth. "Tell her I don't appreciate having to clean up after her. She's sloppy. Please remind her that she has had plenty of time to get her act together."

"Right." I assumed he was talking about the men in the woods. I took Karter by the arm and led him upstairs.

We left Lou's and went to the truck. I felt better after leaning my head against the dash and taking a few deep breaths. Karter sat in the driver's seat, gripping the wheel.

"Saying those things to you like that? What the hell is wrong with him?" He reached over and squeezed my shoulder. "I'm so sorry, Briseis."

I sat back in the seat. "I don't understand how this has been happening in this town for generations and everyone is trying to keep a lid on it. What for?"

"I don't know," Karter said. "I can't get over fuckin' *Lucifer* in there. That guy was creepy as hell. He didn't give off a creep vibe?"

"He did, but he works with dead bodies all day."

"He *looked* like a dead body."

Karter wanted to get as far away from Lou's as he could, but I was the one who'd just discovered that a bunch of my relatives had died horrific deaths and that a lot of them, my birth mother included, had been murdered. Lou was clearly involved in a cover-up but his insistence that there was a good reason for it unnerved me.

Karter drove me home, and I texted Marie to tell her I'd seen Lou and that we needed to talk face-to-face. She hit me back right away to let me know Nyx would pick me up in a few hours.

CHAPTER 24

Karter dropped me off at the house and I went straight to my room. I sat on the bed and tried to let my mind settle enough to piece together what Lou had shared with me. I wasn't any closer to finding out what I was supposed to do with the Heart and who might have been trying to get to it through me. The plants on the hearth turned toward me, acknowledging in their own little way that they understood my frustration. It made me feel better.

I went down to the apothecary and collected a few perfectly cultivated rosary peas to replace the broken ones on Marie's necklace. I folded a square of scrap paper into a makeshift envelope and slipped them inside.

My phone dinged. An email notification hung at the top of the screen with Dr. Kent's name in the subject line. I stuck the envelope with Marie's gift in my pocket and opened the email.

Hello Briseis,

Angie told me you are thinking of majoring in botany when you get to college, but if you change your mind and want to venture into classical studies, please let me know. You seem to have a passion for it. As for your questions, I'll try to address them in order.

1) Yes, I charge a consulting fee, but not for this conversation. I cannot express how touched I was that you understand the value of picking another person's brain. You are a gem. Truly.
2) Oftentimes, the stories we think of as purely legend are based, at least in part, on real-world events. There are stories, for example, of the Priestesses of Apollo and the Oracle at Delphi. Many believed these were tall tales, but we've found the actual temple where the Pythia sat to give her predictions. We've uncovered the palace at Knossos where King Minos ruled. His wife, Pasiphae, was the mother of the Minotaur in Greek mythology. We now know the location of Troy, where the Trojans sent their famed horse full of invaders. Alexander the Great made a pilgrimage to the tomb of Achilles so that he could pay his respects. This is a fact. These people, these stories, are grounded in truths that have been exaggerated and distorted over time.
3) As for Medea specifically, there is less known about her beyond what the classic stories tell, but in my own research I have found evidence that she was a real person and that her origin story may have predated the Greek mythology by hundreds of years. She was indeed described as a witch or sorceress, but not like the witches we think of today. Think of her more as a

priestess, someone initiated into the mysteries of a certain set of beliefs. Most priestesses were thought to be chosen by the gods or goddesses they served. In Medea's case, she was a devotee of the goddess Hecate, but Hecate only arrives in Greek mythology in the fifth century BCE, which means that, like so many other Greek myths, she originated somewhere else much, much earlier. Long before the Olympians i.e., Zeus, Poseidon, and Hades come on to the scene. Hecate was shoehorned into Greek storytelling when people became aware of her later on, but one of her earliest mentions is alongside Medea. They are always linked, implying some deeper connection that has yet to be discovered.

Medea is said to have killed her own brother in an attempt to avoid being married off by her tyrannical father, who happened to be the son of the god Helios. She was said to have been cursed in some way because of this. What I know for certain is that her legend has been twisted, retold, and reimagined so many times that original elements have been obscured. I don't believe she killed her own children, as only in Euripides's play does she do this. There is some evidence to support my theory.

There is a folio in the Vatican Archives that a colleague of mine had access to about twenty years ago. It's an assortment of documents that he believed were saved from the Library of Alexandria. These ancient, priceless relics were in pretty rough shape. One of them was the Medea story, and that version predated the stories we know now by centuries. There was even some talk about it being composed by someone who knew her. My colleague had planned to decipher the ancient Greek and try to mend the document, but his access to the archives was unexpectedly and without explanation revoked. There were rumors that the document had been "misplaced," which is doublespeak for stolen or destroyed. I lean toward destroyed, because it is nearly impossible to remove anything from the Vatican Archives without being caught.

I'm attaching the only known image of the document. I have had it analyzed, but to no avail. It's a poor-quality photograph and impossible to see clearly enough to decipher. But the photo is proof this narrative existed, and that is a tantalizing fact in and of itself.

I hope this helps to answer some of your questions. Mythology is a murky world. It's much like unraveling a centuries-long game of telephone. The messages we see and hear today may be nothing like what was actually intended.

Please email me with any further questions.

Best,
Professor Kent

I clicked on the attachment and a blurry photo popped up on my screen: a piece of crumbling papyrus pressed between plastic, held by the gloved hands of someone in a white lab coat. It was too blurry to make out any of the writing, but something struck me. It looked familiar.

I zoomed in to get a better look, but it only made the resolution worse. The plants on the hearth twisted toward me. One of their tendrils had gotten stuck in the groove where the fireplace had slid open.

Suddenly, I remembered that the key to the secret door in the Poison Garden wasn't the only thing I'd found in the hidden office.

I jumped off my bed and grabbed the sketchbook from under my mattress. I pulled out the paper that was preserved in plastic and held it next to the image on my computer screen. It was impossible to tell if the letters matched, but the broken pieces in each document lined up.

I grabbed my phone and called Marie.

"Hey," she answered.

"Hey. Is Nyx still coming to get me?"

"She's on her way right now." Even over the phone I could tell she was smiling. "You sound excited."

"I need your library, if that's okay."

"Oh," she said. "Using me for my books?"

"No. No, I wouldn't—"

Marie laughed into the phone. "I'm joking. See you soon?"

"Yeah," I said.

I gathered the sketchbook and the document, which I now handled with more care than I had before, and put them in my bag. I went downstairs and checked in with Mom and Mo before meeting Nyx in the driveway as she pulled up. I climbed in the front seat this time, and we headed to Marie's.

Nyx showed me into the library, where Marie was already waiting. She practically bum-rushed me, sweeping me into a hug. I gasped. Mostly because my feet were dangling a full six inches above the ground but also because as she'd gathered me up, her face had brushed against the bare skin of my neck.

"Sorry," she said, setting me down. She let her hands trail down my sides, gently resting them on my waist. "After what happened, I thought you might never come back. I'm really happy to see you."

"Me too," I said quickly. "Are you literally gonna sweep me off my feet every time I see you?"

She lowered her eyes. "A side effect of the Heart. I've been like this since it happened."

I rested my hand on her arm. "I'm good with that." I reached into my back pocket and handed her the envelope with the rosary peas inside.

She peeked inside and her fingers gently danced across her necklace. "Thank you."

"I have a bunch of stuff I need to tell you, and I don't know where to start."

She took my hand and gently pulled me to the couch.

"Me and Karter went to see Lou," I said.

Her eyebrow arched up. "How'd that go?"

"Um, he hates you," I said. "I thought he was going to spontaneously combust. He was so angry when I mentioned your name."

"The feeling's mutual."

"But he did tell me some information about my birth family, and none of it's good." I ran through what Lou had shared with me: the strange deaths, the homicides, the disappearances. Marie didn't say anything until I finished.

"You're telling me Circe isn't in that grave?"

I shook my head. "Not according to Lou."

"I'm sorry you had to hear that from him." She put her hand on my knee. "He's a ghoul, but I don't think he's dishonest. If that's what he said, then it's probably true. After Astraea died, I left Rhinebeck for a long time. I'd come back and leave again. I kept watch, but from a distance, you know? I got to know Circe, but she was guarded. I didn't know they'd lost so much over the generations."

"And he's doing exactly what you said, covering up the deaths, making it seem like nothing out of the ordinary is going on here. I still don't understand why but there's something else." I pulled the sketchbook and the other document out of my bag and handed them to her. "I found this in the house and I need to find out what it says." I showed her the email and the blurry picture from Dr. Kent on my phone.

"So Medea was a real person?" Marie asked. "And she had some of the same abilities as you?" She looked concerned, and she sat staring off for a moment before abruptly turning to me. "Come with me."

She pulled me up off the couch and I followed her down the hall. She led me to a set of double doors at the end of a narrow hallway. She knocked, but didn't wait for whoever was on the other side to answer before she turned the handle and went in.

"We talked about you walking in on me," a man's voice said.

I peered around Marie. Alec sat behind a wide mahogany desk with ornately carved legs strewn with books and several computer monitors. He looked much better than the last time I'd seen him.

"I have something you need to look at," Marie said.

Alec caught sight of me and stood. "Miss Briseis. Good to see you again."

"Is it?" Marie asked. "You pulled a machete on her last time."

"I brought the machete to cut through the brush and I pulled it on the vines that were trying to kill me," he corrected. "I'd never hurt you."

"Not if you know what's good for you," Marie said.

Alec looked queasy.

"Anyhoo," said Marie nonchalantly, like she hadn't just threatened his life. "Look at this." She handed him the document encased in plastic. "Bri was going to use the library to look into this but maybe you can save her some time."

His face contorted—first in confusion, then in shock as he studied the parchment. He straightened. "Where in the world did you get this?"

"You know what it is?" I asked. "Can you tell me what it says?"

He sat down, his hands trembling as he held the document in front of him. "This is ancient. It's in Proto-Greek, similar to Classical Greek, but with a few distinct markers. It was common in the Early Helladic period."

"Which was when, exactly?" Marie asked.

"Fourth millennium BCE," Alec said. He threw on a pair of thick wire-rimmed glasses and cleared a spot on his desk to lay the document down. He pulled something up on his computer and clicked on a folder labeled *Reconstructed Proto-Greek Phonemes*.

"I'm fluent in several languages. Greek is one of them."

"We get it, you're smart," Marie said. "Nobody asked how many languages you know."

"Jealous?" Alec asked.

Marie rolled her eyes.

"I'll read it aloud," said Alec. "But I'll need a minute to translate accurately. Bear with me."

Marie perched herself on the edge of his desk and I moved around to look at the papyrus as he translated.

"'Medea was the daughter of King Aeëtes of Colchis, beloved niece of the sorceress Circe, and most importantly, the—'" Alec paused. "The word is illegible here. We know from other ancient texts that Medea was a devotee of Hecate and those words might fit, but so would a hundred others." He jotted down a few notes and continued. "'Medea was gifted with the power of immunity to any and all poisons.'"

I dropped my phone. Marie was at my side, handing it back to me before I could blink.

"Are you all right?" Alec asked.

I nodded, but no, I wasn't all right.

He continued, looking between the computer screen and the document. "'Medea became the most powerful sorceress in the land. Her brother, Absyrtus, was her ever-present protector.'" He stopped, double-checking his work. "Here, the word 'δηλητήριο' is in conjunction with the word 'μάγισσα.' 'Poison' and 'witch,' but I don't recognize the way it's being used here."

He made another note, then continued reading while I tried not to hyperventilate.

"'Medea was known throughout the land, so it was only natural that powerful men seeking money and power came to her, hoping she would lend her talents to their quests. She could not be bought. She could not be convinced.'"

I'd been gripping my phone so hard my palm had become sweaty, and pieces of the already-fractured screen flaked off on my palm. Medea wasn't just a woman in an old portrait. She wasn't just a character in a bunch of old stories. She was a person who came from a place called Colchis, who was immune to poison, who had a brother named Absyrtus.

"'Jason, commander of the *Argo*, sought Medea out and devised a plan to deceive her. Jason told her Absyrtus and her father plotted against her, intending to marry her off to a man of their choosing. Medea was devastated. Jason professed his undying love for Medea and told her that he would protect her from Absyrtus and her father, but that in order to do so, he needed to find the fabled Golden Fleece, which would allow him to become king.

"'Medea agreed to help him find it, and after abandoning her home and her family, they sailed the world in search of the Golden Fleece. But after many years and the births of their three children, they had turned up nothing and Jason grew weary.'"

Alec paused again. "Do you know the story of Medea?"

"I read it," I said. "But the version I read isn't like this."

Alec shook his head. "Not at all. But if the language is what we're going by, this document has to predate what is considered the original." He let out a little laugh. "It's impossible but the familiarity and informality of it reminds me of the kinds of documents we see that came out of the time period when people began writing their family histories down instead of passing them down orally." He leaned in and read the next part.

"'Unbeknownst to Medea, Absyrtus had been searching for her. When he found her, he told Medea the truth. There had never been any plan to marry her off. Jason had lied to her. He tricked her into helping him attain the Golden Fleece. When confronted, Jason and his men took their children and Absyrtus as captives and threatened to kill them if Medea didn't find the fleece and turn it over to Jason.

"'Medea sought the help of the goddess and was told the fleece was in the sacred grove of Ares, guarded by a never-sleeping dragon. Medea poisoned the dragon, procured the fleece, and then, understanding that she would never be free from him, decided to kill Jason. She concocted the deadliest poison she could, distilled it into a goblet of wine, and had it served to him. Medea watched in horror as Jason made his children taste his food and drink before him. The children fell to the floor, writhing in pain. Jason seized Medea, took the fleece for his own, and executed Absyrtus by cutting his body into six pieces.

"'Medea, in her bottomless sorrow, called to the goddess for help. Hecate appeared with a . . .'"

Alec stopped and checked his notes and computer screen again. "The document is damaged here. A partial word, 'Κυν——λο,' is written, and the word 'κυνηγόσκυλο,' meaning 'hound,' could fit in the space."

He went on. "'Hecate appeared with a hound and opened the gates to the underworld. Jason fled with the fleece, and Medea looked on as Hecate swept everyone in attendance to their deaths. In an act of grace, Medea's immunity flowed in the veins of her children and they were saved.

"'Jason made use of the fleece and took the princess Glauce as his wife, and so became King. Medea and her children retreated to the island of Aeaea, home of the sorceress Circe. She spent her days wandering her Poison Garden, where she buried the six pieces of Absyrtus's body. In the spot where the earth covered each piece of his remains, peculiar plants grew, plants only Absyrtus's beloved family could tend. Medea nurtured them with drops of her own blood and slivers of moonlight.'"

I felt like I'd fallen off the edge of a cliff. That sickening feeling of free fall made my stomach turn over. Marie's hand was firm on the small of my back.

"This is fascinating," Alec said as he continued to study the parchment. "The way the story's told here, its age—I've never seen anything like this outside of a museum." He eyed me carefully. "Where did you say you got it?"

Marie reached down and snatched the paper off his desk. He winced, reaching for it.

"Be careful!" he said angrily. "It's delicate."

Marie handed the document to me, gently nudging me toward the door. "Thanks, Alec. You can go back to illegally accessing the MoMA's encrypted files."

"History belongs to all of us," he said as we closed the doors behind us.

I looked Marie dead in the eye. "I found the key."

She blinked. "The key to what?"

"The door in the garden."

"You didn't open it."

It wasn't a question as much as it was a statement, as if saying it to me like that would make it true.

"I did. I've seen the Heart."

Marie's eyes grew wide. "Briseis." She didn't have to say anything else. I could hear the disappointment in her voice.

"You don't understand," I said. "Everything has been leading me to it, and this document—whatever it is—is proof of that."

She shook her head, avoiding my gaze.

"Do you want to see it?" I asked.

Marie slowly leveled her eyes at me. "You'd take me in there? Circe would never have—"

"I don't care what Circe did and didn't do. How am I supposed to know what she wanted? Everything she left me is a clue or a riddle or both and I'm over it. She wasn't specific, so I'm gonna do things my way."

"That's not fair," Marie said. "Your family has been guarding the Heart for generations. You're just gonna let random people in to see it?"

"You're not a random person. Neither is Karter. I trust you both. And honestly, this entire family has been closed off and secretive, but everybody seems to know our business. I keep running into people who know more about the house and the shop and the garden than I do." I sighed. "Circe had her reasons for the way she did things, but I have mine."

Frustration swelled in me. This wasn't just about the Heart. It was about not wanting to start every new relationship with a lie. "Keeping it a secret doesn't keep me safe. You saw that yourself." I pulled out my phone. "And I'm gonna tell Karter. We can all go together and maybe we can figure out what to do with it."

"No, you can't do that," Marie said. "You can't show him. It's too dangerous—it's your responsibility and yours alone."

I stepped away from her. "If I stay here and run the shop, if me and Karter stay friends, if you and me—"

Marie's eyes lit up. "If you and me what?"

"If we want to see where this goes, then I don't want to keep secrets."

"I'm not asking you to keep secrets. I'm asking you to be selective about who you share certain things with."

I almost laughed. "Are you serious right now? That's literally the definition of keeping secrets. I have had to lie to everybody, even to myself, just to exist. I'm sick of lying and hiding."

"You think I don't know about burdens? About hiding?" Marie asked, her voice tight. "You think I don't know the damage secrets can do or what it feels like to have to leave everyone behind because of them?" She looked away.

I hadn't meant to hurt her, but it felt like I'd hit a nerve. "I'm sorry. I didn't mean to make you upset. Maybe if I can share this with you and with Karter, we won't have to be alone with our secrets. None of us get left behind if we're in it together."

She closed the gap between us in half a blink. The smell of her perfume, her warm breath on my cheek, it was almost too much to handle. I tilted my chin up so that our lips nearly touched. I wondered how that would feel, what her kiss would taste like.

"I'll look at whatever it is you want to show me," she said softly.

"Whatever I want to show you?"

She chuckled. "The Heart."

Heat rose in my face. "Right."

She brushed past me and I followed her out to the car, where Nyx was waiting to take us back to the house. I sent Karter a text asking him to meet us there. I slid into the back seat of the car and Marie crawled in beside me—scooted right up to me, her leg resting against mine. My problem was going to be focusing on literally anything other than her.

CHAPTER 25

Karter pulled up at the same time as us. I got out to greet him and as I did, he looked past me at Marie and his eyes almost popped out of his skull like a cartoon. I couldn't blame him. She had that effect on people. I glanced at her to see if she'd noticed, but she didn't look like she'd seen him at all. She was straightening her T-shirt under her jacket and doing that tug-jump combo people do when their jeans start to slip off their hips.

I gave Karter a hug. "Hey."

"Uh, hi," Karter said, still looking stunned.

Marie came over and stood next to me. "I'm Marie." Her tone was friendly but clipped.

"The same Marie that fool Lucifer was talking about?"

"You thought he was an asshole, too?" Marie asked.

Karter clapped his hands together. "Yup! See? Briseis got a creep vibe from him, but she's tryna downplay it."

"Oh, I like you," Marie said, smiling.

Karter cocked his head to the side. "He said something about his grandpa but you're—"

"Okay," I said cutting off that line of questioning before it could get started. "Come inside so I can show y'all something."

We went in and said hi to my parents, who were watching something on my laptop in the front room. I led Marie and Karter upstairs and into the turret. I turned on the light before flipping to the page in the big book that showed the illustration of the Absyrtus Heart.

Karter stared down at the illustration. "Is this a plant?"

"It's called the Absyrtus Heart."

"Is this in your garden?" he asked. "I didn't see it."

"Yeah, it's in the Poison Garden. I haven't cultivated it. I've never seen anything like it. It's poisonous—the most toxic thing I've ever touched."

"You touched it?" Marie asked.

I shrank back. "I thought it would be like all the other poisonous stuff I can touch, but it felt like my hand was gonna fall off."

Marie crossed her arms over her chest. "I need you to stop trying to get yourself killed."

I gently squeezed her arm. "You were right about it not being like the other plants." I flipped through the drawings in the book. "All the other plants have instructions, but not the Heart. I wouldn't have known how to cultivate it, but now I do."

"What changed?" Karter asked.

"I found a document and Marie helped me get it translated. It's old. Ancient, actually. It told the story of Medea." I gestured toward the painting on the wall. "She was from a place called Colchis, the same name of my birth family." I had to say out loud what my gut told me was the truth. "I think—I think I'm related to her."

Marie gasped so hard she started to cough.

"Wait, wait, wait." Karter shook his head. "You really think your family tree goes back that far?"

"It makes sense," I said. "I thought Circe and Selene were obsessed with her, but it's not that. It's normal to have portraits of your relatives hanging up, right?"

Karter shrugged. "I guess?"

"And she was a poisonist," I said.

"What's a poisonist?" he asked.

"Someone like me," I said. "Somebody who can work with poisonous plants and not be affected. All the things I've found out about this house and my family lead to Medea and to *that*." I pointed to the drawing of the Heart. "The people I've met since I've been in Rhinebeck know it's out there, but they don't mess with it. They don't even want to talk about it, like it's an open secret. They make it seem like it's my responsibility. Medea was the Heart's original caretaker. She could do everything I can." I stood up. There was only one thing I wanted to do. "Come on. I want to look at the Heart again."

Marie started to protest, but I headed downstairs before she could say anything. Karter and Marie followed me out the front door and across the lawn. I didn't even pause as I approached the hidden trail. The vines and branches parted.

"Stay close to me," I reminded Karter.

"I know the drill." He glanced at Marie. "What about her?"

"I'm good," said Marie.

I hadn't asked about the limits of her power. She didn't seem too worried for her safety, so I pressed on.

About halfway to the garden, I noticed the shadows growing

long. The sun had been at the horizon when we'd ducked onto the path, but after the email from Professor Kent and what I'd learned from that ancient document, I couldn't wait another day, another hour.

When we came into the clearing, I took out my phone and switched on the flashlight. Karter did the same. The trees leaned away to reveal the gate and I unlocked it, nudging him and Marie through. It clanged shut behind us.

Even in the encroaching darkness, I could see Marie's eyes alight with wonder. She'd been honest with me when she said she'd never been inside the garden.

"Wait till you see this," I said, pulling her toward the Poison Garden.

Devil's Pet wound itself around the moon gate.

"We are going straight to the back wall," I said. I turned to Karter. "Wait here until I tell you to come through."

"I could . . . help," Marie offered. She made a motion like she was picking up a baby and rocking it in her arms.

I looked at her and then to Karter. She was suggesting she could pick him up and rush him through the Poison Garden. I had to bite the inside of my cheek to keep from laughing. How ridiculous would it be to see Karter carried around like a small child? He was way too scary to let that happen, so I shook my head no.

"How could you help?" Karter asked.

Marie pretended she didn't hear him, and he shoved his hands in his pockets, glancing around nervously. I walked through the Poison Garden and stopped in front of the rear wall. The vines pulled back, and I opened the hidden door. The crimson brush bloomed and pointed toward the door. I held up my hand. The plant retreated.

"Ready?" I called to Karter. "Hold your breath and run. Now!"

Karter sprinted forward, stumbling once and nearly falling flat on his face. Marie was suddenly there, hoisting him up and pulling him toward the door. They slid to a stop in front of me.

"Oh, wow," Karter said, staring down at Marie. "You work out?"

I yanked him through the door and Marie slipped in after him. I stood between them and the crimson brush's star-shaped blooms.

"Down there," I said, gesturing to the stairs.

They disappeared below and I followed once I was sure the crimson brush wasn't going to act up. I descended the stairs into the dank little room. Karter and Marie were both completely silent. The lights from our phones illuminated the small space. The plant stood in its glass enclosure. Karter leaned in and I quickly put my arm in front of him.

"This is the Absyrtus Heart," I said. "It's the deadliest plant I've ever come in contact with. I don't want either of you to get hurt. You shouldn't even be in here, but I had to show you this. It's real. It exists."

I examined the hole in the ceiling, and Karter followed my gaze.

"I think when the moon rises, it shines through there," I said.

"What kind of plant grows in the dark?" Karter asked. "Don't plants need sunlight?"

"Queen of the Night cacti only bloom in the dark." I unlocked the glass door and we peered inside. "But this is something else."

Marie stood as still as the shadows. "I don't even know what to say."

I'd felt the same way when I first saw it. If I hadn't seen the shriveled stalk and crumbling leaves underneath it, I would have thought I was looking at a real human heart, somehow preserved.

For my AP Biology class, we'd taken a field trip to the museum and seen a human heart suspended in a jar of formaldehyde. We'd had to label the parts on a worksheet, and all those parts were there on the strange plant. The flat waxy plain of the right and left ventricles was pointed upward. The tangle of what might have been arteries snaked off the bottom and fed into long, thick stalks.

Karter leaned over my shoulder. "What the hell? Have you tried watering it? Tried to get it to come back like the stuff up top?"

"No. But I don't think water would make a difference. I don't think that's what it needs."

"What does it need?" Karter asked.

"If it were a real heart, what would it need?" I asked.

Karter's eyes grew wide in the moonlight. "Are you saying it needs blood?"

Marie put her hand on my shoulder, concern in her eyes. "Do you know what will happen if you do this?"

"Do you?" I asked.

She shook her head. "No."

"Do you know if Circe kept it alive? Or did she let it die?"

Marie avoided my stare. "She kept it alive. So did Astraea. She said she had to."

This was the work Circe had mentioned. Not the shop or even the Poison Garden, but this—the care of this very special plant.

"I've seen you do all kinds of impossible things," Karter said suddenly. He walked over and stood next to Marie. "So I'm not really surprised that we're out doing some kind of blood ritual in the dark, in a stank-ass underground vault. But for real—this feels dangerous. Especially for me, because clearly your homegirl is not concerned." He gave Marie the once-over, but didn't push further.

"Oh, I'm concerned," said Marie. "Just not in the way you think." She looked at me. "I'm worried that if you don't keep track of the Heart and look after it the way Circe and Selene did, that it'll be lost—or stolen. If you really think you're related to Medea, your family tree branches back hundreds of generations." She sighed. "I always wondered why they'd risk it, why this family felt like they had to do all this after the toll it seemed to have taken on them."

I gestured at the plant. "They kept it because it's him—it's Absyrtus. The Hearts are his mortal remains."

"Hearts?" Karter asked. "There's more than one?"

"There was," I said. "Originally there were six."

Marie moved closer to me. "What could be lost if you don't do this?"

"Briseis," Karter said softly, his voice trembling. "What are you gonna do?"

I removed one of my earrings and held it against my index

finger until the skin broke. I held my hand over the Absyrtus Heart and squeezed my finger. A single drop of blood fell onto it.

The veiny surface of the plant expanded slightly, like it was being pushed out from the inside. I jumped back, my heart racing. Karter gasped. Marie's mouth fell open as she backed away.

"It moved," I said.

"No shit," said Karter.

The plant shifted again. Karter hit the stairs, taking them two at a time.

"Karter! Wait!" I screamed.

I scrambled up the stairs behind him. He was heading out the door as the crimson brush turned to face him, its blooms opening and taking aim, preparing to shower him with its deadly powder. I threw myself between him and the plant and caught a plume of rust-colored poison right in the face.

Ice-cold numbness stole my breath. Something brushed past me as my vision blurred. I staggered back, my ankle twisting painfully as I slipped on the slick green moss. A thick tendril of Devil's Pet wrapped itself around my arms and legs, keeping me from tumbling down the steps. It righted me and I raced out into the Poison Garden.

Karter stood, eyes wide, chest heaving on the other side of the moon gate. Marie stood next to him, shaking her head. She'd pulled him to safety, probably with enough strength and speed to make him think he was losing it.

"Great," I said to myself. Now I was going to have to tell him secrets that weren't mine to share, and I didn't know where to start. I closed the hidden door, locking it. A dull ache throbbed in my right ankle. I hobbled over to Karter.

"Are you hurt?" I asked. I didn't see any cuts or scrapes, but I couldn't tell if the shock on his face was from almost being poisoned to death or if he was trying to process all the highly weird shit he'd just seen.

"What—what was that?" Karter asked. "Did you see that?"

My sock suddenly felt too tight. My ankle was swelling. "I gotta get home. I think my ankle is broken."

Marie was immediately at my side, taking my entire weight as she slipped her hand around my waist.

"I—I think I need to lie down," said Karter. "Something's not right."

My heart cartwheeled in my chest. "Did you touch something? Were you holding your breath?"

"He's not poisoned," Marie said. "I made sure he didn't touch anything. Me, on the other hand . . ." A ragged cut lay open on her upper forearm. A lacework of veins, black as the night sky, traced a path up her arm.

I grabbed her hand. "Oh no."

"It's fine," she said. "I'll be okay."

Karter glanced at me, sweat beading on his forehead, his mouth stuck in a hard line. He shook himself from his panic-induced stupor. "Come on," he said. "Let's get out of here."

With Marie practically carrying me, we left the garden and I locked the outer gate. The darkness was complete and stifling as Karter led the way home, lighting the path ahead of us with his phone. I kept putting my foot down to at least keep up the illusion that Marie was only assisting me, not effortlessly taking my entire weight, but each attempt sent a bolt of pain straight through the side of my leg. I winced.

"If you keep trying to 'help' me, I'm gonna lift you up so high you can't touch the ground at all," Marie said.

"Like you did me?" Karter asked, glancing over his shoulder. "We not gon' talk about that? You think I didn't notice that you scooped me up like it was nothin'? Like I don't see Bri's feet dangling off the ground this whole time we've been walkin'? I'm a grown—almost grown—man—"

"I could've left your ass there," Marie snapped. "And if I had, your skin would be peeling away from your bones and your throat would be closed up."

Karter's entire demeanor changed. He opened his mouth to speak but nothing came out. "I—I'm sorry. I just— How did you do that? Who are you?"

Marie said nothing.

"I don't think we should tell anybody about what we saw," I said. "Not the Heart, not Marie's abilities, none of it. Not right now."

"I'm not even sure what I saw," he said, glancing at Marie.

"I'll explain everything," I said. "I promise. But right now I need to get home. My ankle is killin' me."

Karter nodded but his expression remained tight and his gaze kept flitting back to Marie.

Marie walked me to the front door, with Karter trailing far behind. Mo was waiting.

"They're back," she called. Marie gently lowered me to the ground. A strangled yelp escaped me as the pain in my ankle flared again. Mo's brow furrowed. "What happened to you?"

"I tripped," I said. "It's pretty swollen."

Mo and Marie helped me inside and onto the couch. My mom knelt and removed my shoe and sock.

"Shit," she said. My ankle was already starting to bruise.

"Can you move it?" Mo asked.

I wiggled my toes. The pain was only on the outside of my ankle. "It hurts, but maybe it's just a bad sprain."

"We should go to the ER," Mom said.

"No," I said. "Not happening." I leaned back against the pillows. "I can put something on it. Can y'all help me get into the apothecary?"

Mom and Mo exchanged glances. Marie and Karter both held out their hands to help me up.

"You could do it yourself, huh?" Karter asked, looking Marie dead in her eyes.

"You know what?" I said. "Never mind. I'll do it."

I pulled myself up and limped down the hall with Marie and Karter following close behind. I turned on the lights in the shop and tried to hoist myself onto the counter but slipped. Marie slid her hand around me, grabbing hold of the back of my shirt and pulling me up before anyone saw. Mom and Mo came in and helped me prop my leg on the counter.

"I need that book." I gestured to a large book I'd brought down from the turret that had the handwritten instructions for a salve to help with bruising and pain. Marie handed it to me and I leafed through. "I need the jar of arnica."

Karter pulled the ladder over, making his way to the top row.

"Mom, can you get me the mortar and pestle?"

She massaged her temples. "Baby, I don't think this is the right time to make a potion or whatever it is you're about to do."

"Please?" I asked.

She begrudgingly slid the stone mortar and pestle set over to me, and Karter handed me the jar of dried arnica. I double-checked the instructions in the book, then took out a handful and crushed it into a fine powder, added some olive oil, and stirred until it became a thick paste. I slathered the mixture on my ankle and covered it in plastic wrap. The relief was immediate.

Mo came over to me. "I don't know what kind of witchcraft you're doing, but it's about to save me some money on healthcare, so I'm with it. You need something, you let me know. One of them pots, those big pots that witches use?"

Marie bit back a smile.

"A cauldron?" Mom prompted.

"Yeah," Mo said, smiling. "A cauldron, a pointy hat, a broom, some green face paint, whatever you need."

"I should get home," said Karter.

"Thanks for helping me get back," I said.

"I didn't really help, but I'm glad you're okay," he said. "I'll call you tomorrow."

He squeezed my hand, gave Marie a quick nod, then disappeared down the hall.

Marie turned to me. "I'm gonna head out, too." She gently gripped her arm where I'd seen those streaks of black. Poison was working its way through her body, but she'd said not to worry. I didn't think I was going to be able to do that.

She leaned in and kissed me on the cheek, letting her lips linger for half a second longer than they needed to. She turned and walked to the door. "Mamas Greene, it was good seeing you both."

Mo grinned. "You come back any time you want. I'll make waffles."

"No, the hell you won't," said Mom. She tucked Marie's arm under hers and steered her out into the hallway. "I'd never let her do that to you, baby. Don't you worry."

Mo helped me off the counter.

"I think I'm gonna go to bed," I said.

"Let me help you upstairs," Mo said.

"No, I'm good. I got it. Love you."

"Love you more," she said.

I shuffled out into the hallway and made my way upstairs as Mo joined Mom in the front room. I crawled into bed and pulled the covers up to my neck.

The image of the Absyrtus Heart was burned into my mind. I Googled "human heart" and a video came up in the search results for a donor heart that was kept pumping by a system of tubes and machines. If it had been flipped upside down and rooted in the ground, it would have been the same as the plant in the garden. I closed the video, tossed my phone toward the end of my bed, and tried to fall asleep.

CHAPTER 26

The next morning, I found Mo in the kitchen scrambling eggs and making toast.

"Need me to get the fire extinguisher?" I asked.

"Hush," she said.

I eased myself onto a seat at the table. The swelling in my ankle had gone down, but it still ached. I didn't think I'd be able to get back into the garden yet, but I couldn't stop thinking of the Heart.

Mom came into the kitchen wearing a billowy red bonnet and a raggedy robe that looked like Freddy Krueger had used it for practice before he sliced those kids up on Elm Street.

"This pollen is tryna kill me today," she said, sniffling. "Bri, baby, I know you're laid up, but your arm still works, right? We gotta stay on top of the dust if y'all want me to live. All the sills I cleaned last week already have a layer of green dust on them."

"Yes, ma'am," I said. Only thing getting me out of Sunday morning cleaning was probably death, so after I finished breakfast, I found the broom and a bunch of clean rags, then hobbled to the apothecary to get started.

I opened the windows in the shop, letting a warm breeze waft through. The sun slanted through the stained glass window on the outer wall, casting blue and green columns of light onto the floor. Down the hall, I heard the familiar notes of Sam Cooke's crooning, and I smiled. They'd played that song at their wedding and I loved it—but now, it was house-cleaning music, which would be followed by either Earth, Wind & Fire or Zapp & Roger. Broke ankle or not, it was time to clean.

I grabbed a rag and dampened it under the faucet. A thick layer of dust sat in the grooves of the open window, tinged green from all the pollen wafting through the air. I cleaned it out and moved on to the overhang of wooden trim that went around the entire room. Dragging the cloth along, I made my way back behind the closet-sized drying rack.

A frayed piece of the rag caught on the trim where it had come away from the wall. I yanked hard, trying to pull it free. It broke loose with a soft click, and a small, narrow door opened in front of me. A gust of sweet-smelling air wafted out.

"Mom! Mo!"

Mo came first, holding a kitchen knife, and Mom barreled in behind her, her Taser crackling in the midmorning sun.

"What is it?" Mo asked frantically.

"Look!" I pointed toward the door. Its seams were perfectly aligned with the wood paneling. Nobody looking at it would have even known it was there. "The rag caught on some kind of latch when I was dusting. It just popped open." Mom pulled me back a step.

"Wait a minute," Mo said. She hurried out of the room and came back a moment later with a flashlight. She clicked it on and shone it into the room behind the door. The column of light cut through the darkness to reveal a space the size of a large bedroom. There were no windows or other doors. Mo stepped in and Mom and I followed her. The walls were painted black, making the space feel smaller than it actually was. The sweet smell was more pungent inside the room. It reminded me of honey and burned paper.

There was a small table at the back of the room. As we approached it, the light from Mo's flashlight danced in her trembling hand.

"What is this?" Mom asked, her voice barely a whisper.

The surface of the table was covered in a black cloth. In the center was a large statue of a woman with three faces—Hecate, the goddess Medea was in service to. Objects were arranged on the table: three rusted skeleton keys, bundles of what I was sure was mugwort, garlic skins, black candles with trails of wax that had run down and dried in layered mounds, and onions that had sprouted and snaked across the black cloth before rotting away to almost nothing. There were small bowls, black stones, and a wreath of decayed flowers around the statue's neck—even a glass jar stuffed with black bird's feet.

"It's an altar," Mom said.

"Auntie Leti has one," I said.

"But it's not like this," she replied. "Hers is for working, for . . ." She trailed off. Her eyes narrowed and I followed her gaze. Sitting at the base of the statue was a photograph, ripped on one edge and stained brown at the bottom like something had spilled across it, soaking it all the way through. I immediately recognized the bubbly little girl, no more than a year old.

It was me.

Mo reached for it, and Mom caught her by the wrist. "Don't touch it. Don't touch anything." Her voice was higher, her face drawn tight. Mom pulled out her phone and dialed a number. "Leti, I—I need your help."

I didn't like the way she sounded. There was real fear in her tone, and I suddenly became uneasy. Mo came and stood next to me, putting her arm around my shoulder, and I hugged her tight.

"There's an altar in this house," Mom said on the phone. "There's a statue of a woman with three faces." She paused as Auntie Leti asked her a question. "Garlic, onions, black flowers, crow's feet." Her face relaxed as my aunt spoke. "Leti, hang on, I'm putting you on speaker." She held the phone out. "Go ahead."

"This isn't my practice, Thandie. You know that."

"I know," said Mom. "Just tell them what you told me."

"The triple goddess is Hecate. Also known as the Queen of Witches, Keeper of the Keys, Guardian of the Crossroads. In Greek mythology, she's said to have aided Demeter in her search for Persephone."

The hair on the backs of my arms stood straight up.

"She's ancient," Auntie Leti said. "An original goddess, or an entity that the goddess label was slapped onto because they didn't have a name for what she was. The black flowers, the crow's feet, black stones, candles—those are all for her. Like an offering. She's often said to be accompanied by a black dog. She's the guardian of women and children, so I wouldn't be overly concerned."

"It's too late for that, Leti," Mo said.

"There was a picture of Briseis on the altar," Mom said.

There was a sharp intake of breath and a long pause.

"Take me off speaker," said Auntie Leti.

Mom talked to her for a few more minutes, while Mo moved behind me to examine something on the wall. "Briseis, look," she said.

Something was drawn there—an intertwined maze of twisting lines, like vines, each new leaf bearing a name. There were hundreds of branches, each bough sheltering dozens of generations beneath it. "Colchis" was painted in a flowing script at the very top, and directly underneath was the crest—from the hidden door in the Poison Garden, from the desk in the room behind my fireplace, from the drawing Mrs. Redmond had given me.

"Shine your light up there," I said.

Mo pointed her light at the top of the wall. The unmistakable face of Medea emerged from the gloom, her dark eyes staring down at us. Her name was written under her portrait, and every branch stemmed from her. She was the founder of this family tree. I traced the branches until I found, near the bottom where the leaves were sparse, my name nested under Selene's: Briseis Colchis.

Mom came up behind me and seemed to take in the wall in one sweeping glance. "Baby, this is incredible. Look how far back this goes."

I scanned the wall. Near the top, directly to the right of Medea's painted face, was another portrait—a man. His branches intermingled with Medea's, but abruptly split off.

"What did Auntie Leti say?" I asked.

"She's gonna get back to me," said Mom. She exchanged

glances with Mo, who nodded, and they steered me out of the room.

"That tree goes back so far," Mo said. "You really think this is real? I mean, how can we know for sure?"

It was real. It had to be. There was a reason my blood woke the Heart from its slumber. My blood was Medea's blood, and she had been the plant's original guardian. I needed to tell them about that and about me. It couldn't wait anymore. "Listen, I have to tell you something and it's going to sound impossible but it's important."

"Baby, you can talk to us about anything," Mom said. "You know that."

I should have trusted them with this sooner. I hoped they'd understand why I'd waited. "Since we've been here, I know things have been weird. Strangers showing up, this shop, the garden. But I think it's all connected." I tried to think in a straight line. "Circe left me some letters."

Mo straightened up.

"They led me to the garden. She knew what I could do with the plants. But she also knew something about me that even *I* didn't know until a few days before we came here, when I cut my thumb." I took a deep breath. "Mo, when you scared me that day, I was working with a water hemlock. It's one of the most poisonous plants in the world."

"Where'd you even get something like that?" Mom asked.

"I grew it in the park and brought home a piece to study. I was just gonna take a few notes and then get rid of it. I cut it open and there was poison on the blade of the scalpel when I sliced my thumb. It should have killed me."

Tears welled up in Mom's eyes. "Baby, you should have told us. We'd have taken you right to the hospital."

"There wouldn't have been time. There *shouldn't* have been time. I should've died within the first five minutes, but I didn't."

"What are you saying?" Mo asked.

"I'm completely immune. I've come in contact with every poisonous plant you can think of since we've been here and nothing has happened. Circe knew I was immune and that I could cultivate the garden I found. And there are plants in there that are too toxic for anyone besides me to handle. That's why people have been showing up here. I can grow things they can't get anywhere else. So could Circe and Selene, and the Colchis family has been running this shop for generations."

Mo and Mom continued to stare at me, speechless.

I took a deep breath and continued to the part that I knew would be the hardest for them to understand. "Also, I found a document that says the goddess Hecate—the exact same goddess that altar is dressed for—gave the power of immunity to Medea, and her children inherited that power from her. It's been passed down to everyone in her line. Now I have it, but—" I stopped short.

"'But' what?" Mom asked.

I gripped my hands together in front of me. "Circe and Selene were keeping a plant called the Absyrtus Heart. Absyrtus was Medea's brother and he was murdered. Dismembered. Medea kept the six pieces of his body buried in her garden. The pieces seeded a plant that isn't like any other plant in existence—the Absyrtus Heart, and there's one right out there in my garden. The Colchis family has been running this apothecary and protecting the Heart, but I think Selene was trying to keep me from having anything to do with this place." If it hadn't been for Circe I never would have known any of it. That was a detail that still made no sense if she and Selene were as close as everyone else made it seem.

"Someone was after the Heart," I continued. "It has some very special properties. It's why . . ." I hesitated. The tendrils of everything I had learned twisted together like the vines in the Poison Garden—inescapable and deadly. The people who'd come after me wanted the Heart. Maybe someone had always been after it, killing off members of the Colchis family to try and get to it. A piece of the Heart had made Marie immortal, and clearly, somebody wanted that power for themselves, wanted it enough to kill for it. Everything I'd learned pointed to one conclusion. "I think that's why Selene was murdered."

Mom blinked, then put her hand on her chest. "Briseis, are you serious? Who told you that?"

"The medical examiner," I said.

"I thought she was sick," Mo said. "That's what the agency told us."

"There's been some issues with record keeping," I said. I felt like I was lying and telling the truth at the same time. The issue was that Lou had a job to do in Rhinebeck and it was inextricably linked with trying to keep the Colchis family secrets intact.

An alarm went off on Mo's phone. She sighed. "I'm supposed to go into the shop and touch base with Jake. I need to do the bank deposit, too, but it can wait."

"You can go ahead and go, Mo," I said. "It's okay."

"Seems very not okay, Briseis," she said.

"We need that deposit to get put in the bank," Mom said. "I don't want you to go, babe, but I kind of *need* you to."

Mo sighed and pinched the bridge of her nose. "I know. I know."

"Until Leti gets back to me, let's take things one step at a time," Mom said. She put her hand on my shoulder. "We can talk about Selene if it's bothering you, and we can damn sure see that her death gets a thorough investigation if it hasn't already. You've been learning all these new details and not telling us? Baby, that bothers me."

"I'm sorry," I said. "I didn't want to ruin this for us."

"We are not that fragile, baby," Mom said. "And you're not ruining anything." She took my hands in hers and held them tight. "I've watched you and your power grow over all these years. Sometimes I wonder what it means, where it comes from. Now it looks like we have some answers."

"You don't think it sounds impossible?" I asked.

Mom shook her head. "What it sounds like doesn't make a difference to me. This isn't just something in your blood. It's *you.* It's who you are. How could I doubt what you're telling us when I've seen what you can do?"

Tears streamed down my face. There were still questions that I needed answers to but they could wait. Mom put her arms around me and pulled me close. Mo came over and wrapped us up like she always did when me and Mom got to ugly crying.

CHAPTER 27

Mom dropped Mo off at the train station so she could commute to Brooklyn and check in with Jake. The rest of the day passed in a haze. In the early afternoon, I snuggled up next to Mom on the couch as we waited for Auntie Leti to call back. I sent Karter a bunch of texts asking him if he was okay, but he didn't text back.

The doorbell rang.

"I got it," Mom said. She went out into the hall and a few seconds later, I heard Karter's voice.

I stood up to meet him but when he came into the front room, he looked upset. The whites of his eyes were bloodshot. "Can I talk to you?"

"What's wrong? I've been texting you."

"Can I talk to you alone?" he asked.

Mom huffed. "It's not a good time, Karter."

He stepped toward me with the most desperate look on his face. "I'm sorry, but you have to listen to me. You gotta leave. All of you. You gotta get out of here."

"What? Why?" I asked, confused.

Karter reached out and took hold of my arms. "Can you trust me? Can you please just listen to what I'm saying?"

"I'm listening, but you're not making sense," I said. "If this is about the Heart, you don't have to worry. I told my parents. They know. It's okay."

"That's not it. I mean, it's part of it, but listen—have you ever heard of something called the Living Elixir?"

I tried not to show any expression on my face as shock coursed through me. I'd seen instructions for something called Living Elixir but they'd been in a sketchbook behind a hidden door in my room. Something didn't sit right. How did he know about that?

Mom stepped forward to nudge him toward the door. "Karter, baby, this isn't a good—"

"Listen to me," Karter said, raising his voice. "You and I both saw that plant. We saw what it did, and I think that plant makes the elixir. Do you know what people would do to get their hands on something like that? Do you know how much danger you're in? You heard what that Lou guy said. You think this is a game?"

Mom stepped between us. "You need to go," she said. "Walk out before you get put out."

The doorbell rang again.

"What, are we having a damn party?" She angrily pulled the door open. "Nice to see you, doctor," Mom said loudly. "Karter here was just leaving."

Dr. Grant came into the front room and locked eyes with Karter, tilting her head to the side. I didn't know if she was somebody's mama, but she gave Karter one of those looks that meant she was not to be messed with. He turned around and left without another word. His footsteps pounded the porch steps and his truck skidded out of the driveway.

"My pops asked me to stop by," Dr. Grant said. "And I have some information to share with you, but first, do you mind if I ask you exactly how you much you know about Karter?"

I was caught off guard by the question. "Karter?"

"After I ran into you the other night"—she regarded my mom cautiously—"I did some digging." She took out a small notepad and flipped it open. "He was born here the same year you were, but he didn't go to school in Rhinebeck. Not under that name, anyway. The bookshop has only been open for six months. Before that, it was a coffee shop. The tags on his truck belong to a man who died two years ago. That can sometimes happen when someone forgets to transfer the title, but it struck me as odd. What else do you know about him?"

"He's been working in the bookshop way longer than six months. His mom has an office upstairs. She's an estate lawyer. She's the one who brought us out here. But wait, I thought your *investigation* was over." The guys she was supposed to be looking into, the men who'd come after me at the theater, were dead.

Dr. Grant caught my meaning. "It is. I wanted to make sure you know the people you're bringing around."

"Why?" Mom asked, an edge of annoyance in her voice. "I'm her mother. I think I can handle who she's bringing around."

"No, I know. I—" She stumbled over her words and looked down at the floor. "I'm sorry. I failed you."

"I don't understand," I said. "Are you talking about what happened with Marie?"

"What happened with Marie?" Mom asked.

We hadn't gotten to that yet but now was not the time.

"I'm talking about Selene," Dr. Grant said. "I was in the station the night she died. I was working with the department on another case when I heard the address, and I recognized it immediately. I rode in with the responding officer."

"You knew how she died?" I managed to ask. My throat felt dry, my chest heavy. "You knew somebody killed her? You—you were there? And you didn't say anything to me about it?"

"She was my friend," Dr. Grant said. "My friend and I couldn't save her," she continued. "When I realized who you were, I swore I wouldn't let anything happen to you."

Mom reached out and put a hand on her arm. Her tone was firm but comforting. "What happened wasn't your fault. I don't think you should be shouldering that kind of guilt."

"But I do." Dr. Grant sighed. "I do, except I'm not sitting around feeling sorry for myself. I've used all my resources to try and solve Selene's murder and Circe's disappearance."

"Hold up," Mom cut in. "This Circe woman is missing? I thought she was dead. She willed this place to Bri."

"She was declared dead earlier this year. That wasn't made clear to you?" Dr. Grant asked.

Me and Mom shook our heads.

"She disappeared after Selene died," Dr. Grant said. "We never found any evidence of foul play. It's possible she set something up to make sure you inherited the house in the event of her death but that's something the estate lawyer should be able to answer for you." Her phone rang and she glanced at the screen.

"I have to take this but I'll be in touch." Mom walked her out and I sat down on the couch.

My chest was tight and I could feel a headache creeping up from my temples. Mom came back and plopped down next to me.

"I guess we found the catch, right?" I asked. "We thought this was too good to be true. Big house that's paid off, but it comes with all the sad memories of my dead relatives and a bunch of deadly plants."

"I thought the catch would be bad plumbing or termites, not secret bloodlines and goddesses and a Poison Garden," said Mom as she closed her eyes and rubbed her neck. "They should definitely have put that in the paperwork. I'm gonna find some Tylenol and see if your auntie has come up with anything else." She gave me a hug. "It's gonna be okay, baby. I promise."

She disappeared upstairs, and I went back to the hidden room in the apothecary, this time armed with two flashlights and a lighter from the kitchen drawer.

I lit the black candles that flanked the statue of Hecate. The picture of me sat among the offerings on the altar. A shiver ran through me as the light from the candles danced across the space. Auntie Leti kept her altar stocked with fresh flowers, rum, cigars, and black coffee, and while I didn't know the ins and outs of her practice, I knew it was important to keep the stuff on the altar fresh.

I went to the apothecary and grabbed the waste bin behind the counter. I swept the rotted garlic and onions into the basket, making a note of where everything was, then went to the kitchen and brought in fresh garlic and a damp rag to dust off the figure.

If I was willing to believe everything I'd learned about the Colchis family, Medea, and her brother Absyrtus, then that meant I also had to believe that the goddess this shrine was dedicated to was the one responsible for the immunity to poison I now possessed. If Hecate was real and willing to reward Medea for her loyalty, maybe she'd do the same for me.

The doorbell rang again, and Mom let out a string of curse words before stomping down the stairs. I went into the hallway to see who it was.

"Mrs. Redmond?" Mom sounded surprised. "Is everything okay? You look . . . rough."

As Mrs. Redmond limped into the foyer, I tried my hardest to keep my expression unchanged, but I was horrified by her appearance.

Her right eye was swollen completely shut. The skin around it was so purple it was almost black. The left side of her face and neck was splotchy. Her left knee was bandaged but a dark red stain was seeping through. The wounds on her hands were weeping, and her hair was a mess.

Mom shook her head. "What the hell happened to you?"

"There has been some confusion with the bank," Mrs. Redmond said, avoiding my gaze. "Apparently Circe and Selene owed several years of back taxes, and there is now a lien on the property. The house and land will be sold at auction. You must vacate immediately."

"Excuse me?" I said, stunned. "You said the house was mine, that they wanted me to have it. You said the taxes were paid through a trust."

"I know what I said," Mrs. Redmond snapped. Her professional exterior was gone. "I was finalizing the title search for you and found the error. Circe should have been a better businesswoman. You'll need to surrender the keys." She shot me a pointed glance. "All of them. And vacate the property in twenty-four hours."

"Wait," I said. "Maybe we can talk to the bank. We can pay the taxes, make a payment plan or something."

"Why didn't you know about this?" Mom asked, glaring at Mrs. Redmond. "You're a property lawyer, right? Shouldn't you have known earlier?"

"This is news to me, too, but I assure you, I have done everything in my power to honor Miss Colchis's wishes. Turns out she was a liar and wasn't being honest when it came to being free and clear on the property. Do you know how much time I've wasted trying to facilitate this handover to you?"

"I'll go to the bank myself," I said.

Mrs. Redmond opened her briefcase and pulled out a stack of papers. "Everything is right here. There's nothing that can be done." On top of the stack was a notice ordering us to vacate the property. She tossed it onto the coffee table. She looked at me and held out her hand. "The keys."

Mom stepped between us. "Get out."

"Wait a minute," I said. "Mrs. Redmond, what's wrong with you? Why are you acting like this? And did you know that Circe was missing this whole time? How did she know to leave me letters and—"

"You can't even begin to understand the time and resources

I have put into this transaction," she said angrily. She stepped closer to me. "Don't make this more difficult than it has to be. Give me the keys." She reached out and Mom slapped her hand away.

"Reach toward my daughter one more time and see what happens," said Mom.

"Are you threatening me?" Mrs. Redmond asked.

"Take it however you want," Mom said, squaring up. "You look like somebody already went upside your head once today. You might not wanna make it worse."

Mrs. Redmond peered around her. "When you vacate the property, make sure you leave the keys, or I'll have a warrant issued for your arrest. The police have already been apprised of the situation. I'm sorry it had to be this way."

"You don't seem sorry at all," I said. "Maybe if you were better at your job, this wouldn't have happened. Dr. Grant told me Karter didn't grow up here like he said. What else are you two lying about?"

Mrs. Redmond glared at me. "Dr. Grant should mind the business that pays her." She turned and walked toward the front door. Mom and I followed her out.

She limped to her car, pausing on the bottom step. "Maybe it's for the best." She glanced at our car, sitting at an odd angle. The tires were once again cut clean through.

"Seems like people don't really want you around here anyway."

Mom kicked off her house shoes, and, with an angry grunt, dove forward. I grabbed a handful of her shirt, trying to keep her from leaping off the porch and pummeling Mrs. Redmond.

"Mom! It's not worth it! Stop!"

Mrs. Redmond grinned with air of superiority, like she'd won this little battle. As she sped off, we retreated into the house. Mom was angry-crying as she called Mo to tell her what happened. I sat down on the floor and thumbed through the paperwork Mrs. Redmond had left behind.

"There's an eviction notice," I said, puzzled by all the legal terminology on the paper. "How can they evict us if this is my house?"

"You gotta pay taxes," Mom said while she still had Mo on the phone.

"Yeah, but shouldn't Mrs. Redmond have known that? Like, wouldn't there be notices or something? They skipped right to eviction?" I wasn't an expert, but it didn't make sense to me. I flipped through page after page of paperwork but didn't find any notices about taxes owed or past due bills. Some of the paperwork had lines that were blacked out. There was no phone number or address for the bank. "How do we even know who we're supposed to talk to about this?" Frustrated, I tossed the papers back onto the table. "I need some air."

I went and stood on the porch. This wasn't right. I couldn't just sit around and wait for Mrs. Redmond to show back up, police in tow. I thought about calling Nyx to see if she could give me a ride, but a Lyft was only five minutes away. I set a pickup, slipped back inside, shoved the stack of paperwork into my bag, and kissed my mom on the top of the head.

"Where are you going?" she asked.

"I'll be back. Try not to worry too much, okay?"

I went out the front door and got into my Lyft.

There were a half-dozen banks in Rhinebeck and I decided to go to all of them with my ID and Mrs. Redmond's paperwork to see what I could find out.

The first three stops turned up nothing. It took a half an hour at each place for them to check their records and tell me they didn't have any information for me. As the afternoon drug on, I was afraid I wouldn't get through my list before the other banks closed. I walked between the different locations, my ankle throbbing, frustration building with each dead end.

At the fourth place, a branch of Hudson Valley Bank & Trust, I gave my ID to the woman at the counter. She looked puzzled and I felt like I was going to scream.

"Let me guess," I said. "You have no idea what I'm talking about?"

The woman shook her head. "No, it's— Can you hang on for a moment?"

I sat in the lobby while she went off with my documents. She came back a few minutes later and led me to a private office where an older woman in a harsh green blouse was seated behind a wide desk, my stack of paperwork in front of her. A small fern sat on the windowsill and it slowly shifted toward me.

"Miss Greene," she said. She leaned forward and stuck out her hand. "I'm Evelyn Haley, the branch manager here. Please have a seat."

I sat down as the other woman left the office, closing the door behind her.

"I'm really sorry to bother you," I said.

"It's no bother at all," she said. "I have to tell you, Miss

Greene, I think you may want to have a parent or guardian here with you before we proceed."

"Why?" I asked. "I mean, I know taxes are owed on the property, but if we could please make a payment arrangement or something. We just need a little time." I was so angry at how casually Mrs. Redmond had ripped the rug out from under us. "Please. Tell me what to do. I'll find a way to pay the money."

"Miss Greene, I can see that this has caused you quite a bit of stress, but I have to admit that I'm very confused right now."

"Confused?" I asked.

She reached into her drawer and pulled out a stack of neatly organized papers, setting them on the desk. She placed her hand on top of them. "Miss Greene, *these* documents are the official documents for the property on 307 Old Post Road. They were drafted in January of this year when Miss Colchis was legally declared deceased. You have to understand that when there is no will—"

"Wait. Mrs. Redmond said that Circe left me the house in her will."

The woman shook her head. "There was no will, no paperwork, nothing. The house is paid for, and the taxes have been paid through a trust for over one hundred years."

"I don't understand." It felt like a rock was sitting in the pit of my stomach. "Why do we have to leave, then?"

"Miss Greene, you shouldn't be in the house in the first place. Not yet, anyway." Ms. Haley pursed her lips. "These documents"—she touched the ones Mrs. Redmond had left with me—"are invalid. We logged their information as invalid because they went missing."

CHAPTER 28

I gripped the armrests of the chair. "What?"

"Until Miss Colchis was legally declared dead, the house couldn't be auctioned or sold or any other such thing. In January of this year, when the declaration was made and certified, we prepared to auction it off. However, we received a visit from a woman representing an adoption agency in Red Hook. She told us that Circe had a living relative and provided your information to us. The documents were meant to be given to you several weeks ago, but there was an unforeseen circumstance that delayed the processing. Mrs. Taylor, the client specialist in charge of this transfer, didn't come into work. She was in possession of the original paperwork, but unfortunately . . ." Her voice wavered. "Unfortunately, we were informed several days ago that her body was found nearby. The police now believe there was foul play involved."

The news report I'd seen in Mrs. Redmond's office had said something about a body being found.

"We immediately established new account numbers for Miss Colchis's estate to protect the security of the estate. But the process of reestablishing everything took much longer than we had anticipated." She took a long, deep breath, cleared her throat, and straightened up. "Where did you get the voided paperwork?"

"A woman came to our apartment in Brooklyn. She reached out to my mom first, and then she showed up in person. She had this paperwork with her and said we could move in. We drove all the way up here—"

"She was able to give you access to the property?"

"She gave me the keys."

The woman looked bewildered. "We'll need to sign the actual paperwork, and your legal guardians will need to be present, but this eviction notice is fake." She shook her head as if she were disgusted. "I've heard of these types of scams. There are con artists that exploit families of the recently deceased, but this doesn't seem like she was trying to get money or even the property itself. It seems like she was trying to put you in the house under false pretenses. It's so odd." She shook her head, flustered. "We need to call the police."

My mind went in circles. "Were you here when the woman from the adoption agency came in? Did you see her?"

"Yes."

"What did she look like?"

She thought carefully. "It was some time ago, but she was tall, black hair with a gray streak right down the center of her head."

Mrs. Redmond.

"Call the police," I said. "Call Dr. Grant. Right now."

The woman immediately picked up her phone and started

dialing. I stepped out into the lobby and sent texts to Mom and Mo, letting them know what was going on. Then, I messaged Karter.

Bri: Did you know what your mom was doing this whole time?

I didn't want to believe that he had known. After everything I'd shown him, everything I'd shared with him. I felt stupid. My phone buzzed with his reply.

Karter: You should go back to Brooklyn. Right now. It's not safe for you here.

I tried calling Mom. No answer.

A flurry of activity in the front of the lobby drew my attention. Dr. Grant came rushing in.

"What's going on?" she asked

I steered her into the bank manager's office. "You were right about Karter, and his mom is even worse. She's been lying to me and my family and to everyone this whole time." I looked at the bank representative. "Please fill her in. I gotta go."

"No," Dr. Grant said. "Don't leave."

"I'm gonna go get my mom and we'll meet you back here." I didn't wait for her to protest. I quickly left the bank and called Mom, then Mo, and then Mom again. No one answered. I set a pickup for another Lyft. My phone rang.

"Mo!" I yelled.

"What's wrong?"

"Where are you?" I asked.

"I'm on my way back, but it'll be a while. Your mom was so upset. What's going on?"

"When's the last time you talked to her? To Mom?"

"Earlier, when she asked me to come back. Why?" Fear invaded her voice. "Briseis, what is going on?"

"You gotta get here. Are you taking the train?"

"No. I rented a car. I'm driving, but I'm not even halfway back yet."

"Mo, Mrs. Redmond was lying. There's nothing wrong with the house, at least not in the way she said."

"Oh," Mo said, heaving a sigh of relief. "Okay. That's good. Wait—why are y'all so upset then?"

"She's not the person who was supposed to get in touch with us about the house. All those papers were with a woman from the bank who disappeared and then turned up dead."

Mo gasped.

"Mrs. Redmond knew about me," I said. "She pretended to be from the adoption agency and gave the bank our information to have the house papers drawn up. Circe didn't will us this house, and I don't think she left me those notes. It was Mrs. Redmond the whole time."

"Why?" Mo asked.

"The Heart," I said. "That's all this has ever been about."

My Lyft pulled up and I jumped in. "You gotta get here," I told Mo. "I'm gonna go get Mom and meet Dr. Grant back at the bank."

"I'm coming," Mo said. She hung up.

I called Mom ten more times, back-to-back. I texted her over and over. Each time she didn't answer, my chest grew tighter, and time seemed to slow to a crawl. I couldn't allow my mind to wander to the negative possibilities. Maybe she was in the shower. Maybe she was in another room where she couldn't hear her phone. I told myself I was overreacting, but Karter's message replayed in my mind.

You should go back to Brooklyn. Right now. It's not safe for you here.

We pulled into the driveway and I jumped out before the car came to a full stop. My ankle throbbed as I raced inside.

"Mom!"

The silence that met me was louder than the rush of blood in my ears as my heart leaped into a furious rhythm. I sprinted up the stairs, ignoring the pain in my leg, and checked her room, the guest rooms, then ran back downstairs. An all-consuming sense of dread overtook me.

I ran into the apothecary. "Mom!"

I fumbled with my phone as I tried to text Mo again. I stopped. There, on the counter, was a sheet of paper with four words scribbled on it.

Look out the window

I ran to the window and pushed it open. My mom stood at the tree line and Mrs. Redmond stood behind her.

I dropped my phone and sprinted outside. All around me, the grass twisted violently, angrily. As I cut across the rear lawn and approached Mrs. Redmond, Mom flinched. I stopped in my tracks. Mrs. Redmond held a knife to my mom's throat.

Her hair was wild, her one good eye wide. "One more step and I will kill her."

"Please don't hurt her," I pleaded. I took another step forward.

Mrs. Redmond pushed the knife against Mom's throat. "Are you stupid?"

"What are you doing? I know about the house and the paperwork and—"

"You don't know anything!" she screamed. "I don't have time for this! I've been waiting too long already!" She gestured toward the curtain of vines. "Open it. Take us to the garden, and if you try anything, if a single blade of grass moves in my direction, I'll kill her. Understand?"

I locked eyes with my mother. "Stay on the path and don't touch anything when we get to the garden."

"Quiet!" Mrs. Redmond shouted. Her hand was steady on the knife's handle. She would do exactly what she'd threatened without a second thought.

The curtain of vines guarding the hidden trail parted as I approached. We stepped onto the path as the sun sank below the horizon. Pushing forward, Mrs. Redmond kept the knife at my mom's neck, cursing and complaining with every step. The trees groaned, contorting their trunks to bend toward me, their boughs like eager arms reaching to embrace me. I had to ignore them. They might lean in and pluck Mrs. Redmond out of her own skin, but not before she cut my mom's throat. I focused on the ground in front of me, which became harder to do in the encroaching darkness.

When we came to the clearing Mrs. Redmond gazed up at the garden wall as thick ropes of euphorbia snaked their way to mingle with the ivy.

"I tried to get here on my own," Mrs. Redmond said

breathlessly. "Knowing *it* was there and not being able to reach it . . ." She laughed lightly.

Her injuries made sense now. "How'd that work out for you?" I asked angrily.

Mom let out a choked yelp as Mrs. Redmond pushed the knife against her throat. "Wanna keep running your mouth?"

I clenched my teeth so hard I thought they'd break.

"I tried to reason with Circe and with Selene," Mrs. Redmond said, pushing my mom toward the gate. "They wouldn't listen. Maybe you'll be smarter than they were." She shot me a pointed glance. "Open the gate."

My mind was racing. Mrs. Redmond had the knife so tight against my mom's neck that droplets of blood were running down her throat. I didn't have any other options. I took the keys from around my neck and unlocked the gate.

"Mrs. Redmond, please don't do this." I didn't know what her plan was, but she seemed absolutely desperate. She had no idea how dangerous this was.

"In," she said firmly.

I led the way into the garden.

Mrs. Redmond surveyed the front part of the garden. "Keep moving."

"We can't go back there."

"Why not?" Mrs. Redmond asked.

"You know why," I snapped.

She smirked. "So you've started to put it all together?"

She prodded my mom forward. At the threshold to the Poison Garden, and as the full moon began to shine down on us, I turned to face her.

"Please," I said. "Mom can't go in, and neither can you. It's not safe."

Mrs. Redmond glared at me. "You think I don't know that? You think you're special? Descended from Medea herself, immunity running in your veins! What good does it do when you don't even know what to do with it?"

"How do you know so much about me?"

"You think you're the only one descended from greatness? Think harder, sweetie." Mrs. Redmond scowled as I struggled to understand what that meant. "You're a descendant of Medea, but I am descended from the man who made her what she was—Jason himself, great-grandson of Hermes." She tilted her face to the sky in silent reverence.

The story said Jason had taken another wife after Medea, and now I understood why Mrs. Redmond was on the verge of killing my mother so she could get her hands on the Heart. She and I were on opposite sides in a millennia-long family feud.

"Jason didn't make Medea who she was," I said angrily, remembering the story Alec had helped me decipher. "Her abilities came from something else, not from some murderous, power-hungry asshole."

"Nobody even remembers her name. Everyone knows of Jason and the Golden Fleece. Medea is an afterthought. She was pathetic."

"You think you know everything about her? About me? You're wrong."

"I know you're uniquely situated to cultivate the Absyrtus Heart," said Mrs. Redmond. "You are the only one left who can. But can you wield its power? Are you fit to handle that kind of responsibility? You didn't even feel a pull to this place. I had to lead you here."

She was wrong. I *had* felt a connection with the house, the people who'd lived here before, and the garden itself. It was why I didn't want to leave, but her taunts revealed what I'd suspected. "You forged all the letters."

"All of them except the map. Circe left that behind. Did you enjoy your little scavenger hunt? This place is impossible to get into even with the key to the outer garden, but I did try, Briseis." She held up her mangled arm. "And then to realize it was locked away even farther than I'd imagined *and* I didn't have the god-damned key?" She laughed maniacally. "Maybe it was luck or fate or magic that led you to the final key, but now that you have it, you can get me the one thing I've been searching for my entire life."

A sickening thought bloomed in my mind. "Did you kill the woman from the bank?"

Mom inhaled sharply.

Mrs. Redmond narrowed her eyes. "I did what I had to."

"You said she was your friend."

She flashed a crooked, wicked grin. That had been a lie, too.

"I won't get it for you," I said. "You can't have the Heart."

Mrs. Redmond raised her hand and brought the butt of the knife down onto my mom's head. She crumpled to the ground. Mrs. Redmond bent over her, pressing the tip of the knife over her heart.

"Don't!" I screamed.

"I want the Absyrtus Heart, and I want it now." Her voice

cracked. For the first time, I saw something in her eyes that wasn't pure malice or fake kindness. It was raw desperation.

"I need to know why," I said. "Why do you want it so bad? You really wanna live forever? What about Karter?" I was so angry at him. He'd lied to me, broken my trust in the most awful way by pretending to be my friend when I needed one so badly. But he'd also warned me that I wasn't safe. I wanted to believe that there was some part of him that was on my side.

"I don't give a damn about him," Mrs. Redmond growled. She shook her head and clenched her teeth like she'd said something that was supposed to be a secret. "My family has always sought the Heart, and their reasons were petty and selfish. I want it for something bigger and more profound than they could have imagined." She drew a slow breath. "My forefathers still walk the earth. Imagine it. Gods among us. And if I have to leave Karter behind to take my rightful place among them . . . so be it."

Her contempt for her own son was clear, but I struggled to comprehend the rest of what she was saying. "What do you mean, they still walk the earth?"

"Hermes lives," she whispered. "As do so many of the others. I come from them. I belong with them. I've been searching and I've found hints of them—clues." She was trembling as she spoke. She looked like she would come undone at any minute. "I know they're out there, but I can't keep searching in this mortal body. I need more time. The Heart will give that to me—all the time I could possibly need and when I find them, they will welcome me home." She pressed the knife down and a circle of blood seeped through my mom's shirt.

"Stop!" I yelled. "I'll get it for you! Please don't hurt her!"

Mrs. Redmond stood and marched toward me. She stuck the knife under my chin, her eyes wild, her hand trembling slightly. "Take me to it."

Her motivation for this elaborate inheritance scheme made more sense when I understood she expected to take her place among some kind of ancient, godlike beings. I didn't think it was possible that she could be telling the whole truth, but it didn't matter. *She* believed it, and she was willing to hurt me and the people I cared about to get what she wanted. I tried to think of a way out of this while protecting Mom and the Heart, but I couldn't see how.

I glanced at my mom's crumpled frame. Her chest rose and fell, and the whites of her eyes were visible under their half-open lids.

Mrs. Redmond gestured to the Poison Garden. "You took my son in there. You showed him the Heart."

"I wish I hadn't," I said. "Do you have any idea how poisonous it is?"

"Obviously," she said, rolling her eyes and glancing at her watch. "That's why I need you. I'm going in with you, but know that if anything happens to me, Mo might have an unfortunate accident when she arrives home. Bad things happen all the time, Briseis. You know that though, don't you? But Mo won't have some unworthy abomination to protect her."

My blood turned to ice as I realized she was referring to Marie protecting me from the men at the cemetery. "How did you know about that?"

She gripped the knife. "Karter set up the trip to the theater perfectly, but not everything went to plan. I had to adjust course."

"Karter?" I'd played right into their scheme. Betrayal burned away any shred of hope I had that he might not have been as bad as his mother. "You had those men come after me?"

Mrs. Redmond pulled a cloth mask out of her pocket and strapped it across her face. But even with her mouth covered I could tell she was smiling.

"Move," she said.

Mrs. Redmond prodded me in, the tip of her knife at my back. I led her to the back wall, where the vines pulled away from the hidden door. As I fumbled with the keys on the lanyard I stole a quick glance at her. She wasn't coughing, but her eyes were bloodshot and she'd pulled her shirt up over her nose and mouth. Apparently the mask wasn't providing her enough protection. I lingered at the door, hoping the poison in the air would take its toll on her.

"Hurry up!" she said.

She shoved me into the metal door and my head collided with the carved crest. A searing pain shot across my skull. I grabbed my head to stem the ache.

"Immune to poison but not head injuries, I see," said Mrs. Redmond.

I wrenched the door open and stumbled into the darkened space. Mrs. Redmond stepped in behind me, so close I could smell the sweat on her. She grabbed my shoulder, digging in her fingers, and pushed me down the stairs as the crimson brush aimed its poison darts at her.

"If I'm not back at the house by eleven, Mo is a dead woman," she quickly reminded me.

I held my hand out in front of the crimson brush blooms. They folded closed and retreated.

We entered the underground chamber as the light from the moon outside shone down the shaft in the ceiling, bathing the still-withered plant in pale light. I unlocked the enclosure.

Mrs. Redmond peered inside. "You haven't fed it?"

"Fed it?" I hated the way that sounded, like it was some kind of monster. "I pricked my finger."

"Pricked your finger? Who are you, fucking Sleeping Beauty? Hold out your hand."

Mrs. Redmond grabbed my wrist and dragged the knife across my palm, opening a deep gash. I screamed as she shoved my hand into the enclosure. Blood rushed from the wound and spilled across the surface of the Heart.

This time it did more than shift inside the glass enclosure. The Heart contracted, then flushed pink on the rounded bulbous lobe where my blood had fallen. Ribbons of red rippled down the stalks that snaked into the dirt. And then, as slivers of moonlight filtered down from the hole in the ceiling, the Absyrtus Heart began to beat.

CHAPTER 29

The Heart beat like it remembered powering a flesh-and-blood body. The steady pulse was audible and reverberated in my bones. The fresh infusion of my blood pumped through its stalk and down into the ground.

"Pull it up," Mrs. Redmond ordered.

I'd barely brushed one of its dried and crumbling leaves before and it made me feel like I'd broken every bone in my hand. How was I supposed to uproot it completely?

Mrs. Redmond backed away from the enclosure. Desperate as she was, she knew its power, and she was afraid of it. I thought of tossing it at her. I was sure it would kill her, but Mo wasn't back yet, and I didn't know who Mrs. Redmond had waiting for her to return.

I reached in and grasped the base of the plant, my hand still oozing blood. Blistering cold numbed my palm. One hard tug, and the Heart's roots broke from the soil. The icy cold spread up my arm and into the right side of my chest. The shock of it took my breath away. I stumbled, falling onto my knees, dropping the plant. It continued to beat, flopping around on the floor like a fish out of water.

"Get up!" Mrs. Redmond barked.

I grabbed the Heart, tripping up the steps as the cold invaded every part of me. It had spread to the side of my neck and face. A wave of nausea washed over me. I leaned against the damp rock wall to steady myself as the Heart dangled from my hand, bits of earth and blood dripping from its freshly exposed roots. Mrs. Redmond screamed at me to keep moving.

Staggering up and out to the Poison Garden, I fell to my knees, dropping the Heart and clutching my chest. The numbing pain began to subside—but not before Mrs. Redmond was threatening me again. I picked up the plant and the cold intensified. I couldn't catch my breath.

Lurching forward, I managed to make it to the moon gate before I had to put the Heart down again. Mrs. Redmond ripped off her mask and stood over my mom, who had rolled over, clutching her head, still dazed. Mrs. Redmond grabbed her under her arms and pulled her to her feet.

"I can't breathe," I heaved. My heart felt like it was beating too fast. Lights danced around my vision. "I can't. I can't carry it."

Mrs. Redmond plunged the knife into my mom's arm. She screamed as Mrs. Redmond twisted the handle.

"Stop!" I pleaded.

She pulled the knife out and my mom swayed on her feet, but Mrs. Redmond held her tight. "Back to the house. Let's go."

We left the garden with Mrs. Redmond prodding my mom along behind me. Vines slithered around my ankles; groans and rustling surrounded us on all sides as we staggered down the path.

"If a single thing comes toward me, I'll slit her throat," Mrs. Redmond said.

I moved forward as quickly as I could, but the Heart's poison had spread into every joint of my body. Every step was excruciating, like my bones were grinding together.

When we finally emerged onto the rear lawn, my arms and legs were heavy, my vision blurry through my glasses. Mrs. Redmond shoved my mom toward the house, and she groaned. She hadn't said a word since she'd regained consciousness, and she still had a dazed look on her face.

When we got inside, I attempted to set the plant down again, but Mrs. Redmond shook her head. "To the apothecary."

She marched us back and sat my mom in a chair, keeping the knife trained on her.

"Go get something to tie her with," she ordered.

I put the Heart on the counter and tried to steady myself. Was this really what being immune to the Absyrtus Heart felt like? There was no way anyone else could have come in contact with this plant without dropping dead.

I found a roll of duct tape in the hall closet and took it back to Mrs. Redmond.

"Lie down on the floor," she said, shoving me in the chest. "Face down, with your hands behind your head, and don't even think about moving."

I didn't hesitate. Mom was still bleeding from the wound in her arm, and a trail of dried blood traced down her forehead where Mrs. Redmond had struck her. I lay still and Mrs. Redmond secured my mom to the chair with the tape, then stood behind her with the blade at her throat.

"Get up," she said to me. "Get the oleander." She motioned toward the ladder.

I clung to the rungs, barely able to coordinate my arms and legs enough to climb up and grab the jar. When I finally managed to retrieve it and set it on the counter, I felt like I'd run a marathon. My bones ached. My muscles spasmed. My hand throbbed. The gash in my palm looked like a bloody, toothless mouth. Mrs. Redmond took out her phone and made a call.

"Come to the apothecary," she said.

A few minutes later, there was the sound of a car door closing and the front door opening. Footsteps came down the hall, and Karter appeared in the doorway.

As he stood there and looked over the scene—my mother duct-taped to a chair, bleeding, me on the verge of collapse—his expression didn't change. He closed the door and turned the big brass lock. As it clicked closed, a new rush of panic set in.

"I thought you said no one else was going to get hurt." Karter stared at my mom.

"And I thought you said you were going to stop complaining," Mrs. Redmond said coldly. "I wouldn't have had to hurt anybody if they'd cooperated. Did you bring the other supplies?"

Karter set down a bag he'd been carrying. He rummaged through it and pulled out a stone bowl carved with strange symbols, two small vials of liquid, and a mason jar full of amber-colored honey, setting them on the counter.

"Karter, what are you doing?" I asked. "How could you do this to me?"

A wicked grin spread across Mrs. Redmond's face. "What,

you thought he liked you enough to betray his own mother? You thought you had a friend?" She laughed. "He's been helping me this entire time. Slashing your tires, keeping you busy when I needed him to." She shook her head. "Why are all the people in your family so stupid?"

"Mom—" Karter began.

"Shut up," Mrs. Redmond snapped. "Come over here and hold this."

Karter walked over and took the knife from her. He pressed it against my mother's neck without any hesitation. Mrs. Redmond went to the counter and arranged the items he had set out.

"Do you have any idea how long I've dreamed of this moment?" she asked, her voice trembling. "Collecting the rarest ingredients on the planet, bringing them together, only to feel like a failure because I couldn't get this one missing piece." She smoothed out her hair and pressed her hands to the countertop. "Selene was stubborn. So was Circe. Their convictions, their loyalty to Medea's memory, and their affection for the ancient ways wouldn't let them stray from their course. When they were out of the picture, I thought my quest had come to end." A devious smile crept onto her lips. "But I didn't know about you, the girl they tried to save."

A sudden and terrible rumble reverberated through the ground. Dust rained down from the ceiling and fear darkened Mrs. Redmond's face.

"We have to hurry," she said. She grabbed my arm, digging her fingers into my skin. "Grind up the Absyrtus Heart. The whole thing. Now."

She shoved me to the counter and I stared at Karter. He looked away. Coward.

Mrs. Redmond followed my gaze. "Kill her if Miss Briseis here tries anything."

Karter let his gaze drift to the floor but he nodded.

My fingers still ached as I took hold of the plant. The Heart had stopped beating. The leaves had wilted and the lobes were ashen. The smell of rot was just as intense as the cold sensation. I ripped the Heart to pieces and placed them in the mortar, then crushed them together.

Mrs. Redmond pushed the stone bowl toward me. "Dump it in here."

I tipped the mortar, and the ground pieces of the Heart slid into the bowl. She picked up the two vials of liquid—one gold, one silver—and dumped them in. She added three spoonfuls of honey. The contents shimmered and a thick ash-gray mist billowed out. Mrs. Redmond stood transfixed, but I took several steps back. The bowl rattled and the jars on the shelves clanged together.

"Put your hand in there," Mrs. Redmond said. "Complete the transfiguration."

I didn't move. Mrs. Redmond motioned toward Karter. He sank his fingers into the wound in my mom's arm. She cried out weakly, then sobbed, her body convulsing with each heave.

"Okay! Okay!" I shoved my cut hand into the bowl, trying to recreate the feeling I had when Dr. Grant's father had shown me how to transfigure the contents we'd put on the copper plate. I closed my eyes and tried to concentrate. A warm sensation built in my palm, chasing away the cold. The liquids and pieces of the Heart combined under my hand. I pulled back as my muscles spasmed.

Mrs. Redmond stared into the bowl as a deafening crack split the air. Then, silence. She grabbed the bowl and poured the contents into an empty glass vial. The liquid was red as blood and thick like honey.

CHAPTER 30

"The Living Elixir," Mrs. Redmond said breathlessly. She held up the vial, admiring its contents. "It has had a thousand names over as many years, but the Absyrtus Heart was always the most important piece of the formula. Do you have any idea what this means for me?"

Karter was staring at his mother—not with reverence or admiration, but sadness. His jaw was set, his fingers twitching on the handle of the knife. I couldn't stand it. I had to put an end to this.

As Mrs. Redmond gawked at the elixir, I edged around the counter, lowered my shoulder and rushed her, catching her in the gut. We crashed to the floor and my shoulder struck the counter on the way down, sending a stab of pain through my arm. The glass vial flew out of her hand and skidded across the floor.

"Get it!" she screamed.

Karter leaped over me, grasping at the elixir. I grabbed his leg and he fell face-first onto the floor with a sickening crack. He was still for a second, then scrambled forward, groaning, holding his unnaturally situated jaw. He writhed on the ground and

I tried to grab hold of him, but he thrust his leg out, catching me on the side of my head. Everything went black.

"Briseis," Karter mumbled. "I—I'm sorry."

As my vision came back into focus, I could feel blood trickling from the top of my ear and into my open mouth. It tasted the way the Absyrtus Heart smelled, like wet metal. Karter grabbed the vial as I clawed at him.

"Get away from it!" Mrs. Redmond screamed. She really didn't give a single thought to her son. All she cared about was the elixir. She'd moved behind my mom, holding a fistful of plant matter. The jar of dried oleander leaves lay at her feet. "Selene tried to keep me from the Heart." Anger burned in her eyes. "She paid for that with her life."

It took a moment for me to register what she'd admitted to. I scrambled to my feet. "You—you killed her? *You* killed Selene?" A numbing ache coursed through me that had nothing to do with handling the Heart.

Mrs. Redmond glared at me. "It seems I'll have the very rare privilege of making you a motherless child twice in your life." She shoved the oleander into Mom's mouth and clamped her hand over her lips. I lunged toward them, but Karter caught me by the arms, holding me back. My mother struggled against her bindings, but she'd lost so much blood, she didn't have the strength to fight back.

"*Mom!*" My legs went out from under me. Blistering sores erupted on her face. She gasped as Mrs. Redmond shoved another handful of leaves in her mouth, her own fingers blistering as she did.

The damage was done. Mrs. Redmond rushed to the sink,

holding her hand under the tap. Karter loosened his grip on me and I wrenched away from him, scrambling to my mother's side. I pulled the leaves from her mouth and cradled her head as her eyes rolled back. A gurgling sound erupted from her throat.

I couldn't breathe. I couldn't see straight. Karter handed his mother the vial, and they embraced. I hated them with everything in me.

Suddenly, Mo was kicking in the door, screaming and scrambling across the floor. She tore the tape from my mom's hands and feet. We lowered her to the ground and Mo held her, tears running down her face.

My mom didn't speak or cry. The color drained from her face. I knew the poison was quick, and Mrs. Redmond had given her enough to kill fifty people. She became so still, she didn't look real.

And then, she was gone.

A ragged scream broke from Mo and split the air. Anger and grief pooled inside me. I stood and balled my fists at my sides. There was no reason to hold back anymore. Roots and vines by the hundreds crashed through the windows and burst right through the floor, tearing up the wooden slats. They twisted like tentacles, slithering in through every crevice.

Mrs. Redmond screamed as vines wrapped around her waist. A smaller one tangled itself around Karter's leg, and he slashed at it with the knife. I focused on Mrs. Redmond, moving toward her as I completely gave myself over to my anger and my grief. A trio of slender roots broke through the window and gripped her legs. I wanted them to squeeze the life out of her.

Karter broke free and sprinted for the hallway, but he stopped short.

A hulking beast-like shape darkened the doorway.

My heart, already beating wildly in my chest, almost stopped.

A guttural growl erupted from the shadows, and a dog the size of a bear lumbered into the room, its wet lips pulled back over its gleaming yellow teeth. Karter tripped over his own feet as he scrambled away from the creature. Mrs. Redmond struggled against the vines. I was frozen where I stood.

Just then, a tall, hooded figure appeared from the shadowy hall.

They wore a sweeping black robe that melded so perfectly with the darkness that I thought my mind, racked with fear and anger and grief, was playing tricks on me. Only Mo's terrified gasp let me know it was real.

As the figure crouched to fit through the doorframe, their hood fell down around their shoulders. A cloud of lustrous coils framed her head. Her skin, the rich color of black calla lilies, shone in the darkness. Circling her head was some sort of crown with six or seven points radiating like the golden rays of the sun. Her black eyes narrowed as she glided into the room. The dog heeled to her like a puppy, and she stroked it between its ears.

I tried not to scream.

"Calm yourself," she said to the dog. Her voice was a symphony of thunder, wind, and fire.

Karter stumbled into the counter, sending the mortar and pestle clambering to the ground. The mysterious woman made a noise like a sigh and the dog leaped on top of him, clenching his shin in its mouth. Karter cried out, and Mrs. Redmond struggled again.

The woman turned to me. "Release her," she said, pleasantly enough.

I let out a long, slow breath. The vines dropped away from Mrs. Redmond and came slithering over to me. Mrs. Redmond stumbled and the tall woman caught her by the throat, lifting her off the floor like she weighed nothing. It was only in that moment that I realized the woman had to be pushing ten or eleven feet tall.

She took hold of Mrs. Redmond's hand, crushing it inside her own. Mrs. Redmond let out a howl like a wounded animal. The vial of Living Elixir fell from her fingers and landed on the counter. Karter squirmed in the grip of the black dog.

"Heel," said the woman. The dog retreated and Karter grabbed his leg to stanch the bleeding. The woman turned back to Mrs. Redmond. "Katrina Valek."

"Wha—what?" I stammered.

The woman narrowed her eyes at Mrs. Redmond in a way that sent a bolt of pure, unfiltered terror straight through me. "You've denied your own name? Melissa Redmond, Louise Farris, Angela Carroll. Lies."

My mind looped back on itself. Those were names from the apothecary's ledger. She'd been here, trying to get access to the Heart for years, decades.

"How did you find them?" the cloaked woman asked. She closed her hand tighter around Mrs. Redmond's—Katrina Valek's—throat when she didn't respond. "The guardians of the Heart. How did you find them?"

Katrina kicked her legs wildly. The woman loosened her grip slightly.

"Jason's line remains," Katrina gasped. "We've been hunting them since the Heart's inception. *We* should be the ones to reap the benefits of its magic." Blood trickled from the corner of her mouth.

"The keepers of the Heart determine who is and is not worthy of possessing it," said the woman.

"Why?" Katrina asked, angrily. "Why do they get to decide? Selene was selfish. She wanted to keep it for herself!"

"To protect it," said the woman. "And you slaughtered her like an animal."

I flinched. It hurt to hear what Mrs. Redmond—Katrina—had done to Selene. The woman paused for a moment, glancing back at me. Her gaze was hypnotic. There was something unnatural about the way she moved, the way she spoke.

"You will not wield it," said the cloaked woman. "You are not worthy of the power it will grant you."

"I deserve to be among them! Among the gods!"

The tall woman tilted her head back and let out a laugh that shook the walls and rattled the floor. "You deserve no such thing."

Katrina struck the woman in the face. She didn't even flinch. With a flick of her wrist, the woman tossed Katrina onto the floor. The dog descended on her, sinking its teeth into her shoulder. She wailed in agony.

I stumbled back to where Mo sat with Mom's lifeless body. My ears popped like the air pressure in the room had changed. A huge, black void appeared by the door. Heat radiated from it, so stifling I threw my hand up to cover my eyes. It burned my nose and the inside of my throat.

The dog pulled Katrina toward the opening. Somewhere inside was a light like a smoldering ember. In one angry motion, the dog whipped its head and tossed her into the void. The last thing I saw before Katrina disappeared were her wild, terrified eyes.

The woman picked up the vial of Living Elixir and walked over to where Karter lay. She crouched over him. "Leave this place and never return."

Karter stumbled to his feet. Limping toward the door, he glanced at me. The giant dog growled angrily and Karter rushed out of the apothecary.

The tall woman rose and came toward me. Mo scooted back, dragging my mom with her, but I stood and faced her. She reached out and cupped my face in her hands. Her skin was cool and smooth to the touch. She smelled like fire.

A strange feeling swept over me. It was like I knew her. My deep fear was tempered with a deep sense of understanding. "Please. My mom, she's—she's hurt."

"She's dead," the woman said.

Grief washed over me again. The woman wiped away my tears with the sleeve of her cloak. "Death is only painful for the living." Her gaze moved over my face. She traced my jaw-line. Her hand, from palm to fingertips, was longer than my entire face. Her shoulders were inhumanly broad, and she was taller than me while kneeling. I stared at the woman whose appearance seemed to shift as we stood in the shadows.

Her face grew softer, her eyes more luminescent. "Do you know me?"

"I—I don't know," I stammered. I didn't, but I felt like I should.

"You all look so much alike, the members of this ancient family. *My* family."

I blinked. This wasn't Medea if the portraits that hung around the house were accurate, but she did look a bit like her. The women were connected somehow . . .

It suddenly dawned on me that I knew exactly who she was. "Hecate."

Her eyes turned to liquid gold in the darkness. She nodded gently.

"But Medea—the stories—she was your devotee."

"My daughter," she corrected. "And Absyrtus, my son."

My heart raced as the revelation seeped into my brain. This family wasn't just made up of people who were devoted to a goddess. They were a *part* of her, as Medea and her brother Absyrtus were, as I was.

Hecate stood. "I will guide your mother on her journey to the underworld. She will be safe under my watch." The vial of Living Elixir glinted in her hand.

"Can't we use it? To bring her back?" I asked.

She shook her head. "To make life everlasting, there must still be life. Alone, it is not enough to bring the dead back. But . . ." She trailed off.

"But what? Please. I'll do anything. Please help me. Help her."

She glanced toward Mom and then back to me, leaning down, putting her face very close to mine. "Can you do what has never been done? What no one has been able to do since the pieces of the Heart were first separated?"

I thought of Circe's journal. *Absyrtus made whole, master of death.* "The six pieces. If I bring them together, I can save her?"

"She must come with me now," Hecate said. "I cannot stave off death forever, but I can keep it at bay for a full cycle of the moon. Reunite the six pieces and resurrect her."

"But I don't know where they are! What if I can't find them?"

Hecate pressed her palm to the side of my face, put the vial of the transfigured Absyrtus Heart in my hand, then turned and knelt at my mom's side. Mo stiffened, but didn't move. I stood watching as the cloaked goddess slipped her arms under Mom's body, cradling her like a child. She walked to the void, her dog at her heel, and disappeared into the abyss.

CHAPTER 31

Hecate was real and Mom was dead—but we had a chance to save her if we could bring together the six pieces of Medea's brother, Absyrtus. I was the only one who could do it. I was all that was left of Medea's descendants. Hecate's family.

I called Dr. Grant. When she arrived, Mo and I tried to recount everything that had happened. She looked at us like she couldn't believe what she was hearing. We sat in the front room, stumbling over our own words, trying to lay it all out.

I called Marie and told her everything as she rushed to the house. When she arrived, she didn't speak. She looked exhausted, and she kept her injured arm covered, but she held my hand as Nyx stood by the front door.

"What do we do now?" Mo asked through a torrent of tears. "What do we do?"

"We have one month," I said quietly. "And we have this piece." I held out the vial. "It's already transfigured."

Marie took my hand in hers. "I drank the elixir Astraea gave me," she said in a whisper.

"So we have one vial and one person who consumed the

elixir. That's two." I stared at Marie. Was she now considered a piece of the Heart itself? I couldn't see how, but Hecate said the six pieces could be reunited. Looking into Marie's face, I didn't like the questions that posed—or the way those questions made me feel.

"Where are the other four pieces? If Circe was looking and couldn't find them, if nobody in this family has been able to find them after all this time, how are we supposed to locate four pieces in a month?"

There were pins in that map behind my fireplace, but that was my only lead.

"Where do we even start?" Mo asked. She collapsed into tears again and Dr. Grant handed her a tissue.

"There's also the issue of Karter, or whatever his real name was," Dr. Grant said. "You said he was injured pretty badly. I'll check the hospitals and clinics, but he probably didn't stick around."

I felt the tears coming again. I got up and walked out of the room.

"Love, wait," Mo said.

"I need a minute." I felt like I was trapped in a nightmare. All I wanted to do was wake up.

I wandered back to the apothecary. Fragments of broken jars lay scattered on the splintered floor. The counter sat crooked on its base. The jar of oleander lay open on the ground and a large circle of blackened wood where Hecate had disappeared with my mom stained the ground by the door.

I weaved through the shattered remains of the apothecary and went into the room behind the hidden panel. I gazed up at Medea's portrait, avoiding Jason's branch of the tree. I couldn't stand to look at it. I sat down in front of the altar and hung my head and cried until I felt like I couldn't breathe.

A commotion drew me out of my despair—Dr. Grant was shouting, and suddenly, everything went quiet. I raced down the hall and into the front room.

Mo and Nyx were standing next to each other. A tall woman with a head full of waist-length braids held Marie by her arm. Marie wasn't struggling but she seemed upset. Dr. Grant cowered in the corner of the room. There was one other person there, and she stood over Dr. Grant, her back to me.

The woman in the braids took notice of me and her hands flew to her mouth as she inhaled sharply.

"I'm sorry!" Dr. Grant shouted.

"Have you been here this whole time?" the stranger asked angrily. "You didn't guess what might be going on? After what happened to my baby sister, you didn't think maybe you should be extra vigilant? You're smarter than that but Jesus Christ, Khadijah, what is wrong with you?"

"I *have* been vigilant! Fourteen years I been here trying to fix this!" Dr. Grant insisted. "I've been trying to help!"

"Circe," the tall woman standing with Marie said. "Circe, look."

The woman turned and met my gaze. She wore a dark green head wrap twisted into an elaborate knot. Strands of her jet-black curls stuck out from underneath it. We shared the same dark brown eyes and she even wore a pair of oversized glasses that she pushed up the bridge of her nose.

"Briseis," she said, her voice choked with emotion. "I—I never thought I'd see you again."

A thudding noise drew my attention to the foyer.

Not thudding. Beating. Like the rhythm of a heart.

Sitting in the entryway were two identical glass enclosures, padlocked shut, their panes painted black. The sound was emanating from them. I turned back to the woman—to Circe, who smiled warmly.

"I have so much to tell you," she said.

ACKNOWLEDGMENTS

When I was three, the *Little Shop of Horrors* movie came out and soon after went into my regular rotation of *Annie*, *The Wiz*, and *The Wizard of Oz*. For years I was obsessed with the carnivorous plant to the point I actually entered several flower-arranging contests (did y'all know those exist?) and won a few first-place ribbons all in the hopes that one day I would get my shot at tending to a weird and wondrous plant. When I was ten, the *Secret Garden* film came out, and I took it as a sign that I was meant to live on some windswept estate where I could have my own "bit of earth." But being the kind of kid I was, I wondered what it might be like if I had an Audrey II behind that locked gate.

I toyed with this idea for years when I started thinking about writing professionally but put it on the back burner while I was working on *Cinderella Is Dead*. It wasn't until 2017, when I found an article on the Poison Garden at England's Alnwick Garden—a gated plot that houses some of the world's deadliest plants, that I decided to revisit the idea of a hidden garden sheltering a rare and deadly plant. After reading the article, I sat down and wrote a very rough outline of what would become *This Poison Heart*.

So many of the weird and wonderful things I love went into this story—poison plants, Greek mythology, hidden legacies, and old creepy houses—I had the time of my life writing it.

To my partner, Mike, my babies, Amya, Nylah, Elijah, Lyla, and my brother, Spencer, I love y'all so much. Thank you for being my biggest supporters, my loudest cheerleaders. To my dad in heaven, Errol Brown, I miss you so much. I know you would be proud of me. Keep showing me the way and I'll keep putting in the work.

Thank you to my agent extraordinaire, Jamie, who did not immediately drop me for bringing her an idea that was essentially poison plants, Greek myth, and Gothic-inspired atmosphere. No plot, just vibes. Thank you for being an unfailing champion of my work.

To my amazing editors on this project, Mary Kate Castellani and Annette Pollert-Morgan. Thank you for your invaluable input and brilliant, insightful feedback. Thank you as well to everyone at Bloomsbury, Bloomsbury UK, and Bloomsbury AU/NZ, including Ksenia Winnicki, Erica Barmash, Beth Eller, Lily Yengle, Lucy Mackay-Sim, Namra Amir, Claire Stetzer, Phoebe Dyer, and Tobias Madden, for all your support, hard work, and enthusiasm. I could not have asked for a better team, and I'm so thrilled that we get to bring this story into the world together.

I am forever grateful to the wonderful authors, publishing professionals, and bookish folks I've met along the way. Thank you for your support and encouragement, and I hope to be able to do the same for you all whenever I can. This community has been a lifesaver. Big shoutout to the Squad. You know who you are. I'm so happy to be in community with you all.

To all the book bloggers, booktube rockstars, bookstagramers, and the book TikTok crew—I love y'all so much! Thank you for all your hard work, for every post, every boost, every photo, every cosplay. A special shoutout to Melody Simpson with Melanin in YA.

Every writer has certain things that make their writing life a little easier, so I'd like to take a moment to say a big thank you to coffee, Biscoff cookies, and my trusty AlphaSmart. I couldn't have done it without y'all!

As always, to the readers—I am so grateful for your continued support, your boundless creativity, and your endless enthusiasm. Seeing my work make its way into your hands is the honor of my life. I hope we'll be together on this journey for a good long while. Happy reading.